EMPIRE
OF GOLD

By Andy McDermott and available from Headline

The Hunt for Atlantis
The Tomb of Hercules
The Secret of Excalibur
The Covenant of Genesis
The Cult of Osiris
The Sacred Vault
Empire of Gold

ANDY McDERMOTT

EMPIRE OF GOLD

headline

First published in 2011 by
HEADLINE PUBLISHING GROUP

3

Cataloguing in Publication Data is available from the British Library

Hardback ISBN 978 0 7553 5467 2
Trade paperback ISBN 978 0 7553 5468 9

Typeset in Aldine 401 by Avon DataSet Ltd,
Bidford-on-Avon, Warwickshire

Printed and bound in Great Britain by
Clays Ltd, St Ives plc

Headline's policy is to use papers that are natural, renewable and
recyclable products and made from wood grown in sustainable forests.
The logging and manufacturing processes are expected to conform
to the environmental regulations of the country of origin.

HEADLINE PUBLISHING GROUP
An Hachette UK Company
338 Euston Road
London NW1 3BH

www.headline.co.uk
www.hachette.co.uk

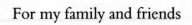
For my family and friends

Prologue

Afghanistan

The barren landscape was simultaneously alien yet oddly familiar to Eddie Chase. The young Englishman had grown up in the rugged hills of Yorkshire, the topography of the northern county in many ways similar to the gnarled ground below the helicopter. But even at night, one difference was obvious. The hills and moors around his home town were green, a living countryside; beneath him now, everything was a parched and dusty brown. A dead land.

More death would be coming to it tonight.

Chase looked away from the window to the seven other men in the Black Hawk's dimly lit cabin. Like him, all were special forces soldiers, faces striped with dark camouflage paint. Unusually, though, the participants in this mission were not all from the same unit, or even the same country. Five were from the 22nd Special Air Service Regiment, one of the United Kingdom's most admired – and feared – elite units. The remaining three, however, were from other nations, the team hurriedly pulled together by the Coalition for the urgent operation.

Despite this, Chase doubted they would have trouble working together. He already knew two of them, even if his previous dealings with Bob 'Bluey' Jackson of the Australian SAS had only been brief. Jason Starkman of the United States Army Special Forces – the Green Berets – had, on the other hand, been a friend for years.

The third foreign soldier was the unknown quantity, to Chase at least. Although he had been vouched for by the team's commander, Major Jim 'Mac' McCrimmon – and to Chase there were few higher recommendations – he still wanted to get a handle on the beaky-nosed Belgian's personality before they hit the ground. So he had taken the seat beside him with the intention of teasing out information about the Special Forces Group's Hugo Castille.

As it happened, no teasing was necessary. The genial Castille had volunteered so much that even a trained interrogator would have struggled to keep up. 'So we found a little bar off Las Ramblas,' he was saying now, 'and I met the most beautiful Spanish girl. Have you ever been to Barcelona?' Chase shook his head, wondering how the conversation – well, monologue – had moved from a military operation in Bosnia to chatting up women in Spain in the few seconds he had been looking out of the window. 'Its architecture matches its women! But as for what we did that night,' a broad smile, 'I am a gentleman, so I shall not say.'

Chase grinned back. 'So there actually *is* something that stops you talking?'

'Of course! I—' Castille stopped as he realised he was being ribbed, and sniffed before taking a polished red apple from a pocket and biting into it.

A Scottish voice came from across the cabin. 'Eddie, you accusing somebody of talking too much is a definite case of the pot calling the kettle black.' The comment prompted laughter from most of the other men.

'Ah, sod off, Mac,' Chase told his commanding officer cheerily. The tightly knit, high-pressure nature of special forces units allowed for a degree of informality uncommon in the regular military – to a point. 'At least I talk about more interesting things than bloody cricket and snooker.'

The stiff-backed man beside Mac had conspicuously not joined in with the laughter. 'Your definition of interesting isn't the same as everyone else's, sergeant.' Like Chase, Captain Alexander Stikes was in his late twenties, but the similarity ended there. Chase was fairly squat with a square, broken-nosed face that could at best be described as 'characterful', while the six-foot-tall, fair-haired officer had the high brow and straight nose of a throwback to Prussian nobility. 'I think we'd all prefer a bit of quiet.'

'Quiet is the last thing we'll get in this tub, Alexander,' said Mac, a hint of chiding audible even over the roar of the Black Hawk's engines.

Amused by Stikes's telling-off, Chase turned back to Castille. 'That's the third bit of fruit you've had since we left the base. Last I had was a banana for breakfast, and one end was all smushed.'

Castille took another bite. 'I always bring lots of fruit on a mission. Much nicer than rations, no? And I have my ways to stop them getting bruised. My father taught me how to take care of them.'

'So he's some sort of . . . fruit vet?'

The Belgian smiled. 'No, a grocer. Nobody wants to buy mushy fruit. What about your father?'

The question caught Chase off guard. 'My dad?'

'Yes, what does he do?'

'He works for a logistics company. Shipping,' he clarified, seeing Castille's uncertainty. 'He transports stuff all over the world, gets things through customs. Oh, and he's also an arsehole.'

'Like father, like son, eh, Yorkie?' said one of the other SAS men, Kevin Baine. Unlike Mac's earlier remark, the estuary-accented comment was devoid of playfulness.

'Fuck off,' Chase replied in kind. Baine's flat face twisted into a sneer.

'An arse-hole,' echoed Castille, the word somehow comical in his Belgian French intonation. 'You do not like him, then?'

'Haven't spoken to him since I left home ten years ago. Not that I saw much of him even before then. He was always off travelling. And having affairs behind my mum's back.' The admission took him somewhat by surprise, Castille's affable questioning having drawn more out of him than he had intended. He gave his SAS comrades warning looks, daring anyone to make a joke. Stikes's expression suggested that he had stored the fact away in his mental database, but nobody said anything.

'Ah, I am sorry,' said Castille.

Chase shrugged. 'No problem.' He had exaggerated – as far as he knew, there had only been the one affair.

But that was enough.

Castille was about to add something when the pilot's voice crackled over a loudspeaker: 'Ten minutes!' The mood instantly changed, the eight men straightening sharply in their seats. The red interior lights went out entirely, the only remaining illumination the eerie green glow of the cockpit instruments. Combat lighting, letting the troops' eyes adapt to night-time conditions.

'Okay,' said Mac, now entirely serious, 'since we were a little short on prep, let's review the situation one last time. Alexander?'

Stikes leaned forward to address the other men. 'Right, now listen. As you know, we've got eleven United Nations aid workers – and one undercover MI6 officer – being held hostage by the Taliban, and twelve spare seats in our choppers.' He glanced towards a window; flying a hundred metres from the US Army Black Hawk was a smaller MH-6 Little Bird gunship. 'I want all of them occupied on the way back. And I want *that* seat,' he pointed at one in particular, 'to have our spy friend in it, alive and well. He's got information on al-Qaeda that we need – maybe even Osama's hidey-hole.'

'Makes you wonder if we'd be going on a rescue mission if one of 'em wasn't a spook,' said Bluey.

'I don't wonder,' Chase told the shaven-headed Australian with dark humour.

Stikes was unamused. 'Keep it closed, Chase. Now, the GPS trackers on the UN trucks showed they'd been taken to an abandoned farm, and as of thirty minutes ago they're still there. A satellite pass earlier today showed one other vehicle and a couple of horses, so we estimate no more than ten to twelve of Terry Taliban. We go in, reduce that number to zero, and recover the hostages.'

'Just to clarify the rules of engagement here,' said Starkman in his Texan drawl, 'we're not only rescuing the good guys, but taking out the bad guys, am I right?'

Even in the green half-light from the cockpit, Stikes's cold smile was clearly visible. 'Anyone who isn't a hostage is classified as hostile. And you know what we do to hostiles.' Grim chuckles from the team.

'Any more word on air support, sir?' asked the fifth SAS trooper, a chunky Welshman called Will Green.

'Nothing confirmed as yet,' said Stikes. 'All our aircraft in the region are engaged on another operation – the ones that aren't broken down, at least. If anything becomes available, it'll almost certainly be American.'

'Fucking great,' muttered Baine. 'Anyone got spare body armour? Nothing I like more than dodging friendly fire.'

'That's enough of that,' said Mac sharply. 'If it wasn't for our American friends, we wouldn't even have these helicopters. Be glad we're not driving out there in Pink Panthers.' The SAS Land Rovers, painted in pinkish shades for desert camouflage, had inevitably acquired the nickname.

'Sorry, sir.' Baine gave Starkman a half-hearted nod of apology.

'Any further questions?' Stikes asked. There were none.

'One last thing,' said Mac. He regarded his men, focusing particularly on Chase. 'You've all been in combat before, but this might feel different from anything else some of you have experienced. No matter what happens, just stay calm, keep focused, and remember your training. I know you can get these people to safety, so stick together, and fight to the end.'

'Fight to the end,' Chase echoed, along with Green and Castille.

The next few minutes passed in as near to silence as it was possible to get inside the Black Hawk's industrial clamour. Then the pilot's voice boomed again: 'One minute!' Chase glanced out of the window. His eyes had now fully adjusted to the darkness, revealing that the landscape was climbing towards ragged mountains to the north. There were still expanses of desert plain, but they were broken up by steep, knotted hills. Tough terrain.

And they had six miles of it to cross.

The Black Hawk's engine note changed, the aircraft tilting back sharply to slow itself before landing. Chase tensed. Any moment—

A harsh thump. Green slid open the cabin door on one side, Bluey the other, and the team scrambled out. Chase already had a weapon ready – a Diemaco C8SFW carbine, a Canadian-built variant of the American M4 assault rifle – as he ran clear of the swirling dust and dived flat to the ground, the others doing the same around him.

The Black Hawk heaved itself upwards, hitting Chase with a gritty downblast as it wheeled back the way it had come. The Little Bird followed. With surprising speed, the chop of the two helicopters' rotors faded.

The dust settled. Chase stayed down, scanning the landscape for any hint that they were not alone.

Nothing. They were in the clear.

A quiet whistle. He looked round, and saw Mac's shadowy figure standing up. The other men rose in response. Still wary, they assembled before the bearded Scot as he switched on a red-lensed torch to check first a map, then his compass. 'That way,' he said, pointing towards the mountains.

Chase regarded the black mass rising against the starscape with a grumbling sigh. 'Buggeration and fuckery. Might have bloody known we'd be going the steepest possible route.'

'Enough complaining,' snapped Stikes. 'Chase, you and Green take the lead. All right, let's move!'

For most people, traversing six miles of hilly, rock-strewn terrain – in the dark – would be a slow, arduous and even painful task. For the multinational special forces team, however, it was little more than an inconvenient slog. They had night vision goggles, but nobody used them – the stars and the sliver of crescent moon, shining brilliantly in a pollution-free sky, gave the eight men more than enough light. After covering five miles in just over an hour and forty minutes, the only ill effect felt by Chase was a sore toe, and even Mac, oldest of the group by over fifteen years, was still in strong enough shape to be suffering only a slight shortness of breath.

Not that Chase was going to cut him any slack, dropping back from Green to speak to him as they ascended a dusty hillside. 'You okay, Mac?' he asked jovially. 'Sounds like you're wheezing a bit. Need some oxygen?'

'Cheeky sod,' Mac replied. 'You know, when I joined the Regiment the entrance exercises were much harder than they are now. A smoker like you would have dropped dead before finishing the first one.'

'I only smoke off duty. And I didn't know the SAS even existed in the nineteenth century!'

'Keep your mouth shut, Chase,' growled Stikes from behind them. 'They'll be able to hear you half a mile away, bellowing like that.'

Chase's voice had been barely above a conversational level, but he lowered it still further to mutter, 'See if you can hear *this*, you fucking bell-end.'

'What was that, *sergeant*?'

'Nothing, Alexander,' Mac called back to Stikes, suppressing a laugh. 'That's enough of that, Eddie. Catch up with Will before he reaches the top of the hill. We're getting close.'

'On it, sir,' said Chase, giving Mac a grin before increasing his pace up the slope. By the time he drew level with Green, his levity had been replaced by caution, senses now on full alert. Both men dropped and crawled the last few feet to peer over the summit.

Ahead was a rough plain about half a mile across, a great humped sandstone ridge rising steeply at the far side. A narrow pass split the ridge from the mountains, a large rock near its entrance poking from the ground like a spearhead. The obvious route to the isolated farm was by travelling up the pass.

So obvious that it had to be a trap.

Unless the Taliban were complete idiots, which whatever his other opinions about them Chase thought was unlikely, there would almost certainly be guards watching the ravine's far end. It was a natural choke point, easy for a few men to cover, and almost impossible to pass through undetected. And if the team *were* detected, that would be the end for the hostages. One gunshot, even one shout, would warn that a rescue was being attempted.

Which meant the guards had to be removed. But first . . . they had to be found.

Chase shrugged off his pack and extracted his night vision goggles. He switched them on, waited for the display's initial flare to fade, then donned them. The vista ahead became several times brighter, picked out in ghostly shades of green. He searched for any sign of movement. Nothing.

'See anything, Eddie?' Green asked quietly.

'Nothing on the ground . . . just checking that ridge.' Chase raised his head. The top of the rise would be a good place to station a lookout, giving a clear view of the plain, but it would also be a lot of effort to scale.

Too much effort, apparently. There was nobody there. He closed his eyes to ease the transition back to normal sight, then removed the goggles and waved to the waiting soldiers. By the time Mac joined him, his vision had mostly recovered. 'Anything?' his commanding officer asked.

'Nope. Thought they might have put someone on the ridge, but it's empty.'

Mac surveyed the scene, then took out the map. 'We'll go over the ridge, come at anybody watching the pass from the southeast. It's a closed canyon; they won't be expecting anyone from that direction.'

Starkman examined the closely packed contour lines. 'Steep climb.'

Bluey regarded his bulky Minimi machine gun – and its 200-round ammo box – disconsolately. 'Aw, that's great. I'm hardly going to spring up there like a mountain goat with this lot.'

'Starkman, Chase, Castille,' said Stikes impatiently, 'get to the top and see if you can snipe them, otherwise go down the other side and take them from the canyon. The rest of us will wait by that large rock for your signal.' He gave Mac a brief glance, waiting for affirmation; the Scot nodded. 'Okay, move it.'

After checking their radios, the trio made their way across the plain. Chase looked up at the moonlit ridge. 'Should be able to get up there without ropes,' he said, indicating a likely path. 'We— What the bloody hell are you doing?'

Castille had peeled a banana, wolfing down half of it in a single bite. 'For energy,' he mumbled as he chewed. 'We have a big climb.'

Chase shook his head. 'Hugo, you're weird.'

'Literally bananas,' Starkman added. He and Chase laughed, prompting a snort from Castille, who polished off the fruit before bagging and pocketing its skin.

'So, we all ready?' Chase asked. 'Or have you got a bunch of grapes an' all?'

'You may laugh,' said Castille, starting up the ridge, 'but you British should eat more fruit. It is why you are all so pale!'

Grinning, Chase followed, Starkman taking up the rear. The climb proved a little more tricky than it looked, the three men having to help each other scale a couple of particularly steep sections, but before long it flattened out.

By now, the trio were again all business. They advanced along the top of the ridge. About two hundred metres from the pass, Castille let out a sharp hiss. All three immediately dropped into wary crouches, weapons ready. 'What?' Chase whispered.

The Belgian pointed. 'I see smoke.'

Chase narrowed his eyes, picking out a faint line wafting into the night sky. Its source was near the far end of the pass.

No need for further discussion; they already knew what they had to do. They quietly headed across the ridge. Below was the closed canyon – and at its head a small patch of glowing orange amidst the darkness. A campfire.

Chase raised his C8 and peered through its scope. As expected, the Taliban had left guards to watch the pass, positioned amongst broken boulders for cover. Two men in dusty robes and turbans sat near the fire. One had an AK-47 propped against a rock beside him; another rifle lay on a flat rock not far away. Of more concern, though, was a different weapon – the long tube of an RPG-7, a Russian rocket launcher with its pointed warhead loaded.

He lowered his gun, judging the distance. Slightly under two hundred metres: well within range of his Diemaco, even with its power reduced by the bulky suppressor on the end of its barrel. An easy shot.

Starkman had come to the same conclusion. 'Let's do 'em,' he said. 'You take the left guy.'

Chase nodded and shifted into firing position. The Taliban member reappeared in his scope. He tilted the gun up slightly, the red dot at the centre of his gunsight just above the man's head. The bullet's arc would carry it down to hit his temple . . .

A part of his mind intruded on his concentration. *You've never killed anyone before.* Not that he knew of, at least; he had

11

been in combat, fired on people shooting at him . . . but this was the first time he had ever prepared to kill an unsuspecting man.

He shook off his doubts. The Taliban were enemies in a war, and the man in his sights would kill his friends and comrades if he got the chance. It was up to him to make sure that didn't happen.

'On three,' Starkman whispered. 'Ready?'

'Ready.'

'Okay. One, two—'

'Hold fire, hold fire!' Chase hissed. His target had just hopped to his feet. He tracked him. 'Wait, wait – shit!'

The Taliban disappeared behind a boulder. Chase quickly panned past it in the hope of reacquiring him on the other side, but after a few seconds it became clear that he wasn't coming out. 'Arse! Lost him.'

Castille searched through his own gunsight. 'I think he has sat down. The other one is still talking to him.'

'We need to get both those fuckers at once,' Starkman muttered. 'If one gets off a shot . . .'

'We'll have to get 'em from the ground,' said Chase. He saw a large rock near the ridge's edge. 'Tie a rope round that – I'll go first.'

A line was quickly secured to the rock. Chase glanced down. This side of the ridge was roughly sixty feet high, more cliff than slope. He slung his rifle and took hold of the rope. 'Okay, if the guys by the fire start moving, pull on the rope twice.' Castille gave him a thumbs-up, Starkman nodding before aiming his rifle back at his target.

Chase began his descent. Even with two hundred metres separating him and the Taliban, he still moved stealthily, a shadow against the ridge's craggy face. Ten feet down, twenty.

Sandstone crunched softly under his boots with each step. Thirty feet, halfway. The fire was now out of sight behind the rocks, though its glow still stood out clearly. Forty. He checked the cliff's foot. He would have to clear a small overhang, but another few feet and he would be safely able to jump—

A crunch beneath one sole – then a louder *clonk* and hiss of falling grit as a loose stone dropped away, hitting the ground with a thud.

And a voice, a puzzled 'Uh?' below—

Chase froze. Another Taliban! The overhang was deeper than he had thought, enough to conceal a man. Pashto words came from below. Chase didn't know the language, but from the tone guessed that the unseen man was asking, 'Who's there?' A flashlight clicked on, a feeble yellow disc of light sweeping across the sand.

More Pashto, the tone annoyed, not concerned. That was something, at least; the Taliban wasn't expecting anyone but his comrades to be nearby. But if he remained suspicious and decided to investigate further, all he had to do was look up . . .

The C8 was hanging from Chase's back on its strap. Gripping the rope with his left hand, he tried to reach back with his right to take hold of the rifle . . . but as his weight shifted the weapon swung round, the suppressor almost scraping against the cliff. He held in an obscenity. Even if he got hold of the gun, he would still have to fumble it into firing position with just one hand, an awkward – and almost certainly noisy – task.

He had a handgun, a Sig P228 holstered across his upper chest, but it was unsilenced. The shot would be heard for miles.

That left his combat knife, sheathed on his belt. He slowly reached down and released the restraining strap, then drew out the six-inch blade.

The yellow circle danced over the ground as the man emerged from the overhang. He gazed towards the campfire, then looked round. Chase knew what he was thinking: none of his companions was nearby, so something else must have made the noise.

The dangling Englishman stepped sideways across the cliff, bringing himself closer to his target.

Target. A human being, enemy or not. *You've never killed anyone before, not close enough to look into their eyes . . .*

The Taliban turned in place. The beam found the dislodged stone, a jagged lump the size of a grapefruit. He peered at it, started to turn away – then some flash of curiosity made him look up—

Chase dived at him, slamming the man to the ground and driving the knife deep into his throat as he clamped his free hand over the Afghan's mouth. Blood gushed from the wound, an arterial spray jetting over his cheek and neck. The Taliban kicked and thrashed, the fallen torch lighting one side of his face. His visible eye was wide, filled with agony and terror. It fixed on the soldier's camouflage-blackened features, their gazes meeting . . . and then he fell still, staring emptily at the stars.

Chase regarded the corpse for a moment that felt like half a lifetime, then yanked out the knife and sat up. 'Jesus,' he whispered, a bilious nausea rising inside him. He forced it back down, wiping the knife clean and returning it to its sheath, then switched off the torch. Darkness consumed his vision for several seconds before his eyes adjusted.

The body was still there, the neck wound glistening accusingly.

He looked away, unslinging his rifle and aiming it towards the distant fire. If the fight had been heard, the other Taliban would be on their way . . .

No movement. He had been lucky.

He returned to the rope and tugged it three times – *all clear* – before investigating the space beneath the overhang to see what the Afghan had been doing. The smell from the little nook provided the answer. He had interrupted the dead man during a call of nature.

A fall of sand announced Starkman's descent, the American dropping down beside his friend. 'What happened?'

'He got caught short,' Chase replied, the grim gag escaping his lips before he had time to process it consciously.

Starkman grinned, then moved back as Castille descended the rope. 'Are you all right?' the Belgian asked.

Chase didn't want to think about it any more. 'Fine.' A wave of his gun towards the fire. 'They'll soon start thinking their mate's been gone too long just to be constipated.'

Keeping low, they advanced, stopping behind a rock some sixty metres from the campfire. Chase's erstwhile target sat with his back against a large boulder, gnawing the meat off an animal bone. The other Taliban had moved closer to the fire, within reach of the RPG.

Chase was about to take aim when Castille touched his arm, a hint of sympathetic concern in his voice. 'I can do it, if you want.'

He brusquely shook his head. 'That's okay.' A pause, then more lightly: 'But thanks anyway.'

'No problem.' They shared a brief look, then Chase returned his attention to the scope.

The red dot fixed on the Taliban's forehead. 'Ready?' he whispered to Starkman.

'Yeah. One, two . . . *three*.'

This time, nothing disrupted the shots. Each rifle bucked once, the retorts reduced to flat *thwaps* by the suppressors.

Chase blinked involuntarily, his eyes reopening to see a thick, dark red splash burst across the rock behind his target's head.

'Tango down,' Starkman intoned.

'Tango down,' Chase echoed. The body of his victim slowly keeled over, leaving a smeared trail over the stone. 'Okay, let's bring the boys through.' He reached for his radio.

The rest of the team arrived three minutes later, Mac leading the way. 'Good work,' he said as he took in the bodies. 'Just these two?'

'There was another one back there,' Starkman reported. 'Eddie took him out. Stabbed him in the neck.'

Mac looked at Chase, raising an eyebrow at the sight of his uncharacteristically expressionless face. 'Your first kill, yes?'

'Yeah,' Chase replied, his voice flat.

'Well, it's good to know there's more to you than just talk, Chase,' said Stikes sarcastically as he checked one of the corpses. When no reply was immediately forthcoming, he went on: 'What, no smart-arse comments? Not going wobbly on us, are you?'

Mac's face creased with irritation. 'Alexander, take Will and Bluey and check that the way's clear.' He gestured at the dusty slope to the north. Stikes gave him a puzzled look, prompting him to snap, 'Well, go on!' Annoyance clear even under his face paint, Stikes summoned the two men and started up the hillside. Starkman took the hint and nudged Castille to give Chase and Mac some space.

'How do you feel?' Mac asked.

'I dunno,' Chase replied truthfully. 'Shaken, I suppose.'

'A bit sick?'

An admission took a few seconds to emerge. 'Yeah.'

'Good.' Mac put a reassuring hand on Chase's shoulder. 'If

you hadn't, I would have been concerned.'

'How come?' Chase asked, surprised. 'I mean, after all the training I thought I could just do it without thinking. Without worrying, I mean.'

'Training can only take you so far, Eddie. The first time you actually have to kill someone for real . . . well, it's different. Some people find they can't do it at all. Others do it . . . and enjoy it. I'm glad you're in the third category.' He squeezed his arm. 'You did the right thing – you protected your teammates, the mission and the lives of the hostages. You did well, Eddie. I always knew you would.'

Chase managed a faint smile. 'Thanks, Mac.'

'So let's get back to work.' He waved, telling the rest of the team to move out. As the men set off, his radio clicked. 'Yes?'

Even over the headset, Stikes sounded concerned. 'Major, we have a slight problem.'

'He wasn't fucking kidding,' Chase growled.

The team hid amongst desiccated scrub at the top of the slope. Before them was a relatively flat expanse backed by the rising mountains, a few tumbledown buildings about three hundred yards away: the abandoned farm where the Taliban had taken their prisoners.

In its description of the location, the mission briefing had been accurate. In its assessment of the enemy forces, however, it had not.

'Where the fuck did this lot come from?' said Baine. They had expected at most a dozen Taliban, but at least that could be seen beside the single-storey farmhouse alone, and the number of tents pitched nearby suggested many more. The three white-painted United Nations vehicles – two medium-sized trucks and a Toyota Land Cruiser – and the battered pickup spotted by satellite had been joined by another three well-worn off-roaders, and the 'couple' of horses had multiplied to at least ten. There were even some motorcycles.

'Doesn't really matter, does it?' said Starkman. 'Question is, what do we do about 'em?'

Mac looked through binoculars. 'If this were a search-and-destroy mission, nothing would change – we've still got surprise and firepower on our side. But with hostages to worry about . . .' His gaze fixed on a barn-like structure a hundred yards from the house. 'There are two men guarding the barn, but no lights inside. That's probably where they're being held.'

Movement at the main building; several Taliban, chattering loudly, went inside, while others headed for the tents. A few men remained outside. 'That's useful,' said Stikes. 'If they stay in the house, we can bring the whole thing down on top of them.' He indicated the Heckler & Koch AG-C 40mm grenade launchers mounted on Green's and Baine's rifles. 'Get a lot in one go.'

'Still plenty left,' Mac replied. He pointed at a shallow irrigation ditch not far away. 'Eddie, Hugo, see if the hostages are in the barn. And check for any more tents behind the house.'

Chase and Castille slipped off their packs, then, weapons in hand, crawled across the dusty ground and slithered into the ditch. It took them almost ten minutes to reach the barn, moving at a silent snail's pace to avoid alerting the guards. The dusty channel passed about forty feet from the dilapidated structure; once out of the guards' field of view, Chase cautiously raised his head. Nearby was a rubbish pile that would provide additional concealment as they approached the barn. He ducked back down and signalled for Castille to follow, crawling onwards until they drew level with the garbage heap.

He peered up again – and froze as a guard came into view, AK hanging from one shoulder. The man trudged along the side of the barn, passing the pile of rubbish with barely a sideways glance.

Chase expected him to round the rear of the building, but instead he continued across open ground to a small shack. He unbolted its door and went inside.

A woman's fearful shriek cut through the night air. Chase whipped up his gun. It couldn't be any of the hostages – mindful of Afghanistan's repressive attitudes, the UN workers were all men. The Taliban had another prisoner.

Prisoners, plural. A second woman wailed a plea, which was cut short by the thud of a foot hitting flesh and a pained squeal. The man shouted, his tone filled with disgust, and reappeared, slamming the door and bolting it before stalking away.

Chase waited until he was out of sight, then emerged from the ditch and took cover behind the trash heap. Castille followed. 'What was that?' the Belgian whispered.

'I don't think these fundamentalist fuckwits are running a women's refuge,' Chase snapped. 'Come on, let's get them out of there.'

'Wait, wait, wait! We have to find the hostages first.'

Chase frowned, but knew Castille was right. 'Okay. You watch for—' He stopped, sniffing. The stench of garbage was unpleasant enough, but there was another, more ominous odour mixed in with it. 'You smell that?'

Castille's large nostrils twitched, and his face fell. 'Yes. Do you think . . .'

'Yeah, I think.' Chase peeled away a mouldering piece of sacking to reveal what he had feared – a corpse. White skin, not olive or brown. One of the hostages. 'Shit!'

'There is another here,' Castille reported mournfully. 'No,

19

two more. Their throats have been cut.'

'Saves on bullets,' Chase said bitterly as he found a fourth body beneath the first. Even in the moonlight, he recognised the face from the mission briefing. 'I've found our spook. Fuck!' He sat back on his haunches, fuming. 'Any more?'

'No. So, they've killed four of them.'

'Which still leaves eight.' He looked at the barn . . . then an object beside it. A large, old-fashioned refrigerator lying on its side, the door missing. Churned-up dirt showed where it had been dragged from the trash and pushed against the wall. 'Keep an eye out, I'll check the barn.'

Castille covering him, Chase crept forward. As he suspected, the fridge had been moved to act as a barricade, blocking a gap. He peered between the planks.

Holes in the roof provided pools of moonlight inside, enough for him to make out the slight movement of somebody's breathing. The man was bound, his face darkened with bruises and blood. Another man's tied legs were visible nearby, other forms in the shadows.

The mission wasn't over, then. He moved to the corner of the barn and glanced round it, seeing another half a dozen large tents behind the house, as well as more tethered horses. He returned to Castille, and they dropped back into the ditch. Another long crawl, and they reached the scrubby bushes where the others were waiting. 'They've killed four of the hostages,' Chase reported. 'Including the guy from MI6.'

That prompted a round of muttered obscenities. 'The mission's down the lavatory then,' said Stikes.

'There are still the other hostages,' Mac reminded him. 'Did you see them?'

'Yeah,' said Chase. 'They're tied up in the barn. But there're another six tents behind the house, and more horses. I think we're talking at least forty Terries altogether.'

'Hrmm,' Mac rumbled, thinking. 'Jason, get on the radio and see if any additional air support has become available. It's a long shot, but it's worth a try.'

'You don't think we'll be able to take 'em?' Baine asked.

'Not all of them, and if we have to make a run for it with the hostages I'd like to have as much firepower covering us as possible.'

'There's something else,' said Chase as Starkman made the call. 'There's a hut past the barn, and there are more prisoners in it. Women.'

'So what are you proposing we do?' said Stikes with a sneer. 'They're not our problem – our only concern is rescuing *our* hostages.'

Chase stared at him in disbelief. 'Are you fucking serious? These Taliban arseholes hate women. Whatever they're planning on doing with them, it won't be giving 'em flowers and foot massages!'

'Watch your language with me, *sergeant*,' Stikes hissed. 'Much as you might want to play the white knight, we can't take them with us. There isn't enough room in the helicopters.'

'Four of the hostages are dead,' Chase insisted, 'so we've got spare seats – and if there's more of them some of us can ride on the skids.'

Baine snorted. 'I'm not hanging off the bottom of a fucking chopper so some silly bitch in a burka can get a free ride, Yorkie. Fuck that!'

Chase made an angry move towards him, but Mac raised his hand. 'Eddie, I'm sorry, but Alexander's right. The hostages are our priority. The women will . . .' He shook his head, downcast. 'They'll have to fend for themselves.'

'Can I at least let them out of the hut?'

Mac considered for a moment. 'If the situation allows.'

Chase nodded, then everyone looked round as Starkman finished his radio call. 'Good news and bad news,' the American announced.

Bluey chuckled. 'There's a surprise.'

'Good news is, there's a Spooky, call sign Hammer Four-One, in the air. Bad news is, it's currently on another op and they don't know when, or even if, it'll be able to get to us.'

'No helicopters?' asked Mac. Starkman shook his head. 'That settles it, then. We can't wait for backup – it won't be long before somebody realises those sentries are missing. We move in now.'

Ten minutes later, Chase was back at the barn. This time Stikes, not Castille, was with him. The captain lurked by the pile of garbage and corpses, while Chase squatted in the shadows against the rusting refrigerator.

Minutes ticked by. Chase's calf muscles started aching, but he ignored the discomfort, staying focused on his task. This time there was no self-doubt, no uncertainty; the knowledge of what the Taliban had done to the four dead hostages, and what they were likely to do to their other prisoners, had eliminated any concerns about whether he was doing the right thing. He flexed his legs, trying to keep them from stiffening. He couldn't afford to be even a second late in reacting . . .

'Psst!' Stikes, signalling that a guard was beginning another patrol round the barn. Completely still, Chase listened to the plodding crunch of the Taliban's footsteps, the rustle of loose clothing as he drew level—

Chase leapt up, left hand locking firmly over the Afghan's bearded mouth as his right whipped up the knife. This time, though, he didn't drive the blade deep into muscle and sinew, but pressed it flat across the man's throat to choke him. Simultaneously, Stikes rushed to them, yanked up the Taliban's robes and jabbed his own knife up between the man's legs as he hissed in Pashto: 'Make a noise and I'll cut off your balls.'

Chase felt the Afghan tense in utter terror. 'I think he gets the point,' he whispered.

Still holding the knife to the Taliban's groin, Stikes straightened and waved at the ditch. Two figures emerged: Castille and Starkman. Stikes spoke again in Pashto, his intense blue eyes glinting in the moonlight as they fixed on the prisoner's. 'If you don't do exactly what I tell you, I'll gut you like a pig. Nod if you understand me.' The trembling man did so. Starkman and Castille pressed against the wall just short of the barn's front corner. 'Good. Now, call to the other guard – not too loudly – and ask him to come here. Okay?'

Another feeble tip of the head. Stikes nodded to Chase, who took his hand away from the man's mouth, keeping the point of his knife pressed against his windpipe. The Afghan took several long, gasping breaths, then spoke in quavering Pashto. Stikes pushed his knife harder against the man's testicles. 'Again. Less frightened.' The Taliban repeated himself with fractionally more confidence.

The other guard, out of sight round the front of the barn, replied dismissively. One look into Stikes's eyes was enough to convince the prisoner to be more insistent. Complaining, the second man padded round the corner – to find five figures in the moonlight where he had expected only one. Fumbling for his AK, he opened his mouth to yell a warning—

Bullets from the silenced C8s of Green and Baine, the two SAS men still concealed in the scrub three hundred yards away, blew out the back of his skull in a spray of brain and bone. His body flopped grotesquely forward – to be caught by Castille,

23

Starkman lunging to grab his Kalashnikov before it could clatter to the ground.

Stikes withdrew the knife from his captive. For a moment, there was a faint flicker of hope in the Taliban's eyes, but it vanished when Stikes placed the blade's point over his heart. The captain spoke again, this time in English. 'Give my regards to the seventy-two virgins.'

The man stared in fearful incomprehension – and the blade sank to its hilt into his chest. With a hint of a smile, Stikes twisted it, then yanked it out. The man's robes darkened as spewing blood soaked them. Chase clamped his hand back over the Afghan's mouth as he struggled, trapping an animalistic sound inside his throat . . . until both noise and movement dwindled to nothing.

Suppressing shock, Chase let go. The corpse slumped to the dirt. Without even giving it a look, Stikes turned away as Mac and Bluey emerged from the ditch. 'Bluey, watch the front of the barn; Alexander, cover the back,' Mac ordered. He pointed at the fridge. 'Everyone else, move that. Let's get them out of there.'

With four men to lift it, the corroded fridge was hauled clear in moments. Chase looked into the barn. The confrontation had caught the hostages' attention, and the bound man he had seen earlier was staring at him in alarm. 'It's okay,' he said quietly. 'We're here to get you home.' He squeezed through the gap, Mac, Starkman and Castille following. The prisoners' bonds were quickly cut.

'Mac!' An urgent whisper from outside. Bluey. 'Two blokes coming from the house.'

The guards' absence had been noticed. 'Hugo, take them to the ditch, then join Bluey,' said Mac. 'Eddie, you go with Alexander. Jason?'

'Already on it,' Starkman drawled, extracting a pair of Claymore mines from his pack and placing them facing the barn doors before connecting their tripwires.

The hostages were in a bad way, Chase realised as he followed the eight men out through the hole and watched them stagger after Castille. That would slow their escape – not good with forty pissed-off Taliban on their heels.

They would have to reduce that number.

He joined Stikes at the barn's rear corner. A couple of bearded men carrying AKs were now standing by the horses, another ambling amongst the tents. Behind him, he heard Mac on the radio, alerting the helicopters that they were about to evacuate – most likely under fire.

The hostages were hiding in the ditch. Castille ran to join Bluey. Starkman emerged from the barn and readied his weapon. Chase's heart pounded, adrenalin rushing into his system.

Someone at the front of the barn called out in Pashto, then with a creak of wood pulled open the doors—

Both Claymores detonated, a pound and a half of C-4 explosive in each mine blasting seven hundred steel balls outwards in a supersonic swathe of destruction. The doors were obliterated, the two Taliban outside disintegrating into a bloody shower of shredded meat and bone.

Before the boom of the twin detonations had faded, Chase and Stikes stepped out into the open and fired. The two Taliban by the horses fell to Chase's bullets, the walking man tumbling before Stikes switched his aim to the closest tents. Screams came from them as the dirty fabric puckered with bullet holes.

More gunfire from the front of the barn, the suppressed thumps of Castille's C8 almost lost beneath the chattering roar of Bluey's machine gun as the pair opened fire on the Afghans outside the farmhouse. More screams, and shouts from within as the Taliban realised they were under attack and piled for the exit—

The house's front wall blew apart, the roof crashing down on the men inside. It had been hit by high explosive grenade rounds fired by Baine and Green. A huge dust cloud burst from the ruins, roiling over the tents and the panicked horses.

A man with an AK leapt out from a tent – only to fall dead as Chase picked him off. Stikes was still shooting into the other tents to slay their occupants before they could even move. The Minimi's hammering stopped, angry yells reaching the team as the surviving Taliban started to regroup – then they were drowned out again as Bluey resumed firing.

Chase glanced back, seeing Mac and Starkman herding the hostages along the irrigation ditch. Castille and Bluey retreated to provide covering fire. He knew he should join them, but there was something he had to do first.

The swelling dust cloud covered the tents behind the destroyed house. This was his chance. He broke away from Stikes, and hurried to the hut.

'Chase!' Stikes roared. 'Get back here!'

Chase ignored him, yanking the bolt and throwing open the door. A cry of fear came from the darkness inside. He fumbled for his penlight torch, shining it quickly round the interior to see five dark, almost formless shapes: the women, even their eyes only part visible through the netted slits in their all-encompassing *chadris*. Their hands were tied behind their backs, their ankles also bound under the heavy robes.

'Don't be scared,' said Chase. 'I'm here to help. British, not Taliban.' Despite the netting, he could see that the women's eyes were swollen and blackened. 'Bastards,' he muttered as he drew his knife. One of the women made a terrified keening sound and tried to wriggle away. He put down his Diemaco. 'Here to help, okay?' She got the message and turned so he could reach her ties. From outside came another grenade explosion, followed by the thump of a fuel tank detonating: Green or Baine had destroyed one of the trucks.

'Chase!' Stikes appeared at the door, gun raised. 'What the hell are you doing?'

'What I said I would.' He started to saw at the rope.

'Leave them – that's an order. We're moving out. Now!'

'We can take them with us.'

'Leave them!'

'No, there're enough seats in the choppers. I'll—'

Stikes fired. Even with its suppressor, the noise of his rifle on full auto was painful in the confined space. The stream of bullets sliced down the five women and spattered Chase with blood.

'Jesus fucking *Christ*!' Chase yelled, rolling out of the line of fire. He whipped up his C8 at the captain – to find the smoking barrel pointing straight back at him. 'What the *fuck* are you doing?'

'I told you the rules of engagement,' said Stikes coldly. 'Anyone who isn't one of the hostages is a hostile.' A thin, malignant smile. 'And as I said, you know what we do to hostiles. Now lower your weapon.'

'You *fucker*,' Chase snarled. The black tube of the suppressor was still aimed at his head. Slowly, unwillingly, he let his own rifle drop.

'Good. Move it,' said Stikes. The Diemaco not wavering, he backed out of the shack, then turned and ran for the barn.

Chase jumped up, rage flooding through him. He should shoot the bastard in the back—

No. He shouldn't. There was a mission to complete. He

went to the door, then hesitated, his gaze drawn back to the sprawled bodies. With an angry growl, he ran after Stikes.

Castille and Bluey were still firing as they advanced along the ditch after the fleeing hostages. Stikes ran past the pair, but Chase joined them. One of the UN trucks was aflame, and the other vehicles had all taken damage. There were at least fifteen Taliban survivors, judging from the muzzle flashes from behind the collapsed house. It was mostly panic fire, the shots smacking harmlessly into the ground short of the trench. Chase matched the timing of the closest impacts to the flash of the most accurate gunman, then dropped him with a single round to the head.

'Good shot,' said Castille. 'What were you and Stikes doing back there?'

'I'll tell you later,' Chase replied grimly. He looked along the ditch to see that Stikes had caught up with Mac, at the tail of the shambling line of hostages. Starkman, leading, was almost at the bushes. 'Time to go.'

'Can't argue with that,' said Bluey, releasing a sweeping burst before scuttling crab-like down the ditch. Chase and Castille trailed him. A hollow *whomp* came from the scrub, and a moment later one of the 4×4s was bowled on to its roof in a huge fireball as another AG-C round found its target. A man, robes and beard aflame, ran screaming into the night. 'Don't think they'll be driving after us now!'

'They've still got bikes, though,' Chase told him. 'And horses.'

'Well, they shoot horses, don't they?' With a cackle, Bluey fired another sweep to force the Taliban into cover, then hurried after Stikes.

Chase grimaced at the joke, then took up the rear. The AK fire was now more intermittent, but also better aimed. The remaining Taliban had overcome their initial shock.

The hostages were past the bushes, Mac directing them down the slope. A small object, spitting sparks, arced from the scrub – a smoke grenade. A thick grey cloud spewed from it. A second followed, putting an obscuring curtain between the team and the Taliban.

'Hugo, Eddie, come on!' Mac called as Green and Baine jumped up from their hiding place. 'Choppers are on their way. Move it!'

The two stragglers needed no further prompting, Chase catching up with his commanding officer on the hillside. 'Mac, those women – they're all dead!'

'What? How did the Terries even get near them?'

'They didn't. It was Stikes – that bastard shot them!'

Mac's expression was one of shock, but before he could reply a shout from Starkman interrupted them. 'Mac! Hammer Four-One is inbound, three minutes away. They want to know if we need support.'

A crackle of AK fire came from behind them. The Taliban were through the smokescreen. 'I'd say that was a yes,' Mac told Starkman with a wry grin as the soldiers shot back. He raised his voice. 'Strobes on, strobes on! Gunship inbound!'

Chase switched on the infrared beacon attached to his equipment webbing. The strobe light's pulses were invisible to the naked eye – but would flash brilliantly on the approaching aircraft's targeting screens, warning its gunners of the location of friendly forces.

In theory.

'Alexander!' Mac shouted as Starkman made the call. 'Get the civvies to the landing zone – take Will and Kev. The rest of us will cover you. Go!'

Stikes gave him a thumbs-up and took the lead. Chase saw that despite the danger the hostages were slowing, already worn down by maltreatment and hunger. And the landing zone was still over half a mile away.

Worse, the Taliban were gaining. They were moving cautiously down the slope, keeping in cover behind rocks, but they had the tactical advantages both of moving forward and having the higher ground, while the rescue team had to back up as they fired uphill.

'Should we hold 'em off here?' Chase shouted to Mac as they crouched behind adjacent boulders.

Mac expertly assessed the area. 'Further back, nearer the entrance to the pass. If we can hold them from there, it'll give the hostages time to reach the choppers.' He pointed at a large rock. 'Behind that. We can—'

'*RPG!*' screamed Starkman. Chase immediately scrunched down, covering his face and ears as a rocket-propelled grenade streaked down the slope and exploded less than thirty feet away. The rock protected him from the direct effects of the blast, but the detonation was still painfully loud at such close range. Stones and dirt rained over him. The warhead had been high explosive, not a shrapnel-filled anti-personnel charge, but this near it was no less dangerous.

Bluey, though further away, had been without cover and unable to do more than throw himself flat on Starkman's warning. Chase saw the Australian clutch at his head. 'Bluey! You okay?'

'Those dirty little bastards!' Bluey yelled back. 'Copped a stone to my fucking noggin!' Still on his stomach, he slithered round and fired his machine gun up the hill, then scrambled behind a jagged rock.

Bluey wasn't the only person affected by the explosion. The hostages were still a hundred yards short of the pass – and panic consumed one of them. He broke from the group and ran for the closed canyon. 'Green!' shouted Stikes. 'Get that idiot back here!'

Green followed – but the Taliban had already spotted the running figure. AKs barked, gritty dust spitting up from the ground around him. The Welshman rushed to tackle him—

Too late. The man was hit, spinning before dropping like a discarded doll. Green, only a couple of feet behind, was caught too, a round ripping into the side of his chest. He fell with a choked scream, trying to crawl behind the hostage's body for what little protection it provided.

'Man down!' Mac cried. Chase swore. Green was exposed, over twenty yards from any usable cover. The Taliban kept firing. If they had another rocket, it would soon follow their bullets.

He knew what Mac's plan would be before he said it. 'Alexander, get the civvies to the choppers!' the Scot yelled. 'Kev, Jason, get Green. Everyone else – give them cover!'

Chase sprang up from behind his rock and opened fire, his C8 now on full auto. Conserving ammo was no longer a consideration; all that mattered was for himself, Mac, Castille and Bluey to force the Taliban to keep their heads down until Starkman and Baine recovered their wounded comrade.

He picked one AK flash and sprayed it with bullets until it stopped, then moved on to another. His magazine ran dry; he ducked and thumbed the release to eject the empty mag, pulling a replacement from his webbing and slotting it into place with a precise, intensely practised move before tugging back the rifle's charging handle to chamber the first new round. The entire process took barely three seconds, and he rose to fire again.

Mac and Castille were just as efficient, the rattle of their guns getting louder as sustained fire burned out the suppressors.

A shriek came from the hillside. Another Taliban down. But he couldn't tell how many remained. Too many.

The onslaught had achieved its purpose, though – the AK fire had all but stopped. Chase glanced towards Green, seeing Starkman haul him upright, Baine running to assist. It would take both men to carry the wounded trooper to the landing zone, and while they were doing that the amount of fire they could provide would be extremely limited. The team was effectively down to five fighting men.

And it would soon be just four. Bluey's withering storm of lead was now reduced to intermittent bursts as the Minimi's ammunition supply ran low. The Australian only had one ammo load: two hundred rounds was normally more than enough.

Baine and Starkman supported Green, moving at a jog towards the pass. 'Keep firing!' Mac ordered as the thud of Kalashnikovs resumed. Chase sprayed one of the muzzle flashes with fire. He scored a hit. The AK flailed madly, blazing skywards before falling silent. Another magazine change, and now conservation *was* an issue – he only had one spare mag remaining.

Stikes and the hostages were out of sight, Baine, Starkman and Green nearing the pass. In the distance, Chase heard the thud of rotor blades.

'Hugo, Bluey, move out!' Mac called. 'Eddie, cover them!' He was about to say something else when his radio squawked. He crouched, struggling to hear the message over the noise of Bluey's machine gun as the Australian and Castille retreated for the ravine.

Chase switched his Diemaco back to single-shot, trying to pick off the shooters up the hill. Bullets cracked off his cover; he flinched, shielding his eyes from flying stone chips, then snapped his sights on to the source of the fire and pulled the trigger. A dark shape beside a boulder flopped to the ground.

Green and his companions entered the pass, Bluey and Castille not far behind. 'Eddie!' Mac yelled. 'Come on! The gunship's—'

A rising high-pitched whine from the sky drowned him out—

An explosion ripped a crater out of the hillside sixty feet in front of Chase. The blast knocked him off his feet. His senses reeled as if he had taken a fierce punch to the head, a ringing rumble almost blotting out all other sounds. Somehow, he made out another shrill noise and clapped both hands to his ears. A second detonation shook the ground.

The air support had arrived.

Orbiting the battle zone was an American AC-130U 'Spooky II' gunship, a humble Hercules transport turned angel of death. Instead of cargo, it carried three cannons, ranging from a 25mm Gatling gun to a 105mm howitzer, jutting from its port side so they could be fixed on a target as the aircraft circled. The weapon that had just fired was a 40mm Bofors gun, an artillery piece originally designed to shoot *at* aircraft rather than from them. With its battery of sensors, a Spooky could locate and destroy ground forces from several miles away.

And Chase was in its sights. 'I'm on your side, you fucking idiots!' he shouted.

Another explosion, and a fourth, but higher up the hill. Chase hoped that meant the Bofors gunner had finally seen his strobe. He looked round. Mac was now at the pass, signalling frantically for the Englishman to follow.

He shook off the earth and grit the 40mm rounds had thrown on to him, realising he had lost his radio headset, and stood. His hearing returned, the distant *pom-pom-pom* of the

Bofors accompanied by the shriek of incoming shells. More explosions on the hillside. He ran for the pass. Mac gave him one final wave, then sprinted after the rest of his men. The Spooky would keep the Taliban pinned down with its awesome firepower, giving the rescue team all the time they needed to reach the waiting choppers—

The Bofors stopped. One last explosion, and the battlefield behind him fell silent. Either the Taliban had been completely obliterated, or . . .

Chase looked to the sky, and realised the battle wasn't over. The Spooky's orbit had carried it behind part of the mountain, placing a barrier of rock between its weapons and their target. The gunship would already be gaining altitude to compensate, but the surviving Taliban now had a chance to continue the pursuit.

Feet pounding, he reached the pass. Mac was over a hundred yards ahead. No gunfire from behind—

A new noise instead. Engines. Not the AC-130 clearing the mountains, but motorbikes.

The Taliban were riding after him.

Two headlights swept down the hill, glare obscuring the bikes and their riders – but if the Taliban had any remaining rockets, one of the men would surely be carrying the RPG-7.

The entire mission was now in jeopardy. An RPG round could easily bring down a helicopter.

Ahead, the ravine opened out on to the plain. Mac was already clear, running towards a sputtering red flare marking the pick-up point. The choppers had not yet touched down, the Black Hawk moving in while the Little Bird circled. Stikes had radioed the pilots to tell them they were collecting only fifteen men rather than the expected twenty; it would be a tight squeeze, but they could all cram into the Black Hawk to save the MH-6 from having to land.

All the eggs in one basket. They didn't know about the bikes.

Another glance back as he left the pass told Chase that he would never reach the landing zone before the Taliban caught up. Instead he charged for the giant spearhead of rock poking from the sands.

The Black Hawk was about fifty feet above the ground, dust swirling out in concentric rings beneath its rotor vortex. The men at the landing zone shielded their faces from the gritty onslaught. Mac still hadn't reached them, looking for Chase – and seeing the headlights. He tried to shout a warning to the others, but his voice was lost under the helicopter's thunderous noise.

The lead bike, two men aboard, burst out of the pass. It turned to follow Chase – until its driver spotted the more tempting targets on the plain. It swung back, the man riding pillion raising his weapon.

The RPG-7. Loaded and ready.

The second bike roared after its original prey, the passenger firing his AK-47 at Chase as he dived behind the rock. Bullets splintered the stone beside him, but he couldn't shoot back – his attention was fixed on another target.

The Taliban with the rocket launcher took aim, the RPG-7's sights fixed on the Black Hawk as it hovered the final few feet above the ground. The helicopter was two hundred metres away, large, barely moving – an unmissable target.

Mac's shouted warnings finally reached the soldiers. They dropped, pulling the hostages down with them.

Chase fired his C8 on full auto, emptying his magazine into both the bike's riders. The old Soviet motorcycle swerved . . .

But the trigger had already been pulled.

The rocket-propelled grenade burst from the launcher as the bike tumbled. It streaked past Mac and hissed over the men on the ground, heading for the Black Hawk—

Thrown off target, the conical warhead only caught the cockpit canopy a glancing blow. The rocket spiralled away, exploding harmlessly fifty yards beyond the helicopter.

But the danger was far from over. The pilot had jerked in fright at the impact. The Black Hawk rolled sideways. The tips of its rotor blades dropped towards the ground, carving through the air like a giant circular saw . . .

Straight at Castille.

The Belgian froze as he saw the helicopter bearing down on him. The blades buzzed at his face—

The pilot yanked the collective control lever and applied full throttle. The Black Hawk lurched upwards, engines screaming – and the rotor passed six inches over Castille's head, the force of the displaced air knocking him flat. 'Merde!' he screeched, hurriedly patting his hands over the top of his skull to check it was still attached.

The gunman on the second bike kept shooting. Chase scrabbled backwards as more bullets cracked off the rock, but the Afghan would have a direct line of fire in moments.

And he was out of ammo.

Three seconds to reload, but he didn't have even that long—

Instead, he flung the empty rifle with all his might. It arced through the air – and hit the bike's driver hard in the face as he rounded the formation. The bike crashed down on its side, throwing the two Taliban into the sand.

The gunman groaned, then realised he still had his AK. He saw a figure in the moonlight and brought up the rifle—

Chase fired first, four shots from the Sig P228 he had

snatched from his chest holster slamming into the man's upper body. The Taliban slumped lifelessly to the ground. The driver struggled to rise – and another two shots to his head dropped him beside his comrade.

Breathing heavily, hands trembling from a burst of adrenalin, Chase lowered the Sig and looked across the plain. The Black Hawk had finally touched down, the rescue team bundling the hostages into the cabin.

But now he could hear another sound echoing through the pass. Not the roar of more motorcycle engines.

The pounding of hooves.

'Oh, fucking pack it in!' he gasped. The bike's engine was still sputtering, but the front wheel was buckled. Unrideable.

Two options. Either sprint for the Black Hawk, and be trampled or shot before he reached it . . . or make sure it took off safely and got the hostages and his comrades home.

The decision was made before the thought was completed. He recovered his rifle and loaded his final magazine. The last few men boarded the Black Hawk. Even from this distance he could pick out Mac's grey hair, his commander – his mentor, his friend – waving for him to run to the chopper. Chase instead crouched and took aim.

The first horseman emerged from the pass, hunched low on his galloping steed with an AK raised in one hand—

Chase tracked him, firing twice and bowling the Taliban off his horse. But his rifle's suppressor was now completely burned out, and the shots had given away his position. Another horseman appeared, and a third, charging at him.

A mechanical roar: the Black Hawk taking off. Three more riders thundered from the ravine, going after the helicopter as it lumbered into the air. AK-47s chattered, tracers streaking after the rising aircraft. Moonlight flashed off another RPG-7 as a Taliban slowed his mount to take aim. A burst from Chase's C8 cut him down before he could fire. The chopper was safe, but now the nearest riders were almost upon him—

A sizzling chainsaw rasp from above – and men and horses alike were torn apart by a laser-like stream of orange fire.

The Little Bird swooped down, its twin six-barrelled Miniguns blazing as each unleashed over sixty rounds per second at the Taliban forces. It pulled up sharply, pivoting to follow the surviving horsemen, then fired again. Hundreds of spent shell casings hailed down around Chase, one plinking off the top of his head and singeing his scalp. 'Great, now I'll have a fucking bald spot,' he muttered as he fired at the last of the horsemen. The shot hit home, but it became academic a moment later when the man literally disintegrated under the force of the MH-6's firepower.

The Miniguns stopped, but he could still hear more horses approaching. Holding back a curse, he looked up at the Little Bird as it started a rapid descent towards him.

No time for it to land. This would have to be a moving pickup, and he would only have one chance . . .

He glimpsed the pilot in the green light of his instruments, his night vision gear making him look like a cyborg. The Little Bird was coming right at him, slowing, but still travelling at twenty miles an hour.

Chase jumped—

The skid slammed against his chest. He wrapped his arms round the forward support strut and clung for dear life as the MH-6 went to full power. The helicopter surged skywards, Chase flapping beneath it like a banner.

He turned his face away from the downwash to see the plain wheeling below – and tracer fire rising up after him as more Taliban came out of the pass—

They disappeared in a tremendous explosion as the AC-130 reacquired its targets and, friendly forces now clear, fired its big gun. The blast from the 105mm shell collapsed part of the ravine, burying the Taliban under tons of rubble. More explosions ripped along the length of the pass as the Bofors gunner dealt with any stragglers.

The Little Bird levelled out, flying after the Black Hawk. Chase heard a voice; he squinted up to see the pilot shouting at him from the doorless cockpit. 'Are you all right, man?'

Despite the fact that he was dangling from a speeding helicopter a thousand feet above hostile territory, Chase still managed a grin. 'Never better, mate. What's the inflight movie?'

The Black Hawk landed at the Coalition base, the Little Bird close behind it. The MH-6 had briefly touched down, once both aircraft reached nominally friendly territory, so that Chase could climb aboard; he leapt from the cabin and ran to the larger helicopter. Three men from the Royal Army Medical Corps were waiting, two bearing a stretcher and a third to attend to the wounded Green. He was carried out of the Black Hawk by Starkman and Baine, and quickly whisked away by the medics.

The hostages came next, and were escorted to a temporary building nearby. Finally, the remaining soldiers clambered from the helicopter, Mac ruefully looking after Green. The others were simply relieved to have made it back in one piece. 'Christ,' said Bluey, rubbing his shaved head, 'that was a bit fierce.'

Starkman saw Chase. 'Damn, almost thought we'd lost you,' said the Texan. 'You okay?'

Chase ignored him, eyes locked on another man: Stikes. The

captain stepped out, donning his beret and adjusting it to a precise angle. 'Seven hostages rescued, and it would have been eight if that idiot hadn't panicked. Not bad.' He saw Chase step towards him. 'So Chase, you—'

Chase smashed a brutal punch into his face. Stikes's regal nose broke with a wet snap, and he fell back against the fuselage. 'You *fucker!*' Chase shouted.

Baine lunged at Chase, but Mac intervened, hauling the Yorkshireman back from the fallen officer. 'Eddie, for Christ's sake!'

A hand to his bleeding nose, Stikes pulled himself upright as the other team members looked on in bewilderment. 'It's a court-martial offence to strike a superior officer, Chase!' he cried. 'You'll get five years for an unprovoked attack – which you all witnessed!'

'Unprovoked, my arse!' Chase said furiously. 'You pointed a fucking gun at my head!'

'Eddie!' Mac snapped. '*Sergeant!*' Still tight-lipped with rage, Chase stood at attention. 'What the hell is going on?'

'This bastard murdered five civilians – five women, sir,' Chase said through clenched teeth. 'They were unarmed and tied prisoners of the Taliban, but he shot them – then aimed his weapon at me.'

'That's a complete lie, Major,' Stikes responded. 'I did no such thing.'

Mac frowned. 'But the Taliban *did* have female prisoners. Did you see them?'

Stikes's cold eyes didn't blink as he answered. 'No sir, I did not.'

'*That's* a complete lie,' Chase hissed.

'The only non-hostages I saw had been designated as hostiles under the rules of engagement.' Stikes moved his hand from his nose; red liquid trickled over his lips. 'Damn it! Sir, if you don't mind, I'd like to get this dealt with. And then' – a venomous look at his attacker – 'I'll make a full written report so charges can be drawn against Sergeant Chase!'

Mac nodded, and Stikes strutted away. The Scot hustled Chase out of earshot of the others. 'If you have a grievance against a superior, Eddie,' he rumbled, 'there are well-defined procedures. That was not one of them!'

Chase forced his anger back under control. 'Sorry, sir. I mean, I'm sorry for causing you any trouble – not for decking Stikes! It's the bloody *least* that he deserved. He murdered those women in cold blood.'

'Nobody else saw anything. It's your word against his.'

'Mac, you know me. And you know Stikes.' He gave Mac an almost pleading look. 'Who do you believe?'

Mac remained silent for a long moment. 'Eddie,' he said at last, 'however this turns out, there will be consequences for you – for your career. The plain and simple fact is that you punched an officer in the face in front of half a dozen witnesses.'

'I'll take whatever comes to me.'

'I'd expect nothing less. But . . . as you say, I know you. And I know Stikes. So when the court-martial comes – which it will, he's got connections that will see to that – I'll do everything I can to support you.'

'Thank you, sir.'

'And' – a hint of a smile – 'I'd be remiss as your commanding officer if I didn't remind you to get straight on with a full written report of your own, describing *everything* you witnessed on the mission. Our well-defined procedures are there for everyone's benefit, not just officers'. If, as a result of that, an investigation is warranted . . . again, you'll have my full support.'

Chase gave the older man an appreciative look. 'Thank you, sir!'

'Well, you'd better get to it, sergeant. In the meantime, I'm going to see if I can find a shower in this bloody hole.' Mac walked off, then stopped and looked back. 'By the way, Eddie, you did excellent work tonight. Well done.'

Chase saluted, and Mac continued on his way. The Englishman stood for a moment, then took out and lit a long-awaited cigarette.

1

New York City:

Eleven Years Later

Eddie Chase strolled into the office with his hands behind his back and a knowing smile on his face. 'Ay up, love.'

His wife looked up from her laptop with a faint frown. 'Where've you been?' asked Nina Wilde, flicking a strand of red hair away from her face. 'We're going to be late.'

'We've still got ten minutes. Anyway, I'm amazed you noticed I'd gone, since you haven't lifted your nose out of that lot all morning.' He glanced at the stacked paperwork on her desk.

'Don't be a smart-ass.' She eyed him more closely, noticing his expectant smirk. 'What have you got behind your back?'

He stepped forward. 'Oh, nothing. Just . . .' With a flourish, he dropped a large brown paper bag beside her computer. 'Lunch.'

Nina did a double-take as she recognised the logo on the bag. 'Aldo's Deli?' Her frown was replaced by surprised delight. 'Wait, you went all the way to Aldo's just to get me a sandwich?'

Eddie shrugged, looking out at the view of Manhattan beyond the windows of the United Nations building. 'It's only in the East Village. It's not *that* far.'

She opened the bag, and her look brightened still further. 'You didn't.'

'I did. Your favourite. Extra-peppered pastrami on rye, with lettuce, tomatoes, pickled onions, not regular ones . . . and Aldo's special chilli sauce. Just like you used to get when we lived down there.'

Nina almost reverently unwrapped the sandwich. 'That was over four years ago. I can't believe you did this.' She was about to take a bite when she paused. 'Why *did* you do this?'

'What, a bloke can't do something nice for his wife once in a while?'

'Not when she knows him as well as I know you.' A sly smile. 'This wouldn't be a peace offering, would it?'

'Pfft, don't be daft. What've I got to apologise for? I'm right.'

Her green eyes narrowed, the smile fading. 'Don't even start.' A discussion the previous night about the week's main news story had somehow degenerated into a full-blown argument, and the atmosphere had still been frosty even over breakfast. A New Yorker named Jerry Rosenthal was on trial for having killed the man accused of raping his daughter after the case against him collapsed. To Nina it had been an open-and-shut case of revenge-driven vigilantism, but Eddie had very different opinions.

Which he still held. 'What, so you're saying that if it had been your daughter, you'd be happy to let the guy walk the streets because of some forensics cock-up? We know he did it, he just got away with it on a technicality.'

'We *don't* know he did it,' she said irritably. 'You weren't there – you didn't see what happened.'

'Neither did you.'

'Which is why we have courts to decide whether a person's guilty or not. And why we have courts to decide on the sentence – rather than some guy appointing himself judge, jury and executioner. That's not justice.'

'Sounds like it to me. You know somebody's done something bad and thinks they've got away with it? *Boom*. Kill the fucker.'

Nina huffed. 'Eddie, I really don't want to get into this again. You know what? I'm just going to eat my sandwich – for which thank you very much, by the way. And,' she added, 'you are *not* going to get the last word just because my mouth's full!'

'As if I would,' said Eddie, who had been planning to do exactly that.

She was about to take a bite when there was a knock at the door. Before she could ask who it was, Macy Sharif entered. 'Hey, Nina. Hi, Eddie.' The archaeology student, who had helped them discover the Pyramid of Osiris beneath the Egyptian desert the previous year, had accepted Nina's invitation to spend part of her summer vacation as an intern at the International Heritage Agency before completing her final year of study. 'Dr Bellfriar sent me to get you.'

'Bet I know what he's going to say,' said Eddie with a mocking grin. 'Eight months of looking at the things, and he'll tell us . . . they're made of stone. Thank you, that'll be fifty grand plus expenses.'

'Oh, he's got way more to say than that,' said Macy, the Englishman's sarcasm fluttering past her unnoticed. 'I should know. I had to make all his PowerPoint slides.'

'Not enjoying your current assignment?' Nina asked in an impish tone.

'No, no, it's fine!' said Macy hurriedly, not wanting to seem ungrateful. 'Just that I was hoping to do something a bit more fieldworky. With you.'

Nina patted one of the stacks of documents. 'Funny, I was hoping to do some fieldwork too! But then some idiot tried to kill a bunch of world leaders, and we made a find that changes the face of archaeology, and, well, high-up people want to know about it. In triplicate.'

'Maybe Bellfriar's found something that'll give you an excuse,' Eddie suggested.

Nina looked hopefully at Macy, who tried unsuccessfully to hide an apologetic expression. 'Anyway,' said the young woman, 'you can see for yourself. He's with Mr Penrose and the others in the conference room.'

Nina took a quick bite from her sandwich before getting up from her desk. 'What?' she asked Eddie as she chewed. 'I haven't had lunch yet; I'm hungry. Come on.'

'Do I have to?'

'If I do, so do you.' She shooed him from the office.

Macy led the way to the conference room. As well as Dr Donald Bellfriar, also present were several United Nations officials headed by Sebastian Penrose, who acted as liaison between the UN proper and its semi-independent cultural protection agency. 'Ah, hello, Nina,' said the bespectacled, officious Englishman.

'Sebastian,' Nina replied. 'I didn't expect so many people.'

'Everyone loves a mystery,' Penrose said. 'I think they're hoping Dr Bellfriar has the solution.'

Nina shared a knowing look with Macy. 'We'll find out soon enough.'

Everyone took their seats, Macy working a laptop and projector as the Oregonian geologist carefully smoothed his sweeping silver hair before addressing his audience. 'Good afternoon, everyone. Before I start, I'd like to say how great it's been to work with the IHA on this. I suppose that when archaeology can't provide the answers, it's time to call on the rock stars!' He chuckled immodestly at his pun, which was received with appropriately stony silence. '*Rock* stars? No? Anyway, thank you, Dr Wilde – and thank you, Miss Sharif, for all your assistance. And for being enjoyable company.' Macy beamed.

'He was probably enjoying the view more than the conversation,' Eddie whispered to Nina.

'Shush,' she whispered back, although he had a point. While Macy had spent her internship modestly dressed by her standards, in the formal surroundings of the UN the beautiful Miamian's predilection for tight designer clothing made her stand out like a bikini model in a Saudi mosque.

Bellfriar began his presentation proper, opening a case to reveal his subjects: a pair of small statues, crude human figures carved from an odd purple stone. The first had been found by Nina, Eddie and Macy inside the Pyramid of Osiris; the second, stored with stolen cultural treasures in a former Cold War bunker beneath the glacial ice of Greenland. He summarised the circumstances of each discovery before continuing: 'Now, despite their best efforts, Interpol have so far been unable to find out where the second statue was stolen from, and since neither relic appears to be the product of any known ancient culture that would seem to be a dead end in the search for answers. Fortunately, other branches of science can provide a different perspective. Miss Sharif?'

Macy tapped at the laptop, projecting the first slide on to the conference room's screen. It showed the two statues placed side by side. 'As you can see,' said Bellfriar, 'the statues are clearly part of a set, and meant to fit together. Note how the arms are positioned so they'll interlock. But as you see here,' he nodded, and Macy clicked on to the next slide, 'it's obvious that the set is incomplete.'

The new image showed the statues from directly above. They had been positioned in such a way that, facing outwards with one shoulder touching, they formed two sides of a triangle – and, as Bellfriar had said, it was evident that a third figurine would perfectly complete the group. 'Using simulation software,' said the geologist proudly, 'I can show you what the missing one would look like.' Another slide, and the two statues were shown flanking a computer-generated image of a third. All three were broadly similar, the only appreciable difference being the position of the arms. 'And here's how they fit together . . .'

The photos of the figures were replaced by CG copies which began a showy animated display, spinning round each other before slotting into a shoulder-to-shoulder triptych. The UN observers seemed impressed, but Nina was less so, having seen the IHA's own computer simulation of the missing figure over seven months earlier. 'That was one of the first things we realised when we received the second statue,' she said. 'There was – and hopefully still is – a third. The question is, where?'

'Well, before we can ask where,' said Bellfriar amiably, 'we first have to ask what. As in, what are the statues made of?' He indicated the two figures in the case. 'As you see, they have an unusual colour, this strong purple, with a rather vitreous lustre. Some form of bornite was my first thought, but the copper content in the scrape sample I took was far too low – almost non-existent, in fact. But the density of the rock was surprisingly high, so it had an appreciable metal content . . .'

Nina glanced at Eddie as Bellfriar launched into a detailed account of his mineralogical tests. His eyes had glazed over.

She tapped his foot with hers. 'Sorry,' he muttered. 'Geology's even more boring than archaeology.'

She was about to jab his foot again, this time with her high heel rather than her toe, when Bellfriar's words caught her full attention. '. . . which brought me to my conclusion: the rock from which the statues were carved was probably mesosideritic.'

It took a moment, but the term produced a match from Nina's mental database. 'A meteorite?'

Bellfriar was impressed. 'You know about meteorites, Dr Wilde?'

'From an archaeological standpoint. There was a dagger made from meteoric iron in Tutankhamun's tomb, and some Eskimo and Native American tribes also made ceremonial weapons from it. And there was an East African tribe that worshipped a fallen meteorite. But apart from that, only really what I remember from Astronomy 101.'

'Well, I can give you a brief refresher course,' said Bellfriar, chuckling again. 'A mesosiderite is a stony-iron meteorite, which as the name suggests is made up of a combination of rock and metal. They're very rare – there are fewer than a hundred and fifty known examples, I believe.'

'You said it's *probably* a . . . a mesosiderite,' said Penrose, almost stumbling over the word. 'Can't you be sure?'

'Not without cutting one of the statues in two to make a microscope slide, and I doubt Dr Wilde – or the Egyptian government – would be happy about that! But the tests I could do seemed reasonably conclusive. Although,' he added, 'if there's any way at all I could get a larger sample, I'd very much like to carry out further tests. The rock has some unusual properties.'

'In what way?' asked Nina.

'The density, for one thing – either the iron content is much higher than I'd expect, or there are heavier metals in there as well. There are also traces of organic compounds.'

Eddie gave the statues a deeply suspicious look. 'Wait, there was something *alive* inside the meteor? Like the Blob?'

Bellfriar laughed. 'No, no. If a compound is "organic", then chemically it just means it contains carbon. Meteorites might have carried the precursors of life to earth, though; there was a famous find in Australia, the Murchison meteorite, which contained amino acids. I don't know if that was the case here – but I did notice something else.' He turned to Macy. 'Miss Sharif, can you skip forward to . . . I think slide seventeen?'

Macy tapped the keyboard. Slides flashed on the screen, stopping at an image of one of the statues' surface taken through a microscope. At extreme magnification, the stone was a fractal microcosm of a rocky landscape, with what seemed almost like man-made features running through it: a fine grid-like pattern.

'Looks like a developer's laying the ground for a new subdivision,' said Nina.

'It does, doesn't it?' replied Bellfriar. 'I wouldn't want to live there, though – not a lot of space. The lines are only about fifty micrometres apart, less than the width of a human hair.'

'What is it?' Eddie asked.

'Some kind of carbon matrix infused into the meteoric iron. Naturally formed, of course – it looks artificial, but on this scale so do a lot of processes. What's interesting is that it's greatly increased the hardness of the rock, as if the whole thing has been reinforced with carbon nanotubes. Normally, this kind of stone would be around a five or six on the Mohs scale – diamond tops the scale at ten, by the way,' he added for the benefit of the non-scientists. 'The statues are actually harder than the porcelain streak plate I initially tried to use to test them, so on the Mohs scale they're at least a seven – stronger than quartz.'

His description had sparked another of Nina's memories – this time from personal experience. 'The rock,' she began, her cautious, probing tone immediately catching Eddie's attention, 'does it have any other unusual properties? Like, say . . . high electrical conductivity?'

'Actually, yes,' said Bellfriar, surprised. 'It's down to the iron content, of course, but it was higher than I expected. How did you know?'

'It just reminded me of something I'd seen before,' she said, trying to sound casual. 'But it's not important. What else have you found out?'

Bellfriar returned to his presentation, but Nina was no longer listening, instead running through theories of her own. When he finished, twenty minutes later, she thanked him for his work, then waited for the United Nations officials to conclude their pleasantries, trying not to seem too eager for everyone to leave.

'What is it?' whispered Eddie.

'I'll tell you in private,' she replied under her breath, before calling across the room. 'Macy?'

Macy was shutting down the laptop. 'Yeah?'

'Can you take the statues to my office, please?'

'Taking them back off me so quickly, Dr Wilde?' said Bellfriar in jovial mock offence. 'I hope you're not disappointed that I didn't pinpoint where they came from?'

'No, not at all,' Nina told him as the puzzled Macy closed the case containing the statues. 'You've given me a lot to think about. Oh, Sebastian,' she added as Penrose was about to leave, 'can I have a quick word with you? We need to finalise the details of, uh . . . the Atlantis excavations.'

Penrose covered his momentary confusion – the IHA's undersea archaeological work at the ruins of Atlantis was already under way – and nodded as he left. Macy, carrying the case, went out after him. Nina and Eddie followed, and the four met again in Nina's office.

'Okay,' said Eddie, 'what the hell was all that about?'

'A good question,' said Penrose. 'I take it you've realised something, Nina.'

'I think so,' she replied, shoving the papers – and the sandwich – on her desk aside to clear a space. 'Macy, put the case down here.'

Macy obeyed. Nina opened the case and regarded the two crude statues. 'When Bellfriar mentioned carbon nanotubes, it made me think of something I've seen before. Excalibur.'

'Excalibur?' exclaimed Macy. 'What, *the* Excalibur? As in King Arthur?'

'That's the one,' said Eddie.

'Wow! I knew you found King Arthur's tomb, but I didn't know you found Excalibur as well.'

'We did, but we . . . lost it,' said Nina. That wasn't quite true, as she knew exactly where it was: she and Eddie had decided to hide it again to keep it out of the wrong hands. 'But it had some very special properties . . . and they sounded a lot like what Bellfriar just described. Eddie, can you close the blinds? I need the room as dark as possible.'

Eddie began to lower the blinds. 'We've been married for a year and a half – we don't *have* to do it with the lights off any more.'

'Ha ha,' said Nina, not amused. 'Ignore him, he's joking,' she added to Macy, sensing that the younger, far less inhibited woman was about to ask a very personal question. 'But one of Excalibur's properties was that it was made from a superconductive metal – and it could conduct more than just electricity.'

The blinds were now closed, the office in a gloomy twilight. Nina reached for a statue. 'Okay, let's see if I'm right . . .'

She picked it up – and the stone glowed faintly, the light quickly fading to nothing.

Penrose's eyes widened, and Macy gasped. 'What was *that*?' she said.

'That was earth energy,' said Nina. 'It's a network of lines of natural power that flow around the planet, and converge in certain places. If you're in one of those places and the earth energy is strong enough, you can tap into it and use it – if you have a superconducting material to make the connection.'

'Should Miss Sharif be seeing this?' asked Penrose, a stern tinge to his voice making it clear that he thought she definitely shouldn't.

'I'll vouch for her,' said Nina, giving Macy a quick reassuring smile. 'Besides, she discovered this statue, and I gave her the job of finding out more about it – I think this counts. And it beats making PowerPoint slides.'

'Nice slides, by the way,' Eddie told Macy with a grin. 'Almost no spelling mistakes!'

Macy pouted as Nina returned the first statue to the case and picked up the other. Again, a shimmering glow ran briefly over the figure's surface before disappearing. Nina was about to put the statue back down, then changed her mind and picked up the first once more. This time, nothing happened – until she put the two figurines together, linking them shoulder to shoulder in the same way as Bellfriar's slide. Both statues glowed, the light slightly stronger than before. The effect lasted for a few seconds before dwindling.

Macy hesitantly touched the figures, but nothing happened.

'Why did they do that? And how come it never happened before? Dr Bellfriar had them for months, and he never saw anything like this.'

'It never happened before because only certain people can cause the effect,' said Nina. 'People like . . . me. I don't know how or why – the best theory is that it's genetic – but there's something about my body's bioelectric field that lets me channel earth energy through a superconductor.' She opted, for now, not to explain to her friend that her genetic heritage went all the way back to the lost civilisation of Atlantis, destroyed eleven thousand years before – and that the actions of other Atlantean descendants had almost brought about a global genocide. 'We discovered it when we found Excalibur.'

'But you've held the statues before,' said Eddie. 'Loads of times. They never lit up like that.'

'Maybe they did, and we just didn't notice. Open the blinds.' Nina put down the figures as Eddie did so, daylight flooding back into the room. She picked up the statues again. If the strange glow had returned, it was impossible to tell, the feeble effect overwhelmed even by indirect sunlight from outside.

'So how are we going to proceed?' asked Penrose. 'The statues are somehow connected to earth energy, it seems – and earth energy is an IHA security issue. We know how dangerous it can be if the wrong person controls it.'

Nina looked into the roughly carved face of one of the statues, little more than a child's drawing in three dimensions with a bump for a nose and vague indentations for eyes and mouth. 'We've got two of the statues. There might be a third . . . somewhere. If there is, we have to find it. But first, we need to find out more about what we're dealing with – and what these things can do.'

Macy looked surprised. 'They're just statues. What *can* they do?'

'Excalibur was more than just a sword. When it was charged with earth energy, it could cut through literally anything. We know the Egyptian statue had some great significance – it was considered important enough to be sealed in the tomb of a god along with his greatest treasures. Maybe Osiris could channel its power – maybe that's why he was regarded as a god. So we—' She broke off as her desk phone rang, putting down the statue to answer it. 'Hello?'

It was Lola Gianetti, Nina's now four-months' pregnant personal assistant. 'Hi, Nina. Is Eddie with you? There's a call for him.'

'Can it wait? We're in the middle of something.'

'They said it was very important.'

'Okay, he's here. Hold on.'

She passed the phone to her husband. 'Yeah, hello?' he said, eyebrows rising as he recognised his sister's voice. 'Lizzie, hi. Haven't heard from you for a while. What's up?'

He moved away to continue the call with a modicum of privacy, leaving Nina, Penrose and Macy to regard the statues. 'What do you have in mind?' Penrose asked.

'We need to find out what the earth energy effect actually does,' said Nina. 'Which means we need to take the statues to a convergence point.' She chewed her lower lip, thinking. 'There are four places where I know for sure that I can find earth energy. Problem is, one is in a Russian military base, another's in the middle of the Arctic Ocean, and one's buried under thousands of tons of rock out in the desert in a country where I'm not exactly welcome.'

'Jeez,' said Macy. 'So where's the fourth one? Inside a volcano?'

'Fortunately, no,' said Nina, smiling. 'It's somewhere a bit easier to reach – and a lot less hot. England. In King Arthur's tomb at Glastonbury, actually.' She looked across at Eddie to see if the mention of his home country had caught his attention, but he had his back to her, holding his conversation in a low voice.

'And you want to take the statues there?' Penrose asked.

'Yes. I think the glow we saw just now is only a residual effect – if there are any lines of earth energy around New York, they're either too weak or too far away to produce much power. If I take the statues to Glastonbury, with luck I'll see what happens when they get a full charge.'

Penrose shook his head slightly. 'I'm not sure the Egyptians will want their statue to leave IHA security. Or Interpol theirs, for that matter.'

'We'll work something out. But we should do it fast. As you said, it's a security issue now.'

He thought for a moment, then nodded. 'I'll speak to Dr Assad in Egypt and the Interpol CPCU, see if I can persuade them to speed things along. I think you're right, though; we need to look into this – and if there's a third statue out there, we have to find it. When were you thinking about starting?'

'About ten minutes ago,' said Nina.

Penrose shot a rueful glance at the paperwork on her desk. 'And the backlog relating to the Vault of Shiva? Or the meeting of the non-executive directors? Mr Glas particulalry wanted to meet you.'

'That's what I like about being in charge,' she said with a broad grin. 'I get to delegate!'

'I'm sure Bill and Simone will be delighted to hear that,' said Penrose, returning the smile. 'Okay, I'll make the calls.

Keep me posted.' He tipped his head to the two women, then left the office.

'So you're going to England?' said Macy excitedly. 'Can I come?'

Nina was caught off guard. 'What?'

'Well, you did give me the job of finding out more about these little guys . . .' She indicated the statues. When Nina didn't respond immediately, she adopted a pleading tone. 'Aw, please, Nina. It won't cost the IHA anything – I can pay my own way.'

'You mean your parents can.'

'Well, what are parents for? And I'll learn a hundred times more from you in the field than I would in an office.'

Nina reluctantly conceded the point; since Macy was an unpaid intern and not an IHA employee, there was technically nothing she could do to stop her from simply buying a plane ticket and tagging along. 'Okay, I guess.'

'Awesome!' Macy clapped her hands together. 'I've never been to England before. I'll need new clothes. What should I wear?'

Before Nina could make a facetious suggestion, Eddie put down the phone. 'Was that Elizabeth in England?' she asked.

'Yeah,' said Eddie, voice oddly flat.

'Kind of a nice coincidence. I think the best place to find out more about the statues is Glastonbury, so we can visit your folks while we're over there.'

'I'd be going to see them even if we were supposed to be flying to Timbuktu tomorrow,' he said, grim-faced. 'Nan's in hospital.'

2

England

The Royal Bournemouth Hospital was on the coastal resort's eastern outskirts, and Eddie and Nina's first stop after leaving Heathrow airport. Eddie practically skidded the rented Ford Mondeo into a space in the car park and jumped out. Surprised at being left behind, Nina hurried after him. Entering the hospital, she found him at reception, demanding to know where to find his grandmother. The woman at the desk wasn't keen on his uncharacteristically brusque manner, but gave the information. Again, Nina was left trailing behind as he strode through the corridors.

She caught up outside a room on the next floor, where familiar faces waited: Elizabeth Chase, Nina's sister-in-law, and her daughter Holly. Both looked drawn and tired, but relieved to see the new arrivals. 'Uncle Eddie!' said Holly, hugging him. 'And Nina, hi!'

'How is she?' asked Eddie after the greetings were concluded.

'Much better than when I called you yesterday,' said Elizabeth. 'It's lucky I was with her when she collapsed – the ambulance got her here very quickly, and she responded well to treatment. They're probably going to discharge her this afternoon – they're just doing a couple more tests.'

'Thank God. Is it okay to see her?'

'Yes, fine. Come on.' Nina noted that Elizabeth checked her watch before opening the door, but thought no more of it as she followed them into the room.

The smell alone, the tang of industrial-strength disinfectants, set Eddie's nerves on edge. Like most people he had a dislike of hospitals, but in his case it was enhanced by the memory of friends who had been taken into one and never come out. His unease increased when he saw the frail figure in the bed. 'Hi, Nan,' he said, more quietly than he had intended.

'Edward!' replied his grandmother, delight evident even behind the oxygen mask covering her mouth and nose. 'Oh, my little lambchop, come here! Give your poor old nan a kiss.'

He went to the bedside and kissed her cheek, letting her embrace him as best she could around the mask's hose. 'How are you, Nan?'

She released him, a small but deep cough escaping her throat. 'I've been better. But it's really picked me up, seeing you. And Nina too! It's lovely to see you both again.'

'We got here as fast as we could,' he told her. 'So they've got you on oxygen therapy?'

'The best treatment for emphysema with a side effect of pulmonary hypertension, so we've been told,' said Elizabeth. 'Which would have been much less likely to have happened if you'd stopped smoking.'

Nan laughed faintly, coughing again. 'At my age, there aren't many pleasures left in life. Except seeing my family. Oh, I'm so happy that you came, Edward. I worry about you over there in America.'

'How come?' he asked.

'Well, what if you get ill or have an accident? I've heard horrible stories about American hospitals, the way they throw you out on the street if you don't have enough money, being charged hundreds of dollars for an aspirin . . .'

'It's not *quite* that bad,' said Nina, amused.

'So they're going to let you go home this afternoon?' Eddie asked.

Nan nodded. 'Elizabeth wants me to stay with her, but I'd rather go back to my own house.'

'No, you're staying with us, Nan,' Elizabeth insisted. She indicated the oxygen cylinder beside the bed. 'You need to keep the mask on until the doctors say you're better, and you can't possibly carry that tank up the stairs on your own.'

Nan seemed less than happy at being told what to do by her granddaughter, but acquiesced. 'Don't worry, Nan,' Eddie said. 'I'll help you with all this stuff.'

'Oh, thank you. Are you going to be here long? I know you're both very busy.'

'Don't know yet. Nina's got a work thing, but we'll probably be around for a few days.'

'Good. It would be lovely if you could take me for a walk while you're here.'

'Ahem,' said Holly, pointing at a wheelchair.

Nan frowned. 'Oh, all right. If you could take me for a roll!'

'No problem, Nan,' said Eddie. He glanced round as the door opened, expecting to see a doctor entering. 'Maybe tomorrow . . .' He tailed off at the sight of the man who came into the room.

At first, Nina had no idea who the new arrival might be – until with a start she realised that his eyes were just like those of Eddie and Elizabeth. A relative. Beyond that, his appearance had more in common with her sister-in-law than her husband; he was taller than Eddie by at least four inches, face lean and tapered rather than square, lithe even through the inevitable spread of late middle age – she guessed him to be around sixty. Despite this, he was still clearly highly active, carrying himself almost with a swagger in his expensive smart-casual clothing.

'Well, well,' he said on seeing Eddie. 'What a surprise!' The wink he gave to Elizabeth showed it was nothing of the sort.

'Yeah,' Eddie replied, glaring at his sister.

'So,' said the man, 'long time no see, Edward.'

The scathing reply Eddie wanted to give was tempered by the presence of his grandmother and niece. Instead, he said, 'Yeah, it's been a while. Twenty-two years.'

The uncomfortable pause that followed was ended when Holly skipped across the room to embrace the newcomer. 'Hi, Grandad!'

'Hiya, hiya!' he replied. 'How's my favourite grand-daughter?'

'Your *only* granddaughter,' she pointed out.

'Well, that makes you even more special, doesn't it?' He kissed her cheek, then released her and regarded Nina. 'And Holly's told me a lot about you. You must be Nina.'

'That's right,' Nina said. 'So you must be . . .' She knew, but still nudged Eddie for a proper introduction.

Eddie's contempt was barely concealed. 'This is my – dad.' The momentary pause, Nina realised, was to cover what had become almost a conditioned reflex; on the rare occasions when he mentioned his father, the younger Chase almost invariably preceded it with an insulting adjective.

'Larry Chase,' said the man in question, extending a hand. She shook it. 'Great to meet such a big celebrity.'

'I wouldn't call myself that,' she replied, extricating herself from his firm grip.

'But you're certainly famous. I don't think anyone who saw the opening of the Sphinx on TV last year will forget you!'

Her cheeks prickled at the reminder of her unplanned global television appearance. 'It's an unfortunate by-product of the job.'

Larry smiled. 'You're being too modest.' He turned to Nan. 'So, how are you, Catherine?'

While he and Nan spoke, Eddie none too gently ushered Elizabeth into a corner. 'Fucking hell, Lizzie!' he hissed. 'Why didn't you tell me he was coming?'

'Because if I had, you would have found some excuse to avoid him,' she replied in an icy whisper.

'Yeah, because I don't want anything to bloody do with him!'

'I told you in New York last year that it was time you tried to mend some bridges. And when you asked me for his phone number, I thought you were going to do that – but since it's now eight months later and nothing's happened, I decided to move things along.'

Eddie *had* asked for the telephone number, after witnessing another estranged father and son reconciling, but in the end his deep-rooted resentments had prevented him from making the call. 'You should have minded your own fucking business.'

'And you should grow up,' she snapped. 'Like you said, it's been over twenty years since you last saw each other. Dad's changed; it's time you did too.'

'Only thing that's changed about him is that he's got less hair and more gut.'

'The same could be said about you. For God's sake, Eddie, the least you can do is be civil. For Nan's sake, if nothing else.'

He couldn't offer a counter to that. Fuming, he turned away from his sister, to see Larry engaged in conversation with Nina once more. He quickly returned to them, interposing himself to give his father an overt cold shoulder.

But it was too late. 'Larry's invited us for dinner tonight,' said Nina, narrowing her eyes in disapproval of his unsubtle blocking manoeuvre.

'Yeah? Shame we can't make it.'

'I've accepted.'

His face darkened. 'Oh, you have, have you?'

'Yes, I have. For both of us.' She leaned round him to address Larry. 'It'll be a pleasure.'

Larry smiled. 'I'll tell my wife to make something special. Look forward to seeing you. Both.' He said goodbye to his other family members, apologising for having to return to work, then with a wave and a jingle of his expensive gold wristwatch he departed.

'Ooh, that was an unexpected pleasure,' said Nan. 'Wasn't it, Edward?'

'Yeah, it was unexpected,' he replied through his teeth.

A doctor entered and went to Nan's bedside. She had recovered enough to be discharged, he said; she would need to continue oxygen therapy for several days, but the severe breathing difficulty that had caused her hospitalisation had been eased and her blood pressure lowered. Eddie offered to help, but Elizabeth insisted that she and Holly could handle it, and that he and Nina should check into their hotel before meeting them at Elizabeth's house. 'That way,' Elizabeth added, 'you'll have plenty of time to get ready before going to Dad's tonight.'

'I can't wait,' Eddie growled.

★

A few minutes later, he was less restrained. 'For fuck's sake, Nina!' he barked as they cleared the hospital doors. 'Why did you say yes to dinner? Lizzie sticking her bloody nose in I expect, but you? You're my wife, you're supposed to be on my side!'

'Yes, I'm your wife,' Nina shot back, 'and hey, guess what that means? Larry's my father-in-law! When he invites me to dinner, I can hardly flip the bird in his face. You're the one who's got problems with him, not me – I just met the man. I'm not going to be rude to him for no reason, especially not in front of Nan and Holly.'

'Told you plenty of bloody reasons.'

'You're hardly an unbiased source. And it all happened a long time ago—'

'It still fucking happened, though.'

'Then maybe it's time you put it behind you!' she cried. 'What happened with Girilal and Shankarpa in India certainly made you think about contacting him, so why didn't you?'

'Changed my mind.'

'Why?'

''Cause my mind changed.'

'That's not an answer!'

'I don't fucking care! I don't like it when people think they know what's best for me, that's all. I decided I didn't want to see him; that should have been enough. But no, Lizzie had to stick her oar in, and then you backed her up!'

'He's still your father, Eddie. What would you have done if it had been Larry in that bed instead of Nan?'

They reached the car. 'I wouldn't have come.'

She was shocked by his coldness. 'What?'

'Look, he had an affair while my mum was dying of cancer!' Eddie snarled. 'Some things you just don't forgive. I don't, anyway. To be honest, I couldn't give a shit if I never see him again as long as I live.' He got into the Mondeo and slammed the door.

Nina entered on the other side. She sat in silence for a moment, then turned to him. 'There's something I never told you,' she said quietly. 'I once got into a huge fight with my parents – they were going on their expedition to Tibet right in the middle of my exams, and they absolutely refused to let me go with them, said my exams were more important. And I was *so* mad at them. I was a teenage girl being denied something she really wanted, so I said all kinds of things I wish I hadn't. But they went without me anyway, and . . . that's when they died.'

She lowered her head. 'It was just a one-off thing, a stupid argument. I loved them. But . . .' She looked up at him, tears glistening in the corners of her eyes. 'I can't change the past, I can't bring them back. But I would give anything to have been able to apologise to them before they left. I'm not saying you've got anything to apologise for, but if you've got a chance to settle your differences you should take it. If this *is* the last time you ever see him, do you really want it to be like this?'

After a long pause, Eddie blew out a frustrated breath. 'All right. We'll go for dinner,' he said, reluctance clear in every word. 'But I'm only doing it for you, okay? Not for Lizzie, and definitely not for him.'

She wiped her eyes and smiled. 'Thanks. But you're not only doing it for me – you're doing it for yourself too.'

He squeezed her hand, then started the car. 'Well, whoever I'm doing it for, let's hope it's not a huge fucking mistake.'

3

Larry Chase's home was not in Bournemouth, but further east along the coast, about nine miles from the busy port of Southampton. 'Wow,' said Nina as the Mondeo pulled up. 'Your dad's place is huge.' It was an old red-brick farmhouse, but one that had been extensively renovated, surrounded by a couple of acres of lush grounds. A brand new silver Jaguar XKR sports coupé was parked outside, an open double garage revealing a black Range Rover and a lipstick-red Mazda MX-5 roadster within. 'He must be doing well for himself.'

'Making a few quid was never one of his problems,' Eddie said. '*How* he makes it . . . that's another story.' He got out of the car before she could ask him to elaborate.

Nina had made an effort to dress up, wearing a skirt and a pair of high heels. Eddie, however, was in his usual jeans, T-shirt and black leather jacket, not even having bothered to shave. He trudged to the front door and rang the bell as Nina joined him.

Larry opened the door. 'Hello, welcome!' he proclaimed. 'Come inside. Here, let me.' He took Nina's jacket as she entered and hung it in a small cloakroom before turning to his son, but Eddie had already removed his own jacket and pointedly placed it on top of Nina's. 'I'm glad you're both here. Elizabeth's been on at me for ages to get in touch with you.' He became more sombre. 'I just wish it hadn't taken your grandmother giving us all such a scare for it to happen.'

'Yeah, mc too,' Eddie said flatly.

'But,' Larry went on, brightening again, 'it's still an opportunity for us to bury the hatchet, I hope. Twenty-two years – it's a long time. Too long, wouldn't you say?'

'Yes, I would,' said Nina, when Eddie showed no sign of answering.

'So would I. Anyway, come and meet my wife. Julie! Company's here!'

A pretty blonde woman entered the hall, the heels of her black leather boots clacking on the polished tiles. 'Hi, how are you?' she said enthusiastically, kissing Nina on the cheek before doing the same to Eddie, to his discomfiture.

'This is my wife, Julie,' said Larry, putting an arm round her shoulder. 'Julie, I'd like you meet my son Eddie, and his wife, Nina.'

'So, when did you get remarried?' Eddie asked, tone more accusing than interested.

'Two years ago,' Julie told him.

'Surprised Elizabeth didn't tell you,' Larry added.

Eddie smiled, with no warmth. 'I didn't ask her.' He regarded the blonde, who was wearing a tight, low-cut satin dress in a vivid electric blue, as well as a plenitude of gold jewellery. 'So, Julie. How old are you?'

'Ah, come on, Eddie,' said Nina, trying to keep things light. 'You know you shouldn't ask a lady her age.' Admittedly, she was curious herself. Julie was considerably younger than her husband.

Julie flapped a hand, bracelets tinkling. 'Oh, I don't mind. I'm thirty-six.'

'Thirty-*six*?' Eddie exclaimed.

'I know, it's a bit of an age gap. But that doesn't matter when you love each other, does it?' She rested her head on Larry's shoulder.

Eddie was still dismayed. 'You're younger than me!'

'Yes, I know – when Larry told me about you I thought it might be a bit weird, me being your stepmother. But if you want you can think of me as more like a stepsister!'

Eddie's silence and fixed expression told her exactly how well her joke had been received. 'So,' said Larry after a moment, 'Julie, why don't you sort us out some drinks? I'll show Nina and Eddie round the house.' Julie gave her guests a hesitant smile, then clicked back down the hall.

Larry went to a flight of stairs. 'Come on, we'll do upstairs first.' He started up them.

'Half his age plus seven years,' Eddie muttered to Nina as they followed.

'What?'

'That's the rule, remember? For how old a woman has to be to stop the bloke from being a creepy old pervert.'

'So?'

'He's sixty. You're the mental arithmetic genius, work it out.'

Nina sighed. It was already obvious that the evening was not going to be a roaring success; the best result would simply be getting through it without a fistfight.

The house's interior was impressive, expensive . . . and decidedly masculine. If there were any rooms where Julie had been given free rein to apply a feminine touch, Larry opted not to include them in the tour. Instead, he showed off those parts he considered most important: a well-equipped gym; a sauna; a home cinema with a floor-shaking sound system and practically a whole wall of DVDs and Blu-rays, Nina awarding him a few approving brownie points when she noticed that the collection included the complete works of Monty Python. Slightly to her surprise, a large attic was filled by a model railway. It wasn't a hobby she would have expected of such an obvious Type A personality, but as Larry explained, 'I've had model railways since I was a kid. That way, I know there's at least one place where the trains run on time.'

'Yeah, you always did like being in control, didn't you?' said Eddie. He tweaked a dial, and a train jerked into motion.

'Do you mind?' Larry snapped.

'What? I'm not going to break it.'

'It wouldn't be the first time.' He flicked a master switch to turn off the power.

Eddie shook his head. 'Christ, I crash a toy train once as a kid, and I'm banned for life.'

'They're not toys,' his father said with irritation.

'It's really amazing,' Nina cut in, hoping to forestall an argument. She examined one of the little buildings, a replica of an English country pub. 'And it's so detailed!'

'Detail is everything,' said Larry. 'If you want to be successful, you need to cover every last detail, whether you're doing something yourself or delegating. Like this.' He swept a hand over the layout. 'I don't have the time to make everything myself, but I always make sure that when someone else works for me, they know exactly what I expect from them.'

'You paid someone to make this for you?' Eddie said scathingly. 'Where's the fun in that? You might as well hire someone to stand here and drive the trains.'

To Nina's relief, a call came that dinner was almost ready, and they trooped downstairs. Drinks were served, then the meal began. With the addition of the chirpy Julie to the mix, the conversation became less tense. However, halfway through the main course of beef carpaccio with marinated salad, Nina realised she would have to be the designated driver as Eddie, keeping pace with his father, poured himself a third glass of wine. Not even having finished her first glass, she switched to water. 'I'm no expert on the linguistic ins and outs of England,' she said to Larry, 'but I can tell you don't have the same accent as Eddie. Are you not from Yorkshire originally?'

'Oh, no,' he replied. 'I'm from Bucks.' Nina gave him a blank look. 'Buckinghamshire, in the Home Counties. The rich parts around London,' he clarified. 'I used to spend a lot of time travelling between the ports at Liverpool and Hull for work, and the M62, the motorway between them, was just being finished. So I picked somewhere to live that was right in the middle. Same reason I moved down here, actually. A lot of my work goes through Southampton, so it made sense to be near the port. Turned out well in both cases. I met Julie down here – she used to be my secretary – and met my first wife in Yorkshire.'

'You mean *Mum*,' Eddie rumbled.

'What is your work?' Nina asked quickly. 'Eddie said it was something to do with shipping.' His actual words had been 'shipping, or some bollocks', but she kept that to herself.

Larry gestured at a shelf. 'Julie, there are some of my cards on there – can you get one for Nina?' Julie stood and retrieved one, and handed it to Nina.

'Thanks,' Nina said. A stark, modern logo in deep blue stood out at the card's top above the company name. 'Chase International Logistics?'

'That's right,' said Larry with a smug smile. 'I left the old firm ten years ago and went into business for myself. And it's worked out rather well.'

'So what does international logistics entail?' Not wanting to seem rude by discarding it, she slipped the card into her breast pocket.

'Getting things from where they are to where they're wanted as quickly as possible with the minimum of hassle. Including from officials. I go all over the world, getting to know the right people. A word in someone's ear can mean the difference between a package being held up by red tape for a week or clearing customs in an hour.'

Eddie took another chug of wine. 'And it's all totally legal, obviously.' His voice was full of sarcasm.

'Everything's above board, if that's what you're implying,' said Larry, frowning.

'Well, yeah. After that time you got investigated by Customs and Excise, I suppose you'd want to make sure all the paperwork's in order.'

Nina and Julie exchanged awkward looks as Larry stabbed his fork into his last piece of beef. 'That was just a random audit. They do hundreds of them every year.' He put the meat in his mouth and chewed on it ferociously.

'But they don't normally come round to people's houses and take all their files away, do they?' It was Eddie's turn to look smug.

Mouth full, Larry couldn't reply, but from his scowl it was clear he was planning a retaliatory shot. 'So, everyone finished?' Julie said hurriedly. 'Larry, love, can you help me put the plates in the dishwasher?'

Once they had gone, Nina put her head in her hands. 'God, Eddie.'

'What?' he said, shrugging innocently. 'Just being nostalgic.'

'Can you be less *aggressively* nostalgic? Please?'

Dessert was served, baked peaches stuffed with mascarpone

and almonds, both Eddie and Larry washing it down with more wine. Nina was grateful to Julie for steering the conversation away from anything that might spark another round of sniping between father and son. 'It sounds like you have an amazing life,' she said to the archaeologist. 'One great big adventure!'

'It's not all adventure,' Nina assured her. 'I spend more time than I'd like in an office. But we're doing some fieldwork at Glastonbury tomorrow, in King Arthur's tomb.'

'Wow. And archaeology's how you met Eddie?'

'Yes – he'd been hired as my bodyguard. He's kept me safe from the bad guys since then.' She smiled and put a hand on his arm.

'That's really romantic,' said Julie, ignoring Larry's faint but dismissive huff. 'And exciting, too. Eddie, how many bad guys have you had to deal with?'

'Oh, a fair few,' said Eddie, for the first time that evening giving an answer without any snarky undertones. 'But I used to be in the SAS, so I can handle myself.' Julie was highly impressed by the revelation, deepening Larry's irritation. 'A punch in the face usually sorts 'em out.'

'Well, that's one thing you were always good at as a kid,' said Larry loudly as he took another drink. 'Hitting people, I mean. What was the name of that boy you used to bully? Peter something – Peter Clackett, that was it. I remember when his parents came round to complain about you beating him up.'

'Larry . . .' Julie implored.

But he was on a roll. 'Of course, it was the police who started coming round when you got older. Still,' he continued, addressing Nina, 'I'm glad he's finally put his, ah, talent to constructive use.'

'Well, personally, Larry,' said Nina defensively, 'I think Eddie's a fantastic man, and I wouldn't change a thing about him.' That wasn't entirely true, but she hoped it would divert the discussion down a less argumentative path. Though in truth she was startled to hear that her husband had been a bully as a child – and that he had made no attempt to deny it.

'Thanks, love,' said Eddie, to her relief sounding cheery rather than angry. He ate a piece of peach, following it with more wine, then said, 'Mind you, I might have turned out better as a kid if I'd had a good role model. Not someone who was hardly ever there 'cause he was off giving backhanders to crooked customs men and shagging other women behind his wife's back.'

Larry banged down his spoon. 'Oh, God,' Nina moaned under her breath.

'But after I left home,' Eddie went on, 'the army knocked some sense into me, so I turned out okay in the end. You know, serving my country, saving lives . . .'

'Marrying terrorists,' said Larry, turning to Julie. 'Did you know his first wife was Sophia Blackwood – the woman who tried to blow up New York?' Julie was too embarrassed to reply.

'Still, I managed not to cheat on her,' Eddie snapped. A sarcastic sneer. 'So, what contributions to humanity have you been making for the last twenty years? Bit of this, bit of that, makin' deals . . . playing with your toy trains.'

'Maybe I *should* have been around more,' Larry growled. 'I would have knocked some *respect* into you.'

'Oh, you would, would you?' said Eddie, challenging. 'Big man, hitting his kid, eh?'

'I certainly wouldn't have let you run riot like your mother did.'

Eddie jumped up, jolting the table and knocking over his wine glass as he jabbed a finger at his father. 'Don't you fucking *dare* criticise Mum! Not after what you did to her.'

Larry also sprang to his feet. 'Don't you swear at me in my own house!'

'Why, what're you gonna do? Spank me? Or maybe you're going to knock some respect into me. Come on, give it a try!'

Both wives stood too, trying to calm their husbands. 'Eddie, *Eddie*, come on,' said Nina. 'We should probably get moving, huh? It's getting late.'

'Suits me fine,' said Eddie. 'Thanks for dinner, Julie. We'll see ourselves out.' He stormed from the room.

Nina shot Larry a disgusted look – he had, after all, been just as responsible as Eddie for the evening's unpleasant turn – before facing his wife. 'I'm sorry, Julie.'

'So am I,' she replied, equally apologetic. 'I hope the rest of your stay is . . . better.'

'Me too. Bye.' With a sigh, she followed Eddie, who had already donned his leather jacket and was waiting at the door. 'What the hell was that?' she hissed as she collected her own jacket. 'You couldn't stay civil for two hours?'

Eddie walked out. 'What? He bloody started it.'

'You were both as bad as each other,' she said, catching up. 'Yes, he was acting like an ass, but you didn't have to do the same!'

'I didn't want to fucking come at all, remember? The whole thing's your fault for dragging me here.'

'Oh, right, blame me! That's really goddamn mature, Eddie.' They reached the car, Eddie heading for the driver's side. 'What are you doing?'

'Getting in the car, what does it look like?'

'You're not driving, not after all that wine.'

He slapped the key on the roof with a clang. 'Whatever, fucking fine. Maybe I'll walk back instead.'

'Don't tempt me,' said Nina, tight-lipped. She took the key and unlocked the Mondeo.

Eddie dropped heavily into the passenger seat and slammed his door. 'Well, if you're so fucking embarrassed to be seen with me, I'll save you any social humiliation and not go to Glastonbury tomorrow. You can find your own bloody way there. I'll spend the day with Nan, like I promised. At least I know there's one member of my family who appreciates me.'

'Fine. What-*ever*.' Teeth clenched, Nina started the engine and, over-revving, powered down the drive.

4

Eddie departed the hotel the next morning without breakfast or even a word, leaving Nina in a bad mood. She was still mad at him – and Larry – for their sheer *childishness*.

Her outfit from the previous night was on a chair; she folded the skirt and blouse to return them to her suitcase. The creased business card dropped to the floor. She glowered at it, then found her wallet and slipped it inside. Amongst the phone numbers was Larry's home; though she had no particular desire to talk to him, she might still want to speak to Julie, if only to apologise again.

But for now she had work to do. Though she had spoken to the trustees of Glastonbury Tor from New York, the hastiness of the arrangements meant she wanted to check that all was in order before setting out. She started making calls.

Half an hour later, everything was confirmed. Nina tied her hair back in a ponytail and was gathering her belongings when her phone rang. Eddie? No, Macy. 'Hello?'

'Hi, Nina!' From the background noise, Macy was apparently in a car, and going at considerable speed.

'Hey, Macy. Where are you?'

'On the freeway. M3, I think it's called. I'm on my way to you.'

'Did you bring either of the statues?'

'I've got both of them! Mr Penrose persuaded Dr Assad to

let the Egyptian one go on vacation, and your friend at Interpol – Mr Jindal? He said yes right away about the other one. Are you still in this Bournemouth place?'

'Yes, I'm at the hotel.' Nina gave her the postcode.

'Okay,' Macy said after entering it into the satnav, 'it says I'm seventy-five miles from you. Also says it'll take an hour twenty-five to get there, but pshht! I can do better than that.' The engine note rose.

'There's no rush, Macy,' Nina told her. 'They're not expecting us there until lunchtime.'

'No problem. You and Eddie can show me round England first.'

'Eddie's not coming today.'

'No? Huh. Why not?'

'Personal reasons,' was the only answer Nina felt like giving. 'I'll see you soon.'

'Where's Nina today?' asked Nan.

She and Eddie were on a clifftop road overlooking the sea, Bournemouth's pier jutting into the English Channel to the west. He was pushing her along in a wheelchair, an oxygen cylinder on its back connected to her breath mask; though unhappy about the enforced helplessness of her situation, for now she had resigned herself to it. 'She's gone to Glastonbury, Nan,' he told her. 'Some archaeological thing.'

'Oh, I see. Why haven't you gone with her?'

He was still simmering from the previous night, but kept it to himself. 'Because you wanted me to take you out for a walk,' he said instead. 'So here I am!'

'But what if something happens to her?'

'Like what?'

'I don't know, but things always seem to happen to you two.

Like the last time you were here, and the Imax got blown up.'
She pointed at a tower crane inshore of the pier, marking the
site where a group of Russian mercenaries had come to a fiery
end. 'They had to demolish it, you know. Which was marvellous,
it was a hideous building! But I do worry.'

'Well, there's nothing to worry about at the moment. Far as
I know, we haven't upset any cults, there aren't any ancient
civilisations somebody wants to keep secret and nobody's trying
to kill us.'

'That's as may be, but I can't help it. And I'm sure Nina
would feel better with you there.' They continued along the
road for a short while before Nan spoke again. 'What are you
going to do today if Nina's not here, then?'

'You make it sound like I can't do anything without her
permission.'

'You know what I mean – you're a couple, you usually do
things together.'

He hadn't actually thought any further ahead than what he
was now doing. 'I dunno. Maybe spend the afternoon with you
and Holly and Lizzie.'

'Holly's gone out with her friends.' She looked back at him
with a knowing little smile. 'But I'm sure you and Elizabeth
will have lots to talk about.'

'Yeah, right.' His relationship with his older sister was brittle
enough at the best of times, and since she would certainly have
called their father for a report on the previous night, Eddie
didn't doubt that she would have plenty to say on the matter.
'But I don't want to just abandon you.'

'Oh, don't be silly! You don't have to hang around all day
with an old goose like me. There must be other people you can
see while you're here. What about your friend, the Scottish
gentleman?'

'Mac?' Nan had met him on a couple of occasions, most recently a party to celebrate Eddie and Nina's first wedding anniversary.

'Yes, him. He was very charming. Where does he live?'

'London.'

'Well, that's less than two hours away on the train. You should call him.'

Eddie considered it. 'You know, I think I will.'

'You see? Your old nan still knows what's best. You should always find the time to catch up with your friends – you never know when you'll see them next.' She pointed again, this time to a scenic overlook. 'Oh, Edward, can you take me over there? It's one of my favourite spots.'

At the height of the summer holiday season the clifftop was thronged with tourists, but people were good-natured enough to clear a space for an old lady in a wheelchair. 'Will you help me up?' she asked Eddie.

'You're supposed to stay in the chair, Nan.'

'I'm not a cripple, Edward. Come on, give me a hand.' She pushed herself from the seat.

Reluctantly, Eddie helped her to her feet, aware how light and fragile she felt in contrast to the firm and busy figure from his childhood. It was evidently a struggle, as she took several heavy breaths and forced back a cough, but she managed to stand and lean against the fence. 'Thank you. Oh, look at that! Isn't it lovely?'

It was indeed quite a sight. The air was clear, providing a panoramic view along the coast to Poole Harbour and beyond. The sea glittered under the noon sun, the long beach dotted with hundreds of sunbathers. Seagulls drifted lazily overhead, gliding on the warm rising air. 'Yeah, it is,' Eddie agreed, the view lifting his mood.

Nan regarded it in silence for some time, taking the sun on her face, before eventually lowering herself back into the chair. Eddie helped her sit. She coughed again, harder, then cleared her throat. 'I'm glad I got to see it again. Especially with you. I do like the sea. You know, I've told Elizabeth that when I go, that's where I want my ashes to be scattered.'

Eddie didn't like the new turn in the conversation at all. 'You can see it again whenever you want, Nan. And I'll be back to see it with you before too long, don't you worry.'

'Oh, I'm not worried about me, Edward. I've had a good run. But your old nan is . . . well, starting to fall apart.' She tapped the oxygen mask. 'I don't want to hang around if I have to be tubed up in some hospital. I'd rather just fall asleep and never wake up.'

He had heard her say similar things before, but always jokily. This time, though, it was almost in resignation. 'Don't talk like that, Nan. You'll be around for a long time yet.'

She smiled up at him. 'You're a good lad, Edward, thank you. But I've done everything I wanted. I've got grandchildren, I've got great-grandchildren, and about the only thing I still want is to see you and Nina give me another one.'

'Not sure when that'll be,' said Eddie, 'but if that's what it takes to make sure you don't go anywhere, then I'll see what we can do.'

Another smile behind the mask. 'That's nice. But it's your world now. Nobody should stay around past their time.'

Her words made Eddie's throat tighten as though he was being choked. He looked away, following his grandmother's gaze across the peaceful sea.

Nina didn't need the satellite navigation system of Macy's rented Range Rover Evoque to tell her how far they were from their destination. The tiered hump of Glastonbury Tor, the ruined tower of a medieval church atop the green hill, stood out for miles on the plain of farmland surrounding it. 'There it is.'

'Good,' Macy replied. 'I didn't know driving in England would be so stressy.' After being stuck behind a slow-moving horsebox for several miles, she had finally lost patience and blasted past it on a near-blind corner, to Nina's armrest-clutching dismay.

'Because of being on the wrong side?'

'That, and these roads.' She jabbed a manicured finger at the winding lane ahead. 'I've used Scotch tape that's wider! And what's with all the twists and turns? Did the Brits lose straight line technology after the Romans left?'

Nina smiled. 'Well, not much farther now. And I think you'll find Glastonbury relaxing. I know I did.'

'Didn't you get chased and shot at?'

'I meant apart from that!'

Before long, they arrived at the Tor. There had been changes since Nina's previous visit; following her discovery of King Arthur's tomb beneath the hill, a large part of the southeastern face was now fenced off, portable cabins acting as headquarters and labs for the ongoing dig.

They were met by the archaeological team's leader, Dr William Barley. The elderly man wore thick round glasses and had a pipe clenched between his teeth. 'Dr Wilde, welcome. A great honour to have you here.'

'Thank you,' Nina replied. 'This is my assistant, Macy Sharif.'

'Very good to meet you,' said Barley. 'Now, Dr Wilde, you said your visit was a potential security matter?'

'That's right,' said Nina, removing the case containing the

two statuettes from the Evoque, as well as a larger one which she presented to Macy, who stared at it uncomprehendingly before realising she was expected to carry it and grudgingly taking it. 'The IHA came into possession of artefacts that may have a connection to Glastonbury.'

Barley sucked wetly on his pipe stem. 'Not sure what to think about this cloak and dagger business you have at the IHA. I can understand keeping things quiet to stop treasure hunters, but it's hard to imagine how anything found in an archaeological site could pose any risks to global security.'

'You'd be surprised,' said Nina. 'Can we see the tomb?'

'Of course. This way.' Barley plodded to the tomb entrance, which was now covered by a wood and brick structure watched by CCTV cameras. He unlocked the door to reveal a narrow tunnel leading down into the heart of the Tor. Apart from the addition of a string of electric lights, it was just as Nina remembered finding it two years earlier, the Roman numerals inscribed into one of the stone supports marking the year of its construction: 1191 AD. The monks of Glastonbury Abbey had secretly excavated the tomb and moved the bodies of Arthur and Guinevere – and Arthur's legendary sword, Excalibur – to a new resting place to prevent their abbey's greatest treasures from being plundered.

She also remembered other things she had discovered within. 'You've, ah, found all the death traps, I hope?'

Barley chortled. 'No need to worry, Dr Wilde. Everything's been made safe.'

'Glad to hear it! Okay, if you'll lead the way?'

He knocked out his pipe against the wall before picking his way down the steep tunnel, Nina and Macy following. At the bottom of the incline was the start of a literal maze, one of the tomb's defences, but Barley led them briskly through it. Past the statue of the Lady of the Lake, down through what on Nina's first visit had been a flooded labyrinth, up into a foul-smelling space where a great grinning relief of Merlin once marked an explosive end for the unwary, and finally into the vaulted chamber of the tomb itself. The side room containing the black stone coffins of Arthur and his queen was open.

Macy took it in with awe. 'Wow, this is incredible. I only saw pictures before – didn't think I'd get to see it for real.'

'Working for the IHA has its perks,' Nina joked. She became more serious as she examined the object between the coffins. It was a cube of granite, three feet to a side, with a narrow slot in the top from which Excalibur had once protruded – and a chunk sliced from one corner where she had inadvertently discovered that in the right hands, Arthur's weapon was more than a mere sword.

'So, what are these artefacts?' Barley asked. Nina opened the case. The British scientist seemed underwhelmed by the figurines within. 'I don't recognise them.'

'Nor do we – and that's the problem. I'm hoping that bringing them here will prove . . . illuminating.'

Nina hadn't planned on making a pun, but couldn't resist. She touched one of the statuettes. As she had hoped, the tomb was still a confluence point for lines of earth energy – and whatever it was about her that had allowed Excalibur to slice effortlessly through solid stone now caused the figurine to light up with an eerie indigo glow.

'Good God!' cried Barley.

Macy's response was much the same. 'Whoa!' she yelped, flinching back. 'It's not radioactive, is it?'

Nina lifted her finger from the statue, and the glow vanished. 'Open the case, and we'll find out.'

Macy was about to put the case on Arthur's coffin when a

stammered protest from Barley prompted her to switch to the granite block. She opened it, and Nina took out a piece of equipment. 'Geiger counter,' she explained. 'Macy, you hold it while I touch the statue again.'

Macy held the counter at arm's length, cringing as the figurine lit up. Nothing came from the machine except the intermittent crackles of normal background radiation. 'I wish you'd checked that first, before maybe zapping us with gamma rays,' she complained.

'What causes that glow?' Barley asked, stepping closer.

'It's a phenomenon called earth energy,' said Nina, 'but as for exactly how it works, I can't tell you. Not because it's classified – although it is – but because I genuinely don't understand it myself. I'm not a physicist. All I know are its effects.'

'Which are . . . ?'

'Classified.'

Barley sighed. 'I suspected as much.'

Nina placed the first statue on the block, then took the other from the case. It too reacted in the same way to her touch, filling the chamber with an unnatural light. But she noticed something as she put the second figure down beside the first: the effect was not uniform.

Macy saw it too. 'It's brighter on the side facing the other one – like it's responding to it.'

Nina picked up the second statuette again and slowly moved it in a circle round the first. There was indeed a somewhat stronger band of light on one side of the figure, which changed position as the stone was moved, so that it always shone in the direction of the statue's near-twin. 'Like holding a magnet to a compass,' Barley mused.

'There's a compass in the case,' Nina said. 'Macy, get it out;

we'll see if it's some kind of magnetic effect.'

It wasn't, the needle unmoving. Nina picked up both statues experimentally, wondering if each would show a bright band when they were aglow. They did, pointing towards each other no matter the figures' relative positions. Whatever caused the earth energy effect, whoever made the two statuettes had found a practical use for it – if somebody who could utilise the phenomenon had one statue in their possession, they could use it to find the other.

But there was something else – another, barely discernible line of increased illumination on each. Whatever this pointed towards, it was unmoving. Still holding the statues, she walked back and forth across the chamber in the hope of spotting a parallax effect. None was evident. The cause was apparently some distance away.

'What if it's the third statue?' Macy suggested.

'There's another one?' Barley asked.

'Yes – they fit together.' Nina returned to the block and slotted the statues together, arms interlocking. This time, there *was* a change: the two lines merged into one, much brighter, still pointing in the direction of the fainter bands she had seen moments before.

She turned the linked figures. The glow remained stationary, the band of light rippling over the crude carved features as she rotated them. It *was* a pointer. One that led to the missing third of the triptych.

But what was the statues' purpose, and who had created them?

Nina let go, the illumination instantly vanishing. Macy tapped at the figurines, but nothing happened. Barley warily followed suit, with the same lack of result. 'It's only you, Dr Wilde,' he said.

'Must be my electrifying personality.' Silence. 'Oh come on, that was funny.'

'Mm,' said Macy, not quite a ringing endorsement. 'Touch it again – I want to check something.' Nina brought her hand back to the statues and the strange light returned. Macy held the compass above the glowing figures, taking a bearing. 'So it's pointing . . . just about exactly southwest. If there really is a third statue, it's somewhere that way.'

'Southwest . . .' Nina echoed. She turned to Barley. 'Do you have a globe?'

The Tor's Arthurian archaeological team did not in fact have a globe of the world to hand, but they had the next best thing; a virtual equivalent on Barley's computer. 'Are you sure you want to rule out any potential sites in the UK?' he asked in response to Nina's request for him to zoom out. 'Dartmoor alone has over eight hundred Neolithic and Bronze Age sites, and that's southwest of here.'

'I have a hunch that we're looking for something more far-flung,' she said. 'The first statue was found on another continent – in a chamber that was sealed centuries before the start of the European Bronze Age.'

The image on the screen pulled back more and more, until the Earth's curvature appeared at the edges of the screen. Nina followed a line running diagonally down and to the left from Glastonbury, at the map's centre. Though it passed close to the Azores, out in the Atlantic, it didn't touch land until it reached South America, visible only as a line of green along the very edge of the visible hemisphere. 'Can you switch it to a cartographic view?'

Barley fussed with the controls. The image changed, continents distorting as they morphed from a three-dimensional representation to a flat one. The line now made landfall near the great delta of the Orinoco river, on the continent's northern coast. 'Venezuela?' said Macy.

'And Colombia. And Brazil, *and* Peru,' Nina added, following the line southwest through more countries until it reached the Pacific.

'Rather a lot of ground to cover,' said Barley. 'And I think you'll find Dartmoor a lot easier to reach!'

'The best sites are always in the worst places . . .' She regarded the map. South America: home to numerous ancient civilisations. Could one have possessed the third statue? It was possible. But which – and why?

She thanked Barley, gently reminding him of the need for discretion, and headed back to the Range Rover with Macy. 'So what now?' Macy asked.

'I don't know. Like Dr Barley said, there's a lot of ground to cover. And we don't have a distance, only a direction.'

There was one thing she was sure of, though. Ancient artefacts that could conduct earth energy definitely fell within the IHA's remit. If there was a third statue somewhere in South America, it was up to her to find it.

Before anyone else did.

Eddie put a pint of beer and a whisky on the table. 'There you go.'

'Thanks,' said Mac, leaning forward to pick up his glass. His left leg creaked faintly, metal and plastic rather than flesh and bone; he had lost the limb from the knee down in Afghanistan. He took a sip of whisky, then looked round the sunlit beer garden. 'Nice afternoon for a trip to the seaside. I'm glad you called – it was looking to be a rather boring day otherwise.'

'Any excuse to get out of work, right?' said Eddie, grinning.

'Hmph. I wish. The jobs from Vauxhall Cross seem to be drying up of late.'

Vauxhall Cross in London was the location of the headquarters of Britain's Secret Intelligence Service, better known as MI6. Since his retirement from the military, Mac had on occasion worked for the agency as what was euphemistically described as a 'consultant', even though some of his operations had been very hands-on. 'Really?' said Eddie. 'Alderley not appreciating you, is he? Miserable sod. After everything you've done for him . . .'

Mac shook his head. 'Peter's not the problem. It's more that everything I've got to offer – contacts, local knowledge, intel . . . it's all getting a bit out of date. The whole world's moving on, Eddie, and when you're not at the centre of things you start to get left behind, unfortunately.' A small sigh, then his expression changed to one of curiosity. 'And speaking of being left behind, you seem to have been abandoned by your other half. Where's Nina today?'

'Glastonbury. Work stuff.'

'And you're not with her?' Eddie's lack of an immediate response told his friend volumes. 'Things all right with the two of you?'

'Just having a rough patch,' the Yorkshireman admitted. 'You know what it's like. Everything seems to end up in an argument. And we had a pretty big one last night.'

'About what?'

'My dad. We had dinner with him and his wife, and . . . it could've gone better.'

'You actually met him?' Mac was surprised. 'A long time since that last happened.'

'Twenty-odd years, yeah. Lizzie basically tricked me into it. I would've told him to fuck off when he invited us to dinner, but Nina insisted that we go. And that turned out fucking brilliantly. He hasn't changed – he's still an arsehole.'

'Hrmm.'

Eddie eyed the older man. 'Hrmm what?'

'Oh, nothing.'

'Bollocks, nothing. That wasn't a "that's interesting" hrmm or an "I need to think about this" hrmm – that was a "you're being an idiot but it's not my place to comment" hrmm. What?'

'Well, since you ask,' said Mac, sitting up with a faint smile, 'I don't think you're an idiot—'

'Cheers, always good to know.'

'—but I know you well enough to imagine that . . . well, perhaps he wasn't the only one who hadn't changed.'

'You saying *I'm* an arsehole?'

The smile reappeared. 'Never crossed my mind,' said Mac, before his face became more serious. 'But he made the first move – he was the one who put out his hand.'

'So?'

'So he was trying to have some sort of reconciliation, at least. Apparently it didn't go well, but still, he made the effort.'

'Doesn't mean that I should've been all fawning and grateful.'

'I'm not saying that. I know there are some rather large issues between the two of you. But it could be worth trying to deal with them while you have the chance.'

The older man's tone made Eddie suspect there was more behind his words than he was saying. 'Sounds like something that's been on your mind.'

A silence, then: 'It has,' Mac admitted. 'I got in touch with Angela recently.'

'After so long? You've been divorced for, what, seven years?'

'Eight. But we met up a couple of months ago. It went rather well, actually.'

'Are you thinking about getting back together?' asked Eddie in surprise.

'No, nothing like that – it's been too long, too much water under the bridge. But it was . . . *nice*. It reminded me how much we had in common. And in all honesty, the older I get, the more I've realised how easy it is to lose contact with people. You can't rely on them just being there any more – you have to make an effort. It might be hard, but it can be worth it.'

'And you reckon I should make an effort with my dad?'

Mac took another drink. 'Just a thought.'

'It might get Nina off my back, I suppose.' Eddie's phone rang; he recognised the ringtone. 'Speak of the devil . . .' He answered it. 'Hey, love. Where are you?'

'Just leaving Glastonbury with Macy,' said Nina. 'Heading back to Bournemouth.'

'Did you find anything interesting?'

'You could say that.' Enthusiasm was clear in her voice. 'We need to get back to New York. I think we're going to be busy.'

5

New York City

'You know, if these things react to earth energy,' said Eddie, peering at the statuettes inside their display case in Nina's office, 'maybe we should ask DARPA where to look. They know how to find the stuff, after all.'

'I don't think they'd be too happy to hear from us,' Nina replied sarcastically, looking up from her laptop. 'Since we blew up their top-secret billion-dollar ship.'

'All right, Christ, just a suggestion,' Eddie snapped back. The bad feelings left over from the disastrous dinner had faded, but things were still prickly. 'How about President Cole, then? He owes us a favour – we saved his life. And a whole bunch of other world leaders too. Come to think of it, the Russian president was one of 'em. Ask him if we can go back to Grozevny. We can get a triangulation from there.'

'Oh yeah, great idea. Remember the nuclear submarine that sank there? Still kind of a sore point with the Russians.'

'Hey, it wasn't our fault it sank. Well, not entirely . . .'

'Besides,' she said, going to a large map of the world on one wall, 'even if we got another result from Grozevny, I don't think it would help much.' A red thread had been strung from a pin placed over Glastonbury, angling southwest across the map to South America. 'We got the best bearing we could, but it was still only an approximation. And Grozevny,' she tapped the map on the northern coast of Russia, 'isn't that far off the same bearing. Even if we got a triangulation from there, it still wouldn't be accurate enough. The search area would cover hundreds of square miles.'

'Better than half a continent.'

'I know, but . . .' She sighed. 'We need a break, more information.'

The phone rang. Nina put the call on speaker; it was Lola. 'Ankit Jindal from Interpol is here to see you. He says it's about the statues.'

Eddie raised his eyebrows. 'That was quick.'

'Send him in!' Nina said.

'We need a million dollars, an' all,' said Eddie with a hopeful glance at the phone. It remained silent. 'Tchah! Worth a try.'

A knock, and Ankit Jindal entered. The handsome Indian's glossy black hair had developed into even more of a quiff since they had last seen him. 'Hello,' he said, beaming.

They shook hands. 'This is an unexpected pleasure, Kit,' said Nina. 'Why didn't you tell us you were coming to New York?'

'I could have done, but what would be the fun in that? Besides, considering why I'm here, I thought it would be better to discuss it face to face.'

'So why are you here?' Eddie asked.

Kit indicated the display case. 'Your little purple friends. Mr Penrose sent me a copy of your report about what you discovered in England.'

'He did?' Nina was slightly surprised. Certainly, it was part of Penrose's job to keep other international bodies like Interpol informed of the UN's activities, but he didn't normally do so with such promptness. 'What's Interpol's interest?'

Kit opened his briefcase, taking out several files. 'After that business with the Khoils, the Cultural Property Crime Unit tried to track down the owners of the unidentified items found in their vault. Most of them we eventually located, but a few we couldn't find.' He opened a file. 'But we had a breakthrough. Most of the Khoils' computer records had been wiped or encrypted, but our experts managed to recover a shipping manifest.'

He handed Nina a copy of a document. Much of it was gibberish to her, the computerised tracking of a container from port to port, but the final destination – Nuuk in Greenland, the country where the Indian billionaires had been preparing to sit out a global collapse – was clear enough. 'It doesn't specifically name the container's contents, although that's not surprising if it was filled with stolen art treasures. But the shipping agent is based in Singapore.'

She found a name at the top of the page. 'Stamford West?'

'Sounds like a Tube station,' said Eddie.

'Interpol has been watching Mr West for some time,' Kit told them. 'He's been linked to the smuggling of artworks and antiquities from several countries, although there has never been enough evidence against him to make a case.'

'But you're sure he was involved with the Khoils?' said Nina. Kit nodded. 'Which might mean that he knows where the second statue came from originally.'

'He might. But that's only part of the reason I came here.' The Indian opened another file. 'There is also evidence – only circumstantial, unfortunately – linking him to another black market operation. Look at these.' He laid several glossy photographs on the desk.

Nina picked one up. 'Oh, this is beautiful,' she said,

fascinated. The image was of a small statue of a broad-faced man sitting cross-legged, eyes closed as if in meditation. The figure gleamed under the photographer's lights; it was made of pure gold. 'Inca?'

'Yes.' He indicated the other photos, which showed similarly spectacular pieces. 'Our experts confirmed they're genuine, dating from no later than the sixteenth century.'

'And these were found on the black market?'

'No, in a drugs raid on a mansion in Mexico a few weeks ago. The man had a taste for ancient art. But his records contained a paper trail that led back to their illegal source.'

'Peru?'

Kit shook his head. 'Venezuela.'

'What?' Nina shook her head. 'That doesn't make sense – the Inca empire never extended that far from the Andes. Are you sure they weren't just smuggled *through* Venezuela?'

'After these were recovered, we checked with our informants to find out if any other Inca artefacts had come on to the black market. They had, and apparently some were being sold for very large sums, tens of millions of dollars. We didn't find out who was selling them or exactly where they were coming from, but there are two things we are certain about.'

'Which are?' Eddie asked.

'They are definitely coming from somewhere in Venezuela, most likely the south of the country. And they are all completely unknown artefacts. Nobody has ever seen them before.'

The implication of that struck Nina almost physically. 'Unknown?' she echoed. 'But if all these pieces are genuine Inca artefacts, that would mean . . . there's an undiscovered Inca settlement somewhere in Venezuela!'

'*Somebody* must've discovered it,' Eddie pointed out, nodding at the photos.

She wasn't listening. 'That would be an enormous change to what we thought we knew about the Inca empire. They made incursions into the Amazon jungle, but never settled there – they were a mountain people.' She went to the wall map, holding her thumb and forefinger apart above the scale before moving her hand in steps across the map. 'Venezuela is a good nine hundred miles from the empire's outer reaches. Any Inca outpost that far away would be . . .' Her eyes widened. '*Legendary*. No, it couldn't be!'

'What couldn't be?' Eddie demanded.

'The Spanish conquered Peru in the 1530s,' she explained excitedly. 'Francisco Pizarro, the leader of the Conquistadors, captured the Inca emperor Atahualpa, who tried to make a deal – in return for his freedom, he'd give Pizarro enough gold to fill his cell from floor to ceiling. Pizarro agreed, after demanding that he also get enough silver to fill the neighbouring cell. Atahualpa told him it would take two months to collect the gold and silver from throughout the empire, so Pizarro sent messengers to issue his demands, while keeping Atahualpa as a hostage.'

'How big was the room?' asked Kit.

'I can't remember exactly, but quite large. So enough gold to fill it would be worth millions of dollars in today's money – maybe even billions.'

Eddie whistled appreciatively. 'Did this Pizarro get the gold?'

'I don't know if anyone ever literally tried to fill the room with treasure, but Pizarro certainly became extremely rich. Although that didn't stop him from putting Atahualpa up before a kangaroo court, forcing him to convert to Christianity, and then executing him.'

'Ungrateful git!'

'Yeah, the Conquistadors weren't exactly shining beacons of integrity. But the thing was, when Pizarro took control of Cuzco, the capital, the Spanish realised there was much less gold there than they'd expected from previous expeditions. They melted down everything they could get their hands on, tens of tons of it – but they thought they were going to find *hundreds* of tons. And it didn't take long before they started thinking that Atahualpa's message hadn't only been to send gold for his ransom, but also to warn his people to hide as much treasure as they could from the Spanish.'

'This treasure,' said Kit, 'it might have been hidden in Venezuela?'

Nina looked at the map again. 'Nobody knows. But there's a legend of a hidden city where the Incas kept their greatest treasures. It's called—'

'El Dorado!' Eddie cut in.

'No – you've fallen into the same trap as the Spanish,' she said. 'That really *is* a myth, or rather a misinterpretation. The Chibcha Indians in Colombia had a ritual where they covered their king in gold dust and he went out into their sacred lake to wash himself clean. The Spanish, who only heard about it second-hand, thought El Dorado meant a golden *city*, not a golden man.'

'Huh. And I thought I'd actually learned something from cartoons as a kid!'

'Hey, I loved that show too – it was one of the few cartoons my parents didn't mind me watching. Even if it was just so they could point out all the historical inaccuracies . . . Anyway, the real legendary city, if that's not an oxymoron, was called Paititi. The story was that it was somewhere in the jungle, but since we're talking about the Amazon rainforest, that doesn't really narrow things down.'

Eddie shrugged. 'So much for that, then.'

'Ah,' said Nina with a knowing smile, 'but there's more to it. About sixty years after Atahualpa's execution, Sir Walter Raleigh went to South America in search of El Dorado, which he thought was somewhere along the Orinoco river.' She indicated the river on the map; the red thread crossed it inland of its massive delta – and again much further to the southwest, along the border between Venezuela and Colombia. 'He was exploring there because of the story of a Spanish sailor who was set adrift on the river by his men. He claimed that he was rescued by an Indian tribe, the Manoans, who took him to a city deep in the jungle . . . where he met a man who said he was the last heir of the Inca empire.'

'Did Raleigh find the city?' Kit asked.

'No, he never did. He met the Manoans, though. They were traders, who covered hundreds of miles of rivers and could easily have been in regular contact with the Incas.'

'And maybe told them a good place to hide a city?' Eddie wondered. 'Even helped them shift the gold?'

'Maybe. But Paititi could well have been the city Raleigh was searching for. The timescale fits with the fall of the empire.' She turned to Kit, thoughtful. 'So, there's a possible connection between the Khoils' statue and the Inca artefacts on the black market – this guy West.'

'That's right,' he said. 'The reason I came here is because in your report you said a third statue may be somewhere in South America. Perhaps the second was there too – Stamford West would have been able to smuggle it out of the country without it being found by customs agents.'

Nina pursed her lips. 'I'm not sure about that. There's been nothing to suggest that the second statue came from there.'

'Well, it is just a theory,' Kit said with a shrug. 'But the third statue could be in southern Venezuela, and these Inca treasures are coming from southern Venezuela. Perhaps the same place. I think – Interpol thinks – it is worth investigating. Mr West may have some answers.'

'He's in Singapore, you said?' Eddie asked. 'I've got a friend in the Singapore police; she'll be able to help us out when we go and see this bloke.'

'Wait, "we"?' said Nina. '*We* are not going anywhere – there's too much to do here.'

Eddie waved dismissively at the piles of books and papers on her desk. 'That's not exactly my kind of reading. If I go to Singapore with Kit, at least I'll be doing what I'm good at.'

Kit looked between them, noting Nina's glare at her husband. 'A personal connection with the Singapore police could be very useful.' The glare turned on him. 'But I will, er . . . let you both decide what you want to do. I'll be in New York until tomorrow, so call me. Good to see you again.' He gathered up his files and left the office.

Nina rounded on Eddie. 'So you're going to Singapore, huh?'

'Oh, so it's all right for you to jet off round the world whenever you feel like you need a break, but not me?'

'You think you need a *break*?'

'I didn't mean it in a Ross and Rachel sense,' Eddie said irritably. 'You heard Kit. I can help him out.'

'But you still meant it in an "I don't want to deal with my issues, so I'm going to run off to the other side of the world" sense, right?'

'What bloody issues?' Eddie protested. 'You got a bit embarrassed in front of two people, neither of who you're ever going to see again—'

'So you've decided that, have you?'

'Why, do you *want* to see them again?'

'They're my family now, so maybe I might.'

'Oh, might you? Just don't expect me to go with you. Anyway, the only *issue* is that you've blown everything totally out of proportion.'

'Oh, for—' Nina dropped heavily into her chair. 'I sometimes wonder why I married you. Fine, okay, go to Singapore. Try not to get arrested for chewing gum.'

Eddie gave her a sarcastic look. 'I'll go and pack.' He departed, leaving Nina to knead her forehead in frustration.

Once outside the UN building, Kit made a phone call. 'It's Jindal. I've just left the IHA.'

'And?' said a terse male voice.

'It took a while to convince Dr Wilde that the Venezuelan connection is our best lead to the third statue, but she seems to have accepted it. And Eddie has offered to help with West.'

'Eddie?'

'Mr Chase.'

'Don't get too involved with these people, Jindal,' came the disapproving response. 'Once the Group has all three statues we will still need Dr Wilde, but Chase is irrelevant. Just make sure you maintain your cover at Interpol until we have them.'

'Yes, sir. I'll report again when I've found out if West has the information we need.'

A sound of confirmation from the other end of the line, then the abrupt click of disconnection without a further word. Not that Kit had expected anything more. He pocketed the phone and walked away into New York.

6

Singapore

The port of Singapore was one of the busiest in the world, its sprawling docks occupying several square miles of the island state's limited land. Tens of thousands of shipping containers were stacked throughout the great concrete expanse, huge long-legged gantry cranes trundling back and forth from the moored globetrotting megaships in an intricate computer-directed ballet, gripping the steel boxes in their cable-mounted 'spreader' mechanisms.

On the port's fringes, the walls of containers gave way to warehouses and offices. One in particular was the subject of Eddie's attention as he waited with Kit and several officers from Singapore's police and customs forces, sheltered from the rain beneath an awning. Across a wide road leading deeper into the metal maze was a two-storey cabin with a sign reading *S Q West Import-Export*, the upper floor's windows illuminated behind Venetian blinds. 'He's working late,' he said, looking at his watch. It was after nine p.m.

'Many nights, Mr West doesn't leave until almost midnight – and some nights he doesn't leave at all,' said Go Ayu. The Singapore Police Force staff sergeant was in her early thirties, of mixed Japanese and Thai descent, prim and formal in her dark blue uniform despite the humidity and the rain.

'Can't have much of a social life, then.'

'He has enough to keep good friends with some of Singapore's most important people. He is a very well-connected man.'

'Connected enough to keep him out of trouble?' Kit asked.

'Yes,' said Rosman Jefri, one of the customs agents. 'Three years ago, Mr West was suspected of involvement in smuggling. His office and home were raided, but nothing was found – and he sued the government. Not only did he win, but the officer in charge was demoted.'

'But now Interpol is involved, it will be harder for West to get his friends to apply pressure,' said Ayu. 'And it gives us another advantage. We have thought about trying to entrap him by asking him to transport an illegal cargo, but he is a clever man and will spot undercover agents.'

Eddie cocked his head, puzzled. 'Wouldn't that get chucked right out of court?'

'Entrapment is legal here,' Kit explained. 'So if a stranger asks if you want to buy drugs . . . don't.'

'Good job I forgot my crack pipe. So, if we use someone from outside Singapore, you reckon that'll make West more likely to do something dodgy?'

Rosman nodded. 'If he agrees to an illegal act, that gives us the pretext we need to arrest him and seize his records.'

'Before he can destroy them, we hope,' added Ayu.

'I think we can make sure of that,' said Eddie.

'You keep saying "we", Eddie,' objected Kit. '*I* will be going to see West – alone. I appreciate your working with Sergeant Go to move everything along, but you're a civilian, not a police officer. This is up to me now.'

'What, with that cover story you came up with? It's too obvious – he'll be suspicious right from the off.' He rubbed the lapel of Kit's pale blue suit jacket; it was obvious from its fit alone that it was not an expensively tailored garment. 'No offence, but you're dressed like a cop.'

Kit looked offended. 'Then give me *your* jacket. No policeman I know would wear anything like that!'

'Ooh, listen to Derek bloody Zoolander 'ere!' said Eddie, pretending to be outraged. 'All right, swap.' He took off his leather jacket and traded it for Kit's. 'Still think it's a bad idea for you to go in on your own, though.' He turned to Ayu. 'Does West have any history of violence?'

'Not Mr West himself,' she said. 'But he employs security guards . . . and some of them have violent backgrounds.'

Eddie looked at the cabin. Figures moved behind the slats; West had company. 'So, Kit, your plan is to go alone into the office of a dodgy bloke with nasty bodyguards and try to entrap him. Yeah, that's sensible.'

'We are right outside,' Rosman pointed out.

'Not close enough if things turn bad in a hurry – and you can't see much through those blinds. Ayu, he needs support, and you know it. Let me go as well – if he's the client, I can be his bodyguard.'

'Eddie, you are not going with me,' insisted Kit.

He didn't listen. 'Come on, Ayu. It's your turf, not Interpol's.' With meaning, he added: 'A favour for a favour.'

Ayu was conflicted, her eyes flicking between Eddie and Kit. 'It . . . would make sense for Mr Jindal to have backup,' she finally said. 'And since Mr West would spot any of our own men . . .'

'There we go,' said Eddie, grinning at Kit. 'I'll watch your back.'

The Indian was displeased, but grudgingly nodded. 'Okay. But Eddie, leave all the talking to me, yes? Just stand behind me and look menacing.'

Another grin. 'I think I can manage that.'

Five minutes later, having tested the tiny microphone concealed under Kit's clothing, the two men set off for the cabin, shielded from the rain beneath umbrellas. 'I still think this is a mistake,' Kit grumbled. 'How did you get Ayu to agree? Why does she owe you a favour?'

'I helped her out of a tight spot about six years back,' said Eddie. 'She went after some drug dealers without backup. Not a smart move.'

'Well, no. They would have been desperate – Singapore has the death penalty for drug smuggling.'

'Turned out to be redundant for this lot after I finished with 'em.' They crossed the road. 'Still not sure about your cover story, though. It's all a bit too convenient, your supposed mutual friend just happening to be unavailable right now because he got arrested.'

'It's the best we have. But it's time for you to be quiet. I'm sure even you can manage that for five minutes.'

'Cheeky bugger,' said Eddie as Kit pushed the buzzer.

A light came on behind the door, which opened to reveal a thick-necked Malay man. He regarded them suspiciously. 'Yeah? What you want?'

Kit opened his mouth to speak, but Eddie beat him to it. 'Good evening!' he boomed, doing his best Roger Moore impression. 'I'm here to see Mr West.' The man stared at him; he continued irritably, 'Come on, it's a bloody monsoon out here. Let us in!'

The man frowned. 'Who are you?'

'Smythe's the name, James St John Smythe. Now chop-chop,

I've come a long way. There's a lot of money at stake, so don't keep me waiting.'

The mention of money did the trick, and the man waved them inside. 'Your name again? Mr . . . Smith?'

'*Smythe*,' proclaimed Eddie. 'With a y and an e. Now, where is he?' A flight of stairs led to the top floor. 'Up there? Marvellous. Lead on, there's a good chap.'

The man ascended the stairs, gesturing for them to follow. 'What are you *doing*?' Kit hissed through his teeth.

'I told you, you're too obviously a cop,' Eddie whispered back. 'But he'll never suspect a posh Englishman.'

'Wait – that was meant to be posh?' said Kit in disbelief.

'Why, what did you think it sounded like?'

'Like you had something stuck up your nose!'

Eddie huffed as they reached the top of the stairs. 'What do you know? Anyway, we're here.' The man opened a door. 'Thank you,' he said, reverting to his affected accent and self-consciously trying not to sound too nasal.

Tinny jazz music from a CD player reached them as they entered the office. Racks of floor-to-ceiling shelving containing hundreds of box files ran along the rear wall. Another Malay man, even more hulking than the first, sat at a desk piled with documents. He looked up suspiciously.

The room's far end was incongruously homely, a hefty antique desk of lacquered teak positioned almost like a barricade to cut its occupier off from the rest of the workspace. As well as a pair of telephones and several trays of papers, the desk was home to not one but two computers: a modern black and chrome laptop and, less impressively, an extremely outdated PC, its beige casing discoloured with nicotine. A faded picture of what Eddie assumed was Singapore some decades ago hung on the wall, an only slightly less old portrait of the Queen of England beside another door.

The man behind the desk was obese, a triple chin cupping a sun-reddened face. Despite the whirring desk fan fluttering the strands of his comb-over, he was glistening with sweat, in large part because he was wearing a three-piece tweed suit and a cravat. Eddie guessed him to be in his early sixties. His underling spoke in Malay, getting a fluent reply in the same language, then the fat man switched to English to address the new arrivals. 'And what can I do for you gentlemen?' He too had a plummy accent, but unlike Eddie's attempt it sounded genuine. 'I don't often take meetings after normal business hours, but since the weather is so ghastly it would be rude to turn you away.'

'I'm delighted to hear it,' Eddie replied. 'My name is Smythe, James St John Smythe. This is my associate, Mr Jindal.'

'Stamford West. Please, sit.'

'Thank you.' Eddie took a place on a folding chair facing West, Kit beside him. The man who had shown them in, he noticed in his peripheral vision, remained standing with his arms folded, one hand slipped slightly inside his jacket to give him easy access to whatever weapon was concealed there. 'Now, I know these are unusual circumstances, but I wish to engage your business.'

'I see.' West's eyes were piggy, but also sharp and intelligent, already suspicious. 'And how did you come to hear about me?'

'We have a mutual friend, Kazim bin Shukri.'

'Ah. And how is old Kazim?'

'Having a spot of bother with the customs folk in South Africa, poor chap.'

'Inconvenient,' said West, the first syllable barely audible.

Eddie didn't rise to the bait, pretending not to have noticed the vague accusation. 'For me, definitely – he owed me ten thousand dollars at backgammon.'

'Oh, another player?' said West. 'I do enjoy a match, although Kazim is too good for my liking. Where did you play?'

Bin Shukri's regular gambling haunt was an item that had come up during Kit's cover briefing . . . and its name had slipped Eddie's mind. 'That little place in Macao,' he said, remembering one scrap of information and struggling to recall the rest. He could tell that Kit was desperate to mouth the name, but with West watching them both intently the prompt would be spotted instantly. 'Some flower, what's its name? The, ah, the Red Lotus, that's the one. Nice place. Good martinis.'

He had no idea if the Red Lotus even had a bar, but West appeared satisfied – for the moment. 'You had better luck than I did playing against him there, Mr Smythe. Now, what's this business of yours?'

Again, a cover story had been worked out, but to Eddie's mind it was too contrived for West to accept. Instead, he took something he had heard about from Nina as a starting point . . . with his own embellishments. 'Well, old chap, I'm sure you've heard about the archaeological dig the Chinese have been doing at the tomb of the First Emperor, at Xi'an.'

'Hard not to in these parts,' said West, with a faint chuckle that set his chins rippling.

'Quite so. They've been picking at the tomb for a while to excavate the outer chambers – they're afraid to go too deep inside because they think it's cursed, can you believe it? Anyway, they've brought out various artefacts, all of which are obviously extremely valuable. I have, shall we say, come into ownership of one of them.'

The corpulent man appeared surprised. 'I wasn't aware that the Chinese government was selling them.'

Eddie smiled. 'Nor are they. One of the archaeologists had built up quite a gambling debt in Macao.'

'Interesting. What is the artefact?'

'A jade pagoda.' He held one hand above the other, eighteen inches apart. 'About yea high. Quite exquisite. Problem is, I need to get it out of China. They're rather keen to recover it.'

'I can imagine.' West leaned back in his chair. 'And you think I can somehow help you with this?'

'You came highly recommended as someone who can transport goods . . . while avoiding official checks.'

'I would point out that smuggling is illegal.'

'I'm aware of that. But can you help anyway?'

A long silence. Kit shifted in his seat, the intense interest of a cop staring down a suspect plain on his face. Eddie pretended to stretch, nudging him to break his concentration. 'I obviously can't agree to be part of anything illegal,' said West at last. 'And for all I know, you might be working for the Singapore police, trying to entrap me.'

Kit tensed again, but Eddie held out his arms with an expansive gesture. 'Oh, come now. Do I really sound Singaporean?'

'I'm not sure *what* you sound like, Mr Smythe.' Now it was Eddie's turn to stiffen. Had West realised the deception – or had he known all along and simply been toying with them? 'But . . . I must admit, your story is unlikely enough to be true. No policeman I've ever met had that vivid an imagination.'

'They are a block-headed bunch, aren't they?' Eddie said. Kit laughed flatly.

West leaned forward and worked his laptop. 'This artefact of yours, where is it now?'

'Hong Kong.'

'And where are you planning to take it?' He was still being slippery, Eddie realised; not saying anything that could be taken as agreement to participate.

'England.'

'A tad vague. Where in England?'

'Near Tenterden, in Kent. Blackwood Hall, my estate.' It had actually been the estate of Sophia's father, where Eddie received an extremely chilly welcome the one and only time he was invited there in the company of his first wife.

West was impressed. 'Really? Did you know Lord Blackwood?' he asked as he continued tapping at the keyboard.

'Only slightly. Bought the estate from his, er, estate after he died. Got it for a song – he was massively in debt, don't you know.'

'So I heard. I assume you want the item shipped as soon as possible.'

'The sooner the better.'

West nodded, then swivelled his bulk round to face the second, older computer. He pushed a button, and with a bleep and a shrill whine of fans it started up. Eddie could just about see the screen from where he was sitting: green text on a black background. He also noticed that a modern memory card reader had been connected via a black box to one of its rear ports. 'Rather an old machine,' said Eddie. He nodded towards the laptop. 'Why not use that one?'

'For security. Older hardware has its advantages,' said West. He bent down with a grunt to collect something out of sight behind the desk. 'For one, it has no Internet connection, so it's immune to viruses and spyware. For another, the hard drive doesn't act as a cache.'

Eddie gave Kit a puzzled look. 'He means it doesn't keep a copy of your open files in virtual memory,' the younger man explained.

'Quite so,' said West, levering himself upright. In one hand he had a small transparent case, which he popped open to reveal a MicroSD memory card, a sliver of black plastic the size of a thumbnail. 'You can be betrayed by your own computer, you know – its hard drive is full of invisible copies of your files that any half-competent technician can recover.' He slotted the little card into the reader, then typed commands. Columns of green text scrolled up the screen. 'This may be slow and outdated, but it can still run a spreadsheet.'

Eddie and Kit exchanged glances. West obviously kept the sole records of his illegal operations on the memory card. If they could take it from him, they might find the information they were after.

But the fat man wasn't likely to give it up without a fight, even if he wouldn't be the one to throw the punches. The goon who let them in had taken up a more alert stance, and the second man had left his desk and was lurking behind the two visitors. In the time it would take the cops outside to reach the office, the card could be hidden, even destroyed.

And now West's expression had changed. It wasn't outright suspicion, but caution, a feeling that he needed one more test to be passed before being fully satisfied. 'It must have been very gratifying to beat a player as good as Kazim,' he said. 'Especially for such high stakes. How many times did you redouble?'

Eddie had no idea what West meant. His entire knowledge of backgammon came from one scene in the James Bond movie *Octopussy*, and since both players had been cheating that wasn't a great deal of help. He assumed it was some kind of bet, like raising in poker, but what would be a believable answer?

And what if the question was a trick? Maybe redoubling, whatever that was, wasn't allowed at the Red Lotus . . .

West expected an answer, though. So did his men, the two Malays tensing as the silence drew out.

He would have to bluff. 'Oh, I don't really remember. The whole evening went by in a bit of a haze!'

The overweight man stared at him . . . then his eyes flicked up to his men in an obvious sign of warning. Shit! He had failed the test; however hazy the evening, he would have been expected to remember if the Red Lotus allowed redoubling – and it was now clear that it didn't.

West pulled the card from the reader and sat back. 'You know, Mr Smythe, I'm afraid I won't be able to help with your shipping needs after all. I don't want to be involved in anything illegal. Terribly sorry. Now, it's rather late, so my associates will escort you out.'

Reluctantly, Eddie and Kit stood, the Interpol agent shooting the Englishman an angry look. Eddie couldn't blame him. The fish had shunned the bait, and without West's entrapment the listening Singaporeans had no pretext on which to raid the office.

Unless they responded to some other incident . . .

The two Malays ushered Kit and Eddie to the door. Eddie glanced back. West was returning the memory card to its case, pudgy fingers fumbling with the tiny plastic sliver. They passed a window—

'Oi!' Eddie suddenly yelled, bogus accent gone as he whirled to face one of his escorts. 'Get your fucking hands off me!'

The man froze, startled . . .

And Eddie hurled him bodily through the window.

7

The Malay screamed as he plummeted to the concrete amongst shattered glass and the clattering slats of the blind. He landed with a heavy thump, bruised but alive.

Eddie spun to face the other man – and took a hard punch that sent him crashing against a desk, scattering papers. Kit hit the goon in the jaw, knocking him back, but the thick-necked man straightened immediately and lunged at him.

Recovering, Eddie saw West grab a black object. Fear surged through him – *a gun!* – but it was just a walkie-talkie. Like a walking walrus, the obese man lumbered for the other door.

The Malay swung Kit round, slamming him into Eddie just as the Englishman started after West. Both men tumbled to the floor. The bodyguard tried to stamp on Kit's head, but the Indian jerked away in time to avoid all but a glancing blow to the side of his face.

Eddie used a chair to haul himself to his feet, then swept it up and smashed it against the bodyguard's skull. The man cried out, reeling. Eddie tried to swing again, but the piece of cheap office furniture fell apart in his hands, leaving him holding only the backrest. He threw it at the man's face, then kneed the staggering figure in the groin.

The Malay lurched backwards into one of the shelving racks. It toppled over, knocking him to the floor beneath it – and dropping dozens of heavy box files on to Kit. He managed to protect his face, but still took several painful hits.

West was gone, the other door slamming shut. Eddie tried to pull Kit out from under the collapsed shelves. 'No, go after him!' Kit groaned. 'Get the memory card!'

Eddie reluctantly let go and ran to the door. As he expected, it was locked. A couple of kicks took care of that. The room beyond was a small storeroom, a fire door swinging open in the back wall. He rushed to it and looked out into the rain. Metal steps led down to ground level.

No sign of West, but considering his bulk he couldn't have got far. Eddie clanged down the stairs. If West had gone round to the front of the cabin, he would have been seen by the Singaporean officers. He must have headed deeper into the port. Which way, though? The towering maze of containers, stacked as many as five high, rose just yards away like a giant child's building blocks. He listened for footsteps, but heard nothing. Not, he was reluctantly forced to admit, that he could have picked much out through the hiss of rain and rumble of distant machinery; years of exposure to gunshots and other loud noises had permanently affected his hearing.

He ran to a container and jumped to grab the edge of its roof, pulling himself up. The containers to each side were stacked two high; he leapt again and scrambled on top of one, then pounded along its forty-foot length to jump up once more. He was now over twenty-five feet above the ground, giving him more of a chance of spotting West – he hoped.

The containers were arranged in long blocks, six wide, with roadways between them housing the tracks for the gangling cranes. The nearest was to his left; he looked down into it. Nobody there. He hurried across to the right, rounding a gaping hole where several containers had been plucked from the tier. The other roadway was considerably wider, with room for containers to be lowered on to flatbed trailers. The great yellow crane spanning the block along which he was running was ahead, slowly lowering a container towards a waiting truck.

But the huge machine wasn't what caught his attention. Instead, it was a rotund figure a hundred yards away, shouting into a walkie-talkie as he ran.

A look ahead told Eddie where he was going. The floodlit, slab-like sides of cargo ships rose above the containers. The waterfront.

But West wasn't going to board a ship. He was trying to dispose of the memory card. On the ground, even in the dockland sprawl, the Singaporean authorities could use CCTV and dogs to retrace his steps and eventually find it. But in the water, amongst the currents and traffic and floating garbage, the tiny plastic chip would be lost for ever.

'Not a fucking chance,' Eddie muttered as he set off at a run. He could easily catch up with West on the ground – but first had to get down there.

He was too high up to risk dropping to the concrete. But doubling back and descending that way would cost him too much time. He needed an intermediate step . . .

The crane.

He ran at it, the driver in his elevated cabin reacting in surprise at the sight of the interloper, then hurriedly hitting the emergency stop. The container jolted to a halt above the trailer—

Eddie made a running jump, crossing the gap and landing with a bang on the container roof eight feet below. He ran along the container's length, vaulted the end of the spreader and thumped down on his backside on the truck's roof to slide off and drop the last nine feet to the ground.

The impact jarred his joints. He rolled with a pained grunt

and jumped up. The startled truck driver threw open the cab door and yelled in Chinese, but Eddie was already running after West.

The fat man disappeared round a corner. Eddie pushed harder, reaching the corner of the container block just in time to see West make another turn about fifty yards ahead, still heading for the waterfront. Feet splashing through puddles, Eddie followed. At the turn he saw that he had closed the distance again, West only forty yards away. He would be able to tackle him well short of the sea—

Lights came on behind him, his running shadow stretching ahead on the wet ground.

He looked back – and saw a forklift bearing down on him.

Eddie jinked to one side of the roadway. The forklift changed course, tracking him. West had called for help over the radio, and a dock worker had responded.

The containers were stacked too high for him to climb. The machine charged at him like a bull, its forks great steel horns lowered to punch into his chest. Eddie backed against a container. He could see the driver's face between the headlights, fixed in malevolent expectation—

'Olé!' Eddie cried, whirling and dropping flat as the twin forks speared over him and punched through the metal wall.

He had gambled with his life that the container was full – and it was. The vehicle slammed to a stop just short of him as the forks hit whatever was inside. The corrugated side tore open with a screech . . . and dozens of cans tumbled out of the mangled hole, thunking off him as he scrambled out from beneath the embedded tines. The sickly smell of dog food filled his nostrils.

The forklift whined and jolted as it tried to pull free. Eddie snatched up a can and hurled it at the driver's head. There was a ringing clonk of metal against bone, and the man let out an almost comical squawk of pain before toppling nervelessly from the open cab.

Eddie looked back towards the waterfront. West was out of sight again, having gone down another intersecting roadway. Had the fat man gone left or right? If he followed the wrong path, it could cost him his chance to catch up.

He sprinted for the junction. Left or right? He had only a moment to make a choice—

He made it – and carried straight on.

Whichever way he had gone, West would still be heading for the sea. A broad expanse of rain-soaked concrete glistened in the floodlights between the end of the container stacks and a waiting ship.

He burst into the open, looking left, seeing nobody, right—

West was about thirty yards away – and twenty yards from the oily water behind the ship's stern.

Eddie pounded after him. The gap closed with every step, but West had seen him, fear driving him faster. Nine yards, eight, seven, but the obese man was nearly there, about to throw the memory card into the sea. Yards shrank to feet, the tweed almost in reach—

West whipped his arm forward just as Eddie dived at him and clamped a hand over his, the tackle sending them both over the quayside.

They entered the water with a huge splash. Eddie's eyes and nose immediately started to sting, the sea polluted with oil and anti-fouling biocides and effluent from the hundreds of ships that passed through each week. West thrashed; Eddie kept his grip on his hand, feeling the card's sharp edge digging into his palm.

But it was slipping away, the fat man still desperate to lose the incriminating data even in his panic. If he opened his fingers, it would be gone . . .

Eddie pulled West's hand to his face – and bit it.

A muffled gurgle of shock and pain, the card popping free – and Eddie sucked it into his mouth along with some of the foul water. The vile taste almost made him throw up, but he choked back the reflexive response and swallowed. He let go of West's hand and shoved him away, then kicked upwards until his head broke the surface. Gasping, he shook water from his eyes and swam to the dock, taking hold of a concrete piling.

West surfaced, spluttering and screeching. 'Help! Help me! I can't swim!'

'Oh, for fuck's sake!' Eddie growled. He reluctantly pushed himself back out and grabbed West by his collar to haul him to the quay.

Running footsteps above. 'Eddie!' Kit shouted. 'Eddie, where are you?'

'Three bloody guesses!' he called back.

A head peered over the edge. 'Over here!' said Kit, pointing. Other faces appeared, including Ayu's. 'We'll get you out.'

A lifebelt was tossed down, which West eagerly grabbed, followed by a rope ladder. Before long, both men were on the dock, dripping. 'I see I'm going to have to buy a new suit,' Kit said unhappily at the sight of his oil-stained jacket.

'You got promoted; you can afford it,' Eddie replied, spitting to clear the revolting taste from his mouth. 'Christ, that's rank.'

West was already on the defensive. 'I had no idea this was a police operation,' he protested to the uniformed officers. 'I thought I was being robbed – I was running for my life!'

Ayu struggled to bring his bloated arms together behind his back so she could handcuff him. 'You're involved in smuggling, Mr West. You're under arrest.'

'Smuggling?' West hooted. 'I'm sure you were recording the meeting, so check your tapes – I told them that under no circumstances would I get involved in anything illegal. Where's your evidence?'

Kit turned to Eddie. 'Where *is* our evidence, Eddie? What happened to the memory card?'

He patted his stomach, then indicated the polluted water. 'With the amount of crap I swallowed, it'll come out pretty quickly.' A queasy grin. 'From one end or the other.'

The port's customs officials had all the facilities necessary to catch foreign objects as they left the human body, by whatever route. To Eddie's relief, if it could be called that, a cup of clean but very salty water was enough to make him puke out his stomach contents into a bowl, rather than having to speed nature's course along with a laxative. The memory card was recovered and cleaned; it had not been damaged by its brief immersion in either seawater or digestive acids.

Now, the data contained on it had been extracted. 'This bloke West did ship stuff for the Khoils,' Eddie told Nina via phone from Interpol's Singapore office. 'The statue the Khoils had in their vault, he smuggled it out of Japan.'

'Japan? Do we know who it belonged to originally?' Nina asked.

'No, just which ports he moved it through. He'll be questioned about it, though. Kit said there might be a plea bargain on offer. Oh, and Kit was right about the Venezuelan connection. West moved all those Inca treasures out of the country.'

'Did they originate from Venezuela, though? Or was it just a transit point from Peru?'

'Kit was checking a— Oh, hang on, here he is. You can ask

him yourself.' Kit entered, holding a sheaf of papers and looking pleased with himself. Eddie put the phone on speaker. 'It's Nina.'

'Hi, Kit,' she said. 'Have you got something?'

'I think I may have,' he said, riffling through the pages. 'As well as the files on West's memory card, we also got a warrant for his phone records. A lot of international calls, as you'd expect – and many were to Venezuela. Most were mobile numbers, but there were also some to a landline in a town in the south of the country, a place called Valverde.'

'Valverde?'

'I already looked it up – it's near the Orinoco river, about twenty-five kilometres from the Colombian border. Right on that line you put on the map in your office.'

'What about the smuggled artefacts?' she asked, with growing excitement. 'Did they come from Venezuela originally?'

'It looks that way. West was dealing directly with the seller. I think this is well worth investigating – another Interpol/IHA mission.' Now it was the turn of Kit's enthusiasm to rise. 'I don't believe it's a coincidence that the Inca artefacts are coming from a region that is exactly in the direction you are looking. There's a good chance we could find the source of the artefacts and shut down their black market sales, *and* find the third statue at the same time.'

'Raleigh thought the lost city was somewhere along the Orinoco,' said Nina. 'The Incas might have hidden the third statue near Valverde! I'll talk to Sebastian, get him to speak to the Venezuelans about an expedition. I think you're right, Kit – I doubt this is a coincidence. If we find Paititi, we might be able to kill two birds with one stone.'

'So long as we don't get killed ourselves,' said Eddie. 'Somebody else must have found this place already, remember?'

'I'm sure we'll be able to arrange some local security. And you'll be there to look after us too.'

'And so will I,' said Kit. 'You can make the archaeological discoveries while Interpol stops these smugglers. We have already caught their middleman, and now we can catch them as well.'

'Great,' said Nina. 'Better brush up on my Spanish, I suppose . . .'

8

Venezuela

As it turned out, Nina didn't need to work on her language skills in the four days it took to make the arrangements with the Venezuelan government. The moment she heard about the plan, Macy practically begged to volunteer her services. Though initially dubious, Nina knew one area where Macy's abilities far outclassed her own: with her part-Cuban heritage, the young woman was completely fluent in Spanish. And, she had to admit, while Macy could sometimes be annoying, she was usually fun company.

Which right now was more than she could say of her husband. Though things had thawed, there was still the uncomfortable feeling of tiptoeing over eggshells around each other. Nina hated it – and was sure that Eddie did too – but neither was willing to make the first move and apologise to the other.

That said, there were larger matters on her mind. The United States and Venezuela were not close at the best of times, but over recent months the Venezuelan president, Tito Suarez, had made increasingly vocal accusations of US interference in his country's affairs. The State Department, conversely, had noted increasing civil unrest in Venezuela's cities, to the extent of issuing a suggestion – not quite a warning, but the subtext was clear – that American citizens should postpone all but essential visits to the Bolivarian Republic until the situation improved.

From the penthouse balcony of her Caracas hotel, however, Nina saw little evidence of brewing revolution in the city below, only cars and billboards and a giant video screen on the front of what she assumed from the mast on its roof was a television station. Despite her being an American, the Venezuelan government had rolled out the metaphorical red carpet for the IHA's director and her expedition. She had a shrewd idea why; considering her past record, the prospect of her discovering a legendary city in the jungle would be irresistible, bringing the nation both international prestige and tourist money. She had never visited the country before, and had been surprised and impressed by its capital, a bustling and in places strikingly modern metropolis. There was clearly a lot of money at work.

However, it was also clear that, even under an ostensibly socialist government, that wealth was far from evenly spread. Beyond the skyscrapers, great chunks of the city were packed tight with ramshackle little structures: the *barrios*, home to millions of the urban poor. Yet between these cramped slums were towering condominiums, expansive villas, even golf courses. With a gap so large financially and small physically between rich and poor, it was easy to imagine resentments simmering away until they boiled over.

She wasn't planning on staying long in Caracas, however. Returning to the suite – though it was a beautiful day, the stench of smog was stinging her sinuses – she joined Eddie, Macy and Kit to await their visitor.

He finally arrived over half an hour late, which could have been down to the gridlocked streets, but Nina suspected was just as likely due to his displeasure at being there at all. Dr Leonard Osterhagen, a burly German in his fifties with a trim salt-and-pepper goatee that matched his hair, worked for not the IHA but one of the other United Nations cultural organisations – and in very short order made his opinion of the newer agency plain. 'I do not see why the IHA has assumed control of this expedition,' he said. 'And I resent being shanghaied from our dig in Peru.'

'You weren't shanghaied, Dr Osterhagen,' said Nina in a placatory tone. 'It was simply a request for inter-agency cooperation.'

'Cooperation! It was an order, I think. When the IHA makes a demand, everyone else must dance for it.'

'I'll have to disagree with that interpretation,' she said, her patience already wearing thin.

'Well, of course you do. You are the one who benefits. The IHA takes money away from other agencies, diverts funds from serious research and puts it into grand exhibitions, like Atlantis. Our work is not supposed to be a fairground show.' He gestured at Kit. 'And we are archaeologists, not policemen! Why is Interpol involved?'

Nina passed a folder to Osterhagen. 'Take a look.'

He scowled and flipped it open . . . and his expression became first one of shock, then wonder. Inside were the photographs of the black market artefacts Kit had shown her in New York. He shuffled back and forth through them before looking up at Nina in amazement. 'Where were these found?'

'That's the thing,' Nina said, relieved by his abrupt change of attitude. 'They'd been sold on the black market, which is why Interpol got involved, but they were found here. In Venezuela. And that's why I *requested* this meeting. You're one of the world's foremost experts in Inca history, so I thought you might be interested. But if you'd prefer to leave it to the IHA . . .'

Sourness crept on to Osterhagen's face as his displeasure at being played and his lust for knowledge fought it out, but the latter was quickly victorious. 'The site these came from . . . you think it may be . . . ?' He mouthed a word.

Nina spoke it for him. 'Paititi. Somewhere in the south of the country, along the middle Orinoco.'

'Paititi! In Venezuela? But – of course, Raleigh and the Manoans, Juan Martinez being set adrift. Twenty days' travel along the Orinoco. It could be . . .' His gaze went right through Nina as he focused on the images in his mind.

'So, Dr Osterhagen,' she said, 'are you interested in joining the expedition?'

He blinked, returning to the present. 'I think . . . it would be best if you had an expert like myself accompanying you, yes. In the interests of inter-agency cooperation.'

She smiled thinly. 'I'm glad you agree.'

Osterhagen regarded the photographs again. 'I will need my assistants, of course.'

'I'll make the arrangements,' Nina told him. The German gave her the details, then departed – with an almost pained look as he was made to return the photos of the Inca treasures.

'Wow,' said Macy. 'I didn't realise some people had such a problem with the IHA.'

'Experts get very territorial,' said Nina. 'Especially when there's funding involved.'

Eddie laughed. 'Thank God you've never got stroppy with anyone who's stepped on your turf, eh?' He went to a large map of Venezuela laid out on a desk. 'So we've got the expert on board. What about local support?' He tracked the Orinoco river south along the Venezuelan–Colombian border until it turned back east into the former country, picking out the tiny dot that marked Valverde.

'The Venezuelans are giving us a guide, and a pilot,' said Nina, slightly annoyed by his jibe.

Kit joined Eddie at the map. 'Military?'

'Militia, I think.'

'What's the difference?' asked Macy.

'The militia's loyal to *el Presidente*,' said Eddie. 'The military's loyal to the country. Not always the same thing.' He looked more closely at the map. 'Better take plenty of bug repellent. That's a big load of green nothing around there – jungle and swamps, probably.'

Nina looked at the photographs, then across at the case containing the two statues. 'There's *something* else there. Let's hope we can find it.'

Two days later, the expedition assembled in the little jungle town of Valverde, where Nina discovered to her surprise that their Venezuelan guide and pilot were the same person. Oscar Valero was a heavy-set man in his forties, proudly dressed in the olive-green fatigues and cap of the Bolivarian Militia; it was also clear from his not exactly subtle questions that he had been told to keep a close watch on the *yanquis*.

Osterhagen, meanwhile, had been joined by his assistants – three of them, giving Nina the feeling that he was trying to match the numbers of 'her' team. Ralf Becker, gangling and thatch-haired, was another German and Osterhagen's deputy, while the other two were Americans: Loretta Soto, a plump and shy Hispanic woman, and Day Cuff, a long-faced young man with a pretentious little triangular 'soul patch' beard. Cuff's eyes had immediately locked on to Macy – more specifically, her chest – and it seemed nothing short of a nuclear strike would draw them away.

They met in the bar of the optimistically named Hotel Grande, mostly for the practical reason that it was Valverde's only hotel, but also because of its connection to the Interpol investigation: a payphone in its lobby was the landline through which Stamford West had communicated with his local contact. Like the hotel, though, the payphone was the only one in Valverde. The stream of people using it seemed to rule out any chance of spotting an obvious suspect.

'Lot of soldiers around here,' Eddie noted as another uniformed man made a call. There had also been a visible military presence on the streets.

'There is a base near here, to watch the border,' explained Valero. 'To keep out the drug-running dogs and the Colombian puppets of the gringo imperialists. No offence,' he added with a cheery smile at Nina.

'None taken,' she replied icily. 'You know what we need you to do for the aerial survey, right?'

'Sí, no problem. If there's something out there, we'll find it. You wanna start now?'

The way Osterhagen leaned forward expectantly told Nina that she wasn't the only one impatient to begin the search. 'No time like the present.'

Becker sprang to his feet. 'Great, okay, let's go!' he said enthusiastically as he donned a hat – a rather familiar-looking fedora.

Eddie grinned. 'He thinks he's Indiana Jones,' he whispered to Nina.

'All archaeologists think they're Indiana Jones,' Nina replied as she stood, equally amused. 'Well, except the ones who think they're Lara Croft.'

He regarded the tall, bony German. 'I'm glad he went for the Indy look. I wouldn't want to see him in Lycra and hot pants.' His smile widened. 'Now *Macy*, on the other hand . . .' His wife batted his arm.

Valverde was about two kilometres south of the Orinoco, its airstrip between the two. It was only a ten-minute walk from the Grande to what passed as a terminal, a hut with radio masts rising not quite vertically from its roof. The expedition members had been flown in by government helicopters, but the waiting aircraft was considerably more basic – a Cessna Caravan, a single-propeller, nine-seater light plane that was as unexciting and utilitarian in appearance as its name suggested.

'Oh,' said Cuff in sneering disappointment. 'That's what we're flying in? I was hoping for something a bit less prehistoric.'

Valero seemed insulted. 'It's only twenty-five years old, perfectly safe. What did you expect? A jumbo jet?'

Cuff wasn't satisfied. 'Whatever, it'd better be well maintained if you expect me to set foot in it. Although somehow I doubt Venezuelan airworthiness testing is *quite* up to FAA standards . . .'

Eddie had already taken a dislike to the smug twenty-something, and decided he wasn't going to put up with an entire flight of whining. 'Hey, Dave, how about not pissing off the guy we need to keep us from a fiery screaming death?'

The already nervous Loretta looked even more upset at the thought, but Cuff responded with a haughty huff. 'It's not Dave. It's Day. Day F. Cuff.'

'Oh, of the Boston Cuffs, no doubt,' Eddie said in his Roger Moore voice, guessing that he was supposed to be impressed. 'Well, since it's going to be a long flight, either stop moaning or F. Cuff off.'

'Eddie,' Nina chided, trying to conceal her amusement.

Cuff's mood was far more readable. 'You know, Leonard,' he said to Osterhagen, 'I think I'll sit this out. Aerial surveys aren't my speciality.'

Osterhagen frowned, but nodded. 'And Loretta, you don't look very happy. Do you want to stay here too?'

'Thank you,' Loretta said with a relieved sigh. 'I really don't like flying. I – I'm sure this is a very good plane,' she hurriedly added to Valero, 'but it makes me nervous.'

The Venezuelan shrugged. 'Two less people, it saves me fuel. No problem!'

Cuff set off back towards town, Loretta following. Macy nudged Eddie. 'Thanks,' she whispered.

'For what?'

'For getting rid of him. What a creep. Didn't you see the way he was staring at me?'

'Nah, I was too busy looking at your tits,' said Eddie, grinning – earning him swats from both the remaining women.

Everyone boarded the plane as Valero circled it to make his pre-flight checks. That done, he clambered inside and took a navigation chart from a door pocket. 'Okay, this is where we go,' he said, pointing out the planned search pattern. 'We keep out of this grid, though.' He tapped a rectangular marking near the border. 'Military airspace.'

'Be just our luck if what we're looking for is right in the middle of some army base,' said Eddie, checking the map for settlements and landmarks. It was unlikely that anything would go wrong during the flight, but he preferred to be prepared.

Valero shook his head. 'If the military had found anything, President Suarez would know. No point sending you to look for something he already knows about, hey?' He fastened his seatbelt. 'Okay, you ready?'

'Let's go,' said Nina.

Valero donned his headphones and started the engine, steering the Cessna to the end of the landing strip. He spoke with local air traffic control over his headset, then looked back at his passengers. 'Hold on tight,' he said. 'This will be bumpy.'

He revved the engine to full, then released the brakes. The Cessna surged forward. Macy yelped as she was jolted about, and Nina gripped her seat as hard as she could to hold herself in place. Even though the worst of the unpaved runway's dips and humps had been bulldozed out, it felt like riding a bicycle with flat tyres over jagged rocks.

'Glad we didn't – pack the – fine china for the picnic,' Eddie managed to get out through his rattling teeth.

Valero laughed, adjusting the trim controls and pulling back on the control yoke. The Cessna tipped back, then a few seconds later the battering stopped as it left the ground. Sounds of relief filled the cabin.

'Jeez,' said Nina. 'The only rougher flight I've had was the one that crashed!' Another laugh from Valero, and he brought the Caravan up to two thousand feet before turning to begin the aerial survey.

The Cessna had been chosen for the task because its wings were mounted above the fuselage, giving its occupants an uninterrupted view of the landscape. The low cruising altitude was near enough to the ground to let the observers pick out details, but still give them the expansive overview they needed. The Orinoco, in places an almost mile-wide gently snaking line of reflected sky and patchy cloud, passed below; on each side, green pointillist swathes of dense jungle, dotted with darker patches of swampland, stretched off to the horizon.

Macy gazed down at the rainforest, awed by its scale. 'How are we going to spot anything in all that?'

Osterhagen was the expert. 'We look for straight lines – any sign of artificial construction. It's how the ruins of a pre-Colombian civilisation were found on the border of Brazil and Bolivia about ten years ago.'

'Also watch for sawtooth patterns, zigzags,' added Becker, waving a finger to illustrate. 'The Incas often built defensive walls that way.'

Macy nodded, then looked back out of the window. The others did the same, scanning the ground below with eyes and binoculars as Valero brought the plane into its search pattern.

The first sector contained nothing but trees and marsh. As did the second, and the third. Eddie, however, spotted something in the fourth after they crossed back to the south side of the river. 'Is that a road over there?' he asked Valero, pointing.

The pilot looked through his side window. '*Sí*. It goes through Valverde to Matuso, to the south. Oh, and there is another road off it that goes to the military base.' He gestured westwards. A faint line could be made out, winding through miles of jungle until it reached a distinctly rectilinear patch of brown amongst the greenery.

Eddie peered at it through binoculars. 'Radar station, it looks like.' Even at this distance he could make out a rectangular antenna. He also spotted various small buildings and an empty concrete helipad. No hangar to protect a chopper from the jungle elements, though, so airborne visitors probably didn't stay long.

'Hey, hey!' Valero held up a hand, trying to block his view. 'No spying, okay?'

Smiling at the Venezuelan's paranoia, Nina turned her attention back to the jungle. South of the Orinoco was a mostly flat plain of nothing but rainforest for two hundred miles to the

Brazilian border, and well beyond. If the Incas had come all the way here from their homeland in the Andes, they had picked as good a spot as any to hide their settlement. She knew from first-hand experience how hard it was to pick out even large structures beneath the jungle canopy.

The plane flew on. There was a moment of excitement when Osterhagen saw something that at first glance appeared man-made, but, when Valero circled, it was revealed as nothing more than a low ridge of granite breaking up through the soil. Another sector cleared, on to the next, the Cessna diligently avoiding the restricted airspace surrounding the base. The engine's constant drone and vibration became increasingly wearisome as the flight stretched into its second hour, as did the sheer visual monotony of the greenery below. The only variation came from more rocky scarps pushing their way up into the jungle, but disappointment further blunted the thrill of potential discovery as each flypast revealed nothing but natural stone. Then—

'Is that another road?' Macy asked.

Nina glimpsed a thin brown line amongst the trees. 'Not much of one. More like a track.'

Osterhagen checked a map. 'There is nothing marked on here.'

Valero looked down at the narrow path. 'A logging track,' he said, disgusted. 'This whole region is *prohibido* for logging.' He pulled a notepad and pencil from the door pocket, scribbling down the GPS coordinates. 'I will have to report this when we land.'

'Wait,' said Nina, a thought occurring. 'How far are we from the road between Valverde and that other town?'

Eddie checked the GPS unit, then applied the figures to Osterhagen's map. 'Two or three miles, maybe. What're you thinking?'

'Well, we know somebody discovered a trove of Inca artefacts. What if they were loggers? They went deep into the jungle to look for hardwood trees . . . but found something a lot more valuable.'

'And then used the payphone in Valverde to talk to West after finding buyers,' said Kit. 'It's possible.'

Nina tried to follow the track. It was only intermittently visible, the work of the loggers ironically having exposed their secret to view from the air, but now she knew it was there she could just about make out its course. 'Fly along it,' she told Valero. 'If we don't see anything, we can go back to the search pattern. But if these loggers really did find Paititi . . .'

Valero changed course, reducing the Cessna's speed as its occupants all stared intently at the jungle below. The track curved confusingly in places, the loggers apparently having gone out of their way to fell specific trees, but in general it headed westwards. Nina looked further ahead . . .

A distinct line ran through the trees. She almost dismissed it as another geological feature – until something else about it caught her attention. 'There!' she said, sitting up and pointing. 'Do you see it?'

Osterhagen took a sharp breath, pressing his face against the window for a better look. 'Yes. Yes, I do! Oscar, take us closer.'

Valero complied, turning the Cessna. From some angles the feature almost vanished into the jungle – but from others it stood out clearly, even through the all-covering vegetation. It was faint, like a shadow or a ghostly impression of an item long since removed, but it was definitely there. A shape, a few hundred metres long.

A zigzag. Too regular, too precise to be natural.

Macy turned excitedly to Osterhagen. 'Inca defences, just like you said.'

The German couldn't tear his eyes from the sight. 'It must be, yes. It must be!'

Nina examined the surrounding landscape as the plane continued to circle. At one end of the mysterious line, the ground sloped steeply away to marshland, hints of a cliff visible through the tall trees. A cliff would provide a natural defence on one side; had a wall been built on others to protect a settlement?

There was only one way to know for sure. 'We've got to get down there,' she announced. 'I think we've found Paititi!'

9

The Toyota Land Cruiser picked its way along the narrow track, mud squishing out from beneath its tyres. Another vehicle, a twin save for its colour, followed.

Eddie was driving, Nina beside him and Macy and Kit in the rear seats, the young woman yawning from the early start. Valero piloted Osterhagen's group in the second 4×4, the two men having the most off-roading experience. Even so, it was slow going. The day before, Valero had flown back along the track to find where it joined the road, but this morning, even knowing the approximate location, it took some time to discover the trail; it had been concealed, bushes and a mouldering log covering the turnoff. And the track itself constantly twisted between the trees, bushes and low branches swatting the Toyotas as they crawled past.

Eddie checked the odometer. 'Five miles since we left the road. Can't be much further.' He hauled the wheel over to avoid a large jutting bough, the vehicle lurching over the ruts carved by dragged logs.

Macy liberally spritzed herself with insect repellent. 'I just had a thought—'

'First time for everything,' Eddie cut in.

She slapped his shoulder. 'No, but what if the people who found it come back? They might be armed.'

The same had occurred to Eddie, who had been less than

pleased at the Venezuelans' refusal to let him or even Kit bring weapons into the country. However, he tried to sound reassuring. 'Oscar's got a gun.'

'If he knows how to use it. I was chatting to him last night. You know what he used to be before he joined the militia?'

'A pilot?' Nina suggested.

'Well, *yeah*,' Macy said peevishly, 'but before that, I meant. He was a chef! That's not exactly like being in the SAS.'

'Depends how bad a cook he was,' said Eddie. 'If he got a lot of complaints, he'd have to— Whoa, hang on.' He slowed sharply. 'End of the road.'

They entered a clearing, ragged stumps showing where the loggers had chainsawed down several valuable hardwood trees. A steep bank of earth rose ahead. Layers of tyre tracks in the dirt showed that the area had seen a fair amount of traffic.

'There's another path over there,' said Nina, indicating the bank.

'Not sure it's drivable, though,' Eddie replied. He stopped the Land Cruiser. 'It's probably better to go on foot from here . . . and there's something I want to check.'

'What?' Nina asked, but he had already hopped out, eyes fixed on something on the ground nearby. Curious, she followed.

'Oh, ew,' said Macy, wrinkling her nose as she stepped into the mud. 'What's that smell?'

'That would be the jungle,' said Cuff patronisingly as he got out of the second Toyota. He closed his eyes and waved a hand under his nose as if wafting the scent of some delicious meal into his nostrils. 'The most diverse ecosystem on the planet. The lungs of the world. Just smell that life.'

'I can smell *something*,' Macy said, adding 'like bullshit' under her breath. Despite the repellent, small insects were swarming round her; she flapped a hand before treating them to a burst of spray.

Osterhagen emerged from the Land Cruiser behind Cuff. 'Why have you stopped? We can go . . .' He tailed off as Eddie waved urgently for silence.

'What is it?' Nina whispered.

Her husband crouched and pointed at the mud. 'These tyre tracks, they're recent. Less than a day old – there hasn't been time for any rain to wash them out.' In the humid equatorial climate of the rainforest, downpours were an almost metronomic occurrence. He went to the nearby path. 'And there are some footprints here.'

The others joined them, the atmosphere suddenly tense. Kit peered at the impressions in the soil. 'Different sizes – two men.'

Eddie nodded. 'They go into the jungle . . . but they don't come back out.'

That produced consternation amongst the group. 'Are you saying there are people here?' asked Loretta nervously.

'Guards, maybe,' said Nina. 'A treasure trove of Inca gold . . . they'd want to make sure nobody else found it.'

Eddie checked the surrounding trees. No signs of movement, or sounds beyond the chatter of birds and buzz of insects, but he was now very much on the alert. 'Oscar, you might want to keep that gun handy.' Valero hurriedly drew his weapon and checked it was loaded. Loretta gasped in alarm.

'Oh, come on,' said Cuff. 'Why would they post guards when nobody else knows this place exists? It's not as though anybody's likely to stroll by.'

Eddie gave him a contemptuous look. 'No, the plane that circled it yesterday wouldn't attract any attention, would it, Dave?'

'That's Day,' Cuff mumbled, trying to salvage some dignity under the group's withering gaze.

'So what should we do?' asked Becker. 'If there are guards, we could be in danger.'

'We have to go on,' Nina insisted. 'We've got to know what's out there.'

'I agree,' said Valero. 'If thieves are stealing Venezuela's treasures, the Bolivarian Militia will stop them!' He stood with his hands on his hips, glaring defiantly into the jungle.

'Easy there, Rambo,' Eddie said. 'Let's see what we're dealing with first. If it really is this place we're looking for and there are people keeping an eye on it, we'll call *el Presidente*'s people for backup.' He indicated the satellite phone in the Toyota. 'We're not exactly geared up for trouble.'

'Sounds like a plan,' said Nina. 'Let's get our stuff.'

The expedition members donned backpacks and equipment belts. Valero started up the path, but Eddie waved him back. 'Not that way – we don't want to walk right into 'em.' He gestured at a point further along the earth bank. 'Over there. Keep it quiet.'

Eddie and Valero led, Nina just behind with the others following in a line. Keeping low amongst the undergrowth, they scaled the bank and dropped down on the other side to find themselves in a marshy dip. Despite the humps and hollows, though, the land ahead was on a gentle rise.

It started to rain, drops pattering noisily off leaves and heads. Nina shot a jealous look at Becker's wide-brimmed fedora. But even the downpour gave little relief from the cloying humidity as the group trudged onwards. She peered into the gloom. 'I can't see much out there.'

'Good,' said Eddie. 'Anybody out there won't see much of us.' He paused at the top of another muddy bank, then gestured off to one side. 'I think there's something over there.'

Nina squinted through the rain. There was indeed a vague shape visible beyond the trees. 'A wall?'

She started towards it, but Eddie waved her back. 'Wait here until I've checked it out. Oscar, with me.' Hunching down, the Englishman slowly advanced towards the indistinct shape, Valero behind him. Nina watched anxiously as they disappeared behind the trees. She strained to listen over the constant drum of raindrops for an unexpected shout, a gunshot . . .

Eddie reappeared, waving for her to join him. She breathed out in relief and picked her way forward, Osterhagen and Becker behind her. As she got closer she realised that it *was* a wall, partially hidden by plants, crumbling in places and covered with centuries of dirt and decayed jungle debris, but definitely an artificial structure. At its tallest it stood about nine feet high.

Becker had seen something above it, however. 'Look,' he said, gesticulating excitedly. Set several feet back on its top was a second wall, rising another eight feet higher – and a third above that. 'It's tiered! Just like the walls at Sacsayhuamán.'

Osterhagen was nearly as enthused. 'And look! The shape, the zigzag – these are Inca, I'm sure!'

'Shh, shh, *shut up!*' Eddie hissed, scurrying towards the group. Nina gave him a questioning glance. 'There's a gap like a big gate further along,' he said. 'That path goes through it, so those two blokes *who we don't want to know we're here*,' he glowered at the Germans, 'probably did too.'

Becker looked sheepish, hiding from Eddie's glare beneath his hat brim. Osterhagen, meanwhile, turned his attention back to the wall. 'If we climb it, we can try to spot these men from the top.'

'There's a collapsed bit over there,' said Eddie. 'I'll go up and have a gander. If it's safe, I'll wave.' By now, Valero had returned, and the other members of the group were approaching through the trees. 'Oscar, keep an eye on the gate. Any trouble at all, everyone run like buggery back to the Jeeps. Okay?'

He went to the damaged section and scrambled up it, then searched for a suitable point to climb to the next tier. Finding a section where several large stones had been dislodged, he used the gaps as footholds and ascended again, disappearing from Nina's view. The downpour was easing off, the water torture of the large drops giving way to a clammy drizzle.

After a minute, he leaned over the edge and waved. 'Okay,' she said. 'I'll go up first. Oscar, watch the gate until everyone's clear.' Valero's eyebrows twitched at being given orders by her, but he nodded.

It didn't take long for Nina to reach Eddie's position on top of the wall. By now, the rain had stopped, drips from the overhanging trees gradually slowing to nothing. He was on his stomach, looking out across what lay beyond the fortifications; she dropped and slithered alongside him, taking in the view.

It rendered her speechless. Inside the walls was a town, abandoned and in ruins, but still stunning to behold. The shells of stone buildings were packed tightly together, tall gables marking where roofs of wood and thatch had once been. Trees had taken root amongst them, breaking down walls and concealing the structures beneath the jungle canopy. Narrow streets meandered through the outermost parts of the settlement, becoming straighter and wider as they neared the centre, where the buildings increased in size and grandeur.

Temples, and palaces. The heart of the last outpost of the Inca empire.

Paititi. The legend was real.

But they were not the first to find it. 'Have you seen the guards?' she asked.

'Not yet,' Eddie replied, 'but I heard something over there.' He pointed at one of the larger buildings.

There was a rattle and clunk of loose stones, and they looked back to see Osterhagen, breathing heavily, pull himself on to the uppermost tier. Becker, Kit and Macy appeared behind him. 'Oh, for Christ's sake!' Eddie grumbled. 'What is this, a fucking conga line? I didn't mean everyone to come up here. It's not safe yet.'

Osterhagen didn't hear, spellbound by the vision before him. '*Phantastisch . . .*' he whispered, gazing at the ruins, then fumbled to take a camera from his pack, as if afraid the marvel could vanish at any moment.

Eddie grabbed his wrist. 'If that flashes, it won't just be the Incas who practise human sacrifice – I'll have a bloody go!'

Osterhagen pulled free, but checked that the flash was switched off before taking his first picture. 'Mr Chase, I know you are trying to keep us safe, but I do not like your attitude.'

'You'll like getting shot even less, Doc. Trust me, I know.'

'So do I,' added Nina. Osterhagen looked shocked. 'What do you make of it?'

The German surveyed the ruins. The outer walls, as much as could be seen through the interloping trees, enclosed an area roughly two hundred metres square. 'It is smaller than Machu Picchu, but there may be other ruins outside the fortifications. The architecture is definitely late-period Inca, though.'

'The black market artefacts – where would they have been kept?'

He indicated one of the larger structures, a thick-walled block with numerous small trapezoidal windows high along its sides. 'The royal palace, most likely. Or' – a smaller one, unlike its neighbours in that its walls were curved – 'the Temple of the Sun.'

'If that's where the gold is,' Eddie pointed out, 'it's probably where the guards are too.'

The remaining expedition members had by now scaled the wall, and were reacting with amazement. Loretta put a hand to her mouth, on the verge of weeping with joy. 'Look at it, look! I never dreamed we'd find anywhere so intact!'

Even Cuff's seen-it-all-before smugness had temporarily deserted him. 'Jesus. This is incredible. There's so much of it – where do we start?'

'You start by staying put until I find those guards,' said Eddie, moving cautiously along the wall. Not far away was a stairway down to ground level; it had partially collapsed, but he was able to half climb, half slide down it, jumping the last six feet. 'Oscar, down here. Watch the last bit, it's slippery.'

Valero negotiated the ruined stairs rather more clumsily. Eddie was about to investigate a nearby building when he saw Nina also scrambling down. 'No, I meant all of you to stay up— Oh, never bloody mind.'

'I'm not going to blunder into the guards, Eddie,' Nina said as she dropped to the ground. 'I just want a look around. If there's any trouble, I'll go straight back up the wall.'

'I'm already halfway there,' he muttered.

'What?'

'Didn't say a word.' Running between the high wall and a terrace of what he guessed were small houses was a pathway leading to the outer gate, but a narrower alley nearby would, he thought, give a better chance of reaching the settlement's centre unseen. 'Okay, Nina, we're going to check out that noise. Back soon. And don't wander off!' he added firmly over his shoulder.

'Love you too,' Nina replied with a mocking smile as she entered the building. To her disappointment, the interior, a single room with no other entrances apart from a small window, was wrecked. Rotted remains of the wooden roof were strewn across the floor, plants sprouting from the rich compost that had built up as leaves fell through the open ceiling. Fragments of broken pottery poked from the loam. She nudged one with her boot, then saw something more interesting – a stone sphere, slightly smaller than a tennis ball. A length of thick rope was knotted through a hole in its centre. A bolas? She gingerly lifted the ball, tugging the weapon's other two cords clear of the soil – and felt the mouldering rope start to fall apart.

'Oops! Shit,' she gasped, hurriedly returning it to its resting place and going back outside – to see Osterhagen jumping down from the ruined stairway, Becker and Cuff descending behind him.

'What did you find in there?' he asked, eagerly approaching her. 'Are there any surviving artefacts?'

Nina ignored his question, trying to block his path. 'What are you doing? Eddie told you to wait up there.'

'He told you the same thing,' Cuff sniffed.

Now Macy and Kit were climbing down too. 'Sorry, Nina,' said Macy. 'I tried to tell everyone to stay up there, but only Loretta listened.'

Nina looked up to see Loretta peering over the top of the wall. 'Well, at least one person's got some sense. Okay, look – everybody stay here until Eddie and Oscar come back. This place has been waiting since the sixteenth century, so a few more minutes won't make any difference.'

Eddie and Valero moved cautiously through the ruined town. The Englishman had already confirmed that they were not the first explorers, spotting broken stems where people had forced their way through the vegetation reclaiming the settlement.

None of the damage seemed recent, though; more like weeks or even months old.

He had a theory: the loggers had trampled through the whole place searching for valuables. After picking the outlying buildings clean, they had no reason to return, instead concentrating on the central buildings that Osterhagen said would have contained the greatest treasures. The men whose trail he had spotted in the jungle were probably guarding the remainder of the hoard.

And they were close by. Eddie stopped, waving for Valero to do the same, as the tang of cigarette smoke reached him. He listened intently, picking out the muted sound of men talking in Spanish.

He peered round the corner of a building. Before him was a plaza, dotted with trees that had forced their way up through the cracked stone flags. At the western end, a broad flight of steps led up to the rounded building that Osterhagen had called the Temple of the Sun.

Something less imposing but more modern dominated his attention, though. A small canvas hut had been set up near the steps, its walls a jungle-green camouflage pattern. The entry flap was half open, giving him a glimpse of equipment inside.

So where were its occupants?

He leaned out further. In a gap between the trees was a large, oddly proportioned crate resembling a giant pizza box, about five feet square but less than a foot thick. Beside it were the two guards.

Soldiers.

Both men wore Venezuelan army fatigues, in the same camo pattern as the tent. They were armed with AK-103 assault rifles, updated and locally made versions of the venerable AK-47; one had his gun slung loosely over his back, the other had propped his weapon against a nearby tree. It was obvious from their relaxed stances that they weren't expecting trouble.

Eddie signalled for Valero to take a look. He reacted in surprise. 'What is the army doing here?' he whispered. 'I don't understand. If the government knows about this place, why weren't we told?'

'I don't think your government does know,' Eddie replied grimly. 'This is someone's private little operation. Probably run from that base – it's only about five miles from here.' He nodded to the northwest. 'They take any treasures they find to Valverde, and then they get sold on the black market.'

'But – but that is treason!' said Valero, outraged. 'They are stealing from the people of Venezuela, their own brothers!'

'Family doesn't count for much when there's big money involved.'

One soldier flicked away his cigarette and ambled back towards the tent, skirting patches of mud where the flagstones had subsided. The other checked his watch, then picked up his AK and followed.

Eddie moved back. 'We should leave.'

'No,' Valero insisted. 'As a member of the Bolivarian Militia, if a crime is being committed it is my duty to stop it.' He puffed out his chest. 'I will talk to these men, and if I do not like their answers, I will arrest them.'

'Are you fucking kidding me?' Both soldiers were tall and muscular, and looked to Eddie as if their combined ages matched Valero's alone. 'They're not going to bend over for an ex-chef.'

The Venezuelan scowled, insulted, and put one hand on his sidearm. 'They will do what I tell them. I have a gun.'

'They've got two.'

'I have authority from the President himself! I am in charge here, gringo.'

He started towards the plaza, but Eddie held out an arm to block him. 'Seriously, mate. Bad idea. We should get back to the Jeeps and you can call your people from there.'

Valero pushed him away. 'Wait here. I will deal with this.' He headed into the open.

'Fucking idiot,' Eddie growled, watching from the corner. So inattentive were the soldiers that they didn't notice the approaching militiaman until he was barely twenty feet from them – at which point they reacted with a start, fumbling for their rifles.

Valero drew his gun. They froze. He spoke commandingly in Spanish as he strode up to them, no doubt demanding to know what they were doing. To Eddie's surprise, they responded, if uncertainly; it seemed that he had been the domineering kind of chef. One of them pointed towards the temple. Valero instinctively turned to look—

The other soldier whipped up his rifle and viciously clubbed him in the head.

Valero staggered, and the soldier hit him again, knocking him down. His companion slammed a kick into his stomach, then grabbed the fallen man's pistol before kicking him once more.

'Shit!' Eddie hissed, torn between two instincts. He didn't want to abandon Valero, but he needed to warn Nina and the others. The soldiers would assume that the intruder wasn't alone, and either start hunting for the archaeological team or call for backup—

The decision was made for him as one of the soldiers spotted him lurking in the alley. The man shouted and raised his gun.

Eddie turned and ran as bullets cracked off the stonework behind him.

10

Nina whirled in horror at the sound of gunfire. The echoes of the first burst faded away, the cries of frightened birds replacing them – then came another harsh rattle of shots.

Nearer.

'Get back over the wall!' she shouted to the others.

'Where are you going?' Kit demanded as the explorers rushed for the ruined stairway.

'To find Eddie!' She charged down the alley.

Becker, closest to the steps, was the first to begin his ascent. Osterhagen followed, picking his way up the broken section. Loose stones rattled under his weight. 'Come on, *schnell*!' he called down to his companions, before looking up at the panicked figure on top of the wall. 'Loretta, run to the Jeeps!'

Cuff was right behind him, practically barging his team leader aside as he tried to claw his way up the broken stairs. 'Move it, move it!' he yelled. 'I don't wanna—'

A block burst loose under his foot. He tripped, chest thudding against the hard-edged stones, and fell back down to the ground. The entire base of the stairs collapsed, stones crashing after him. Osterhagen almost slipped as part of his footing disappeared.

'You idiot!' Kit shouted at the winded American. 'You almost brought the whole thing down!' Above, Becker hauled Osterhagen to safety. 'Macy, I'll pull you up.'

'What about Nina and Eddie?' she protested.

'You can't help them – you've got to get out of here!' He jumped to grab the surviving part of the stairway as another burst of fire rolled through the ruins.

Eddie raced through the crooked streets, swatting greenery out of his path. Only one soldier was pursuing, the other holding Valero, but the AK-103's firepower meant that he was completely outmatched. His only chance was to draw his pursuer away from the rest of the team, then either lose him in the maze or stage an ambush—

'Eddie! Eddie, where are you?'

Nina, somewhere ahead. Shit! So much for leading the man away from the others! 'They're soldiers! Get back!' he yelled, rounding a corner to see her running towards him. Another three-round burst cut through the air behind, chipped stone spitting at his head. Nina hurriedly reversed direction, disappearing from view.

He only had a short lead – shorter than the stretch of the alley before him. The soldier would have a clear shot at his back . . .

A gap between two buildings to his right formed a small courtyard, a five-foot-high wall at its rear. Eddie swerved into the space just as the soldier saw him and fired again, bullets hissing through the air in his wake. He leapt at the wall, slapping his palms down hard on its top to vault over it—

The ivy-covered stones broke away beneath his hands.

Thrown off balance, he hit the wall and tumbled over it, realising too late that the drop on the other side was much higher . . .

All that saved him from serious injury as he slammed to the ground twelve feet below was the centuries-old build-up of dirt

– and even that couldn't prevent a bone-jarring landing. The metallic taste of blood filled his mouth as he bit his cheek.

He groaned and spat out a crimson glob, levering himself upright. Footsteps slapped through the alley above. The soldier was right on him. The only way out of the sunless pit was through a narrow passage.

He ran for it.

The AK's thudding bark filled the confined space as the soldier leaned over the broken wall and fired. Bullets kicked up mud as they smacked into the ground, but Eddie was in the passage, the rest of the shots twanging noisily off the ancient stonework. Trampling plants, he darted round a corner to find a flight of steps winding upwards. He hurriedly ascended them, listening for the thump of the soldier jumping down after him.

It didn't come. The Venezuelan wasn't willing to take a leap into the unknown. Instead, he was continuing along the alley.

After Nina.

Nina raced back to the stairway, seeing Kit trying to pull Macy up. Osterhagen and Becker had just reached the top of the wall, but Cuff was still waiting anxiously at its base. 'Soldiers!' she shouted. 'Right behind me – everyone run!'

Macy gave Kit a fearful look – even with his help, she was still having trouble climbing. There was no way she could reach the top of the wall before Nina's pursuer arrived. 'Hide!' the Interpol agent ordered. She nodded, and he released her hands. Arms flailing for balance, she scuttled back down the pile of stones and ran for the roofless buildings.

'Hey! What about me?' yelped Cuff as Kit rushed up the stairs after the two Germans.

'Just *run*, you moron!' Nina yelled as she sprinted past him

147

into another undergrowth-clogged alley. He hesitated, then started to follow—

'Hey! Alto!'

The soldier burst into the open, aiming his gun at Cuff. The American gasped in terror, throwing up his hands. The Venezuelan looked round, glimpsing Macy as she ducked into the house Nina had explored earlier. Movement above – he fired at Kit, but the Indian threw himself the last few feet up the steps and disappeared over the top of the great wall.

His smoking AK-103 fixed on Cuff's chest, the soldier advanced on him. 'Don't shoot, don't shoot me!' Cuff stammered. 'I – I have dollars! American dollars!' One shaking hand reached to a pocket. The soldier's finger tightened on the trigger. 'No, no, no! Please! Dollars, see?' He took out his wallet and tremblingly thumbed it open to reveal a wad of banknotes inside, then tossed it to the ground. 'Take it!'

The soldier regarded the money for a moment, then lowered the rifle. Cuff whimpered in relief – and the weapon's stock smashed into his mouth, spilling blood and broken teeth. He collapsed on the muddy ground, clutching his jaw and moaning. A dark patch spread on his trousers as he wet himself.

His attacker shot him a brief sneer, then turned to hunt another intruder.

Macy.

The archaeology student was already regretting her choice of hiding place. The ancient house was more like a cell; small, devoid of concealment and with no other exit – except the window. She slipped her arms into the hole. It was narrower at the top than the bottom, but she hauled herself through, head and shoulders clearing the sill as she wriggled the rest of her body out—

A single gunshot, the bullet shattering part of the lintel.

Stone chips stung her backside and thighs. She screamed, freezing.

'Well, look at that!' said a man in Spanish with a mocking laugh. 'Now that's a gorgeous ass – and in just the right position.' Macy heard him cross the room. 'Maybe I should keep you there, eh? Have some fun.' She flinched as a hand squeezed her left buttock. 'Now that's—'

There was a muffled crack, followed by the thump of something heavy hitting the floor. Then silence. 'Er . . . hello?' she whispered nervously.

'Get your ass out of there, Macy,' said a familiar New York voice.

'Nina!' Macy cried as another hand pulled her backwards. She found the soldier slumped at her feet, Nina standing over him. 'What did you do?'

The redhead held up the bolas. One of the rotten ropes had fallen apart when she pulled the weapon out of the muck, but its other two stone spheres were still connected. 'I got him by the balls. Or *with* the balls, but same thing.' She dropped them and picked up the unconscious man's AK. 'Tell Kit to come back down and keep an eye on this guy, then help that idiot Cuff.'

'What about you?' Macy asked as the other woman returned to the doorway.

Nina looked back at her, determined. 'I'm going to find Eddie.' She moved off at a run, shouting. 'Eddie! I've got his gun!'

Reaching the top of the long, twisting stairs, Eddie thought at first he was trapped in a dead end, but then he found a low opening almost completely hidden behind a curtain of ivy and creepers. He pushed through the plants to find himself on a narrow street. To one side, he saw what he realised was a battlement along the top of the cliff bounding one side of the ruined city, a collapsed section revealing the foliage of trees beyond. He went the other way, heading back towards Paititi's centre.

Before long, the street opened on to the central plaza and he stopped, looking out cautiously. The second soldier stood near the tent with his gun pointed at Valero, who was kneeling with his hands on his head. If he could approach without being seen, maybe—

The soldier's head snapped round at a shout. Eddie heard it too. Nina! But he couldn't make out what she was saying, echoes and his own less than perfect hearing muffling her words.

The soldier seemed to understand them, though. To Eddie's surprise, he didn't react by bringing up his weapon, but instead backed in concern towards the tent, AK still covering Valero.

Nina called out again, closer. This time he made it out. She had got the other soldier's rifle. No wonder the man here was worried.

But why was he going to the tent? A different weapon wouldn't give him an advantage . . .

He realised what was within the canvas shelter just as the soldier groped inside. He was getting a radio, calling for backup.

Eddie burst out of cover and charged at the tent. A click and a hiss of static, then the noise was cut off as the soldier, still guarding Valero, pushed the handset's transmit button and started speaking in urgent Spanish. The word 'Socorro!' stood out – help!

More troops would be coming . . .

Eddie dived at the tent. The whole thing collapsed, knocking the Venezuelan down under the flapping fabric. The radio hit the stone flags with a heavy *clunk*.

The soldier had managed to keep hold of his AK. He fired wildly, bullets pitting the buildings at the plaza's edge. Valero rolled for cover behind a tree. Eddie scrambled to his feet and kicked, catching the soldier's arm and sending the AK-103 spinning across the plaza.

The Venezuelan grimaced, shaking off the camouflaged shroud. He looked for his gun, saw it was out of reach, turned back to face Eddie – and drew a knife.

Eddie took on a defensive posture, judging his opponent. The Venezuelan was bigger than him, and probably fifteen years younger. He would have faster reactions, but less experience and training – his uniform was regular army, not special forces. The Englishman's gaze flitted between the six-inch blade and his opponent's eyes, waiting for the first sign of the inevitable attack—

The knife thrust at his chest. Eddie twisted to avoid it, then tried to grab the soldier's wrist, but the Venezuelan had already pulled back. Another stab, another dodge, the razor edge this time close enough to rasp against his jacket's steel zip.

Third strike—

Eddie gripped the soldier's arm – but the knife sliced across his chest, tearing his T-shirt. He grunted at the sharp pain, battling to keep hold as the man tried to shake him off. A sweep of his elbow, the point cracking against the soldier's face just under his left eye socket.

The Venezuelan staggered, giving Eddie the chance to chop at his hand, trying to force him to drop the knife. Another fierce blow, the soldier's grip loosening . . .

The man shoved Eddie backwards across the uneven stone slabs into a patch of mud. With one last strike Eddie finally knocked the knife away, but his feet slipped in the ooze. One boot lost its grip, and he fell.

He landed on his back with a thick splash, the soldier on top of him. And now it was the Venezuelan's turn to use his elbow, driving it down with all his weight into Eddie's stomach.

Even tensing his abdominal muscles to absorb the impact, Eddie still convulsed in sickening, breathless pain. His groan was choked off as the man clamped his hands round his throat. He tried to claw at the soldier's eyes, but the Venezuelan pulled back out of Eddie's reach as he squeezed harder—

The pressure abruptly eased. The soldier was no longer looking down at Eddie, but at something above. The Yorkshire-man tipped his head back to see an inverted world, buildings hanging over the empty abyss of the sky . . . and an upside-down Nina pointing an AK-103 at his attacker.

A quick flick of her eyebrows told the soldier to release him. Eddie drew in a hoarse breath as his adversary nervously withdrew, and sat up. 'You okay?' Nina asked.

He coughed. 'Bit of a hairball. What about the others?'

'Macy's fine, Cuff'll need a trip to the orthodontist but looked okay apart from that. Kit's watching the other guy; everyone else got up the wall.'

'Good.' He stood, giving the soldier a threatening glare before calling to Valero. 'Oscar!' He pointed to the fallen AK. 'Get the gun – I'll tie him up.'

Nina kept her rifle aimed at the soldier as Valero retrieved the second Kalashnikov. 'I don't understand,' she said. 'If loggers found this place, what's the army doing here?'

'Maybe loggers did find it,' said Eddie, tugging a length of guy rope from the tent. 'But they wouldn't know how to sell the stuff they found, so they started asking around – and word got back to someone at that radar base. Quick arrest, bit of an interrogation, and now someone with stripes on their sleeve knows all about Paititi – and how much treasure's hidden in it.' He pulled the rope through the last eyelet and lifted the canvas – to expose a field radio lying on its side, the handset trapped beneath it. The transmit light was on. 'Buggeration and fuckery,' he said, lifting the radio and seeing that the handset's key had been depressed by the unit's weight; as soon as it was released, the channel cleared and an urgent voice crackled through the speaker. He hurriedly switched it off. 'He managed to warn his mates – we need to get out of here.'

'Wait a minute,' said Nina as Eddie tied up the soldier. She gestured towards the large buildings at the plaza's western end. 'We need to at least check the temple and the palace first. These guys have already stolen potentially millions of dollars of artefacts – we've got to see if there's anything left before they strip the whole place bare.'

'We don't have time. If they think somebody's found their little secret, they'll probably be on their way here already.'

'No, I agree with Dr Wilde,' said Valero. 'It took us over two hours to reach here from Valverde – it will take even longer from the military base. If we take the road south to Matuso, they will never catch up with us. And when we get to the Jeep, I can use the satellite phone to report to the Bolivarian Militia. The more I know about what is here, the more I can tell my superiors.'

Eddie didn't like the idea of delaying their getaway, but Valero was right; it would take some time for more soldiers to reach them. 'Okay, but be quick about it. Ten minutes, no more.'

It took over half that long just to assemble all the expedition members. Both soldiers were tied to a tree, Eddie and Kit taking their weapons after Valero recovered his pistol. With Eddie pointedly checking his watch, the group hurried up the broad steps to the Temple of the Sun.

Where something incredible awaited them.

11

'My God!' Nina gasped, Osterhagen echoing her words in German. Everyone stared in amazement. The chamber was roofless where the wood had long since decayed, but an overhanging tree blotted out most of the light. At the east end was a single window . . . facing the wonder opposite.

Mounted on the west wall was a metal disc, a stylised face surrounded by elaborate patterns of spirals and interlocking lines. It was some four feet in diameter, at its deepest four inches thick . . . and even covered with the dirt of ages, it was instantly obvious that it was made from solid gold.

'The Punchaco!' exclaimed Becker.

Even through his awe, Osterhagen shook his head. 'No, it is too small, and there are no jewels. It must be a copy.'

'What's a punchaco?' Macy asked.

'A sun disc,' Nina replied. 'One of the greatest Inca treasures.'

'*The* greatest,' Osterhagen corrected her. 'It represented the sun god Inti, and was in the Temple of the Sun at Cuzco. As well as being made of pure gold, it was decorated with thousands of precious stones. But when the Spanish arrived, even though they looted the temple of a huge amount of gold, the Punchaco was gone.'

Eddie moved further into the room. Before the golden face was a large stone slab, which he guessed was an altar – and behind it was proof that someone else knew of the sun disc's existence. 'The Spanish weren't the only ones who wanted to get their hands on this thing,' he said, holding up a length of heavy-duty chain.

Nina rounded the altar to see a trolley made of thick steel with six fat little tyres, as well as a pile of equally beefy metal struts, several of which had been fastened together to form the basis of a truss. She also recognised the pulleys of a block and tackle. 'Looks like they were going to lift the disc off the wall and stand it on this cart.' She went to the window. At one time it would have allowed the light of dawn to shine on the Punchaco. Though the view was now blocked by trees, she could still make out the main gate to the east – and closer, the oddly proportioned crate.

Its purpose was no longer a mystery. It was the right size to accommodate the sun disc.

'It's a good thing we *did* come in here,' she said, with a faintly accusing look at her husband. 'They were about to steal the sun disc. And they were probably saving it until last – it's not something they could carry off in their pocket like the artefacts Interpol recovered. That much gold must weigh tons.'

Kit examined the sun disc. 'It's about one metre twenty across, and . . . ten centimetres deep. So it would weigh . . .'

'The volume of a cylinder is *pi* r squared h,' Cuff mumbled through the handkerchief he was holding to his mouth. 'So that's . . .'

'One hundred and thirteen thousand, one hundred and forty-two cubic centimetres,' Nina announced, performing the calculations in her head, to the surprise of Valero and Osterhagen's team. 'Or zero point one one three cubic metres, more or less. And I think gold is something like nineteen times denser than water, which weighs a metric ton per cubic metre, so . . .' Another moment of thought. 'We're talking over two tons of gold. The weight of an SUV.'

'No wonder they left it till last,' said Eddie. 'Be a bugger to get out of here.'

'But if this is only a copy,' said Macy, 'where's the real thing?'

'Still hidden, somewhere,' suggested Loretta.

Nina looked towards the entrance. 'Somewhere here, maybe?'

Osterhagen had the same idea. 'The palace! We have to search it.'

'Two minutes,' warned Eddie. 'The longer we're here, the more chance we have of getting caught.'

'I know, I know,' Nina snapped, bustling the others to the door.

They hurried out and ascended another set of steps to the building on the highest tier of the jungle city. It too was open to the elements, and in a state of partial collapse where wind-borne seeds had taken root and grown into infinitely patient, subtly destructive trees, but more than enough of the structure remained to reveal its stark majesty. Every block had been carved with painstaking precision to fit exactly amongst its neighbours without needing mortar to secure it, and in contrast to the plain architecture elsewhere in Paititi the palace was decorated, geometric patterns carved into the stonework and sculpted heads jutting from sections of wall.

'Split up,' Nina ordered. Much as it pained her, she ignored the ancient adornments to search the various rooms for any unlooted treasures. Though there were a few remaining artefacts that would be valuable from a cultural perspective, nothing stood out as being so financially. The raiders had been thorough. 'Find anything?' she called.

'It'd help if I knew what I was looking for,' Eddie complained from a neighbouring room.

'Anything obviously valuable – gold, silver, jewels. If it shows up on the black market, we can tie it back to here and give Interpol some legal ammunition.'

'If we just take it with us, we can stop them getting hold of it,' Macy piped up.

Nina was about to give her a refresher course on professional ethics when Eddie called out again. 'Nina! In here.'

She knew from his tone that it was important. 'What is it?'

'It's not gold or silver or jewels,' he said as she entered the small chamber, 'but I'm pretty sure you'll think it's valuable.'

Unlike the palace's other rooms, one end of this had a roof of sorts where an alcove was set into the wall. The space was around six feet deep, slightly wider. Set into its rear was a foot-high arched recess. Something stood inside it.

She took out a flashlight. Its beam revealed that the alcove's walls were painted; though in places split by cracks and scabbed by mould, most of the images were still discernible.

But it wasn't the paintings that had seized her attention. Even before she brought the light on to it, she recognised the shape in the recess. And when she did, she also recognised the colour.

A strange purple stone.

'It's the third statue . . .' she whispered. Like the other two figurines cocooned in their case in her backpack, it was a crude but recognisably anthropomorphic sculpture, arms held out in such a way as to interlock with its near-twins when they were placed together.

Except . . . there was only one arm.

'What—' she gasped. There was *less* to the statue than met the eye. It stood sideways in the niche, its right side to her – but there was no left side. It had been sliced in half down its centre line. 'No!'

'Yeah, I thought you might not be happy about that,' said Eddie as she plucked it from the recess and turned it over in her hands. 'Why do you think they chopped it in two?'

'No idea,' she said, disappointment welling. For all the archaeological wonders of the lost settlement, the statuette had been her primary reason for coming here – but she now had no more clues to lead her to the rest of it.

Unless . . .

She switched off the flashlight. 'Hold this for a minute,' she told Eddie, passing the figurine to him. As the other expedition members filtered into the room, she took the other two statues from their case. No eerie light, but there was a mildly unsettling sensation through her palms, like the tingling of a very low current.

'What are you doing?' Osterhagen asked.

'Seeing if maybe this isn't the end of the line for the Incas.' Nina slid the statues together shoulder to shoulder . . .

The others made sounds of surprise as the linked figures glowed, very faintly but just enough to stand out in the shadows. 'Give me the other one,' she said to Eddie. He slipped it between the pair. She used her thumbs to nudge it into position, the lone arm in place round its neighbour – and the glow subtly changed, strongest on one particular side of the triptych. 'Eddie, you've got a compass, haven't you?'

'Yeah, of course.'

She turned the statues, the brighter glow remaining fixed as they moved. 'What direction is it pointing?'

'Why are they doing that?' asked Valero, entranced.

'They react to the earth's magnetic field,' said Nina, simplifying for convenience. 'And they also point towards each other. That's part of what led us here.'

Eddie, meanwhile, had checked his compass. 'Southwest,' he reported.

'Huh. That's why we didn't realise it had been split into two parts – they're both on the same bearing from Glastonbury, so we only saw one glow.'

'Why isn't it as bright as at Glastonbury?' Macy asked.

'The earth energy mustn't be as strong here. Or maybe it was once, but the confluence point moved.'

'Earth energy?' demanded Osterhagen. 'What confluence point? What is going on?'

'It's why the IHA's involved, I'm afraid. But it means the other piece of the statue is somewhere southwest of here.'

'Have to look for it later,' said Eddie. 'Time's up, and we need to get the fuck out of here.'

'Another minute, please,' said Osterhagen, turning his attention to the alcove's walls. He switched on a torch of his own, sweeping it across the murals. Becker and Macy followed suit, while Loretta brought out a camera and began taking photos. 'These paintings . . . I think they are the story of how the Incas came to this place. Look.' He indicated one section on the left-hand wall: a large building. 'That is the Intiwasa at Cuzco, the Sun Temple – the Spanish destroyed the upper levels to build the church of Santa Domingo on it, but the base is exactly the same.'

Nina carefully put down the statues, then retrieved her light and examined the mural. Though simplistic, almost cartoony in the way everything was broken down into blocks of solid colour, there was clearly a story being told. 'These figures outside the temple, the ones in different clothes – are they the Spaniards?'

Osterhagen nodded. 'Pizarro's messengers. Giving Atahualpa's orders for his people to gather their gold and silver.'

'And hide it from the Spanish . . .' Nina moved her light across the walls. Opposite the representation of Cuzco was one of what she assumed was Paititi, a walled town surrounded by trees, above which was an image of the sun disc in the nearby temple – as well as a small shape that was almost certainly meant to be the half of the third statue.

Murals of other locations were spread out between the start and the end of the Inca exodus. A painted path connected them, marked along its meandering length with symbols: vertical lines broken up by dots. 'These symbols,' she said. 'An account of the route they followed, maybe?'

'I thought the Incas never developed writing?' said Macy.

'They didn't,' said Osterhagen. 'Most of their history was oral. They had ways of storing numerical records such as censuses and taxes, though.'

'Uh-huh.' Tax records were of not the slightest interest to the young woman. She examined another part of the wall.

Nina was still concentrating on the markings. 'I've seen this kind of thing before. My guess is that these give you distances and directions to follow. It's a record of their journey to Paititi.'

'And other places,' said Macy with growing excitement, illuminating another painted scene above the recess. 'Look at this!'

Even Eddie was impressed enough to delay yelling another, more forceful reminder of the time. 'Thought you said El Dorado was just a myth?'

Mountain peaks rose above a city, buildings stacked seemingly on top of each other as they rose to a palace at their summit – above which was another sun disc, but more elaborate than the one above the painting of Paititi, and even its real-life counterpart in the Temple of the Sun. Both city and god-image were coloured in yellow . . . or gold. 'Is that the Punchaco?' Nina asked. 'The real one?'

Osterhagen's nose almost rubbed the faded paint. 'Yes! Yes, it must be! Look at all the jewels – look how big it is!' Even taking the Incas' primitive understanding of perspective into account, it was clear the ornate disc was meant to be larger than the figures kneeling below it. 'It must have been huge!'

Nina gently blew away dirt and cobwebs to reveal more detail. Running down one side of the city were streaks of pale blue that ended in a stippled cloud, which in turn led into a winding blue line that could only be a representation of a river. 'A waterfall?'

'It could be, yes . . .' The German gazed open-mouthed at the scene. 'Oh! And look at these jaguars. They must be symbols of the gods, protecting the city from invaders.' He pointed out a little vignette between the lowest tier of buildings and the river. At one side, a pair of elegantly stylised cats, yellow bodies mottled with black spots, sat and watched with aloof disdain as two figures were swept away by another waterfall; to their right, a crouching jaguar observed a man climbing a steep set of steps.

Nina was no longer looking at the painting, however. With more light on it, the niche was revealed to be not as empty as she had thought. There was something beneath the accumulated dirt behind where the figurine had stood. She brushed it experimentally with a fingertip, finding a braided cord beneath and slowly lifting it. More muck fell away as other lengths of coloured string were revealed, small knots woven into them.

Loretta took a picture. 'It's a khipu!' she gasped.

'Be careful,' Osterhagen urged Nina. 'They are very rare, only a few hundred in the world. The Spanish destroyed any they found.' She carefully lowered the cords back into their resting place.

'What's a khipu?' Macy asked.

Even through broken teeth, Cuff's condescension was clear. 'Khipus are how the Incas kept their records – the word actually means "talking knots". They had a very advanced mathematical system using different kinds of knots in strings to store numbers. I thought everybody knew that, but apparently *not*.' He laughed a little at his own pun.

Macy gave him a scathing look. 'Bite me. Oh wait, you can't.'

But Nina was now fixated on something else. In the heart of the palace atop the painted city was a small oval space . . . and in it was a mirror image of something she had already seen. 'The third statue – that's its other half,' she said. 'It's in this city – wherever that is.'

'Southwest of here?' Osterhagen mused. 'In mountains – that would be the Andes in northern Peru. The eastern mountains and the edges of the Amazon basin in that region were among the last conquests of the Incas before the Spanish invasion, the farthest reaches of the empire. A good hiding place.'

'Not good enough,' said Nina. 'They must have thought the Conquistadors were going to find it, so they moved again, all the way through the jungle to here. Somewhere they could finally be sure it was safe.'

'Until now,' Eddie cut in impatiently. 'If we don't get moving right now, half the Venezuelan army is going to roll up and catch us.'

Osterhagen began to protest. 'But we have to—'

'No, we're going. No more arguments.' He unshouldered his AK-103 for emphasis. 'Nina, I'll give you a hand packing up those statues. Kit, Oscar, get everyone else back to the Jeeps – we'll catch up.'

Kit had also readied his rifle. 'Don't take too long,' he said, ushering the others out.

'We won't, don't worry.' Eddie crouched beside Nina to help return the statues to their case.

'Another five minutes wouldn't have killed us,' she objected.

'Those two arseholes tied up outside would have if they'd had the chance,' he countered. 'I don't think their mates'll be any different. Especially not with millions of dollars at stake.'

'Oscar said we'll be miles away before they get here.'

'Yeah, and Oscar said he was going to order those soldiers to surrender, and look how that turned out.' The two IHA statues were back in their foam beds. 'What about the one you just found?'

Nina hesitated, aware of the hypocrisy of what she was about to say; she had been on the verge of castigating Macy for the same thing not ten minutes earlier. But she justified it – at least, to herself – as a case when the IHA's global security mandate trumped normal considerations. 'We take it,' she said, taking out a penknife and cutting away part of the foam to make a space for the third piece. 'I don't know what it's going to lead to, but I think it's important.' A glance back at the recess. 'And that khipu might be too – it was with the statue, so there could be a connection. I don't want to risk these soldiers getting it.'

'If they wanted it, they'd have swiped it already,' Eddie pointed out.

'But they don't know what we know about the statues.' She swept the dirt from the niche, exposing the rest of the khipu. It was longer than she had first thought, folded over itself several times. 'There should be some Ziploc bags in my backpack. Can you get one for me?'

He did so, and she gently slipped the khipu into the plastic bag, squeezing out the air before sealing it shut. 'Okay,' she said, placing the bag in the case and closing it, then putting the case in her pack, 'I'm ready.'

'About time. Come on.'

They hurried back into the open, passing the temple and descending the steps into the plaza. The soldiers were still tied to the tree, the other expedition members heading for the main gate.

Not as quickly as Eddie wanted. 'What is this, a fucking afternoon stroll?' he growled. 'Oi! You lot! Shift your arses!'

His shout spurred them on, but not by much; Nina and Eddie caught up while they were still short of the gate. 'Some of us are injured, you know,' Cuff whined.

'You don't run on your lips, do you?' said Eddie, devoid of sympathy. 'Oscar, how're you managing?'

The Venezuelan's face was tight with ill-concealed pain; unlike the American, he had suffered blows that were affecting his movement, his torso badly bruised by the soldiers' kicks. 'I'm okay,' he grunted. 'When we—' He broke off, looking round at a noise.

Eddie heard it too – or more accurately *felt* it, a subsonic thumping inside his chest cavity.

He instantly knew what it was. 'Shit! It's a chopper!'

The pounding grew louder, rising to a clattering whump of rotors as a helicopter swept overhead. Eddie glimpsed it through the jungle canopy: a Russian-built Mil Mi-17.

With the yellow, blue and red stripes of the Venezuelan flag standing out from the muted green camouflage paint on its tail boom. A military aircraft.

The soldiers' backup had arrived.

12

'Get through the gate!' Eddie yelled. The group was still short of Paititi's thick outer walls. As everyone ran, he glared at Nina. 'This is why we had to go five minutes ago!'

'Don't you try to put this on me!' she shouted back. 'You said they were coming by road, not helicopter!'

'Well, I'm not a fucking oracle, am I?' They reached the gate, the narrow opening forcing them into single file to pass through.

The helicopter slowed, preparing to hover. The tree cover was far too dense for it to land, even inside the settlement. 'It's going to drop troops,' Eddie warned as everyone scrambled across the remains of a defensive trench. 'They'll be able to shoot you from about two hundred metres away through this much jungle, so keep as many trees behind you as you can. Oscar, get everyone to the Jeeps. Kit, you and me are going to cover the rear.'

'I don't think I like the sound of that,' the Indian said unhappily.

Nina wasn't keen either. 'What are you doing?'

Eddie pointed back towards the lost town. 'In about thirty seconds, they'll have boots on the ground – and another thirty seconds after that, the guys we tied up'll have told them we just did a runner out of the gate. We need to slow 'em down long enough for you to get to the trucks.'

'We're not going to leave you!' she protested.

'It's a tactical withdrawal, not a last stand. We'll be there, you can bloody believe it!' She was still hesitant, so he gave her a reassuring smile. 'We'll be fine. Go on, see you soon.'

'I'll hold you to that,' she said with a faint smile of her own, before going after the others.

Eddie watched her retreat, then turned to Kit. 'You ready?'

'No, but that never seems to matter, does it?' A grim grin from the Interpol officer. 'What do we do?'

'Keep your gun on the gate. Soon as anyone comes out of it, fire a couple of rounds. We're trying to buy time, so we need to keep 'em bottled up for as long as we can.'

'Are we shooting to kill?'

'They will be.' The Mil tipped out of its hover, swinging round to circle the area. 'Okay, they're down,' said Eddie. 'Soon as the shooting starts, we'll do a running retreat. You back up by twenty, thirty metres, get behind a tree and cover me while I move, then I do the same for you.'

'Okay.' They hunched behind an earth mound, about sixty metres from the gate. The team had been extremely unlucky, Eddie thought; the chopper must have been visiting the radar base for it to have responded to the soldier's SOS so quickly. It also still posed a threat – it was a transport, not a gunship, but it could follow the fleeing 4×4s and report their position.

There were more pressing worries, though. He sighted the AK on the gate. How long before the soldiers reached it?

He got an answer a few seconds later. A man cautiously looked out—

Eddie fired two rapid shots. The first went slightly wide, cracking off the stonework. The Englishman immediately adjusted his aim, but the soldier had already pulled back.

'Move,' he told Kit, who started his retreat. Eddie kept his gun fixed on the gate. The man reappeared, unleashing a three-round burst from his AK. Bullets smacked into the mound in front of Eddie. He ducked, then returned fire – but that had been all the time another two soldiers needed to rush past their comrade and dive headlong into the trench.

The soldier at the gate fired again, the rounds whipping over Eddie's head. He crawled back and waved for Kit to shoot. It was going to be a tough escape.

But not impossible.

Kit fired a couple of rounds, and Eddie quickly scuttled backwards. He passed the Indian, and kept moving until he reached shelter behind the vine-throttled trunk of a large hardwood tree. Nobody was in clear sight, but the jolting of a small bush told him that one man was crawling along the trench. The other was probably doing the same in the other direction. They were spreading out, making it harder for himself and Kit to cover them all.

They weren't advancing, though. For now, that was what mattered: it would buy Nina and the others the time they needed to reach the trucks.

'Kit!' he called. The Interpol officer dropped low and backed up to pass him. He readied his weapon—

Two more soldiers rushed out of the gate. Eddie fired again. Somebody yelled, but more in surprise than pain – a very narrow miss, perhaps even a grazing impact. A good scare would make him more reluctant to put his head up.

But there were still at least four other men to deal with. He released another round to encourage them to stay down – then jerked into cover himself as a soldier in the trench opened fire on full auto. Chunks of shredded wood exploded from the trunk.

Kit was in position behind another tree. Eddie fired a single shot, then ducked and hurried to overtake him. The Indian unleashed more bullets, hitting nothing but soil and wood, then moved back as Eddie took up the cover fire.

The man at the gate reappeared. Eddie aimed at him – then snapped his gun round as he saw a soldier rise and rush out of the trench. Two pulls of the trigger, and the man tumbled into the dirt, shrieking in Spanish.

If the soldiers were professionals, some would break off to help the wounded man . . .

Money was their motivation. The screams continued as the gunfire intensified, the angry Venezuelans advancing. Eddie fired again as another man ran for a tree, but a spray of bullets from two others chewed into his cover and forced him back behind it.

But he and Kit had done their job. The others would be almost at the Jeeps by now. He registered that the helicopter was still circling somewhere behind him, but ignored it. Time to go.

'Give me cover, then run!' he called to Kit, who fired again. Eddie bent low and scurried from the tree – then, when he was level with his friend, broke into a sprint. Kit fired a last burst before following. AKs chattered behind them as they ran.

Valero's injuries were slowing him, the Venezuelan clutching his ribs as his run became a faltering plod. Nina moved alongside him. 'Leonard, help me carry him!'

'No, keep going,' Valero wheezed as Osterhagen hurried over. 'We're almost there – go on!'

Nina took his weight on one side, the German supporting him on the other. 'No, we stick together,' she insisted.

Another expedition member didn't share that view. Cuff

broke from the group and raced up the earthen bank ahead. 'Day, wait!' cried Loretta.

'If he takes one of the trucks on his own,' Nina growled, 'he'll need more than a dentist when I'm done with him.'

'I'll help,' Macy added.

'He wouldn't do that,' Osterhagen assured her. 'I think . . .'

Macy ran to catch Cuff as they brought Valero up the slope. At the top, Nina spotted a flash of red through the greenery – one of the Land Cruisers. Osterhagen saw it too, and they guided the winded man towards it.

Cuff reached the nearest 4×4, yanking open the driver's door. Nina expected him to jump in, but instead he stood unmoving. 'Start it up!' Macy yelled to him as she reached the vehicle. 'Come on, get—'

She too froze, suddenly silent.

Nina realised that something was horribly wrong, but it was too late to do anything about it – they were only a couple of dozen yards from the trucks with nowhere to run, nowhere to take cover.

Macy looked back, frightened. Nina now knew why.

Someone was in the Land Cruiser. But how—

The helicopter. She hadn't paid it any attention, distracted by the gunfire. Now, though, she knew what it had been doing. The only way to leave Paititi was along the logging track, and it had dropped more troops ahead to catch them in a pincer.

Figures emerged from behind trees and bushes, weapons aimed at the archaeologists and their guide. Loretta screamed. One soldier pointed at Valero, then gestured towards the ground. With a faint moan of defeat, Valero dropped his gun.

The man in the Land Cruiser emerged, Cuff stepping back in fear. Tall, late forties, tending towards the spread of middle age but still intimidatingly powerful. An officer, his crisp and clean uniform contrasting with the sweaty fatigues of his men. He regarded Nina and her companions coldly from behind a pair of aviator sunglasses. 'Who are you,' he said in thickly accented English, 'and what are you doing in my ruins?'

Eddie and Kit weaved through the jungle, plants whipping at their faces. 'Over there!' Eddie said, seeing footprints heading up the bank. He followed them. 'Just up this, and we're—'

Figures standing around the 4×4s.

Too many figures.

Instinct kicked in and he dropped flat, dragging Kit with him as more rifles fired. Bullets ripped into the ground just above them.

The gunfire stopped. Gesturing for Kit to stay still, Eddie crawled sidelong until he was below a plant's dangling fronds. Very cautiously, he raised his head and peered through the leaves.

The other team members were lined up on their knees before the Land Cruisers, hands behind their heads. Nina was at the centre, between Macy and Cuff. None appeared to have been harmed.

Yet.

A man wearing a tan beret was partially visible behind the nearer 4×4, but Eddie fixed his attention on the person in charge: a Venezuelan officer in sunglasses standing behind the prisoners, one hand on his holstered automatic. 'Throw your guns over the top and raise your hands above your heads!' he shouted.

'What do we do?' Kit whispered.

They were outnumbered, only limited ammo remaining, and, with the prisoners held at gunpoint and more soldiers closing from behind, the chances of taking down the

Venezuelans without suffering multiple losses were almost zero. 'We'll have to give up,' Eddie reluctantly told him. Kit looked shocked. 'Yeah, it's a pisser, I know. But if we don't—'

The officer shouted again. 'If you do not surrender by the time I count to three, I will kill one of your friends!' Eddie looked through the leaves again, his blood chilling when he saw that the man had drawn his gun and moved behind Nina. He started to count, with almost no pause between the numbers. 'One, two—'

'No!' Eddie yelled, flinging his AK over the rise and jumping up with his hands held high. Kit did the same.

The cold gaze behind the sunglasses regarded them for a moment. Nobody moved. Then—

'Three.'

He pulled the trigger.

The bullet hit the back of Cuff's skull from point-blank range. It shattered into fragments as it punched through bone, red-hot metal chunks liquefying brain tissue. One of the pieces exploded from his right eye socket at the head of a terrible gout of grey and red. Cuff slumped lifelessly in his own blood.

Nina had been almost deafened by the gunshot barely two feet from her head. The ringing in her ears gradually faded, only to be replaced by another sound. Screaming. Loretta was wailing hysterically at the sight of Cuff's body. The other prisoners were also in shock.

The officer gestured to two of his men. Weapons locked on Eddie and Kit, they recovered the discarded AK-103s, then brought the explorers to their commander. The three golden stars of his insignia told the former SAS man that he was a major general – one of the highest Venezuelan military ranks. He removed his sunglasses, revealing dark, narrow eyes, blinking as infrequently as a lizard's. 'Are there any more of you?' he asked.

'No,' Eddie replied.

'If you are lying, I will kill you all. Starting with her.' He pointed his pistol at Nina. She looked fearfully at her husband.

'This is all of us. I'm not lying,' said Eddie.

The officer stared at him for several seconds before finally turning away, appearing satisfied. His gaze moved on to Loretta, who was still crying. 'Rojas,' he said to a man nearby, a sergeant. 'That noise. Silence it.'

Rojas stepped up to Loretta and with a swift, savage move smashed a fist across her face, knocking her to the ground. 'You fucker!' Eddie cried, lunging at him, only to have two Kalashnikov muzzles stabbed hard into his chest, then the stock of a third rifle slammed against the back of his head. He dropped to his knees in pain.

The man standing behind the Land Cruiser spoke. 'Always did try to play the white knight for the ladies, didn't you . . . *Chase?*'

Eddie looked up in shock. He knew that voice. The speaker strode out and stood before him, a smug smile on his chiselled face.

It was Alexander Stikes.

13

'You know this guy?' Nina asked, shocked.

'Unfortunately, yeah,' said Eddie. 'He's a complete fucking bell-end called Stikes.'

'Alexander Stikes,' said the man in question, introducing himself to Nina with mock civility. 'Formerly of the SAS. I had the dubious privilege of commanding *Corporal* Chase here.'

Eddie gave him a cutting half-smile. 'Until I got him kicked out.'

Stikes sneered. 'Don't award yourself credit where it's not due. My transfer back to my old regiment had nothing to do with that pathetic inquiry McCrimmon organised.'

'Still stopped you getting promoted, didn't it? Nothing like murdering civilians to fuck up your career prospects.'

'I don't know, striking a superior officer did for yours. Admittedly, a simple demotion wasn't nearly punishment enough, but again, your being McCrimmon's trained poodle helped you.' He slowly circled Eddie. 'You've put on weight, Chase. Two marriages have made you lazy. So how is your ex?'

'Dead as you'll be when I'm done with you. Been stalking me on Facebook, have you?'

'Just keeping tabs on an adversary. But I must admit, it was quite a surprise to hear that coarse northern drawl again when they replayed the SOS at the base. Still, you never could keep your mouth shut.'

The Venezuelan general waved an impatient hand. 'Enough. You know this man, yes, but we need to know who the others are, how much they know about the lost city – and who they have told.'

Stikes ran his hand down the side of Nina's face. She flinched away, Eddie giving him a deadly look. 'Well, since I know Chase, I also know who she is. We have a celebrity in our midst, Salbatore – this is Nina Wilde.'

The general's eyebrows twitched as he recognised the name. 'The one who found Atlantis?'

'The very same. And it appears she's not resting on her laurels. Unfortunately for her, you found this place first.' He stepped back. 'Search them.'

Three soldiers moved along the line, roughly relieving the prisoners of their possessions and tossing them to the ground. Stikes began to examine the passports and wallets.

'You've got me at a disadvantage,' Nina said to the general, trying to maintain a façade of calmness. 'You know my name, so who are you?'

'I know who he is,' said Valero quietly. There was a note almost of betrayal in his voice. 'General Callas.' He looked the officer in the eye. 'You are supposed to be President Suarez's closest ally – his closest friend! Why have you not told him about this place?'

Callas's lips tightened at the mention of Suarez, but he didn't answer, instead turning back to Nina. 'I am General Salbatore Delgado Callas,' he announced. 'I would offer you my hand, but I do not think you will take it.'

'I think you're right,' she replied. He seemed amused by her defiance.

Stikes held up Nina's wallet. 'Well, look what I've found!' he said with exaggerated cheer, thumbing out a business card. She recognised it as the one Larry Chase had given to her. He grinned malevolently at Eddie. 'So, how are your daddy issues these days, Chase? Still mad at him for fucking other women behind Mummy's back?'

Eddie said nothing, but his jaw muscles clenched. Stikes chuckled, pleased at having touched a nerve, then opened the metal case from Nina's backpack. The three statuettes were revealed within.

Callas crouched to look more closely, tapping the half-figure. 'This was in the ruins,' he said, puzzled. 'But the other two . . .'

'You didn't take it?' Stikes asked.

'It wasn't gold or silver, just stone. Broken stone! It is worthless.'

'Apparently not,' said Stikes, shooting Nina a calculating look. He gave the bagged khipu a similarly intrigued appraisal, then carried on with his check of the team's belongings. Kit's was the last; after reading his identity card, he regarded the Indian with surprise. 'Interpol? Inter-esting.' A small smile to match the joke. 'Now, why would the head of the Cultural Property Crime Unit be personally poking around in the jungle?'

'Interpol?' Callas said in alarm. He pointed his gun at Kit. 'Who have you told about this place?'

'Everyone,' said Eddie.

'Nobody,' Stikes said simultaneously. 'If they'd told anyone, Suarez would have ordered your arrest by now.'

'Then we must make sure they never do tell anyone.' Callas stepped back, nodding to Rojas. Loretta started to cry again, trembling. The soldiers readied their weapons.

Stikes raised a hand, as if about to object – but Eddie spoke first. 'Kill us and you'll never find the real treasure – in El Dorado.'

'Eddie!' Nina protested.

Callas laughed. '*This* is El Dorado. The lost city of gold!'

'If you were an archaeologist, you'd know it's not. This place is called Paititi. Didn't pay attention to anything *but* the gold, did you?'

Eddie's eyes were fixed on Callas; meanwhile, Stikes scrutinised Eddie's expression. 'You know, Salbatore . . . he may be telling the truth.'

'What?' Callas demanded.

'Chase here is very protective of the so-called innocent, so he'll say whatever it takes to save them . . . but he's not a natural liar. Blunt, simple-minded honesty is one of his defining characteristics.' He looked towards the ruins. 'It's possible they *have* found something else – especially considering his wife's talent for discovering lost civilisations.'

Callas stood before Nina, gun still in his hand. 'Then we only need to keep one archaeologist alive, don't we?'

She glared at him. 'Hurt anyone else and I'll never tell you anything.'

His lips spread into a lupine smile. 'Oh, you will. I promise you.'

A noise came from the jungle, the whine of a straining engine. A military truck lumbered into view, jolting along the rutted logging track. Eddie tensed, ready to take advantage of the distraction, but the jab of an AK's muzzle into his back told him that his guards were expecting it.

The driver seemed surprised to see them, however; the truck had apparently set out before the SOS was received. It stopped in the clearing. The general shouted an order, and Cuff's corpse was tossed like garbage into the vehicle's open back.

Callas turned back to Nina. 'I have a use for your friends after all.' He clicked his fingers. His troops straightened, ready for action. 'Bring them to the city.'

★

The use Callas had in mind was purely physical: slave labour, to help move his biggest prize. The prisoners were held at gunpoint in the plaza while men went into the Temple of the Sun to complete the assembly of the block and tackle before the two-ton golden disc was prised from the wall with jacks and slowly, carefully, lowered to stand on its edge between supports on the specially built cart.

Once it was done, the explorers were forced to help move the trolley and its weighty cargo to the top of the steps. Other soldiers assembled a makeshift ramp from stout planks so that it could be lowered to the plaza, where the overhanging jungle canopy was thin enough for it to be airlifted out without risking damage. Callas stood nearby, watching the disc's slow progress from behind his sunglasses.

Stikes, meanwhile, disappeared into the palace. When he returned, Loretta's camera in hand, his expression was more calculating than ever. 'I think Chase really was telling the truth,' he told Callas. 'There's a painting on the wall, an account of what I assume is the Incas fleeing the Spanish – I'm hardly an expert on Inca history. But,' he added, gesturing at Nina, 'I know someone who is.'

'She can tell us how to find El Dorado?' Callas asked.

'I'm sure she can, yes. Given the right kind of encouragement.'

Callas nodded. 'She will have it. But after the operation. That must come first.'

'Well, of course. That's why I'm here, after all.'

'Why *are* you here, Stikes?' Eddie demanded as he strained with the others to push the cart to the ramp. 'You've got your knock-off SAS beret on, so I'm guessing you're pretending to be a soldier.'

'Actually, I'm in the same line of work as you used to be, from what I heard on the grapevine. A private military contractor.'

'You're a mercenary?' said Nina disapprovingly.

'Aren't we all, ultimately? We provide our skills to those who need them, in return for money. Mine happen to be in the field of conflict resolution. 3S – that's my company's name, for Stikes Security Solutions—'

'Not Stupid Southern Shitehawk?' Eddie cut in.

Stikes kicked him hard, dropping him to his knees. The guards quickly moved in, AKs raised to deter Eddie from retaliating as he painfully stood back up. 'As I was saying,' Stikes continued, as if nothing had happened, 'my company has been rather successful, what with all the opportunities in Afghanistan and Iraq. But things are tailing off now, so it's time to look for new markets.' A nod to Callas. 'And new clients.'

'There are no conflicts inside Venezuela,' said Valero. 'Only the fight against imperialist aggression.'

Callas laughed sarcastically. 'The voice of the new convert! What were you before you put on that joke of a uniform? A farmhand? A dog from the *barrios*? You have no idea what is really going on in this country.'

'He's right, though,' said Stikes. 'There certainly won't *be* any conflicts in Venezuela – once we're finished.'

Another laugh from the general. 'That is true.'

'Finished what?' Eddie asked.

But no answer was forthcoming, Callas instead walking to the steps in response to a call from below. The ramp was complete. The general issued more orders, and chains were attached to the cart and looped round thick stone pillars at the top of the stairs so the workforce could lower the sun disc slowly to the plaza. It was made very clear to the unwilling members of the group that if the cart broke free and its cargo was damaged, they would all be shot.

After ten minutes of straining, sixteen people struggling to hold the great weight of the Inca treasure on the incline, the sun disc was safely off the foot of the ramp. Arms aching, Eddie nevertheless kept a close watch on Stikes and Callas. Once the golden artefact had been wheeled to the clearing and crated up ready to be lifted by helicopter, the only expedition member they needed to keep alive was Nina. Any opportunity to escape, however slim, would have to be taken.

But even with the majority of the soldiers helping move the sun disc, there were still four guards with AKs, and both Callas and Stikes were armed; the mercenary carried a gleaming nickel-plated Jericho 941 automatic, an Israeli weapon styled to resemble its larger and more famous Desert Eagle cousin, in a hip holster. And the crate was not far away; it would take just a few minutes to reach.

Not much time. There had to be some way they could break loose.

Maybe there was.

The mud near the tent, still churned up from where Eddie had fought the soldier. The cart would be pushed right past it . . .

'Move!' barked Callas, pointing across the plaza.

Everyone resumed their positions: Kit, Osterhagen, Becker and Loretta holding the chains to pull the sun disc, Eddie, Nina and Macy pushing the cart, both groups joined by soldiers. The cart's fat tyres squeaked, bulging under the great weight as it rolled inch by inch across the uneven stone flags.

It drew closer to the patch of sludge. Eddie whispered to Nina, 'I'm going to try something in a minute. If it works, run.'

'What about the others?'

He couldn't speak any louder without risking being overheard. 'Just hope they're quick on the uptake. This mud, coming up – get ready.'

The group pulling the chains were already angling to avoid the obstacle. Eddie checked the mud as the trolley skirted it.

The knife he had knocked from the soldier's hand was still where it had fallen, almost submerged in the thick brown ooze.

He shifted position, moving his feet further from the trolley. Only another couple of steps now. A sidelong glance at the nearest guard. If he saw what he was doing . . .

Last step—

He planted his right foot into the mud – and felt the knife under his sole.

Now!

Eddie pretended to slip, his other foot slithering in the mud. He brought his right sharply forward to regain his balance, dragging the knife with it.

The guard would see if he tried to pick up the blade. Instead, he shoved it forward again and pressed the edge of his boot down hard on the hilt, forcing the blade upwards—

Into one of the tyres.

The point stabbed through the rubber as the cart rolled over it. The tyre exploded with a bang as loud as a gunshot, the sudden extra strain on the two neighbouring wheels causing them to compress.

Top-heavy, unbalanced, the cart tipped over.

Eddie and Nina jumped back—

One of the soldiers tripped, landing beside the cart. His panicked scream was abruptly cut off as the sun disc fell on top of him, two tons of dense metal flattening him with a splatter of blood and mud.

'Run!' Eddie yelled. He punched out a guard and broke into a sprint for the nearest alley.

Nina started to run after him, but another soldier blocked her way. She tried to swerve past – only to slip in the mud, knocking them both to the ground in a tangle of limbs.

Macy fared even less well. She had instinctively leapt back as the sun disc fell, colliding with the soldier behind. Before she could twist away, he tackled her.

Of the other team members, both Osterhagen and Loretta were too surprised to think of fleeing, turning in startled confusion. Kit, sandwiched between two soldiers, got just a couple of feet before he was grabbed. Only Becker managed to break away, barging another soldier out of his path and running for the main gate—

Callas bellowed in Spanish: 'Stop him!' The guards hurriedly brought up their weapons and tracked the gangling German. He weaved desperately as the shots closed in.

One tore a thumb-sized chunk of flesh from his thigh. He fell.

Stikes was hunting another target, snapping the Jericho from his holster and whirling to track Eddie as he ran. He fired – but his target had already ducked behind a tree, the 9mm round smacking into the trunk. Stikes cursed and moved to get a better firing angle.

Too late. Eddie disappeared between two buildings, a second bullet hitting only his shadow. Stikes hissed in frustration and ran after him.

Eddie realised he was heading back towards where he had emerged from the pit. That gave him the advantage, however small, of knowing the terrain. Was there anywhere he could stage an ambush?

Yes. If he could reach it before being shot in the back.

He swatted branches aside, following his footprints in the dirt. He could hear Stikes pounding after him, boots thudding rhythmically down the narrow alleyway. Gaining. The taller, leaner officer had always been faster, and while both men had stayed fit after leaving the SAS, Eddie had spent the better part of five years in an office. Another bullet cracked against the wall behind him, the Jericho's bark echoing through the ancient city. From somewhere deep inside he dredged up an extra burst of speed, swinging round the next corner—

The collapsed section of battlement was ahead – but Eddie was only interested in the vines and ivy hanging from the wall a few yards away, the entrance to the lower level all but invisible behind them.

He dived through, rolling and taking up position at the squat opening. His passage had ripped away some of the creepers – if Stikes spotted the gap and guessed his plan, a few bullets fired through the green curtain would end it instantly.

Footsteps. Stikes had reached the corner. They got closer.

Slowed.

Eddie peered through the leaves. Stikes drew nearer, moving at a cautious walking pace. Eddie tensed, waiting for the best moment to attack – or run. Had Stikes seen the archway, or . . .

The mercenary went past. He hadn't spotted the entrance, instead heading for the doorway of a nearby ruined building. But it would only take him a second to see that there was nobody inside—

Eddie burst out through the vines.

Stikes spun at the crackle of branches – and Eddie slammed him against a wall. He fired, muzzle flame scorching the sleeve of Eddie's leather jacket. Eddie responded by grabbing his wrist and smashing it against the edge of a stone block. Stikes barely held in a grunt of pain as the gun was jolted from his grasp. Eddie shoulder-barged him against the wall, then reached for the fallen Jericho—

Stikes whipped up one knee, catching him in the side and making him stumble. He twisted away from Eddie, then lunged, trying to catch him in a headlock.

Eddie lashed out with a foot, catching his kneecap. Stikes grunted again, reeling – then let out a full-blown groan as Eddie drove a solid punch into his stomach. The Yorkshireman pressed home the attack, delivering another blow to his mid-section before landing an uppercut on his jaw. Stikes fell against the wall, blood round his mouth. 'Always knew you were just a fucking Rupert!' Eddie snarled: army slang for a useless upper-class officer. He pulled back his fist for a knockout blow. 'Can't win in a proper fight—'

Two of Callas's men ran round the corner, raising their AK-103s—

Eddie hauled Stikes away from the wall and shoved him back at the two soldiers. In the confines of the alley they couldn't fire without hitting him, giving Eddie the chance to sprint in the other direction.

Stikes shook off his dizziness. 'What are you waiting for?' he shouted in Spanish, moving aside to give them a clear shot. 'Shoot him!'

They opened fire – just as Eddie reached the collapsed wall and made a running jump into the jungle beyond.

He was over forty feet above the ground, nothing to stop his fall except the branches of a nearby tree. Leaves smacked at his face as he arced through the foliage, arms thrown wide . . .

He hit the damp wood hard, a bough thumping against his chest. Winded, he grabbed it. There was a sudden explosion of movement around him – dozens of small, brightly coloured birds in the tree took to the air in alarm, shrilling and chittering. The branch bounced as if trying to shake him off, but he kept his hold.

He looked for a way to the ground – but the tree chose one for him. The branch snapped. Eddie dropped – and was caught in a knot of creepers, swinging at the trunk.

He braced himself—

Smaller branches absorbed some of the impact, but they also ripped through his clothes, cutting him in several places. He jerked his head sideways just in time to avoid being blinded by one stub, the wood slashing a line across his cheek.

Crackles from above. The creepers were tearing apart. He tried to find a secure handhold, but the branches he clutched all broke under his weight.

He fell again – and hit a twist in the crooked trunk, bouncing off and landing in the overgrown marsh with a thick splash. Despite the pain, he crawled back towards the tree, pushing through the undergrowth.

Above, the two soldiers reached the broken wall and looked into the jungle. Birds whirled madly through the branches, leaves dropping like green snowflakes from the still shaking tree. No sign of the escaped prisoner.

Stikes pushed them aside. 'Give me that!' he barked, snatching the AK from one of the men. He aimed it into the tree, seeing no sign of his former subordinate, then down at the ground.

Movement in the bushes—

Stikes opened fire as Eddie scrambled for cover. Bullets thunked into the tree, bark and splinters spitting from each impact. But his target was now hunched against the other side of the trunk, shielded by over two feet of wood. Stikes fired the last rounds in the magazine, then irritably thrust the AK into its owner's hands. 'Get back to Callas.'

The other soldier still had his weapon fixed on the tree. 'We can climb down and get him.'

'No,' Stikes said. 'We need to get the sun disc out of here. Come on.' He headed back down the alley, retrieving his Jericho. The soldiers followed.

Eddie sat breathlessly behind the tree, wondering if his pursuers had their weapons trained on his hiding place, waiting for him to emerge. After a minute, he risked a peek. Nobody above. They had gone.

Aching, he stood, trying to work out the quickest way to get back into the ruins. Scaling the cliff was out; from here, he would have to go almost halfway round the entire perimeter. He limped away, hearing the rumble of the helicopter drawing closer to the lost city.

'Did you kill him?' Callas called as Stikes and the soldiers returned to the plaza.

'No. He got away,' the Englishman replied.

'You let him escape?'

'He won't go far, not as long as we have them.' Stikes gestured at the prisoners, who apart from the wounded Becker had been forced back to work. 'He'll try to rescue them. I'd advise that we leave before then.'

A faintly dismissive sneer crossed Callas's lips. 'You're afraid of him?'

'Not in the slightest,' Stikes snapped, wiping the blood from his mouth. 'But if we leave him behind, there are only two towns he can reach from here – and you can have men waiting for him at both.' He regarded the blood-spattered sun disc, which had been lifted back upright on the cart. 'How long before the chopper can pick it up?'

'A few minutes.'

'Good. Send two men to guard the trucks – he might try to hijack or sabotage them. The rest, tell them to help load the sun disc as quickly as they can. The moment it leaves the ground, we'll evacuate.'

The Venezuelan stiffened slightly at being given orders by his employee, but nevertheless called out instructions. Two of his men ran for the main gate, the others doing what they could to speed the golden disc's laborious progress. Before long, it reached the waiting crate; a few more minutes of straining, and it was safely in the container. By now, the Mil was hovering directly over the clearing, lowering cables. Soldiers attached the steel lines to the crate as the others forced the prisoners back at gunpoint. Another minute, and a man signalled to Callas that it was ready.

'Take it up!' the general shouted impatiently, waving to the helicopter.

The Mi-17 increased power to full, engines screaming as they took the extra load. The crate lurched from the ground. For a moment it seemed as though it would get no higher, swaying pendulously a few inches above the flagstones; then it slowly began to rise.

Callas watched in satisfaction as the helicopter lifted its precious cargo higher. The crate cleared the trees, then the Mil turned lethargically northwest, heading for the military base. Aircraft and cargo disappeared from view behind the jungle canopy.

It was now Stikes's turn to be impatient. 'Time to go,' he said. His gaze fell on the prisoners. 'What about them?'

'We take them with us,' said Callas. 'I don't want anyone to know we were here.'

'All the bullet holes you've left in the place might give it away,' Nina said scathingly. 'And all the gear you've left behind – as well as Flat Stanley there.' She nodded towards the gory spot where the luckless soldier had been squashed beneath the sun disc.

'I will send more men to collect them later,' the general replied as he started for the gate, signalling his men to bring the explorers. Becker was half carried, half dragged by two soldiers. 'And a bullet hole is a bullet hole. Anyone could have made them at any time. But the bodies of archaeologists known to be in the country on a particular date . . . that would be harder to explain if they were found here.' A sadistic hardness entered his voice. 'But where you are going, you will never be found.'

Despite her outward defiance, a chill of fear ran through Nina's soul.

Eddie climbed back up the outer wall where he had first entered the city, warily surveying the buildings below before scrambling down the ruined stairway and heading for the plaza. He was on full alert, certain that Callas's men would be searching for him – which made the absence of any guards all the more disconcerting as he crept through the alleys.

He peered over a wall at the plaza. Nobody was there. The soldiers, Callas and Stikes were gone. So were Nina and the other expedition members.

And the sun disc.

Callas had what he came for – the golden god-image had been taken away by the helicopter. He vaulted the wall and hurried across the plaza. Tracks in the dirt led to the main gate – and the smaller prints of women's boots amongst them showed that Nina, Macy and Loretta were still alive. Callas presumably had some reason for not wanting their bodies to be found at Paititi, but Eddie was certain that he still intended to kill them. He would be taking them somewhere he could be sure they wouldn't be found. Where?

The military base. A restricted area in the depths of the jungle, what few visitors it might get deterred by barbed wire and bullets. Once Nina and the others entered, they would never leave.

He ran for the gate. As he cleared the ancient walls, he heard something over the noise of birds and insects: a low grumble. Engines.

Receding. The trucks were already heading away down the logging track.

'Shit!' He stopped, forcing back his anger, trying to think. There was only one road, and it took a long and circuitous route back to Valverde and the spur leading to the base. It would take a couple of hours for Callas's convoy to get there. The base itself was about five miles to the northwest . . .

Eddie already knew there was only one course of action he could take.

He raised his wrist, turning in place until the hour hand of his watch pointed at the sun. South, he knew from his military training, was exactly halfway between the hour hand and the twelve o'clock position on the watch face. With that established, it only took a moment to work out which way was northwest. One last look after the vehicles carrying his wife and friends, then he set off at a run into the trees.

14

The bumpy drive from the ruins took two hours, Nina and the others sweating in the back of the troop truck. Ahead and behind it were the Land Cruisers. Kit and Valero looked after Becker, while Macy tried, with limited success, to comfort the weeping, terrified Loretta. Nina's fleeting thoughts of leaping over the tailgate to escape into the jungle were tempered by the AK-103s pointed at her companions – and the presence of Cuff's body. Loretta's hysteria at the sight had forced the soldiers to cover it, but the huddled shape was a constant reminder of Callas's ruthlessness.

She knew he would display that trait again soon enough. The general's greed had convinced him to keep her alive – for the moment – in the hope she could lead him to even greater riches . . . but he had no cause to spare the others. They had witnessed his plundering of Paititi, something he wanted to keep secret even after successfully completing his 'operation'.

They would have to be silenced.

The little convoy turned off the road to Valverde on to a narrower, even rougher track. A warning sign read *Prohibida La Entrada: Zona Militar*. Callas's domain, a private kingdom. Here, he could do whatever he wanted to his prisoners, and nobody would ever know.

The truck slowed. Nina looked ahead, seeing a chain-link fence topped with coils of razor wire stretching into the vine-draped trees to each side. A soldier opened a gate to let the vehicles through. They rumbled on for a short way before emerging in a large rectangular space bulldozed out of the jungle.

The military base.

The Mi-17 was parked on a concrete helipad, being refuelled. The crate containing the Inca treasure rested beside it. At the facility's heart was a giant rectangular radar antenna, aimed towards the Colombian border. The rest of the base was less imposing: an assortment of prefabricated control and admini-stration huts, and tents for the troops luckless enough to be stationed in the sweltering green hell.

The lead Land Cruiser stopped beside the helipad, Callas getting out to check the crate. The other two vehicles pulled up behind it. Stikes emerged from the second Toyota and strolled to the truck. 'Everyone comfortable in there?' he asked mockingly.

'For God's sake,' said Nina, indicating Becker's injured leg, 'he needs a doctor.'

'At least give him something for the pain,' Kit added.

'He'll get something for the pain soon enough, don't worry.' Stikes looked away at a distant noise. 'Ah! Excellent timing. My new toy has arrived.'

Nina followed his gaze. Off to the southwest was the dot of an approaching helicopter – *two* helicopters, she realised, picking out a smaller one flying alongside.

Callas joined Stikes by the truck. 'I wasn't actually sure this friend of yours could live up to his promises,' Stikes said to him. 'For once, I'm pleased to be wrong.'

The Venezuelan spat. 'Pachac is no friend of mine. Maoist scum! If I could do this without him – or that drug-dealing pig, de Quesada – I would, but I need their money. For now, at least. After we succeed, I think I will change the deal. It is time Venezuela was . . . *cleaned*.'

'Well, if you need my services again, you have my card,' said Stikes. Callas smiled darkly, then watched the helicopters.

Valero frowned as they neared, puzzled. 'What is it?' Nina asked.

'The big helicopter – it is a gunship, Russian. You *yanquis* call them Hinds.' Nina looked more closely as the two choppers prepared to land. The subject of Valero's confusion was, she suspected, every bit as deadly as it was ugly, stubby wings bearing rocket pods and a huge multi-barrelled cannon beneath its nose. 'We have them here in Venezuela – but this one is from Peru.'

'Peru?' Now it was Nina's turn to be bewildered. 'But that's Colombia over there. Peru's four hundred miles away.'

'I know. And this Pachac, I have heard of him. He is a communist revolutionary, but a dangerous one, a killer – even the Shining Path threw him out. He is also a drug lord.'

'Sounds like a nice guy,' said Macy.

'If he has got a gunship, that is bad. If he has brought it to my country to give to mercenaries, that is worse! I do not like this.'

'You're not the only one,' said Nina. The Hind moved over the pad, blowing dust and grit in all directions as it touched down beside the Mil, tripod landing gear compressing under its armoured weight. The smaller helicopter, a civilian Jet Ranger, followed suit.

A man climbed from the Jet Ranger, bending low beneath the still spinning rotors even though his short stature meant he was in no danger of decapitation. Like Stikes, he wore a military beret, this one blood-red. Giving the Hind an almost longing look, he approached Callas and Stikes.

'Ah, Inkarrí!' cried Callas, suddenly exuding warmth and friendliness towards the new arrival, who responded with similar, not entirely sincere, enthusiasm. He was not of Hispanic descent, instead having the broad features of a native Indian. While far from tall, he had a powerful chest and muscular arms, his sun-weathered skin showing that his physique was the result of long outdoor labour rather than a gym. The two men briefly conversed in Spanish, then Callas switched to English. 'Alexander Stikes, meet Arcani Pachac.'

Stikes and Pachac shook hands. 'The mercenary,' said the Peruvian with vague disapproval.

'I simply provide a service,' said Stikes. 'Once the job's done, I leave. Quick, clean and efficient, with no messy differences of ideology to cause problems afterwards.' A hint of a smile. 'So, how are your relations with the Shining Path at the moment?'

Pachac's eyes widened with anger. 'Do not mention those traitors! Counter-revolutionary bastards!'

'Well, should you need help to clean house after overthrowing the bourgeois imperialist puppets in Lima,' said the Englishman, still amused, 'give me a call. In the meantime, I'd like to check the general's new acquisition.' Pachac nodded, and Stikes marched to the Hind. Its pilot – a Caucasian – climbed out and saluted him, then took him on an inspection tour of the gunship.

Pachac's reluctance to give up the helicopter was clear. 'The damage we could do if we could make its weapons work again! I would give you back your money, and more.' Revolutionary fervour faded, replaced by businesslike pragmatism. 'But speaking of money . . .'

Callas signalled to a waiting soldier, who lugged a pair of canvas holdalls, one large, one small, to the two men. 'Here. The rest of your payment. Two million US dollars, in cash.'

The Peruvian opened the large bag, revealing bundles of banknotes. 'I'm sure Chairman Mao would be proud,' Nina muttered.

Pachac heard her, and glared up at the truck's occupants. 'Who are these *yanquis*?'

'Prisoners,' said Callas. 'Don't worry about them, they will not be here for long. And speaking of prisoners, I have a gift for you, Inkarrí. Two gifts, in fact. I think you will like them both.' He gave an order to the soldier, and the man jogged away to a nearby hut. By the time Pachac had satisfied himself that the holdall contained everything due to him, the soldier was returning with a comrade, between them hauling a third man, a bound civilian with a bloodied face.

Even through his swollen, purpled eyes he saw Pachac, and gasped in fright, trying to break free. One of the soldiers punched him. The two men dropped him at their commander's feet.

Pachac clapped in cruel delight. 'Cayo! Ah, Cayo, it has been a while since I last saw you.' His voice became a snarl. 'Since you *betrayed* me. Since you stole half a million dollars of my drugs and gave them to de Quesada, along with your loyalty.' He kicked the helpless man in the chest. 'You shit!'

'He was caught crossing the border with two others,' said Callas. 'And ten kilos of cocaine. He tried to pass himself off as one of your smugglers, but used an old password. So my men arrested him.'

'The others?'

A shrug. 'They had unfortunate accidents. They will never be found.'

'And the cocaine?'

'Confiscated, of course. Venezuela does not tolerate drug smugglers. Ones who don't pay, anyway.'

Pachac looked at the nearby soldiers. 'Are all the men on this base . . . yours?'

Callas nodded. 'They are all loyal to me, yes. You may do what you wish with this man.'

'Very good.' Pachac crouched beside Cayo and produced a folding knife, opening it with a loud metallic *snick*. The man jerked up his head, whimpering in fear. 'Yes, you know that noise, don't you? You have heard it before when I have dealt with traitors.' He was still speaking in English, glancing up at Nina and the others as if revelling in the opportunity to perform for a new audience. Cayo wailed and begged for mercy, but Pachac shoved him down on to his back. 'Now, I will deal with you!'

Even with her hands over her eyes, Loretta still screamed at the sound of Pachac stabbing the knife deep into Cayo's torso just below his sternum. His cries became an almost animalistic screech as the blade sawed down his body. Blood gushed from the lengthening wound.

Pachac worked the knife to the struggling man's waistband, then sharply withdrew it. 'And now,' he said, with almost some twisted form of reverence, '*capacocha*.'

Osterhagen was too revolted to look, but still reacted to the word with shock. 'My God . . .'

'What does it mean?' asked the equally appalled Nina.

'It is the Inca ritual . . . of human sacrifice.'

'Oh, Jesus,' she gasped, sickened.

Pachac locked his blood-slicked hands round Cayo's neck. His victim's eyes bulged horribly as he struggled to breathe, coughing up blood. The Peruvian pushed down, cartilage crackling inside Cayo's throat. His legs thrashed, blood spouting from the gaping wound with each kick . . .

Then his movements became weaker, slower.

And stopped.

Pachac released his hands. There was a gurgling hiss from the dead man's mouth, a last release of trapped air, and he was still. His killer lowered his head, speaking in a language Nina didn't recognise, then retrieved his knife and wiped off the blood on the corpse's clothing.

'So that was *capacocha*?' said Callas, having watched the hideous exhibition with an expression of no more distaste than if he had discovered a fly on his food.

'Only the strangling,' Pachac told him. 'The other part is mine. But when I come to power in Peru as the Inkarrí, it will be how traitors and the bourgeois are executed.'

'He's mad,' the trembling Osterhagen whispered to Nina.

'What does it mean?' she asked. 'What's the Inkarrí?'

'An Inca myth – a prophecy, of a leader who will restore the Inca empire to glory. My God! He really thinks he's the Inkarrí reborn!' The German buried his head in his hands.

Callas gestured to the two soldiers, who picked up Cayo's body and slung it into the back of the truck. Loretta was now too far gone even to scream again, curled up tightly and rocking back and forth as Macy held her. Nina, nauseated, looked away from the still bleeding corpse to see Stikes and the pilot returning from the Hind. 'Well,' the Englishman announced, 'everything seems in order.'

'It is ready?' Callas asked.

'It'll need some minor maintenance before the operation, but nothing Gurov can't handle.' He nodded at the pilot. 'It may have been decommissioned, but everything except the weaponry is still working. And we can have the fire control systems reinstalled in twenty-four hours. All it needs is a lick of paint, some ammunition, the transponder code, and we're good to go.'

'Good. Good!' Callas beamed. 'Arcani, I cannot thank you enough. This helicopter is crucial to Venezuela's future. Your support is beyond price.'

'Unlike the safe passage of my drugs through your country,' Pachac replied sharply.

'For your help, you will get a very big discount on the percentage you pay me! But I told you I have another gift.' He presented the smaller holdall to the Peruvian. 'Here.'

Pachac, not sure what to expect, opened the bag. Inside was a polished wooden box, about eight inches square. He lifted the lid – and gasped.

Nina craned her neck for a better look. She was almost as impressed as Pachac by the box's contents: a smaller version of the golden sun disc, with elaborate tongues of 'fire' spiralling out from its edges.

'An Inca treasure,' said Callas. 'I thought you should have it.'

Pachac's wonder quickly faded, resentment surfacing. 'While you sell the other lost treasures of my people to anyone who has the dollars.'

'They were found in Venezuela,' Callas said patronisingly. 'So they belong to my people, not yours. And you could have bid for any of them – if your followers in the True Red Way did not mind you spending millions of dollars of the cause's money on golden trinkets . . .'

The Peruvian snapped the box shut and turned angrily away, taking in the crate next to the Venezuelan helicopter for the first time. Realisation dawned as its odd dimensions suggested what it might contain. He whirled back to Callas. 'That – that is—'

'The Punchaco, yes,' Callas replied. 'Two tons of Inca gold.'

'You must let me have it. You *must*.' Pachac was almost pleading. 'It is the greatest symbol of the Incas – of my people. We must have it back!'

'The gold alone is worth more than you can afford, Inkarrí.' The general's use of the title now held more than a hint of sarcasm. 'And because it *is* an Inca treasure, it is even more valuable. But I have found a buyer.'

Pachac's face paled. 'No . . .' he whispered, then more forcefully, with rising anger: 'No! Not *him*!'

'Yes, your old friend – your old *partner*, Francisco de Quesada. He can afford it. And anything else he desires. You could have been the same, if you had concentrated on business and not politics . . .'

The Maoist's teeth clenched in rage. 'He only wants it to insult me! And you cannot even get it to him. My contacts told me that your smuggler, West, was arrested. Without him, it will never get through customs – and what else can you do, drive it through the jungle? There are many bandits round here. On both sides of the border.' He gave Callas a pointed look. 'You cannot give it to him.'

Callas laughed. 'I am not *giving* it to him. He has already paid me the first twenty million dollars!'

Pachac looked down sharply at the bundles of banknotes. 'You are paying me with that bastard's money?' A burst of invective, again in the unfamiliar language. 'Give me the Punchaco, or this deal is off!'

'The deal has been agreed, Arcani,' said Callas.

'I am not leaving without the Punchaco.' Pachac's right hand slipped inside his camouflage jacket.

The soldiers snapped up their AK-103s. Callas's face was now stone. 'Remember where you are, Pachac,' he growled. 'You have your money, my thanks, and even my gift. Take them, and have your revolution. But do not challenge me in my own country. It will be painful.'

The shorter man glared at him, breathing heavily. Finally, he zipped up the holdall, then picked it up and, the wooden box under one arm, strutted without a word back to the Jet Ranger.

'Communist scum,' snarled Callas once the Peruvian was aboard.

Stikes appeared entertained by the whole confrontation. 'I did rather enjoy the hypocrisy, though. A man who's such a hard-core Maoist that he thinks the Shining Path are counter-revolutionary, making millions by selling drugs. Holding two completely conflicting viewpoints at the same time? No wonder he's insane.'

'He did have a point, though,' Callas admitted. 'Without West, getting the Punchaco to de Quesada will be very difficult. And I need the rest of his payment – even after the operation succeeds, there will be chaos. The only way to calm it will be with money to the right people. Lots of money.'

An odd smile crept on to Stikes's face, and he gave Nina a calculating look. 'I think I may have a way.'

Callas regarded him questioningly, but before he could speak the Jet Ranger took off, sweeping more dust across the helipad. Stikes brushed grit from his sleeves and addressed the Russian pilot. 'Gurov, take the Hind to the staging area and restore the weapons. General,' he said to Callas as Gurov returned to the gunship, 'we should get back to the Clubhouse – there are still tactical issues to discuss.'

Callas nodded, then looked at the prisoners in the truck. 'First we deal with them. Dr Wilde is the only one we need alive. The others—'

'Jindal too,' Stikes interrupted.

'What?' Callas asked, confused, as Nina and Kit exchanged shocked looks. 'The Interpol agent? Why him?'

'I have my reasons.' He let the words hang in the air as he regarded Kit thoughtfully.

'Get them down,' Callas ordered. The soldiers in the truck forced Nina and Kit to their feet.

'Let them go,' Nina demanded. 'If you kill them, you might as well kill me too, because I'll never tell you what you want to know.'

The Venezuelan smiled, a chilling crocodile grin. 'That sounds like a challenge, Dr Wilde. And as I told Pachac, challenging me results in pain. Great pain.'

He shouted more commands in Spanish: for a forklift to load the crate containing the Punchaco aboard the Mil; two men to take a Jeep to Valverde and clear out any personal effects from the expedition's hotel rooms; the prisoners to be driven to 'the hole'. Whatever it was, it was clear that the trip would be one way. Callas began to walk away—

'*Bastardo!*' yelled Valero. He dived for one of the soldiers' weapons, only to be clubbed down and kicked repeatedly in the head and chest. Macy jumped up, shouting for them to stop, but was shoved to the bloodstained floor.

'Let them go,' Nina repeated. This time, it was not a demand but a plea for mercy.

None was forthcoming. Callas waved a hand, and the truck drove away, the prisoners at gunpoint in its back.

15

Panting, muscles stiff and burning, Eddie watched from a
high branch of a creeper-choked tree as the truck set off.
His run through the jungle, stopping every ten minutes to
check his bearing against the sun, had taken just over two hours.
Tough going, but the thought of what would happen to Nina
and the others if he didn't make it had driven him on.

But he was too late.

Even from outside the perimeter fence he had picked out
Nina's red hair immediately in the hot afternoon sun. She and
Kit were being taken to the Mi-17. A forklift hoisted the crate
containing the sun disc into its cabin, and it looked as though
Stikes, recognisable by his beret, and Callas were waiting to
board the helicopter as well.

But his concern was now for those left behind. The armed
guards in the truck told him that at least some of the prisoners
were still alive . . . but they wouldn't be for long. Civilians held
on a military base might arouse questions. Corpses buried in
the jungle would not.

But how could he help them? The truck was too far away
for him to catch up. And he couldn't help Nina and Kit either;
too many armed men around the helipad for him to stand a
chance of even getting close.

The helipad . . .

Part of his mind had already subconsciously registered

something wrong, and as the other chopper's rotors began to turn he realised what. A Hind? That wasn't unusual in itself, as the Russian flying tank had been sold all over the world . . . but this one bore the red-and-white roundel of Peru, not the Venezuelan tricolour. What was it doing here?

He dismissed the question when he saw something more important. On the far side of the base was a small motor pool. A soldier climbed into a Jeep.

His chance—

Eddie leapt down, breaking into a run parallel to the boundary fence. He couldn't catch the truck – but if he was fast enough, he might be able to intercept the Jeep.

The Hind roared into the air and turned northwards. The Mil had been loaded, the forklift backing away to let its passengers, willing and otherwise, board. A flash of red: Nina being pushed inside.

He forced down a surge of anger and kept running. The soldier in the Jeep waved impatiently to another man. The deforested area was only about two hundred metres across – once the 4×4 set off, it wouldn't take long to reach the gate.

A corner of the fence ahead. He swung round it, angling away from the base. Another glance—

The Jeep was on the move.

Shit! Could he catch it? It disappeared from view, blocked by trees, then reappeared. Closer than he had expected. The driver was in a hurry.

So was Eddie. He forced himself on, aware that one stumble on the uneven ground could cost the prisoners their lives. Dangling vines swatted at his face. His heart pounded, leg muscles on fire, but he couldn't stop.

A scrape and clatter of metal – the gate being opened. He heard the clash of gears as the driver set off.

A shallow slope ahead. The muddy road at the bottom came into view through the undergrowth – as did the Jeep. Moving quickly.

Too quickly. Eddie knew he couldn't reach it before it passed.

His chance was gone—

No!

He turned again, aiming ahead of the Jeep, and leapt up, grabbing a clutch of creepers hanging from a high tree. He swung down the slope, reaching the bottom of his arc, rising higher . . .

And letting go.

He fell, landing with a bone-jarring crash in the Jeep's open back as it passed. The two soldiers had put their AK-103s on the rear seat, and it now felt as though they were embedded in his spine.

The pain of his touchdown was nothing compared to the soldiers' shock, however. The driver jumped halfway out of his seat in fright. The 4×4 swerved almost into a ditch before he regained control.

Eddie pulled himself upright. One of the AKs clattered into the footwell. But they were too close to the base for him to use the weapon – the shots would draw attention. Instead, he smashed an elbow into the driver's face as he looked round. The Venezuelan's head snapped back, blood spraying from his burst lip.

The other man twisted in his seat, grabbing for the rifle. Eddie chopped at his throat. He jerked away, the blow catching his jaw.

A retaliatory strike lashed at Eddie's eyes. He threw himself back – and banged his head on the hard-edged bodywork.

The passenger took advantage of his brief dizziness, pulling the AK from the footwell by its barrel. He spun it round, about to empty the magazine into the intruder's chest at point-blank range—

Eddie reached between the front seats and yanked the handbrake.

The 4×4 skidded. The sudden deceleration caused the passenger to be thrown forward, and his head thunked forcefully against the windscreen's frame.

Eddie used the same inertia to fling himself upright. The dazed soldier was halfway out of his seat, and Eddie shoved him with both hands to make the exit complete. With a cry, the passenger tumbled out of the Jeep's open side, and hit a tree at the roadside head first, breaking his neck. The AK bounced into the undergrowth.

One down – but the driver had recovered. He released the handbrake and stamped down hard on the accelerator.

The Jeep fishtailed, kicking up a muddy spray. The sudden swerve hurled Eddie sideways. He clutched desperately for a handhold to avoid following the dead soldier out of the vehicle, but only caught the edge of the rear seat. He hung over the Jeep's side, mud splattering into his face.

The driver jerked the steering wheel. The Jeep swayed, tipping Eddie even further out. The track blurred past beneath him. He tried to hook a foot under the front seats, but couldn't get a firm hold.

Green in his peripheral vision—

He closed his eyes as a plant at the roadside smacked into his cheek, at this speed even mere leaves enough to draw blood. Stinging, he looked ahead again – to see a tree coming up fast.

The driver saw it too. He swerved to scrape off his uninvited passenger against its thick trunk.

Eddie kicked, searching for a foothold. His boot thumped against the hard seatback. He strained to pull himself back into the Jeep, but couldn't get enough leverage.

The tree rushed closer, filling his vision—

His groping foot finally caught the seat's underside, and he yanked himself back inside as the tree whipped past, the leafy creepers dangling from it swatting his head.

Other parasitic growths concealed a danger of their own, though – a branch protruding into the road—

The driver screamed and braked hard – but too late.

The branch hit the Jeep's windscreen. The glass shattered, pieces showering into the driver's face. Chunks of broken wood bombarded both men. The remaining AK fell off the rear seat, ending up beneath the driver.

Eddie recovered first. He grabbed a piece of smashed tree and swung it at the soldier's head, scoring a satisfyingly solid hit.

But the driver wasn't out of the fight, swerving the 4×4 sharply across the track. As Eddie swayed, the Kalashnikov rattled into the front footwell – giving the driver the chance to snatch it up.

With an angry leer of victory, the Venezuelan swung round to shoot his attacker—

Eddie was gone.

The soldier was bewildered by his apparent disappearance – until he realised the Englishman had flattened himself across the rear seat.

He whirled back—

The Jeep had angled off the track – directly under a low, thick branch. There was a crunching thud. Slowed by dense bushes, the 4×4 bounced to a stop amidst the undergrowth. The engine rattled and stalled.

Eddie cautiously looked up. The driver was still in his seat . . . up to his neck. His head was a hundred feet further back, a pulped mess beneath the bough that had chopped it from his body.

'Nice bit of tree surgery,' Eddie said, clambering into the front and kicking the decapitated corpse from the Jeep. He recovered the AK-103, then restarted the engine and backed the 4×4 on to the road.

Now, he had to find the truck.

Before it was too late.

The new track was even more narrow and overgrown than the one that had led to Paititi, trees clawing at the military truck. Macy ducked a clawing branch, then peered fearfully at her surroundings. The vehicle had turned off the base's access road on to the almost hidden path only a few minutes earlier, but even over that short distance the jungle had transformed into a dark, malevolent thicket. The trees were gnarled, as if twisted by the wounds of physically battling each other for the few scraps of daylight. Even the sun seemed to have abandoned this place . . . or turned away in horror.

Because there was something hanging in the air, permeating everything with foulness. A stench, beyond the inescapable jungle odour of decaying vegetation.

Osterhagen had caught it too. 'I did my civilian service in the *Katastrophenschutz* – disaster relief,' he whispered to Macy, his face grim. 'I know that smell.'

The scent of death.

They were at their journey's end.

Macy searched the soldiers' faces for any hint of mercy. She found none. The four Venezuelans holding them at gunpoint were all cold, dispassionate. They had done this before.

One last lurch over some roots, and the truck clattered to a stop. The jungle canopy was so thick it seemed like twilight beneath, all colour sapped away. A soldier unlocked the tailgate and let it fall open with a gunshot bang. '*Muévete!*' he said, pointing out of the truck with his AK.

Soto began to shudder. 'Oh, please no, please, don't do this, please . . .' One of the soldiers roughly dragged her to her feet. She wailed, a keening mewl of helpless despair as he shoved her from the truck.

Valero snarled, about to leap up at him, but received a brutal kick to the head for his trouble. Another soldier threw him out on to the ground.

The two remaining men gestured with their guns. Macy and Osterhagen picked up the semi-conscious Becker and carried him from the vehicle. One of the soldiers plucked the injured man's hat from his head and put it on, earning sarcastic laughs from his fellows.

The driver was waiting, Kalashnikov in hand. He signalled for the prisoners to advance. The guards pushed them forward. Macy could hardly breathe, the stench of rot clogging her nostrils and fear tightening her chest. She rounded the truck to see . . . *the hole.*

It was aptly, bluntly named: just a ragged opening in the earth, steep sides littered with decomposing leaves. But as Macy got closer, she saw that it was not empty.

Bodies were piled inside it, a dozen, more. Most were rotted beyond recognition, insects and animals having feasted on the rich flesh and organs. Only the pair on top of the heap remained recognisably human, just a day or two dead, but even these had already lost their eyes and chunks of skin to the relentless scavengers. Insects swarmed from the blackened bullet wounds in their chests. Cayo's partners, the drug smugglers.

Cayo himself soon joined them. As the other soldiers held the prisoners at gunpoint, two men pulled his corpse from the truck, carted it between them like a sack to the pit, and tossed it in. Flies exploded from the bodies as it thumped down on top of them.

The soldiers repeated the process with Cuff. Macy looked away in horrified disgust. Loretta's pitiful cries became even louder at the sight of the dead American splayed on the pile, his remaining eye staring dully back at her.

'Mother of God,' grumbled one of the soldiers in Spanish, 'that's a noise I could live without.'

'We'll do her first,' said another man, before switching to English. 'Okay, down! On your knees!'

They forced the explorers to kneel at the pit's edge. Valero muttered a desperate prayer. Macy realised she was crying, tears stinging as she started to hyperventilate. Loretta gave her a pleading look as the soldier stood behind her.

Macy wanted to keep her eyes fixed on the helpless, innocent woman, but her fear forced them shut. A last whimper escaped Loretta's mouth—

A gunshot, shockingly loud.

There was a soft thump as her body slumped forward. The dull impact of a boot against flesh, and with a slithering thud Loretta's corpse dropped into the hole.

The soldier moved behind Macy.

She desperately tried to open her eyes again, to take one last look at the world, but they were locked shut by terror.

A rustle of cloth as the soldier raised his gun . . .

And another sound, rising fast—

An engine!

She heard the man behind her turn in surprise. 'Who's that?' Macy opened her eyes and looked back.

A military Jeep charged past the truck. Its driver held the steering wheel with one hand, an AK in the other—

Eddie!

'Duck!' he yelled, yanking at the wheel—

The 4×4 skidded in the mud as Eddie pointed the Kalashnikov out of its side and pulled the trigger. He didn't need to aim – the Jeep's spinning turn swept the bullets in a swathe above the kneeling prisoners' heads.

Three soldiers took hits to their chests and faces, dropping dead to the ground. The man behind Macy was caught in the left shoulder, the impact sending him reeling to the edge of the pit. With his good arm, he pointed his AK-103 at the Jeep . . .

Macy sprang up and barged him over the edge. He landed on the heaped corpses, rolling down them into the rotting sludge at the bottom of the hole.

One soldier was left standing, though. Eddie's wild fire had missed him. He raised his gun—

The skidding Jeep had made a half-turn, and was now pointing backwards. Eddie jammed it into reverse and leaned low across the front seats, stamping hard on the accelerator. Bullets clanged through the bodywork and cracked against the seat backs. He yelled, but held his course.

The Jeep hit the soldier with a bang, scooping him up over its back end. Eddie raised his head, seeing the man bent over the rear seat – still very much alive. In reverse the 4×4 was only doing twenty miles per hour.

The Venezuelan's eyes met Eddie's, widening with anger. He swung the AK round—

Eddie twitched the wheel, and dropped again.

The Jeep smashed tail first into a tree, throwing Eddie against the bullet-pocked seats – and mashing the soldier into the wood.

Eddie pushed himself upright. The Venezuelan was pinned against the trunk, mouth open in a silent scream of agony. His gun had been thrown into the undergrowth.

'Eddie!' Macy cried. Not in thanks, but in warning. The soldier in the pit was still alive, still armed, climbing up over the corpses.

Eddie restarted the engine and put the battered Jeep into first gear, tearing free of the tree. One of the soldier's legs came with it, snared on twisted metal. 'Out of the way!' he shouted. Valero and Osterhagen dragged Becker away, Macy leaping aside as the Jeep surged forward—

Eddie dived out of the 4×4. It sailed over the edge of the pit – just as the soldier reached the top of the piled bodies and aimed his weapon. The Jeep hit like a giant hammer, pounding him back to the bottom of the hole and crushing him into the ooze of his victims.

Macy ran to Eddie and helped him up. 'Oh my God! Eddie! Are you okay?'

'Fucking top,' he groaned, seeing the three men nearby. 'Where's Loretta?'

Macy's tears returned. 'They – they killed her. Right before you got here.'

'Oh, shit,' he breathed, sagging. If he had arrived just a few seconds sooner . . . 'I'm sorry. I'm sorry,' he repeated, more loudly, to Osterhagen.

The German's lips were tight as he struggled to hold his emotions in check. 'You did all you could. Thank you.'

'How did you find us?' Macy asked. 'How did you even get here?'

'I ran,' Eddie told her, standing. 'Got to the base just as they were driving you away.'

'You *ran*? Jesus. You're . . . you're amazing. Thank you.' She embraced him, her tears now of gratitude. 'Thank you.'

Valero, still supporting Becker, limped over. 'We have to warn the militia about Callas.'

'Yeah, we do,' said Eddie, 'but then we've got to find Nina and Kit. I saw Stikes and Callas put them in a chopper. Where are they taking them?'

'Stikes said something about a clubhouse,' Macy remembered.

'A clubhouse?' Eddie echoed. 'What, like a golf club?'

Unexpectedly, Valero laughed, a bitter little bark. 'Not a golf club – but near one. *The* Clubhouse. It is the joke name of a house in Caracas,' he explained to his bewildered audience. 'It overlooks a golf course in one of the richest parts of the city. The government confiscated it from a businessman who did not pay his taxes. It was supposed to be given to the people, but the military took it over – temporarily, so they said. But they are still there.'

'Callas is using it?' Macy asked. Valero nodded.

'Then that's where they've taken Nina and Kit,' said Eddie. He frowned, thinking. 'Is that Peruvian Hind – the gunship – part of what Callas is doing?'

'A drug lord called Pachac got it for him,' said Valero. 'We heard them talking about it. I don't know what Callas is planning, but it is why he has been selling the treasures from Paititi – he needs millions of dollars, tens of millions, to pay for it.'

'He's an army general doing something he doesn't want the President to know about, he's got a helicopter gunship, and he's hired Stikes for some "conflict resolution". There's only one thing this can be about.' Eddie looked grim. 'Callas is planning a coup.' He indicated the truck. 'Sooner we get moving, the more chance we have of stopping it.'

'What . . . what about Loretta?' asked Osterhagen, glancing hesitantly towards the pit. 'I don't want to leave her there.'

'We'll have to,' said Eddie. 'Sorry, but we don't have time to bury her properly. Once we contact the militia we can tell them how to find this place, but right now we've got to get out of here. We're not far from the base, so it won't be long before this lot are missed.'

'I understand,' Osterhagen said with an unhappy nod. 'Oscar, help me with Ralf.'

'Macy, see if there's a first aid kit in the truck,' Eddie said as they took Becker to the tailgate. He collected the dead soldiers' rifles, then searched the bodies, gathering a handful of Venezuelan currency.

Even after the horrors he had witnessed, Osterhagen was still shocked. 'What are you doing?'

'Being practical,' said Eddie. 'We've got no money, and we might need some to make a call. Besides, these bastards don't need it. Okay, let's go.'

He retrieved Becker's fedora and handed it to Osterhagen, then climbed into the driving seat, Macy beside him. The vehicle turned, then rattled away down the path, leaving the dead in silence.

16

Valverde was just beyond a small rise. Eddie stopped the truck and opened the cab's rear window to speak to the men in the back. 'Okay, the soldiers in town'll be looking for us – or at least me. So what do we do?'

'Can we get to the phone in the hotel?' Osterhagen asked.

'That'll be the top thing on their watch list,' said Macy. 'Is there anywhere else we can go?'

'San Fernando de Atabapo is the next town,' Valero told her, 'but to reach it by road we have to drive through Valverde.'

'How about flying there?' Eddie suggested.

'We can – but if we are flying,' said Valero, an idea striking him, 'we should get as far from Callas's men as we can. My plane is fully fuelled. It can reach Caracas.'

'Can we use its radio to contact the militia?'

'Yes – yes, we can! I can put an emergency call through to air traffic control.'

'Okay, so we go for the airfield,' Eddie decided.

Macy made a pensive face. 'Hate to be Debbie Downer, but we kinda have to drive through town to get to the airfield.'

It was true. 'Bollocks! Okay, how about walking? We skirt round town and get to the plane from the jungle.'

'What about Ralf?' said Osterhagen. Becker, lying between the German and Valero in the rear bed, had fallen into a state of drifting semi-consciousness. 'He will slow us down –

and we can't leave him behind. If the soldiers find him, they'll kill him.'

Osterhagen was right; they couldn't abandon the injured man. 'That doesn't leave us much choice, then. We'll just have to charge through and hope we're in the air before they catch up.' He addressed the two men. 'Can either of you drive a truck?'

'I can,' said Valero.

'Good. Get in here, then.'

Macy was mildly offended. 'How do you know *I* can't drive the truck?' she demanded.

'Can you double-declutch?' asked Eddie.

'Can I what?'

'You *can't* drive the truck. Stay in the cab and keep your head down.' He picked up one of the AK-103s and hopped out. Valero clambered inside and took his place. Eddie climbed into the cargo bed and crouched at the rear window. 'Okay, Oscar, soon as any soldiers see us we're in trouble, so gun it through the town.'

'What are you going to do?' Macy asked.

He waved the Kalashnikov. 'Have a guess. Everyone set?'

'No,' she said in a small voice.

He smiled at her, then banged the cab roof. 'Oscar, let's go.'

Valero put the truck in gear and set off. The Russian-built vehicle was designed for carrying heavy loads over poor terrain, not speed; it took more than half a minute for it to reach thirty miles an hour. Eddie looked ahead. They were at the top of the rise, Valverde coming into view.

The town's military presence had increased. A pair of Jeeps was parked at the settlement's edge – not a roadblock, but certainly a checkpoint.

And they would have to go through it.

'Two Jeeps,' Eddie warned Valero. 'Aim for the one on the left – don't ram it, it'll slow us down too much. Just try to smash the front.'

'What about the other one?' Macy asked.

Another shake of the gun. 'Again, guess!'

He checked the road ahead. The soldiers at the checkpoint had seen the approaching truck, but weren't yet concerned.

That would change when they realised it wasn't going to stop.

'Grab on to something,' Eddie warned Osterhagen, before bracing himself for the impending collision.

The truck bore down on the soldiers. One man stood in the road waving his hands over his head – then dived out of its way. Another unshouldered his rifle.

Eddie readied his own weapon as Valero swerved—

There was a colossal crunch as the truck's girder-like front bumper smashed into the Jeep, sending it spinning into a ditch. The second soldier brought up his AK—

Eddie fired first, aiming not at the soldier, but at his vehicle. A burst of fire hit the Jeep, ripping into the radiator and engine.

The panicked Venezuelan had dived when the gunfire started, but now he was back on his feet. 'Get down!' Eddie shouted, ducking. Osterhagen dropped flat, holding Becker. Bullets cracked against the tailgate, and the rear window shattered. Macy shrieked, Valero sliding as low in his seat as he dared.

Eddie held the AK over his head and sent a couple of shots blindly back down the road, forcing the gunman to take shelter. The firing stopped. The truck roared past the hotel, townspeople running for cover.

Eddie rose again, rapidly turning to search for danger. Most of the soldiers on the streets were more interested in their own safety than in opening fire, and were sprinting out of the truck's path. Another couple of shots deterred the others from retaliating.

A bend in the street put the troops out of sight behind a building. Eddie looked ahead. They were almost through the little settlement already; a few hundred metres away was the turning to the airfield. 'Okay, Oscar,' he shouted, 'slow down for the turn. Crash the gate and head straight for your plane – I'll sort out anyone following us.'

Valero complied. The track's condition was even worse than the main road's, and everyone was thrown from side to side. Becker cried out in pain.

The airfield came into sight. Across the track was a wooden barrier, but it snapped like a toothpick as the truck thundered through. An angry civilian ran from the terminal hut after the intruders, but the sight of Eddie's AK made him do an about-face and flee for the ruined gate instead.

Valero skidded to a stop alongside his plane. 'Macy, grab the other gun, then help the doc with Ralf,' Eddie ordered as he jumped down. On foot, at a run, it would only take the soldiers a couple of minutes to catch up, and if they had another Jeep it would be even sooner. He took up position behind the truck to watch the airfield entrance. Macy and Osterhagen carried Becker to the plane. Valero, rather than climbing into the cockpit and starting the engine, was examining something on the wing. 'Oscar, what're you doing? Get it going!'

'I have to do the pre-flight checks,' Valero shouted back.

'There's no time!'

'But if something goes wrong—'

'Don't worry about gremlins, worry about bullets! They'll be here any minute!'

Clearly unhappy, Valero nevertheless abandoned his inspection and climbed into the Cessna's cabin. Osterhagen and Macy lifted Becker through the large main hatch on the port side.

Eddie looked back at the gate. The airfield worker was gone, but the track wouldn't be empty for long. Seconds passed. The plane remained silent. 'Oscar, start the bloody thing!'

'It's not a car!' Valero protested. 'I have to check the circuit breakers and set the engine mixture.'

'Then check 'em and set 'em faster!'

Movement at the gate—

Two soldiers ran towards the terminal hut. Eddie fired two shots; neither hit, but they forced the men to dive for cover. Still no sound from the Cessna's engine. 'Get the fucking thing going, Oscar!'

A third soldier appeared, keeping low. A round clanked off the truck's flank as he took a shot. Eddie returned fire. This time, the bullets were on target, the soldier flailing backwards.

But now another three men had arrived, opening up with their AK-103s. More shots hit the truck like hot hail. Eddie ducked behind the rear wheels, crouching to peer under the cargo bed. The first two soldiers were moving again. If they advanced much further, they would have a clean shot at the plane as it taxied to takeoff position.

Grey and red metal barrels, stacked in a little fenced compound near the hut—

Eddie emptied the AK's magazine into the fuel drums.

A barrel exploded with a *crump* and a great splash of liquid fire, others following in a chain reaction. Burning drums shot skywards on trails of flame, falling back to earth like bombs. A tumbling keg crashed through the roof of the terminal hut, and the entire building exploded in a storm of flying corrugated panels.

The destruction had the desired effect. The soldiers retreated as fast as they could from the spreading flames.

Another loud noise, this time behind him – the Cessna's engine turning over. A choppy, reluctant coughing . . . then the propeller burst into motion. Eddie dropped the empty AK and leapt through the cabin door. 'Oscar, go, go, *go!*'

Valero opened the throttle. The Cessna hauled itself complainingly out of the indentations its weight had left in the earth and jolted over the uneven ground towards the runway.

Eddie faced the door. 'Macy, gun!' She passed him the second AK. He grabbed a dangling strap above the opening with his left hand, then leaned out and pointed the weapon back towards the gate. The soldiers were still scattering as the fires spread, oily smoke boiling into the sky.

Backwash from the propeller whipped past him as Valero increased power, swinging the plane into line with the runway. Eddie braced himself. The last takeoff had been a bumpy ride, and this was likely to be a lot worse . . .

'Shit!' A Jeep raced through the gate, two soldiers inside. The passenger stood in his seat, supporting his AK-103 on the windscreen. 'Take off, *now!*'

Valero brought the throttle to full power. The plane picked up speed, landing gear crashed over bumps.

The Jeep speeded up too – closing in.

Eddie and the soldier fired almost simultaneously. Their aim was thrown off by the rough ride, but the Venezuelan had a larger target. Bullets pocked the wing as Eddie fired again. The Jeep's windscreen crazed, but neither soldier was hit. Another burst from the 4×4, followed by a *crack-crack-crack* of lead punching through aluminium. Valero yelped as the instrument panel was hit.

Eddie pulled the trigger once more. The Jeep's windscreen

shattered. The shooter dropped back into his seat, hanging on tightly as the driver swerved sharply to take the vehicle behind the Cessna's tail.

Out of Eddie's firing line.

'Dammit!' He turned. The Jeep came into view through the rearmost starboard window, but trying to shoot out the toughened acrylic might result in a lethal ricochet. Instead, he gripped the strap more tightly and leaned from the open hatch, swinging round to bring his gun arm over the top of the fuselage.

'Eddie, Jesus Christ!' Macy shrieked. 'Get back inside!'

But he could no longer hear her, the propeller's piercing rasp joined by the rising roar of wind. He fired another burst at the Jeep. The rifle bucked in his hand, banging against the metal roof.

The soldier shot back. Bullets pierced the fuselage.

One of the Cessna's wheels ran through a deep dip. The whole aircraft jolted violently – and Eddie's right foot slipped.

Unbalanced, he swung further out of the plane. The strap creaked, biting into the flesh of his wrist. His other foot was hooked round the hatch's frame, metal digging painfully though the leather of his boot.

His right arm started to slip back down the fuselage's curved roof . . .

The Cessna's nose tipped upwards. The Jeep was falling behind, but still firing. More bullets riddled the plane.

Eddie kept sliding—

With a last straining swing of his arm, he jammed the AK over the base of the tailfin – and swivelled the weapon to fire at the Jeep.

The remaining bullets spewed out, most of them harmlessly hitting soil and grass – but one caught the speeding Jeep's front tyre, which deflated abruptly, the wheel rim shredding it. The Jeep flipped over and tossed both soldiers high into the air.

The Cessna's wings flexed as they took the plane's weight—

The ground made one final attempt to claw the plane back down to earth, a wheel striking a muddy hump. The Caravan lurched – and Eddie's boot lost its grip on the doorframe.

The seventy-five mile an hour wind snatched him out of the hatch. He lost his hold on the AK-103, the weapon spinning away as the Cessna took to the sky. He slapped his hand against the roof, but there was almost no grip to be found on the smooth metal. The strap around his wrist creaked and strained, the fastener attaching it to the hull buckling under his weight.

'Eddie!' Macy cried. She yanked at her seatbelt release.

The plane kept climbing: one hundred feet, one-fifty. Valero struggled to keep the controls steady. 'Close the hatch!' he yelled.

'Eddie's out there!' Macy screamed back. She staggered to her feet, clinging to the seats as she made her way down the steeply sloping aisle.

'No, you'll be killed!' Osterhagen shouted, but she kept moving. With a curse, he unlocked his own seatbelt.

Outside, Eddie felt what little hold he had on the fuselage slipping away as the plane picked up speed. He was flapping like a flag, legs trailing helplessly.

And the strap was giving way. He could feel the fastener breaking . . .

A hand grabbed his wrist. He squinted into the wind. Slim fingers, neat nails. Macy. She poked her head through the hatch, black hair whipping round her face. 'Get back in!' he yelled.

'No, hang on!' she shouted, tugging at his arm. Eddie shook his head, desperately willing her back inside. He didn't want to die – but he wanted to drag her with him even less. Macy just didn't have the sheer physical strength needed to pull him through the hatch against the wind – and his fingertips were slipping off the hull . . .

Another hand seized his arm. Osterhagen. The German leaned out of the hatch behind Macy, gripping the upper frame with his free hand. 'Oscar!' he bellowed. *'Now!'*

Valero jammed the control stick hard to the right, putting the plane into a steep roll – and simultaneously pitching it downwards.

Eddie lost his grip, swinging away from the hull. Macy and Osterhagen both hauled on his arm with all their strength—

And Eddie dropped head first into the cabin as gravity overpowered wind resistance, bowling them with him against the cabin's starboard wall as the plane banked practically on its side.

'Hang on!' Valero howled. They were far from out of danger. The plane was still at a low altitude – and getting lower by the moment. He shoved the stick back over to level out, throwing his passengers to the floor. The Orinoco wheeled ahead. The Cessna was only two hundred and fifty feet above it.

And still in a dive.

'Oh, *mierda*!' he wailed, yanking back the stick.

Eddie looked up, seeing nothing but water through the cockpit windows. Two hundred feet, the Caravan pulling up, but slowly, too slowly. Greenery on the far bank replaced the river as the plane's nose rose, but they were still too low—

Whumph!

A slam of impact – and a huge spray of water came in through the open hatch.

But the plane was still in the air, even if only by inches. The landing gear had skimmed the great river, Valero levelling out just in time. The Venezuelan whooped in relief, then worked the controls to gain height again. The Caravan climbed, trailing sparkling raindrops from its wheels.

'Everyone okay?' Eddie gasped.

Osterhagen crawled back into a seat. 'I feel . . . airsick.'

'Oh, my God!' Macy squealed. 'I'm alive. You're alive. *We're* alive!' She kissed the Englishman. 'I can't believe it, we're all still alive!' She kissed him again.

'Steady on, love, I'm married,' said Eddie. 'Oscar, how's the plane? Can we make it to Caracas?'

'It will fly okay, but some of the instruments are broken.' Valero gave him an almost apologetic look, indicating the bullet damage. 'And so is the radio.'

'What?' Eddie sat up. 'You're fucking kidding me! How are we going to call the militia?'

'More to the point,' added Macy, 'how are we going to land if we can't talk to air traffic control?'

'I can fly a distress pattern to tell the airport we have no radio,' Valero assured her. 'They will give us priority.'

'How long will it take us to get there?'

'About two and a half hours. Although it will be hard to know exactly.' The Venezuelan shot an irate look at Eddie. 'I can't get a proper airspeed reading because you wouldn't let me take the cover off the pitot tube.'

Eddie laughed a little. 'So long as we get there, that's the main thing.' He stood. 'First, can someone shut that hatch? It's a bit draughty in here.'

17

The building nicknamed the Clubhouse was a mansion in the Caracan hilltop district of Valle Arriba, overlooking the perfectly kept greenery of a private golf course, and beyond it the great sprawl of the city itself. Even with the Venezuelan government's increasingly militant push towards the redistribution of wealth, the enclave was reserved for money and privilege. No *barrios* here; even the smallest house was worth several million US dollars.

Nina very much doubted that she or Kit would enjoy the luxury, though.

Callas's helicopter had flown north to the airbase at Puerto Ayacucho, where the group transferred to a military transport plane to travel on to Caracas. A convoy, two SUVs escorted by police outriders, completed the journey to the Clubhouse. Callas and Stikes were in the lead vehicle, Kit and Nina under heavy guard in the second. Nina looked out through the darkened glass as the vehicles turned on to the driveway. Two soldiers stood guard at the main gate, and she saw several others inside the grounds. Off to one side of the mansion she glimpsed a swimming pool and a private helipad. Not exactly a typical military facility.

The SUVs stopped at the front door. Nina and Kit were hustled out and taken down to the building's cellars. One underground room had been converted into a makeshift prison, metal bars dividing it into three small cells. Nina was pushed into one, Kit another, an empty chamber separating them. A soldier locked the cell doors, then took up position on a chair to watch his prisoners.

After half an hour, footsteps echoed down the passage outside. The jailer looked round as the door opened, standing and saluting when Callas entered, accompanied by two more soldiers. Stikes followed them in, carrying the case containing the statuettes. 'Dr Wilde,' said Callas. 'Mr Jindal. I hope you are both comfortable?'

'I'm guessing this is as comfortable as we're going to get,' Nina replied.

'That is up to you. And also to Mr Stikes. If you tell him what we want to know, your discomfort may be kept to a low level.'

'And if I don't?'

'You can work it out,' said Stikes. 'You're an intelligent woman. Although your marrying Chase does make me question that. And speaking of questioning . . .' He opened the case to reveal the three figurines within, two whole and one bisected, and the bag containing the khipu. 'El Dorado. You're going to lead us there.'

'I don't know how.'

'Yes you do. You found . . . what did Chase call it? Paititi.'

'That was the result of years of archaeological research by Dr Osterhagen and an aerial survey,' she lied.

'Then why did you bring these?' He tapped the two complete statuettes. 'How did you know the third one would be there?'

'Because . . .' Her hesitation, her inability to fabricate a convincing excuse in the split second available, told Stikes all too clearly that she was concealing something.

The mercenary gave her an unpleasant smile, then addressed Callas. 'Is the room ready?'

Callas nodded. 'My men will show you.'

'And the item I asked for?'

'Waiting for you. It was not easy to find at short notice, but my people have their resources.'

'Good.' Stikes nodded to the jailer. 'Bring her out.'

'What are you going to do with her?' Kit demanded, rattling his cell's bars.

'The same thing I'm going to do to you later,' Stikes replied, chillingly matter-of-fact.

'Then take me first. I'm an Interpol officer, and Dr Wilde is my responsibility.'

A sound of sarcastic amusement from the general. 'He is quite a hero.'

'Is he, though?' Stikes eyed Kit curiously. 'But that's what I intend to find out. In the meantime . . .' He stepped back as the jailer unlocked Nina's cell and the soldiers moved to bring her out. 'A little chat with Dr Wilde.'

'Get your goddamn hands off me,' Nina snarled, jerking out of one soldier's grip. The other man backed her into a corner, and they both grabbed her. She kicked at them. 'Fuck you!'

'Rather unladylike language,' said Stikes. 'Chase really is a bad influence.' He closed the case. 'General, if you'll excuse me?'

Callas smirked. 'Enjoy yourself.'

'Oh, I will.' He signalled for the soldiers to take Nina, and followed them from the cells.

'Nina!' shouted Kit, but he was cut off as the heavy door slammed shut.

Nina was dragged down a white-painted passage to another small room. It had apparently once been used for storage, but the shelves were now empty – except for two small boxes and a single glove of thick black leather. One box was tightly secured by an elastic band, several little holes poked in its side. A rust-scabbed metal chair sat beneath the glaring overhead light.

Lengths of rope were coiled on its seat.

Nina fought to break loose, but the soldiers forced her on to the chair and held her as Stikes tied her wrists securely to its armrests, then her ankles to the front legs. He finished by looping the last length of rope tightly round her chest. 'Are you sitting comfortably?' he asked.

'Go fuck yourself!'

Stikes was unfazed. 'Then we'll begin.' He told the soldiers to leave, then closed the door and opened the case again, revealing its ancient contents. 'El Dorado,' he said. 'I always thought it was just a myth.'

'It *is* a myth.'

'The paintings in that temple suggest otherwise. This Paititi may have been the last outpost of the Incas, but there was a much greater settlement along the way. El Dorado.' He went to the shelves and picked up the ominous glove. The leather creaked softly.

'Whatever it's called, it's not El Dorado,' Nina insisted, trying to draw out the purely verbal part of his interrogation for as long as possible. The punctures in the box could only be air holes; there was something alive inside it . . . and the protective glove suggested it was deeply unpleasant. 'That's a completely different legend. The Conquistadors got it mixed up with the story of the Incas hiding their . . . gold . . .' She tailed off as Stikes pulled on the glove, clenching his fingers into a fist.

'Semantics,' he said. 'The name may be wrong, but the story, it seems, is true. Somewhere in Peru is an unimaginable fortune.

I did a little Googling upstairs just now. The ransom room, which the Inca emperor said he would fill with gold if the Spanish set him free, was seven metres by five and a half. Thirty-eight and a half square metres. Assuming it was two metres high, that would be—'

'Seventy-seven cubic metres.'

Stikes seemed almost impressed. 'Correct. Seventy-seven cubic metres . . . of gold. Do you know how much that would be worth?'

'Y'know, I forgot to check today's price with my broker.'

He was less appreciative of her sarcasm. 'One cubic metre of gold weighs nineteen point three metric tons. And I'm sure you can use your apparent skills at mental arithmetic to work out how many tons would fill the ransom room.'

Despite herself, Nina couldn't resist the urge to work it out. 'One thousand four hundred and eighty-six tons. Point one.'

'Point one,' Stikes repeated with a sardonic smile. 'Almost one and a half billion grams of gold – using the American billion, that is. The proper imperial billion seems to have fallen by the wayside. But at today's price per gram, that's worth over *fifty billion* dollars. As you can imagine, General Callas and I are rather keen to find it.'

'Flooding that amount of gold on to the market would drop the price to almost nothing,' Nina pointed out, still trying to prolong the discussion. She could hear movement inside the box, sinister little ticks and rustles. 'And Atahualpa told Pizarro he'd fill the room with *treasure*, not actual solid gold. However tightly everything was stacked up, there would still be a lot of empty space.'

'Frankly, even if it were four-fifths air, it would still be plenty. But the point is, he didn't fill the room, did he? Instead, he told his people to hide it all somewhere the Spanish would never find it. And they never did. And nor did anyone else.' His gaze moved to the statues. 'Until now.'

'I'm telling you, I don't know how to find it.'

'Maybe you don't know . . . yet.' Stikes slipped the elastic band off the box. 'But as I said, you're an intelligent woman. And your past record speaks for itself. I'm sure that if you turn your mind to finding El Dorado, you will.'

'Not gonna happen.'

'Oh, I disagree.' He lifted the lid. 'Even if it takes a little, shall we say, encouragement?' He lowered his gloved thumb and forefinger into the box to grab its contents.

That it took a couple of attempts suggested the contents did not want to be grabbed.

'Ah, shall we *not* say? We could . . .' Nina dried up in instinctive toe-curling fear as Stikes lifted the box's occupant into view.

A scorpion.

Dark green with mottled golden spots and bands across its carapace, it writhed angrily in Stikes's grip, jabbing its poisonous sting ineffectually at his thick glove. 'This is a Gormar scorpion, a native of Venezuela,' Stikes announced, as if presenting it for Show and Tell. 'There's some dispute over whether it's the deadliest scorpion in the world, or only the second. Either way, its sting will kill a healthy adult in ten minutes.' He moved closer, holding the thrashing arachnid up to Nina's face. She cringed back in rising terror. 'Once stung, the only hope of survival is to get an injection of antivenom. Fortunately,' he glanced at the second box, 'I have a syringe there.'

'Th-that's good,' Nina gasped, heart racing. The scorpion was mere inches from her eyes, bulbous claws snapping at her. ''Cause accidents can happen.'

'Oh, this won't be an accident.' Stikes moved the scorpion away from her face . . .

To her bound arm.

The hideous little beast lashed out with its tail, the poisonous barb stabbing into the back of her wrist. Nina instinctively yelped, as if stung by a bee – before screaming for real as the full horror of the situation struck her. The jab's initial pain was fading, but already another was replacing it, a burning spreading up her arm. 'Oh God! Jesus Christ!'

Stikes returned the scorpion to the box, then opened the second container and took out a syringe containing a colourless liquid. 'Now, we're going to discuss El Dorado. If you give me good answers, I'll give you the antivenom.'

Nina struggled uselessly against the ropes. The spot where she had been stung had already swollen. The burning sensation pervaded her body, her racing heart spreading the venom faster through her bloodstream. Another kind of pain, an intense cramp, grew in her shoulder muscles. 'I don't know where El Dorado is!' she cried. 'Osterhagen's the Inca expert, not me!'

'You can do better than that. Now, you saw the paintings on the wall. You must have deduced what they meant. I mean, even I did, and I'm not an archaeologist.' He held up the syringe tantalisingly. 'Tell me what you saw.'

The cramp reached her throat, feeling as though an invisible hand was slowly tightening around her neck. 'An – an account of their journey,' she said. 'Showing how they fled Cuzco to escape the Spanish. Along the Andes, then out into the Amazon basin. A map.'

'A map, yes. With a very important stop along the way. El Dorado.'

'Yes,' she croaked. 'But they thought the – the Spanish would find it, so they moved on.'

Stikes nodded. 'So we have a start point, Cuzco; an end point, Paititi; and a map, of sorts. That should make it possible to find El Dorado. How do we decode the map?'

'I don't know.'

He held up the syringe, pushing the plunger slightly with his thumb. Droplets formed at the end of the needle. 'Try again.'

'I don't know, I don't *know*! We never worked that out, we didn't have time!'

'And you don't have much time now. So think fast. There were markings on the map, between the pictures. What do they say? Are they directions?'

She gasped as the pain spread, struggling to remember what she had seen. 'I don't know! The Incas never developed writing – if they're directions, I don't know what they mean! Nobody'd ever seen anything like that before, not even Osterhagen!'

Stikes regarded her unblinkingly for a long moment . . . then, with a look of grudging acceptance, turned away. 'All right. You don't know how to decode the map. Let's try something else. How did you really find Paititi? And don't tell me it was the result of years of patient research.' He picked up one of the stone figurines. 'It's something to do with these, isn't it?'

Nina was losing feeling in her hands and feet as the scorpion toxin paralysed her. But despite the growing numbness in her extremities, the pain within her was getting worse. The hand was tight at her throat, squeezing harder. 'They led me here,' she choked out, struggling to breathe. Any thoughts of resistance had vanished, survival instinct forcing them aside.

'Led you? How?'

'Earth energy, it's called earth energy. Don't know how it works, but – statues glow under certain conditions. Point towards each other. IHA had—' She broke off, convulsing as a searing cramp rolled through her body. 'Oh God! Please, please!' She looked desperately at the syringe.

'The IHA had what?' Stikes demanded. 'Tell me!'

'Two statues, IHA had two statues. I put them together, they pointed to Venezuela. Interpol thought – link to Inca artefacts Callas was selling out of Valverde.' She started to hyperventilate, forcing air through her constricted windpipe. 'I don't know anything else. Please . . .'

Stikes regarded the statuette thoughtfully. 'This "earth energy" effect – can anyone make it work?'

Nina's eyes stung, tears blurring her vision. 'No, only me – something about my body's bioelectric field. Don't know why, it just does . . .' She panted, each breath a terrible effort. 'Please, told you everything I know . . .'

Stikes remained still, gazing at the stone figure . . . then put it down. He pulled up Nina's sleeve, searched for a vein, then jabbed the needle into her. She barely registered the injection through the burning pain – but after a few seconds, the pressure at her throat eased. With a shuddering gasp, she drew in a long, unrestrained lungful of air.

He withdrew the needle. The syringe was still half full. 'So, the first two statues led you to Paititi, where you found half of the third . . . and the other half, according to the painting, is somewhere in El Dorado.' He returned the syringe to its box. 'Which means you can use these statues to point the way there. Very handy.'

'Not gonna . . . help you,' Nina croaked, head lolling.

'We both know that you will. But,' he said, going to the case, 'I have work to do first. No point making retirement plans until I have the money to pay for them.'

Nina blinked away the tears, focus returning as Stikes returned the statuette to its foam bed. He put the bag containing the khipu on top of the three figures and closed the case.

The khipu . . .

Osterhagen had said the collections of knotted strings were valuable; not so much for their intrinsic worth as their rarity. But what had Cuff called them? *Talking knots*. A unique form of record-keeping. The Incas had no written language, but they did have numbers.

Numbers.

Distances. Directions. Any journey could be reduced to a series of numbers, as long as you knew the system—

A new tightness pulled at her chest, but this time not because of the poison. It was an adrenalin surge, sudden excitement as she realised what the knots were silently telling her. Not a *series* of numbers. A *string*. In this case, a literal one. The khipu was somehow the key to understanding the map, its markings connected to the dozens of cords.

Stikes had her, and the statuettes, but he didn't have a source of earth energy. The effect at Paititi had been so feeble it had only provided the vaguest indication of the final statue piece's location.

But with the khipu and the painted account of the Incas' last journey, she wouldn't need the statues. She would have a map.

She stayed silent, trying not to let the unexpected elation of discovery show on her face. Stikes still had the scorpion, still had another dose of antivenom he could use to take her to the agonising edge of death if he thought she was concealing information. He looked down at her, cold blue eyes piercing her soul. Had he realised that she had worked out more?

No. He turned away and opened the door, summoning the two soldiers back in. They untied her and hauled her back through the cellars.

'Nina,' said Kit as she was dumped, rubber-legged, in her cell. 'Are you okay?'

'Super fine,' she moaned. The antivenom may have worked,

but she still felt numb and nauseous, the sting on her arm an angry red lump.

'What did they do to you?'

'Your turn to find out,' said Stikes. The soldiers opened his cell. No attempts to grapple the prisoner here; one of the men simply drove a punch into Kit's stomach, doubling him over.

'You bastards,' said Nina, but she was too weak even to raise a hand in protest as Kit was dragged from the cage. 'He's not an archaeologist, he can't tell you anything about El Dorado.'

Stikes held up a hand. The soldiers stopped. 'Maybe not,' said the Englishman, 'but there's something else he can tell me.' He leaned closer to the Interpol agent, examining him with unblinking intensity. 'Why are you here, Mr Jindal?'

'Smuggling . . . case,' Kit groaned.

'No, why are you *really* here?' A silent moment as the two men locked eyes. Then Stikes clicked his fingers. 'You'll tell me very soon,' he said as the soldiers hustled Kit away.

'What do you mean, why is he really here?' Nina demanded. But Stikes simply gave her a disdainful look before slamming the door behind him.

18

The jungle rolled below, mile after mile of endless green. The Cessna was heading almost due north towards Caracas, detouring slightly to avoid the peaks of the Serrania Mapiche mountains. The sun dropped towards the horizon, casting a golden hue over the landscape. The explorers had left Valverde less than an hour ago, so were not even halfway to their destination, and it would be dark in around forty minutes.

'Is landing at night going to be a problem?' Eddie, in the co-pilot's seat, asked Valero. 'Without a radio, I mean.'

'Don't worry,' the Venezuelan replied. 'I can do it.'

'Great.' He looked down the cabin. 'How's Ralf?'

'Asleep,' said Macy. She and Osterhagen were taking it in turns to watch the injured man, having used the plane's first aid kit to clean and bandage his gunshot wound. There was a good chance he would recover if he reached a hospital.

'What about you?'

She grinned half-heartedly. 'Oh, just kinda wishing I'd worked harder in school so I could have done a medical degree like my parents instead of archaeology. You get shot at less that way. Even in Miami.'

Eddie smiled, then examined a navigation chart. Valero had earlier pointed out a landmark: Cerro Autana, a great flat-topped mountain, standing alone on the jungle plain. The bizarre tower was now many miles behind them, so before long they would pass about ten miles east of the city of Puerto Ayacucho.

He noticed something else. Puerto Ayacucho, as a regional capital, had a fairly large airport . . . but it was also marked as a military facility. 'Is this an airbase?' he asked, pointing at the map.

'*Si*,' Valero replied. 'That is why we are going to Caracas. I didn't want to land in the middle of Callas's friends.'

It made sense, but Eddie was suddenly on edge. An airbase so close to the border would serve a strategic purpose, its planes patrolling the edge of Venezuelan airspace . . .

And intercepting intruders.

'Where are the binocs?' he demanded.

Macy found them, concerned by his change of tone. 'What is it?'

'If Callas has friends in the air force, we don't need to land to meet them. They can come to us!' He looked northwest through the binoculars, following the long sparkling line of the Orinoco until he spotted the greys and browns of civilisation. The airport was south of the city.

Even from this distance, it was easy to make out a couple of parked airliners. He was searching for something smaller, however. He panned away from the civilian terminal to a cluster of hangars and support buildings. Their drab functionality told him at a glance that this was the military facility.

Something was moving in the rippling heat. Camouflage paintwork: a fighter jet, rolling towards the runway.

It could have been a coincidence, the plane about to set out on a routine patrol . . . but he wasn't about to bet his life on it. 'Oscar – take us down as low as you can, and head away from the city. Quick!'

'Why?'

''Cause if you don't, we'll be going down in flames! They're sending a fighter after us.'

Shocked, Valero banked right and put the Cessna into a steep descent. Macy pulled her seatbelt tighter. 'Okay, I don't know much about planes, but aren't we at kind of a horrible disadvantage in this thing?' She gestured towards the propeller.

'That's why we're trying to stay under their radar,' Eddie told her. 'Most of it'll be pointing west, towards Colombia. We might have a chance.' Valero's expression, however, suggested it would be very small.

Macy saw their shared look. 'Oh, great! After everything we've been through, we're going to be blown up by the Venezuelan Maverick and Iceman?'

'We're not going to be blown up,' Eddie growled. He raised the binoculars again.

Perspective flattened the runway against the landscape as the plane descended. Where was the jet? He couldn't see it. Lost in the heat distortion, or—

It was already in the air, a dark dart pulling up sharply atop a cone of flame from its afterburner. Its silhouette triggered his memory of aircraft recognition training: a Mirage 5, a French-built, delta-winged fighter. Some versions lacked radar . . . but not, he remembered, the Venezuelan variant.

It would find them. Soon. 'Buggeration,' he muttered.

'Oh boy,' Macy gulped. 'Not good?'

'Not good.'

'Shit shit *shit*, why didn't I pay attention in biology class?'

The jet levelled out, afterburner flame disappearing – and turned in their direction. 'Oscar,' said Eddie, 'I don't have a fucking clue how, but we're only going to stay alive if you can lose it.'

Valero shot him a disbelieving look. 'I don't have a fucking clue how either!' He eased out of the dive, the Cessna only metres above the rainforest canopy.

Macy pointed. 'There's a river. Maybe we could fly along it, behind the trees.'

Again, Valero's face revealed what he thought of the odds of success, but nevertheless he turned the plane to follow the river, easing back the throttle to give himself more time to react to the waterway's turns as he dropped lower.

The high trees along the bank blocked Eddie's view of the Mirage. He felt a moment of hope. If they couldn't see it, it couldn't see them – and the fighter's radar would also struggle to detect them through the trees.

But all the pilot had to do to find them was head for the river and look down to spot the white cross of the Caravan.

Valero made another turn. Eddie kept watching the sky. The high wing, which had made the Caravan the ideal choice for surveying the ground, now blotted out part of his view. How long before the jet reached them? The Mirage was a supersonic fighter, but even at subsonic speeds it could cover the distance in under two minutes—

Osterhagen made a startled noise as the wingtip thwacked a branch. Eddie winced, but there was no damage beyond a green stain on the paintwork.

Valero slowed the Cessna still further, holding it just above stalling speed. Even so, the plane was still tearing through the jungle at over seventy miles per hour. The river weaved, the rainforest rising on each side like green walls.

Walls that were closing in.

'There is not enough room,' Valero said urgently.

Eddie was still scouring the sky. 'Stay low as long as you can. If it goes past us, we might have a chance—'

'I can see it!' Macy cried.

'Is it going past us?'

Her voice was simultaneously angry and terrified. 'Whadda *you* think?'

'Oscar, *climb!*' Eddie roared. Stealth was now worthless; they needed room to manoeuvre. 'Macy, what's he doing?'

'Coming right at us!' she shrieked over the engine's howl as Valero pulled up sharply.

Eddie finally saw the Mirage again, sunlight flaring off its cockpit canopy. It was approaching head-on. The Caravan would be fixed in its gunsight, the slow-moving aircraft an easy target—

Twin flashes of fire beneath the fighter's fuselage. Glowing orange dots seemed to drift towards him, but he knew all too well that the cannon fire's apparent laziness was just an illusion. 'He's firing!' he yelled.

Valero responded, flinging the Cessna into a hard rolling turn. Loose items bounced around the cabin. A loud crack came from the roof as an aluminium panel split under the stress. Eddie lost sight of the Mirage, but knew the shells were still incoming—

Bright streaks flashed past the windows like meteors. 'He missed!' cried Osterhagen.

'Let's hope he keeps missing!' Eddie strained to hold himself upright as the Cessna wheeled round. The Mirage came back into view. Closer. The guns flared again. '*Oscar!*'

Valero changed course again, climbing . . .

Too late. Some shells seared past – but others hit home. Two fist-sized holes exploded through the starboard wing. Macy screamed as a piece of shrapnel scarred the window beside her.

Valero struggled with the controls. 'Can you keep it in the

air?' asked Eddie, trying to see the damage. Something was coming from the wing. Smoke?

No. A red liquid, sparkling in the light of the falling sun. *Fuel.*

The Venezuelan saw it too. He cursed in Spanish, eyes flicking over the instruments. 'I can't stop the leak.' The wing tank had been punctured top and bottom by the cannon shells; no way to shut off the flow.

'*The plane!*' Macy cried, instinctively ducking. Eddie saw a flash of camouflage green and brown rushing at them—

The Mirage blasted overhead with an earsplitting scream, the Cessna crashing violently through its wake. The jet had come in too fast, unable to slow enough to match the weaving transport's speed. Instead, it ignited its afterburner with another sky-shaking roar and powered into the distance.

Eyes wide, Osterhagen watched it thunder away. 'He's leaving,' he gasped.

'No, he's not,' Eddie replied grimly. The Mirage was making a long, sweeping turn, the pilot about to swing back round . . . and fire a missile. 'Can we get to Caracas without that fuel tank?' Valero shook his head. 'Shit! How much fuel's still in it?'

Valero checked a gauge, the needle of which was slowly but steadily dropping. 'Four hundred litres, and falling.'

Eddie thought for a moment, tracking the distant Mirage as it turned. 'Head away from him, and take us up,' he ordered.

Valero stared at him, confused. 'What?'

'Up, take us up – we need all the height we can get!' He unfastened his seatbelt as Valero put the Cessna into a climb, heading northwest.

'What are you doing?' Macy demanded as he stood.

'The emergency kit – where is it?' The yellow plastic case

had contained the first aid supplies used to patch up Becker, and more besides. He spotted it at the back of the cabin and slid down the sloping floor to retrieve it.

The glowing dot of the Mirage's afterburner cut out. 'Eddie, the jet's turning,' warned Valero.

'Just keep climbing!' Eddie opened the case. Inside were a Very pistol and several distress flares. He loaded one and snapped the breech closed, then looked through the window. The fighter was coming back towards the Cessna. 'Okay, Oscar. Can you dump the fuel from the knackered tank?'

'Yes – but why?'

'Get ready to do it! Level out, and turn so he's directly behind us.'

'But that'll make us a really easy targ— *Oh*,' said Macy, regarding him with sudden hope. 'You're going to use the flare gun to decoy the missile!'

'Nope,' said Eddie, shaking his head. 'That only works in movies. We need something a lot hotter!' There was a small hatch opposite the main door; he unlocked it and swung the top section upwards. Wind shrieked into the cabin – along with the stench of fuel, the leaking avgas swirling in the vortex created by the plane's wing.

Macy's hope was replaced by appalled disbelief. 'You're going to blow up the *fuel*? What happened to the whole us-not-blowing-up thing? We'll go too!'

'Not if I time it right.' The Mirage was moving in behind them, now some miles distant – the ideal range for a heat-seeking missile. 'Oscar! Dump the fuel when I say, then head for the ground.' The jet disappeared behind the tail. '*Now!*'

Valero, with considerable trepidation, pulled the fuel-dump lever.

The plumes of red-dyed avgas streaming from the holes in

the wing were joined by a much denser spray as the main valve opened. The needle on the fuel gauge plummeted. Eddie leaned out of the open hatch, the slipstream tearing at the back of his head as he searched for the Mirage. The dark dot was directly astern. He readied the flare gun—

Another flash of fire from the jet, this time beneath a wing. A line of smoke trailed behind a white-painted speck. A heat-seeking missile, either an American Sidewinder or a French Magic, but it made no difference – neither would have any trouble locking on.

The missile closed in a sweeping arc. Travelling at over Mach 2, it would take just seconds to reach its target.

Fuel was still gushing from the dump valve. Eddie held his breath, feeling droplets soaking his skin. If he fired too soon, Macy's fear would be realised – the igniting fuel vapour would consume the plane and its passengers.

And if he fired too late, they would be dead anyway . . .

The deluge stopped, the tank empty but for the last dribbling dregs.

He pulled the trigger.

The pistol bucked, the flare spiralling into the dissipating red cloud. For a moment nothing happened . . .

Then the sky caught fire.

Flames spread like an exploding star, greedily swallowing up the drifting fuel. Searing tongues lashed after the Cessna, trying to reach the last morsels in its ruptured wing. Eddie threw himself back into the cabin as a wave of heat hit the plane.

The missile was an R550 Magic, carrying a fragmentation warhead of twelve and a half kilograms of high explosive wrapped in frangible steel. Its infrared seeker was overwhelmed by the fireball, the heat source of its target's engine lost amidst a much bigger, hotter signal. It ran through its programmed options in a millisecond. Target lost at close range: only one response.

Detonate.

The missile was less than a hundred metres from the Cessna when the warhead exploded, sending red-hot shrapnel out in all directions. Most of the chunks of metal hit nothing . . . but only a fraction had to strike their target to score a kill.

The Caravan's tail shredded as if hit by a shotgun blast. Other sizzling shards ripped through the wings and fuselage.

One hit Valero above his ear, tearing away a chunk of flesh and hair. Blood splattered the windscreen.

He slumped, unconscious. The Cessna's descent steepened, beginning to roll.

Eddie slid across the rear of the cabin as the plane tilted. 'Eddie!' Macy screamed. 'Oscar's hit!' He hauled himself up and half ran, half fell down the aisle to clamber into the co-pilot's seat. Rows of dials and gauges gazed meaninglessly at him. 'One of these days,' he gasped as he took hold of the control yoke, 'I'm going to learn how to fly a fucking plane!'

He turned it like a steering wheel in the hope that it would counter the roll. Smoke trailing from its tail, the aircraft staggered back to a wings-level attitude – but still with its nose pointing down at the rainforest. The altimeter he understood, at least: two thousand feet.

Falling fast.

He pulled back the yoke, trying to level out. Nothing happened, the control refusing to move. 'Oh, bollocks,' he muttered as he tried again, harder. It gave slightly, then locked again. The damage to the Cessna's rear had jammed the tailplanes. 'Oh, *bollocks*!'

Fifteen hundred feet. He jerked the yoke in an attempt to

free it. The plane responded slightly, producing a faintly nauseating roller coaster sensation, but the controls remained stuck.

But to have worked at all, they still had to be connected to the tailplanes. The problem was a physical obstruction, something preventing them from moving. Maybe they could be forced free . . .

One thousand feet—

Eddie planted his feet firmly against the instrument panel. Macy watched in frightened bewilderment as he gripped the yoke with both hands. 'Everyone hold tight!' he warned as he pulled at the control, simultaneously pushing with all the strength in his legs – trying to force the tailplanes to move through sheer brute force.

The yoke creaked. It seemed to give, but only a little. He pulled harder, aware that if he tore the handgrips clean off their mount, they were all doomed.

Five hundred—

'Come *on*!' he rasped, face twisted with effort. The jungle was rapidly approaching. Three hundred feet. Every muscle trembled as he strained. The glass of a dial cracked beneath his foot.

Two hundred—

Something snapped. The yoke suddenly broke free, the tailplanes slamming upwards to their full extent. The aircraft pulled out of its dive . . .

Not quickly enough.

The jungle's tallest trees stretched up well over a hundred feet above the ground. Even as the Cessna levelled out, it was still heading inexorably into the thick canopy—

Branches and leaves disintegrated as the propeller carved through a treetop like a chainsaw. Eddie wrestled with the controls, still trying to pull up, but the plane hit another tree, branches clawing open the Cessna's skin.

The towering trunk of an emergent redwood rose above the canopy ahead. Eddie shoved down a rudder pedal, but even had the controls been fully responsive there wasn't time to turn away—

The tree scythed past less than a foot from the fuselage's left side, slicing off the port wing at its root. Fuel erupted from the tank inside it as it crumpled. The Cessna's tail, still smouldering, hurtled through the spray – and ignited it. The wing blew apart, an oily mushroom cloud roiling up through the foliage.

What was left of the plane dropped towards the ground, the mangled tail now aflame. '*Brace!*' yelled Eddie, grabbing his seatbelt straps and bending into a crash position—

The Caravan hit on its belly, the impact tearing away the wheels and buckling the hull. The propeller blades bent as they churned through the earth. The starboard wing clipped another tree and was ripped in half, the fuselage skidding onwards in a huge spray of soil and rotting vegetation. The windscreen shattered, dirt filling the cockpit. Jutting roots tore at the aircraft's belly as it crashed over them with a terrible screeching sound.

Which suddenly lessened.

Eddie clung to the straps, eyes shut tight. The plane was still moving – but the ground beneath it was somehow cushioning its passage. The bumps continued, but muffled, fading as the plane slowed . . .

And stopped.

The bent hull tipped back with a thump. Eddie wiped away mud and cautiously opened his eyes. They were indeed stationary. His arms ached where the straps had cut into them, and there was a horrible bruise across his stomach from the steering yoke. He flexed his hands, then his feet. Nothing broken.

Valero had fared much worse. Unconscious, he had been unable to protect himself, flailing as the plane ploughed through the trees. Two of his fingers were bent back at unnatural angles, and blood streaked his face where he had hit the controls. Becker, equally helpless, had come off better; secured in his seat, he was now slumped over the armrest, moaning softly.

'Ow, God . . .' a female voice whispered. Eddie staggered to his feet. Osterhagen sat bolt upright, eyes squeezed shut and breathing loudly and rapidly. Macy, meanwhile, had her head against the window, grimacing.

Eddie staggered to her. 'Macy! Are you okay?'

'I dunno . . .' She tried to stand. 'Ow, that hurts – wait, if it hurts . . .' She rolled her head to clear the dazed fog from her mind. 'I'm not dead?'

Eddie half laughed. 'No, we're alive. That means I've survived two plane crashes in less than a year. Fuck me! Don't know if that means I'm really lucky or really *un*lucky.' A feeble smile briefly turned up her lips, which he returned. 'We need to get out of the plane, though. Something's burning.' He faced Osterhagen. 'Doc. Doc! Can you hear me?'

Osterhagen's eyes snapped open, darting about wildly before settling on Eddie. 'Where are we?'

'On the ground, and that's good enough for me. Are you hurt?'

'Only bruised, I think. But my neck is very painful.'

'Whiplash, but I doubt you'll get the chance to sue anyone for it. Okay, you and Macy get Ralf out of the plane. I'll get Oscar.'

They released the injured men from their seats and hauled them through the main hatch. The reason for the plane's relatively soft landing became clear; they were in a marsh, boots sinking inches deep into the soft muck. Eddie looked at the plane, seeing smoke curling from the tail, then searched for more solid ground. There was a broad hump of earth not far away. 'Lie them down on that,' he said. 'Then I'll—'

A deep rumble shook the rainforest. The Mirage. It was still out there.

Hunting for them.

Osterhagen searched the patches of sky visible through the canopy. 'Where is it?'

Eddie turned, listening. The jet growl was loudest back along the channel gouged out of the jungle by the careering plane.

And still getting louder . . .

He glimpsed movement above the trees to the southeast. The Mirage was circling. But not overhead. He realised why; the exploded port wing had sent up a column of thick black smoke.

And from a fire that large, the pilot might assume that the entire plane had blown up.

The Mirage came round for another low, slow pass. Even something the size of the Cessna slashing through the all-encompassing canopy would only have left a small scratch; the pilot wouldn't be able to spot more than a few scraps of wreckage through the trees.

Or so Eddie hoped. He waited, the engine roar growing louder. Another brief flash of something large and deadly above . . .

And gone. The thunder faded as the Mirage accelerated away, heading northwest. Back to the airbase.

'Think they'll come back?' Macy hesitantly asked.

'Not in a jet,' said Eddie. He carefully lowered Valero. Macy and Osterhagen put Becker beside him. 'They might send a chopper or a foot patrol, but I reckon that pilot thinks we're dead. The wing made a pretty big bang. And speaking of which, better grab what I can before the rest of the plane catches fire.' He hurried back into the wreck, re-emerging with a handful of charts, Becker's hat, a torch and a plastic bottle of water. 'Couldn't find the first aid kit – it must have been sucked out of the hatch.'

'So what can we do to help Ralf?' Osterhagen asked. 'And Oscar?'

'I still think Ralf'll be fine if we get him to a hospital,' said Eddie. 'Oscar, though . . .' Even a cursory glance told him that things did not look good for the Venezuelan. The deep head wound needed sterilising, stitches and bandages – none of which he could provide.

He lifted Valero's hand to get a better look at his broken fingers – and the man jerked awake with a scream. Macy jumped back, startled. Valero cried out in Spanish, writhing. Eddie tried to hold him down. 'Oscar! Oscar, stay still. You're hurt. Don't try to move.'

He tried to wash a little water over the gash above Valero's ear, but he flinched away. 'Eddie, you've got to get to – to Caracas. Tell militia about . . .' His face twisted in pain. 'Callas. Tell them about Callas.'

'We can't leave you behind,' Eddie insisted. 'We're not far from Puerto Ayacucho. We can get you to a hospital.'

Valero shook his head, the movement clearly causing him great suffering. 'No,' he said, his voice falling to a hoarse whisper. 'In my head, I can – I can feel it. Something hurts, it hurts so bad. You have to—' The tendons in his throat pulled tight as he convulsed in agony, a strangled moan escaping. 'Clubhouse, Callas is at – the Clubhouse. Stop . . . him . . .' Another spasm, mouth open wide in silent torment . . . then he relaxed, his final breath softly leaving his body.

Eddie, Macy and Osterhagen stared at him in silence. Macy was the first to look away, eyes brimming with tears. Osterhagen rubbed his head with a shaking hand. 'A burst blood vessel, perhaps . . . I don't know.'

'Doesn't matter,' said Eddie stiffly. He reached down to close Valero's pain-stricken eyes. 'We know who caused it. Callas. And Stikes. All of this is because of them. Oscar was right – we've got to stop them.' He stood.

'Can we really get to this Puerto place?' Macy asked quietly.

'Yeah. We're maybe seven or eight miles away as the crow flies – but if we go due west, we'll get to a main road a lot quicker.' He unrolled a chart and showed her. 'About four miles, a bit more. We can hitch a lift.'

'What about Ralf?' Osterhagen asked.

'I'll carry him.'

'All the way?' Macy exclaimed.

'I can manage. You take this.' He tossed her the torch. 'Once we're out of this swamp, the chart says there's no rivers and the terrain's pretty flat, so it shouldn't be too bad. We've got less than half an hour of light left, so we need to get moving. Doc, give me a hand.' Osterhagen helped him hoist Becker in a fireman's lift. The injured man moaned faintly, but didn't fully wake up. 'Okay, let's get going.'

Time in the cell blurred past as if in a fever dream, the after-effects of the poisoning lingering like a sickness. Nina drifted in and out of consciousness, unsure whether moments or minutes had passed each time she closed her eyes.

She felt the swirling, clammy darkness rising to swallow her again, and shifted her head, resting it against the metal bars for the coolness they provided. But it didn't last long. The awful weariness pulled at her once more . . .

A noise startled her into wakefulness. Two soldiers dragged Kit into the room and dumped him back in his cell before slamming its door and leaving. Nina pushed herself upright. 'Kit,' she said, her voice weak. 'Kit, are you okay?'

The bruises on his face revealed that Stikes had used old-fashioned interrogation techniques in addition to his vile little pet. One eye was blackened, the lower lid puffy and swollen, and there was a smear of blood down his chin from a split lip. 'I've had better hospitality,' he croaked. 'I . . .' His face suddenly twisted with pain, and he let out a choked scream as he clutched his chest.

'Kit?' said Nina, alarm rapidly turning to fear. 'Kit! Oh my God!' She tried to stand, but her legs still felt rubbery. 'Hey!' she shouted at the guard. 'Do something, help him!'

The guard gave her an uncomprehending look, apparently not understanding English, before turning his gaze back to the convulsing Indian . . . and doing nothing.

Horrified, Nina rattled the door. 'He's dying! Help him!' But the soldier's expression remained dispassionate. Appalled, she realised what that meant; now that he had been interrogated, Kit was expendable. She tried to reach across the empty middle cell to him, but he was too far away. 'Kit!'

His moans stopped, and he slowly raised his head to give her a pained wink with his swollen eye. 'It was worth a try,' he rasped.

Nina glanced back at the guard, who still showed no signs of understanding what was being said, before lowering her voice. 'You were *faking*?'

'If he had opened the door, I could have found out how well I remembered my unarmed combat training.'

The guard was younger and considerably beefier than Kit. 'As much as I want to get out of here,' said Nina, 'I'm kinda glad you didn't put it to the test.'

Kit managed a look of mock affront. 'Are you saying I couldn't have taken him down?'

'I'm saying that I know how I feel right now. I'd guess that you probably feel worse.'

'You're probably right.' He slumped on the concrete floor, sweat beading his forehead.

'What did Stikes want from you?' Nina asked, hoping that conversation would help him – and her – stay awake.

A hesitation. 'He . . . asked me lots of questions about Interpol. He wanted to find out how much I had told headquarters about Callas.' He moved his arm to display a reddened scorpion sting. 'He believed me when I said that they knew nothing. Eventually. But what about you?' he went on before Nina could ask another question. 'What did he want from you?'

'El Dorado. How to find it.'

'And did you tell him?'

She looked away, shamefaced. 'Yeah. All about the statues, earth energy, how I used them to find Paititi . . . everything.'

With visible strain, Kit sat up. 'Nina, you did nothing wrong. Nobody can stand up to torture, however strong they think they are.'

'Eddie probably could.' The thought of her husband filled her with sudden guilt; her own suffering had pushed him from her mind. 'Oh, God, I hope he's okay. I don't even know what happened to him at Paititi.'

'I think he is still alive. Stikes seems to be the kind who would enjoy telling you if he wasn't.'

Despite her efforts to stay focused, the sickening tiredness was rising to swallow Nina again. 'I hope you're right,' she whispered, slumping against the bars.

★

The trek westwards was not difficult physically; the thick jungle canopy actually made movement easier by starving the undergrowth of light. Eddie and the others made steady, if plodding, progress.

What made it unpleasant were the humid heat, which refused to lessen even after the sun had set, and the insects. They were bad enough in daylight, but once the twilight gloom forced Macy to switch on the torch they swarmed around the light. 'You know what?' she complained after a particularly huge and loathsome bug batted her in the face with its wings. '*Screw* the rainforest! They can bulldoze the whole place into strip malls for all I care!'

Eventually, to everyone's relief, the jungle thinned, giving way to open ground that had been subjected to slash-and-burn cultivation. Before long they found themselves on a road – not a glorified dirt track like those found in the rainforest, but an actual paved highway. It was only one lane in each direction, but to the exhausted group it seemed like an eight-lane motorway. 'Oh, thank God!' Macy cried. 'Civilisation! Kinda.'

There was no sign of traffic. Eddie checked his watch; it was coming up to nine p.m. 'Let's hope somebody's out at this time of night. And that Venezuela doesn't have laws against hitch-hiking!'

They laid Becker down beside the northbound lane, and waited. After a few minutes, headlights appeared to the south. Eddie stood in the road and waved for the approaching vehicle to stop. Macy joined him. 'What?' she said, to his look. 'If the driver's a guy, he might be more likely to stop for a hot babe, right?'

She was covered in dirt and sweat, clothes torn, hair a ratty, tangled mess. 'Right now you look about as hot as I do. But maybe he likes it dirty . . .'

'Shut. *Up!*'

The vehicle, a beaten-up pickup truck, stopped. Macy did the talking, explaining that they had been in a crash – she left out that it had involved a plane to avoid awkward questions – and forced to walk through the jungle. The driver, an elderly man, chided the *yanquis* for lacking both caution and survival equipment before agreeing to take them to Puerto Ayacucho. Osterhagen rode up front with Becker, while Eddie and Macy sat in the rear bed.

The drive along the empty road didn't take long. They passed the airport, Eddie keeping a wary eye open for military patrols, and entered the city. The driver pulled up outside the hospital. 'Eddie,' said Osterhagen as the Englishman climbed from the truck, 'I am going to stay with Ralf.'

'You sure? They might still be looking for us. Two gringos in the hospital . . . they could make the connection.'

Osterhagen looked at the wounded man. Becker had drifted in and out of consciousness through the entire trek, but never been lucid enough to do more than mumble in German. 'He will need someone to tell him what has been going on. Besides . . .' He regarded the hat he was holding. 'He is my friend. I should be with him.'

Eddie put a hand on the older man's shoulder. 'I can't argue with that. Just be careful, okay?'

'I will. And you be careful too.' They lifted Becker from the truck. 'What about you and Macy? What are you going to do?'

'Rescue Nina and Kit. And kill Stikes and Callas. Not necessarily in that order.'

Osterhagen's face suggested that he thought the latter objective a dangerous step too far, but he said nothing. He and

Eddie carried Becker into the hospital. Macy gave a modified version of her story to a nurse to account for Becker's wound, the 'crash' now happening while fleeing armed robbers. The story seemed to be accepted, and Becker was taken away for treatment.

Osterhagen shook Eddie's hand. 'Thank you. For keeping us alive.'

'Shame I couldn't do it for everyone,' Eddie replied glumly. 'But look after Ralf. And yourself. Hopefully see you both again soon.'

'Thank you,' the German repeated, before following his friend.

'So how *are* we going to rescue Nina and Kit?' Macy asked once they were outside.

The pickup driver had waited for them, keen to learn Becker's condition in the hope of adding a happy ending to his tale of Samaritanism. 'We need to get to this Clubhouse place,' said Eddie. 'I doubt this bloke'll take us all the way to Caracas, but ask him how we can get there – if there's a bus or something.'

Macy did so, learning that there was an overnight bus between Puerto Ayacucho and the capital, with still enough time for them to catch it. 'Ew, I hate using buses,' she added after reporting this to Eddie. 'There's always some really gross guy trying to check me out.'

'You want to walk three hundred miles?'

'Depends how gross the guy is.'

'Can't be as gross as those bugs. Ask if he'll give us a lift to the bus station. Oh, and if there are any payphones there.'

'Yes, and yes,' she said after posing both questions. 'Who are you planning on calling? Someone in the government we can warn about Callas?'

'I would if I knew who to call, but I don't – and I don't know who we can trust, either. If Callas is planning a coup, he'll need more than just the military on his side. He'd have to have people in the militia too. They're the biggest threat to him.'

'Except for you.'

Macy had meant it as a joke, but the smile Eddie gave her had a very hard edge. 'Yeah. Except for me.'

They got back into the pickup and set off. 'So who *are* you going to call?' Macy asked.

His smile this time was somewhat warmer. 'An old friend.'

19

Nina jerked awake, a fierce cramp burning in her arm. For a nightmarish moment she thought the antivenom had worn off, letting the Gormar's toxin continue its work, but as she scrambled to sit up she realised it was only the result of her uncomfortable sleeping position on the hard floor.

She rolled her shoulder to ease the stiffness. The wallowing nausea had subsided, leaving just a hangover queasiness. Examining her wrist, she saw that the swollen sting had gone down, though it was still an angry red.

'Nina? Are you all right?'

She looked round to see Kit sitting against the wall of his cell. 'I'm . . . not great,' she admitted. 'But better than I was.' A glance told her that the guard had been replaced by another man. 'How long was I asleep?'

Kit checked his watch. 'Quite a while. It's after eleven in the morning.'

She had been out for something like fourteen hours while her body did its best to expunge the poison from her system. 'Jesus. How long have you been awake?'

'About an hour. I didn't want to wake you.'

Another look at the guard. This one apparently understood English, his eyes flicking between them as he followed their conversation. 'We've got a new watchman – did I miss anything else?'

'No, he was there when I woke up. I've been spending the time wondering how on earth I ended up in this situation. It seems destiny works in strange ways.'

Nina made a sarcastic sound. 'You think being tortured with scorpions was our *destiny*?'

'I prefer that to it being nothing more than bad luck.'

'Huh. I kind of see your point. Just hope that our destinies don't end in here.'

'So do I. But . . . I do think that things happen for a reason, even if we can't always see it at first. There is order in the universe, but it has to be maintained – whether by the gods, or by our actions. Part of our purpose is to keep that order.'

'Interesting,' said Nina with a faint smile. 'I'm not used to philosophical discussion in the morning. But then, I do live with Eddie.'

Kit grinned back through his puffy lips. 'Not bad for a humble policeman, no?'

'So is that why you became a cop? To maintain order?'

He nodded. 'In some ways. Growing up in India, I saw a lot of corruption, a lot of greed that caused others to suffer. I wanted to do what I could to stop it – to make sure that people who took more than they deserved were punished.'

'Sounds like a good motivation to me.'

The Interpol officer gave her an appreciative look, then sighed. 'It did not always make me popular. Even among my colleagues.'

'Yeah, I know what that feels like,' Nina told him sympathetically.

'But then, this is what I mean about destiny. If I had been the kind of cop who looked the other way when I saw others taking bribes, I probably wouldn't have been "encouraged" to move from regular police work into more specialised areas like art theft. And if I hadn't done that, I wouldn't have been offered a position at Interpol, which means I would not have investigated the Khoils, I would not have met you and Eddie . . . and I would not be here right now.'

Nina raised her eyebrows. 'And you're still upbeat about it? If I'd thought about the course of my life like that, I'd be going "Oh God, where did it all go so wrong?"!'

He smiled. 'I'm a very upbeat person. And I don't regret my decisions. Even though at the moment they seem to have brought me to a rather dark place.'

'You're not kidding.' She tapped the bars. 'Any ideas how we can get out into the light?'

'A few. Unfortunately, they all begin with us being outside these cells.'

'That's not as helpful as I was hoping for.'

'I'm still working on them.'

The door opened and a pair of soldiers trooped in. 'Work faster,' Nina urgently told Kit as they unlocked her cell and entered. 'All right, okay!' she protested as she was pulled to her feet.

They took her back upstairs, ascending a broad marble staircase to the mansion's upper floor. Nina screwed up her eyes, dazzled by the brightness of the morning sun through panoramic windows as she was led through a luxurious lounge with a giant TV on one wall. Beyond, a large balcony overlooked the golf course.

Stikes and Callas, the general in full uniform, waited for her outside, but there was also a third man; tall, tanned, with long jet-black hair swept greasily back from his forehead. His pastel jacket and trousers were clearly of some extremely expensive designer label, though the stylish effect was offset by a vulgar gold medallion. Even this early in the day, he had a glass of Scotch and clunking ice cubes in his hand.

'Ah, here she is!' said Callas as the soldiers brought Nina into the open. 'My expert.'

The third man's eyebrows flickered in recognition. 'Wait, she is . . .'

'Dr Nina Wilde,' Callas announced. 'Discoverer of Atlantis, and the secret of the Sphinx, and now . . . my guest. Dr Wilde, meet my good friend Francisco de Quesada.'

She remembered the Venezuelan mentioning the name at the military base, though in a far from friendly way. Like Pachac, then; another of his allies of necessity.

De Quesada took in Nina's dirty, dishevelled clothing. 'You do not let your guests shower, Salbatore?'

'She's not entirely a willing guest,' said Stikes.

'But she will still tell you how much this is worth,' Callas said, indicating something on a glass coffee table: the khipu, opened out to its full length, knotted strands displayed along the braided central cord. Nina noticed the case holding the statues on the floor nearby.

De Quesada shook his head. 'I am already paying you fifty million dollars for the sun disc—'

'It is worth far more,' Callas smoothly interjected.

'Perhaps. But you are also getting a share of my . . . proceeds.' He looked askance at Nina. 'Is it safe to talk in front of her?'

Callas snorted. 'You can say anything you like – she won't be telling anyone.'

'My drug revenue, then. Now that the American DEA and the government have cracked down in Colombia, I need Venezuela to ship my product. Which means I need you, general. Or should I call you el Jefe?'

Callas smiled proudly, only to be deflated by Stikes's 'Let's not count our chickens before they're hatched.'

'Which brings me to another English phrase,' said de Quesada. He gestured dismissively at the khipu. ' "Money for old rope". You are getting a lot of money from me, Salbatore – cash now, and a share of what will come later. Why should I pay another million for this trash?'

'That is why I brought Dr Wilde,' said Callas. 'Who better to tell you why these strings are worth so much? If you can't trust the world's most famous archaeologist, then who can you trust?'

'Yes, who?' de Quesada replied, his tone suggesting to Nina that the Venezuelan's veiled dislike was mutual. But he sat back, gesturing at her with his drink. 'Very well. Impress me, Dr Wilde.'

'And be honest,' Stikes added in a quiet but threatening voice.

Nina walked to the table, examining the khipu. Fully opened, it was more than three feet long, the number of multicoloured strings attached to the woven spine greater than she had thought; well over a hundred. The number of knots on each string ranged from a couple to over a dozen.

The topmost knot on each string, she noticed, was always one of four kinds. She knew that the Incas had divided their empire into quadrants based on astronomical features: could they be directions? Below the first, the other knots were more varied, strung like beads. If it were indeed a guide to the Incas' journey, it would require considerable work to decode.

But she had seen such guides before – leading to Atlantis, to Eden. It could be done. El Dorado could be found.

If she made the khipu seem dull enough to dissuade de Quesada from buying it.

'Well, it's called a khipu,' she began, slipping into a professorial tone. 'They were used as a system of record-keeping by the Incas. The knots on each string are a way of storing numbers, similar to an abacus.' She tried to remember what Osterhagen had said about them. 'They were used to keep censuses, calculate taxes, track how much food was grown.' *Keep it boring*, she told herself. 'They were the backbone of the Inca accounting system.'

To her relief, de Quesada didn't appear impressed. 'But they are valuable, no?' prompted Callas.

'I suppose, but more because of their scarcity than any intrinsic worth. There are only a few hundred still in existence. The Conquistadors destroyed all the ones they found.'

'The Conquistadors?' De Quesada's eyes flashed with sudden interest. 'Why did they destroy them?'

'They thought the Incas used them to send secret messages,' said Nina, aware that Callas now had a look of greedy expectancy. It seemed she had unwittingly pushed one of de Quesada's buttons. 'I don't think that's true, because as far as we know the khipus only contained numerical information – the Incas never developed a written language. But the Spanish—'

De Quesada regarded the khipu more closely. 'So the Conquistadors destroyed them to show their power over the Incas?'

'You could say that. Really, though, they're just—'

He cut her off again, getting to his feet. 'I will buy it, Salbatore!' He cackled, swigging from his glass. 'You just make sure that my old friend Arcani Pachac knows I have it, like his precious sun disc. That little communist *cagada* thinks he is the Inca emperor reborn? Then I'll remind him what the Spanish did to the Incas. A million dollars, you said? Make it two!'

'You – you're spending two million dollars just to annoy Pachac?' Nina said, shocked and appalled.

'I am spending more than that! The sun disc, this great symbol of Pachac's glorious heritage?' His words dripped sarcasm. 'I have the perfect place for it. When it is installed, I will send him a picture – it will drive him mad!'

'Francisco and Pachac were once partners,' explained Callas. 'Until—'

'Until he turned against me,' said de Quesada. 'He got politics, decided he wanted to restore the poor downtrodden Indians to power.' He mimed wiping a tear from one eye, pulling an exaggeratedly sad face. 'The defeated should keep their heads down. The Spanish nobles were the victors. They still are.'

'But all that money,' said Nina. 'You're spending millions out of *spite*? Why?'

De Quesada shrugged and took another drink. 'Because I can. I already have cars, boats, planes, houses, women . . . I have to spend my money on something. Other than bribes, anyway.' He looked back at the khipu. 'I will take it. What about the sun disc? How are you going to get it to Colombia?'

'It's already being dealt with,' said Stikes.

'You found a replacement for West?'

'Indeed we did.' He gave Nina a smug look. 'As for the khipu, you can take it with you if you like, but I'd recommend using our agent's services for that as well. In case anyone asks questions.'

De Quesada scowled. 'You are probably right. I cannot take a shit in my own country without some government *pendejo* or bastard from the DEA trying to look up my ass. Maybe after tonight I should move to Venezuela, eh?'

'Maybe,' said Callas noncommittally.

'And speaking of tonight . . .' A small but distinctly cunning smile as de Quesada took something from his jacket: a DVD in a transparent case. 'I know you have made a deal with Pachac, giving him control over the southern routes across the border. I want you to give those routes to me.'

Callas stiffened at the challenge, regarding the disc suspiciously. 'What?'

'Capture and kill his runners, and give his drugs to me. The only cocaine shipped through Venezuela will be mine.'

The general shook his head. 'We have made a deal, we will stick to it. Just as I will stick to the deal I made with Pachac.'

De Quesada laughed. 'Yes, of course you will. It never crossed your mind to use your new power to change the deal with him in your favour.' His smile vanished. 'Or the deal with me.'

Callas looked pointedly towards the two soldiers, both of whom were armed. 'I don't like your tone, Francisco.'

'And I don't like being double-crossed, Salbatore. So, let's make sure it never happens, eh?' He held out the DVD to Callas, who hesitated before snatching it from him, then nodded towards the television in the lounge. 'Put it on.'

'Watch her,' Callas ordered one of the soldiers, who moved closer to Nina. The other closed the door behind Callas, Stikes and de Quesada as they went into the lounge. The reflections on the glass made it hard for Nina to see inside, but she could make out Callas putting the disc into a player and switching on the TV.

He watched it for less than a minute before whirling angrily on de Quesada. A brief argument, Callas becoming more furious by the moment, then the Venezuelan stormed back to the player, ejected the disc and hurled it across the room. Still seething, he threw the door open and returned to the balcony, clenching his fists round the handrail as he glared out across Caracas.

De Quesada followed. 'If that became public, your new position would become very unstable.' He finished his drink, crunching an ice cube between his teeth. 'It might even give the Americans an excuse for regime change. However much oil you offer them, they are not going to tolerate a drug lord as president.'

'I am not a drug lord!' Callas spat.

'But you are working with one, and there was the proof.'

'That recording would also be damaging to you,' Stikes pointed out.

'A calculated risk. But,' de Quesada went on, 'it will be much easier if we just make sure it is never seen, eh? Accept my new deal. You will still get your percentage – and you know you would rather deal with me than a psychopath like Pachac.'

The general drew in a long breath before facing de Quesada. 'Pachac is . . . unreliable, yes. Very well. You will have his territory. But if the video is ever seen . . .' He jabbed a threatening finger at the Colombian's heart.

De Quesada simply smiled. 'It will not be.' He rattled the last couple of ice cubes in his glass. 'Now, we should celebrate our new deal with a drink.'

'Not for you, I'm afraid,' Stikes said to Nina. He nodded to the soldiers. As they led her away, he added, in an overly casual way: 'Oh, by the way – your husband.'

'What about him?' demanded Nina, heart sinking.

'Dead.' The word was delivered with a thin smirk. Nina felt as though she had been stung by the scorpion again, her throat clenching tight. 'I must admit, he put up a good show. Even rescued your friends. But then their plane got shot down and exploded in the jungle. The end of the Chase, you might say.'

Fury and despair rose simultaneously inside her, the former narrowly gaining ascendance. She lunged at Stikes, but the soldiers caught her before she could reach him, twisting her arms behind her back. 'I'll fucking kill you!' she snarled.

Stikes merely smirked again as she was dragged away.

20

Caracas baked under the afternoon sun, shimmering beneath a blanket of smog. The streets were clogged with traffic. More so than usual; there was a greater police and military presence than when the archaeological team had arrived four days earlier. Armoured vehicles rumbled through the city, soldiers and cops regarding the sweating Caraqueños with suspicion. The mistrust was mutual, everyone feeling the tension in the air.

Almost everyone. 'Excuse *me*! Jeez,' Macy sniped at a woman who had bumped into her and carried on without a word. 'What was her problem?'

'Same as ours, probably.' Eddie nodded towards three policemen who had thrown a man against their car and were roughly searching him. 'This'll be part of Callas's coup. Stir the shit, find an excuse to get the police and army on the streets. That way, they're already in position when the real action starts.'

'And what is the real action?'

'Something to do with Stikes and that chopper. You don't hire mercenaries and buy a gunship just for mopping-up work. They're the key.'

The man was shoved into the police car, one of the cops gesturing threateningly at bystanders with a baton. 'So what are we gonna do?' Macy asked.

'Find this Clubhouse place. That way, we find Nina and Kit, and probably Callas and Stikes as well. Maybe even stop them before they start.'

A military Jeep bullied its way between cars, armed soldiers glowering at drivers. Macy regarded them nervously. 'How are we going to do that? They've got, like, hundreds of guys on their side. And they've all got guns. And we don't.'

'I don't need a gun.' They reached a crossroads, and saw the giant screen outside the television station. On it President Suarez, wearing militia uniform, delivered an impassioned speech. 'What's he saying?'

Macy listened to the booming audio. 'That everything's okay and there's nothing to worry about, and not to listen to— Hey! He's blaming America! Says CIA agents are trying to undermine the revolution. What a jerk! They're not. Are they?'

'The CIA messes with *friendly* countries,' said Eddie. 'Take a guess what they do in ones they don't like.' The traffic was almost at a standstill; he took Macy's hand and hurried her across the street. 'Okay, the hotel's just up here.'

Coming back to the same hotel was a risk, but when he made his phone call in Puerto Ayacucho Eddie hadn't known anywhere else he could be contacted. Besides, he hoped that Callas's followers thought they were dead. They entered the lobby, getting disapproving looks for their less than pristine appearance. Eddie ignored them and went to reception. 'Hi. Any messages for Eddie Chase?'

To his disappointment, and surprise, there were none. 'Huh. Better find out what's up,' he said, leading Macy to the payphones. The last of the coins he had taken from the dead soldiers at the burial pit got him through to an operator to make a reverse-charge international call, and he soon got an answer.

'Is that you, Eddie?' said a familiar Scottish voice.

'Yeah, Mac, it's me,' said Eddie, somewhere between relieved and impatient. 'I'm at the hotel – I thought you were going to leave me a message?'

'I wanted to deliver it in person,' the voice said from behind him.

Eddie spun to find Mac standing there in a light-coloured suit, holding a mobile phone to his ear. 'Mac! Fuck me, what's you doing here?'

Macy was equally delighted to see him. 'Oh my God, Mr McCrimmon!' she cried, embracing him.

'Well, there goes my suit,' Mac sighed. Macy hurriedly tried to brush away a dirty mark she had left on his sleeve before a wink told her that he was joking. 'Glad to see you both. How was your trip?'

'Thirteen hours on a bus, loved every minute,' said Eddie. 'How the bloody hell did you get here so fast? And what are MI6 doing about Callas and Stikes?'

'It's a long-ish story, so I'll tell it in my room,' said Mac. 'And while we're there, you can take advantage of the shower . . .'

'So MI6 aren't going to do a fucking thing?' Eddie exclaimed, after Mac had described his dealings with the British intelligence agency. 'I *knew* you can't trust a fucking spook. Was it Alderley? And after I invited him to my wedding do, an' all.'

'Funny, I seem to remember you "accidentally" dropped his invitation down a drain,' said Mac.

'Yeah, there was that. But I'm sure he's not bitter.'

'Actually, South America is outside Peter's section, so I didn't speak to him. I did talk to C, though.'

'Who's C?' Macy asked, emerging from the bathroom in an oversized dressing gown.

'Head of MI6,' Eddie told her.

'I thought that was M?'

Mac smiled. 'James Bond isn't real, Macy. But I discussed this with C, although he wasn't pleased at being woken up at four in the morning.'

'So if you talked to him, why aren't they going to do anything?' demanded Eddie.

'Well,' said Mac, leaning back in his chair, 'the official position of Her Majesty's Government is that the internal politics of Venezuela are the country's own affair, and that British interests are not sufficient to justify any kind of interference. Unofficially, of course, HMG would not object to Suarez's being replaced by someone less incendiary. They're also rather unhappy with statements he and his predecessor made about the Queen, and Britain's ownership of the Falklands. In short, they'd be happy to see him go.'

'Even if it means him being replaced by Callas? The guy's a cold-blooded murderer working with drug lords! As soon as he takes power, the country'll be a fucking bloodbath.'

'Same old story,' Mac said, shaking his head ruefully. 'In a choice between two third-world military strongmen, we always seem to support whoever's the more unpleasant.'

'And what about Stikes? He's British, his company's British – he's ex-SAS, for Christ's sake. Doesn't that count as being involved if he's helping overthrow a democratically elected leader?'

'How? He's a private military contractor; he can choose to work wherever and for whomever he chooses. 3S has never worked directly for our government, so there's no conflict of interest or potential for embarrassment there. As long as he doesn't break the law in Britain, his hands are clean.'

Eddie threw up his own hands. 'So that's it?'

'I did convince them to give me something, even if it's not much. I got the address of this Clubhouse place.' He took out his phone and brought up the map app, a pin showing a location in Valle Arriba. 'After that, I went straight to Heathrow and got a standby ticket on the first morning flight to Caracas. Business class, so it cost me a bloody fortune. Still, whenever I get involved with you my bank account always takes a beating, so I should be used to it by now.'

Eddie looked at the map. 'I want to check this place out in person.'

'I thought you might. I've got a hire car. Although there's something I think you should do first.'

'What?'

Mac glanced towards the bathroom. 'Don't take this the wrong way, Eddie,' Macy said, 'but . . . you kinda stink.'

Eddie looked down at his filthy, ripped, bloodstained clothing. 'You mean they aren't going to bottle me as the new fragrance from Hugo Boss?'

'Cool house,' said Macy, regarding the Clubhouse through the rented Fiat's rear window.

Eddie made a non-committal sound. Architecture was not foremost on his mind, but rather the soldiers on duty around the mansion. There were two at the main gate, and even though the building and its grounds were partially concealed behind trees and a wall he had spotted at least three other uniformed men. As Callas's unofficial headquarters, those numbers would be the tip of the iceberg.

'So what do you think?' Mac asked from the driver's seat.

'Unless I dress up as a delivery boy bringing twenty pizzas, I doubt I'll get in through the front gate. And they'll be watching the golf course round the back too.' He looked at one of the nearby houses. Another mansion, though not as grand as the one the Venezuelan government had confiscated. 'The neighbours – they're still all normal houses with people living in them, right?'

'I think so. According to MI6, the chap who owned the Clubhouse was rather outspoken against the Suarez regime. Whether the tax evasion charges were real or trumped up they didn't know, but he was someone Suarez had been targeting for some time.'

Eddie scanned the row of luxury houses. 'Might have to do a bit of garden-hopping. But I'll need a distraction to get into the Clubhouse grounds without being seen.'

'I'm sure we can come up with something,' said Mac. 'But if you've seen as much as you need, we should go. Being parked like this is probably attracting attention.' The tree-lined street was devoid of stationary vehicles; all the houses had drives and garages large enough to accommodate multiple cars. Parking on the road was a giveaway that someone didn't belong.

'Yeah, okay.' Eddie looked back at the Clubhouse – and saw the main gates open, the guards moving aside. 'No, hang on – someone's coming out.'

It was not a car that emerged first, but a police motorbike. Next came a black Cadillac Escalade SUV, miniature Venezuelan flags fluttering from its front quarters. Another bike followed it.

Eddie glimpsed a familiar silhouette behind the tinted glass as the convoy drove past. 'That was Callas!'

'No sign of Stikes?' Mac asked.

'Nope.' He regarded the Clubhouse again, cracking his knuckles. 'He might still be in there with Nina . . .'

'Or he might have gone to do whatever Callas has hired him for.'

'Either way, Nina's still there. Soon as it gets dark, I'm going in. Okay, let's go.'

'So how are we going to distract the guards?' Macy asked as they set off.

Eddie looked at her, an idea forming. Having showered away the sweat and grime of her jungle ordeal, she was back to her usual state of youthful beauty – though her clothes still bore the dirty scars. 'We'll have to get you a new outfit.'

She grinned. 'I'm okay with that.'

'Something that shows off your body.'

The smile broadened. 'Still with you.'

'And some running shoes.'

'Aw.'

'And an iPod.'

'Cool!'

Mac sighed. 'And I suppose all this is going on my card?'

'If we stop Callas and Stikes, I'm sure *el Presidente*'ll pay you back.' Eddie pointed down the street. 'Okay. To the mall!'

In the tropics daylight ends quickly, the twilight sky over Caracas soon fading to black. By the time the last glow had vanished, Eddie was in the garden of the mansion next to the Clubhouse, perched in a tree near the wall separating the two properties. The house behind him was dark; he didn't know if its occupants were simply away for the evening or if the military takeover of their neighbour's home had encouraged them to take a vacation, but either way it simplified matters.

From his position, he had a good view of the brightly lit Clubhouse. It was a big building, with multiple points of entry. More important, none seemed to be guarded. Soldiers were patrolling the grounds in ones and twos, but they had an indefinable air of excitement – or anticipation – about them.

Their minds were on something other than their immediate duties.

The coup? Possibly. Callas hadn't returned, and there had been no sign of Stikes or anyone who might be working for him, just Venezuelan troops. Was tonight the night?

But for now, his priority was finding Nina and Kit. He regarded the house. A swimming pool glowed an unreal cyan, illuminated by underwater lights. A large flatscreen TV near the poolside was showing a baseball game, an excited commentator offering a blow by blow account in Spanish, but nobody was watching it. Handy; the noise would help cover his entry into the grounds.

He looked at his watch, then towards the road. Any minute now . . .

Movement in the grounds: a soldier strolling from the mansion's rear to its front. Shit! He was staying on the wide lawn rather than venturing into the bushes and flower beds near the wall, but would still be close enough to catch any unexpected movement in his peripheral vision. Eddie had replaced his filthy clothes at the mall with a black T-shirt and jeans, but they would hardly render him invisible – there was more than enough light coming from the pool for him to be spotted if he wasn't careful.

He willed the man to move faster, but instead the Venezuelan slowed, taking out a pack of cigarettes and lighting one . . . then stopping entirely for his first drag. 'For fuck's sake!' Eddie muttered.

Another look at the street—

He saw Macy jogging towards the gates. She had gone the other way ten minutes earlier, her low-cut, tight and very bright pink and black running outfit ensuring that she caught the attention of the two young men guarding the entrance. Her smile and wave as she passed had hopefully cemented her in their memories. Now she was returning, the inference being that she lived nearby and was on her way home.

The gate guards definitely remembered her, turning to watch her approach. That was part of the distraction Eddie needed – but now this arsehole with his cigarette was right where he wanted to go. And there wasn't enough time for him to climb a different tree – a pair of headlights had just come into view behind Macy . . .

The soldier remained still, savouring the smoke as if he had stepped out of a 1950s cigarette advert. Eddie glared at him, trying to induce instant and terminal lung cancer, but to no avail.

Macy waved at the soldiers again, then jogged across the street towards them. The headlights drew closer. White earbuds in, she didn't seem to hear the oncoming vehicle. One of the soldiers suddenly realised the danger and shouted a warning. Macy turned—

The car skidded to a stop. Not quickly enough. The screech of tyres was punctuated by a flat metallic bang as she rolled up on to the bonnet, then slid off to land heavily on the road.

Eddie winced. Even though he had been expecting it, and both Mac, driving, and Macy knew what they were supposed to be doing, it still sounded like a bigger impact than they had planned.

The smoking soldier heard the commotion. He saw the guards hurrying into the street, and ran to investigate.

Eddie looked back at the 'accident'. Mac was out of the car, hands raised in an expression of shock. Unsurprisingly, though the collision had been entirely the pedestrian's fault, the soldiers were siding with the attractive young victim rather than the elderly motorist, one of them shouting angrily at the

Scot. Even as he advanced along the stout branch, Eddie couldn't help but be worried – if they decided that Mac was to blame and called the police, or, worse, took matters into their own hands . . .

Macy was back on her feet. She blocked the Venezuelans from reaching Mac, apparently telling them she was okay. This seemed to mollify the soldiers, who began competing with each other over who would help her.

The noise had attracted a couple of other men from the mansion's far side, but Eddie was only concerned with the smoker. Seeing that everything was under control, he stopped – far enough away to give Eddie his chance.

The branch reached almost to the wall, having been trimmed to a stump to avoid encroaching on the neighbouring property. He jumped off it, briefly landing with both feet on the top of the wall, then dropped down on the other side and flattened himself behind an ornamental shrub. He peered through the leaves, hunting for the soldier . . .

The man had half turned to look back.

Some noise, the scuff of the Englishman's boots on the wall or the thump of his landing, had caught his attention. Eddie froze. The soldier's expression changed from confusion to a curious frown.

He started towards the bushes.

Eddie reached into his jacket. Getting hold of a gun in a country where he had no contacts had been impossible; the only weapon he had been able to obtain was a small survival knife from a sporting goods store in the mall. And unless the soldier obligingly walked right up to him without looking down, he would be spotted long before he could use it . . .

Cheers came from the television by the pool as the batter struck a home run. The soldier looked over to it – and then turned away, clearly assuming the noise he had heard had come from the TV.

Eddie returned the blade to his pocket and cautiously raised his head. The soldier was still retreating; at the gate, he saw Mac ushering Macy to his car. She was limping, but seemed otherwise unharmed. The soldiers reluctantly watched her go, then returned to their posts as the car drove away.

He was clear.

A quick check of the area. About sixty feet of lawn to cross to the pool, then round it to one of the entrances. Glass double doors were open at the poolside, but a single door further along the wall seemed the better choice, giving him more cover—

A distant boom, like thunder.

Only it wasn't thunder. Eddie had heard enough explosions to know the difference. Another, sharper *crump*, then the unmistakable rattle of machine gun fire.

And more, from a different direction. And a third harsh clatter, elsewhere again.

The coup had started.

Callas had put his forces into place throughout the city, waiting for the right moment – and that moment had come. A coordinated attack, aimed at taking control of the most vital strategic locations: key roads and intersections, radio and TV stations, centres of operation for the pro-Suarez Bolivarian Militia.

And President Suarez's own residence, the Miraflores palace in the heart of Caracas.

That was what the men at the Clubhouse had been waiting for. Eddie ducked again as soldiers rushed from the building, carrying machine guns and ammo boxes, ready to defend the grounds against attack.

Someone shouted orders. Eddie recognised him from Paititi:

Rojas, Callas's right hand. Callas might not be here, but the Clubhouse was obviously a key part of his plans. The place was being fortified, surrounded by a ring of soldiers.

Not just soldiers. The front gates opened, vehicles entering the grounds. Three Tiunas, Venezuelan near-copies of the American army's ubiquitous Humvee, ripped up the pristine lawn as they took up position by the entrance. They were followed by a pair of even larger and far more imposing pieces of military equipment: a brutish V-100 Commando armoured car with a soldier manning the .50-calibre machine gun mounted on its open parapet, and behind it an even bigger V-300, a six-wheeled slab of steel with a 90mm cannon on its tank-like turret. Both hulking machines pulled up outside the mansion.

As if things weren't bad enough, two soldiers moved to the corner of the house – with a clear line of sight over the swimming pool. Eddie now had no way to get inside without being seen.

And no way to leave unseen, either. He was trapped – as civil war erupted on the streets of Caracas.

21

General Salbatore Callas suppressed a smile as he put down the phone. The first reports had come in to Miraflores of an uprising in the city . . . but the one he had just received was very different from those his agents in the Bolivarian Militia were feeding to the palace's senior staff. The first accounts of events President Tito Suarez received would be vague, conflicting, uncertain even who was responsible for the explosions and gunfire across Caracas.

Callas, however, had accurate intelligence. His forces had struck exactly on schedule, and now controlled a long list of important locations. The only major target yet to fall was one of the state-run – and Suarez-supporting – television stations, where the approach of troops had roused a loyalist mob to defend it, but it would soon be taken.

He left his office and marched down a marble-floored hall to the double doors at its end. Two members of the Bolivarian Militia stood guard, eyeing him suspiciously – for the crime of wearing an army uniform rather than militia fatigues, even an old and trusted friend of *el Presidente* was regarded as a potential threat. But they let him pass. Within, Suarez's secretary was fielding phone calls; she waved him to the next set of doors.

Callas knocked once, then entered. The wall behind the large teak desk facing him held three portraits: Simón Bolívar, the nineteenth-century liberator of Venezuela from colonial rule; Hugo Chavez, the previous Venezuelan president who fancied himself as Bolívar's modern-day socialist successor; and, central and largest, the current holder of the office.

The general kept his contempt hidden. Suarez in person was not nearly as impressive as the artwork, his hair thinning and greying, fuller in face and body thanks to the lack of exercise and rich foods that accompanied high office. Callas made a mental note not to fall into the same trap once he occupied this room.

With Suarez was another man in fatigues: Vicente Machado, second-in-command of the militia after the president himself. He was also number two after Suarez on Callas's long list of enemies, a problem to be eliminated as soon as possible. With its head cut off, the militia's body, a semi-trained rabble of peasants and paupers driven by vapid propaganda or the desire to feel important because they were wearing a uniform and carrying a gun, would soon die.

That time was rapidly approaching. But not quite yet. He had to wait for Stikes.

Suarez finally looked away from Machado. 'Salbatore! What's going on? Who is behind this?'

'Unfortunately, I don't have an answer yet,' Callas replied. 'I've had reports of gangs rioting in the *barrios*, attacks on police stations and military personnel. But it's definitely organised – the first incidents all took place simultaneously. Someone is behind it all.'

'The Americans,' said Machado. 'It has to be. They're trying to overthrow the revolution!'

Callas forced himself not to tut sarcastically at the idiot's naïveté – Suarez had appointed him for his loyalty, not his brains. Instead, he took advantage of it. 'They would be the obvious culprits, yes. And,' he put a conspiratorial note into his voice, 'they could have agents anywhere. For an operation this big to begin without our security forces knowing, the CIA must have corrupted people at all levels. The police – even the militia.'

'Or the army,' Machado said. Stupid he might be, but he still had enough cunning and survival instinct to recognise an attempt to discredit him.

Which was exactly what Callas wanted. 'Or the army, yes. We have hundreds of thousands of soldiers – there's no way to know how many have sold their loyalty to the Americans.' He faced Suarez. 'Which is why we have to get you out of Miraflores and to a secure location.'

'No,' said Suarez. 'The people need to see that I am still in control. Not running away and hiding.'

'But that's exactly what President Chavez thought in 2002,' Callas countered, raising a hand towards the portrait of the former leader. 'The plotters in the coup attempt arrested him here in the palace – in this room! He only survived because his enemies overestimated their support among the people. They won't make the same mistake twice. We have to get you to safety. I've already ordered a helicopter gunship to evacuate you.'

'To where?'

'There's an army base at Maracay. It—'

'Not an army base,' Machado interrupted. 'The Bolivarian Militia are responsible for the President's safety. One of *our* facilities.'

'It . . . is your decision,' Callas told Suarez, making a show of seeming conflicted at the idea of deferring to Machado. 'Your safety is my top priority. I will be at your side whatever you choose, of course.'

'The militia base,' said Suarez after a moment. Machado couldn't contain a smug smile. 'But yes, you will come with me, Salbatore. Both of you will. I need you to fight back against these bastards!'

'The helicopter will be here soon,' Callas told him. 'We should go now, before the rebels move on Miraflores.'

'I'll get some men,' said Machado, hurrying into the anteroom.

Suarez stood, gathering up documents. 'Don't worry, Tito,' said Callas reassuringly. 'We've seen days like this before. We'll get through it together.'

Suarez gave him a faint smile. 'I'm glad to have you behind me, Salbatore.' He shoved the documents into a folder and snapped it shut. 'All right. Let's go.'

They left the room, waiting briefly for Machado as he finished issuing orders by telephone. The two militiamen outside the doors fell into step behind the group as they moved through the palace. 'A squad will meet us at the west exit,' Machado reported.

'The helicopter only has eight seats,' said Callas. 'It can take the three of us, plus five of Vicente's men. Everyone else will have to stay.'

'Yes, yes,' Suarez said dismissively, his own well-being now dominating his thoughts. They reached the outer doors, where a gaggle of armed militiamen awaited them. Machado selected five to accompany them to the helicopter, and ordered the rest to defend the building. With the uniformed men flanking them, the high-ranking trio set out across the grounds.

Callas heard echoing cracks of gunfire from the surrounding city, but his attention was fixed on another noise – the rising roar of rotors. The helicopter was approaching. He slowed slightly, falling a couple of steps back so that neither Suarez nor Machado could see what he took from a pocket.

A pair of earplugs. He quickly pushed the soft silicone into his ears, sound dulling as if he were underwater.

A spotlight stabbed down from the sky, darting over the trees before finding the helipad. Callas followed it up to its source. A Hind, descending for a landing. It passed through the lights illuminating the palace. The Venezuelan tricolour stood out proudly on its flank.

The eight men held back as the Hind dropped on to the pad. Its rear hatch slid open . . .

Six figures dressed in black leapt out.

Callas shut his eyes and turned away, clapping his hands over his ears. Even with the plugs in, he knew that what was about to come would be loud—

The new arrivals, faces concealed behind balaclavas, had timed everything perfectly. The first man to emerge had already pulled the pin from a stun grenade, the fuse burning away as he threw it. It exploded in mid-air a second later – at head height right in front of Suarez and his group. The blinding flash and earsplitting detonation hit the unprepared men as solidly as a physical blow, obliterating all senses.

The utter helplessness of their victims didn't encourage mercy from the attackers. Two men opened fire with suppressed, laser-sighted M4 assault rifles, short, controlled bursts slicing down four of the militiamen. The other survived only by chance, having tripped in his dizzied state and fallen into some bushes.

Callas lowered his hands. Even prepared and protected, the stun grenade's blast had still been painful. But he ignored his ringing ears, instead drawing his gun.

Suarez staggered, groping blindly. Machado had managed to

bring an arm up in time to block the flash, but was still reeling. He opened his eyes, and saw the general standing contemptuously before him—

A single shot from Callas's pistol hit him in the forehead, blowing out the back of his skull in a gruesome spray.

One of the men in black ran to Callas. Though he was holding an M4, the gleam of his holstered pistol instantly told the general who he was: Stikes. 'Are you all right?'

'Yes, I think so,' Callas replied, pulling out the earplugs.

'Good. Get Suarez aboard. We'll cover you.'

Callas grabbed Suarez by the collar and hustled him along.

Even though the mercenaries' rifles were silenced, the grenade and Callas's gunshot had attracted attention. More militia were running towards the helipad. The surviving member of the presidential escort pushed himself to his knees, feeling for his gun—

One of the mercs, a muscular colossus, grabbed him by both ankles and yanked him off the ground as easily as if he were a doll. The giant spun like a hammer-thrower, whirling the man round – and letting go. The Venezuelan flew screaming over the bushes, slamming down like a human bomb on the leading militiamen and knocking them flat.

Stikes's other men used more lethal weapons. The flat thuds of suppressed fire mingled with screams as they picked off other targets.

Callas pushed Suarez to the Hind's hatch. The President was starting to recover from the blast, and resisted. Callas jammed his pistol's still hot muzzle under his chin and forced him inside.

Shouts from above. Two militiamen ran along one of the palace's rooftop balconies, carrying a heavy machine gun. Stikes fired at them, but his shots cracked against the thick stonework as they ducked. One man slammed the gun's bipod down on the parapet, his companion already loading a belt of ammunition as they prepared to fire on the mercenaries—

A black-clad man fired first. Not a rifle, but an RPG-7 rocket launcher. The warhead streaked up at the roof, blasting the parapet and the men behind it to pieces. Chunks of masonry rained down on people running out of the building.

'Let's go!' shouted Stikes. The group retreated to the helicopter. He fired another burst, sending a man flailing to the ground, and followed.

He jumped into the cabin, slamming the hatch. Gurov, piloting from the rearmost of the two bulbous cockpits, increased power. The Hind lurched into the air.

A piercing clang echoed through the cabin: a bullet hit. Stikes hurriedly strapped himself into the seat beside Suarez, Callas holding the President at gunpoint on the other side. The helicopter was heavily armoured, but not invulnerable. He pulled off his balaclava and donned a headset. 'Okay!' he yelled. 'Hose them down!'

In the forward cockpit, the Hind's gunner – an Armenian, Krikorian – grinned and pulled a trigger.

The helicopter's nose cannon pivoted, unleashing a fearsome stream of fire from its four rapidly spinning barrels. Through the infrared display in the gunner's helmet visor, the Miraflores palace was transformed almost into a video game, human beings a hot white against the greys and blacks of the grounds. All he had to do was look at each target, sweeping a cursor over them – and the human shapes exploded into glowing chunks as the blazing Gatling gun followed his movements. Bullets clonked off the cockpit canopy and hull, but the Hind's armour shrugged off the 7.62mm rounds spitting from the militia's AK-103s. The men firing at him were picked out by brighter flashes from their weapons; like a modern-day Gorgon, he killed them with a glance.

The Hind wheeled over the palace. Men on the upper balconies opened fire, only to be cut to pieces by more storms of gunfire. The helicopter kept rising, turning southeast and sweeping past skyscrapers.

'What's our status?' Stikes said into the headset. 'Did we take any damage?'

'No, we're okay,' Gurov replied. 'Did you get him?'

'We got him. How long until we land?'

'We can be there in – yah!' He recovered from his surprise and muttered in Russian before returning to English. 'We have company. Another *krokodil*.'

Crocodile was the Russian nickname for the Hind. 'Where?' Stikes demanded.

'Left side, ten o'clock.'

Stikes loosened his seatbelt so he could look through the hatch window. Formation lights blinked in the darkness over Caracas – the other Hind.

Catching part of Stikes's conversation with the pilot, Callas put on headphones. Still pressing his gun against his president's chest, he peered through the window. 'Do they know we have Suarez aboard?'

'Yes,' said Stikes calmly. 'Otherwise they would have shot at us by now.'

Gurov's voice came over the headsets. 'They are on the radio . . . they are ordering us to fly ahead of them to a military base, where we will surrender and turn over Suarez.'

'Will we now?' Stikes said. He pulled his straps tight once more, giving his client a sly smile. 'General, you've spent a lot on this helicopter. I think it's time you got your money's worth.'

Callas's own smile was more predatory. 'Yes. Do it.'

'Gurov, Krikorian,' the Englishman said into his headset. 'Our friends out there – show them the quickest way to the ground.'

'Okay, roger!' replied Krikorian, excitement clear in his voice.

The Hind banked towards the Venezuelan gunship. Gurov spoke again. 'They are back on the radio – this is our last warning. If we do not turn—'

'I don't waste time with warnings,' Stikes snapped. 'Krikorian, take them down. Now!'

Krikorian switched weapon modes, activating the Russian 'Igla' missile mounted on one of the Hind's wing pylons. The surface-to-air weapon had not been designed for an aerial launch, but the mercenary ground crew had wired it to the helicopter's systems. A warbling tone in his headphones told him that the improvised connection was working – the missile had found a heat source in the night sky.

The other Hind was almost directly ahead, closing fast.

He pulled the trigger.

The Igla shot from its launch tube, searing past the cockpit on a pencil of orange flame. The heavy, clumsy Venezuelan chopper had no time to dodge—

The missile hit the Hind practically head-on at supersonic speed. The explosion blasted apart the rear cockpit, instantly killing the pilot. Shrapnel ripped through the twin engines' air intakes, shattering compressor blades and smashing turbines.

Power lost, the crippled Hind nevertheless hung in the air, supported by its main rotor as it continued to auto-rotate . . . then its great weight dragged it downwards, spinning out of control to explode on top of an apartment building.

'Well?' said Stikes impatiently. 'Did you get it?'

'We got it,' Krikorian reported with glee.

'Good. Gurov, get us back to the Clubhouse.' He leaned back with a satisfied expression as the Hind resumed its course to Valle Arriba.

22

L ying behind the bushes, Eddie watched the soldiers in the Clubhouse's grounds with rising frustration and concern. The sounds of fighting from the city were growing in intensity, so Callas's coup attempt was well under way – and seemed to be succeeding. He could see Rojas listening to messages over a walkie-talkie, and from his satisfied body language it appeared they were what he wanted to hear.

Another squawk and gabble of an incoming message. Rojas issued orders, some of his men hurrying round the mansion. Eddie ducked, but they went past, heading for the helipad. Rojas followed at a more relaxed pace, talking in Spanish over the radio. Eddie couldn't be certain, but the voice on the other end sounded like Callas. The Venezuelan paused to check the breaking news on the TV by the pool, then muted the sound and carried on after the troops.

Eddie stayed low, watching the soldiers as they reached the helipad, awaiting an arrival. Callas himself, most likely, returning to his command post.

His guess was soon proved correct. The thunder of a helicopter overpowered the chatter of gunfire in the city below, the aircraft sweeping in over the golf course. A Hind – the one Eddie had seen at the base near Paititi, repainted in Venezuelan colours. So why had Callas needed it when he had control over the country's own gunships?

The answer came once the helicopter settled on the pad. A man dressed in black combat gear emerged. Blond hair, a Jericho glinting at his waist. Stikes. Of course – Callas needed a gunship crew on whom he could rely one hundred per cent. Even men who thought they were committed to the cause might baulk at opening fire on their own people. So what had they been doing?

More mercenaries emerged, wearing balaclavas – then Callas himself, pushing another man at gunpoint.

Eddie recognised him. Tito Suarez.

'Jesus . . .' he whispered, impressed despite himself at the sheer balls of the plan. They had kidnapped the President, probably right out of Miraflores. And by using Stikes and his mercenaries, Callas had eliminated the risk of any soldiers switching their allegiance when challenged face to face by their leader, as had happened with the capture of Hugo Chavez over a decade earlier.

Stikes donned his beret and spoke to his masked men, who grabbed the struggling Suarez and hauled him into the mansion. Rojas delivered a report to his superior. Callas nodded, then issued orders. Rojas saluted and relayed them over his radio, then turned and jogged back round the building. The soldiers followed him.

The two men guarding the corner of the house joined the group as it passed. Eddie's heart jumped. They were redeploying – with Suarez's capture, Callas probably wanted to secure a wider perimeter around the Clubhouse. This could be his chance to get inside . . .

He watched and waited. The main gates opened and a Tiuna drove out on to the street, followed by a squad of soldiers. One of the armoured cars started up with a diesel roar: the six-wheeled V-300, carving up the grass as it made a wide turn and left the grounds.

Voices nearby. He looked round, seeing Callas and Stikes walking past the swimming pool. The general paused to lift the lid off a dish on a catering trolley near the TV and pop a piece of food into his mouth. 'You want some?' he asked Stikes.

The mercenary shook his head. 'Are you sure you want to set up roadblocks so far out from the Clubhouse? If they were nearer, it would be a tighter defence.'

'I want to cover the intersections,' Callas replied. 'Besides, now that the coup is under way, I no longer care about upsetting the neighbours.' He replaced the lid, then continued with Stikes into the house.

Eddie checked his surroundings. The soldiers at the rear of the Clubhouse were still looking outwards across the golf course, while those at its front were grouped round the vehicles near the main gate. There was a chance someone might glance back at the side of the house, but he would have to take the risk . . .

He broke from cover and ran across the lawn.

No shouts of alarm. He hadn't been seen – yet. The single door was almost directly ahead, but he couldn't just charge in – he had to make sure the room beyond was empty. At the gate, a soldier looked round—

And saw nothing. The headlights of the parked Tiunas had wrecked his night vision.

Eddie reached cover and pressed against the wall. He drew his knife and went to the door.

There was light inside, but only dim. He peered through the window. A darkened kitchen, the illumination coming through a half-open door at the far end. He tried the handle. It turned. He slipped inside.

Where would the prisoners be kept? A cellar, most likely.

He crept to a closed door in the hope that it led to a lower floor, but instead found a lounge with French windows opening on to the poolside. 'Arse,' Eddie muttered, realising he would have to search the whole house. He went to the other door, seeing a hallway beyond.

He was about to go through when he heard boots clumping on the polished floor. He pulled back, watching through the crack as someone approached. One of the mercenaries . . .

Eddie felt a shock of recognition. Kevin Baine. He hadn't seen the former SAS man for over nine years. Stikes had obviously remembered him, though – and recruited him.

Baine's steps faded as he rounded a corner. Eddie entered the hall, heading in the opposite direction. An open door led back into the lounge, so he ignored it, checking that the passage round a corner was empty before proceeding.

A narrow staircase went upwards. A closed door was at its foot. Cellar steps? He reached for the handle—

The door opened.

Eddie found himself face to face – or rather, face to chest – with a huge black-clad man. Another mercenary, a holstered pistol and a stun grenade on his combat webbing. He looked up. Surprised eyes stared down at him through the holes in the balaclava.

He drew back the knife, about to stab the merc in the stomach—

The eyes widened in recognition. 'Little man!' said a delighted Russian voice.

Eddie arrested his strike, jerking the blade out of sight behind his back. He knew the voice, but couldn't believe he was hearing it. 'Maximov?'

The giant peeled off the balaclava to reveal a bearded, heavily scarred face, the worst injury a gnarled knot of tissue at the centre of his forehead. 'What are you doing here?' said Oleg Maximov, grinning at the Englishman.

It was two years since Eddie had last met the huge ex-Spetsnaz soldier, first as a foe, later an uneasy ally during the search for Excalibur. He had then been in the service of a Russian billionaire; that he was here now suggested he had looked further afield for employment. 'Didn't Stikes tell you I was coming?' he said, desperately improvising.

Maximov looked puzzled. 'No. When did you join company?'

He feigned nonchalance. 'Oh, I've known Stikes for years – we were in the SAS together. I had sort of an open invitation to join 3S, but didn't get the chance to take it up until recently. I've been busy with the IHA – plus getting married, stuff like that.'

'You finally picked a day? Congratulations!' Maximov slammed a meaty hand down on Eddie's shoulder. 'To the pretty redhead, *da*? Hey, I saw her on TV. In the Sphinx. What is she doing now?'

So Maximov didn't know that Nina was here? 'Archaeological stuff. Kind of boring, which is why I decided to see if old Stikesy had anything exciting on the cards. Got to admit, regime change in Venezuela was more than I was expecting!'

'Me too,' said Maximov, nodding. 'But job is job, money is money, hey?'

'I know what you mean. Oh,' he added, sensing an opportunity, 'can you come with me to talk to President Suarez? That's why Stikes wanted me here – I've, er, met him before, so I might be able to get him to tell me the information Callas needs.'

He knew that the more he elaborated on his story, the more danger there was of falling into a hole – but he also knew that Maximov had not been hired for his brainpower. The name-dropping seemed to have convinced the Russian that he was here legitimately. 'Okay,' said the big man, nodding.

'So,' Eddie said, stepping back and ushering him into the hallway, 'what've you been doing since the business with Jack Mitchell?'

'Mitchell?' Maximov growled as he headed back the way Eddie had come. 'That little shit, I should have crushed him. What happen to him, anyway?'

'He's dead. Very, very dead. Stabbed, electrocuted, drowned, in that order.'

'Ha! Good. I work a lot in Africa recently. Always little wars, *da*?'

'Do you know Strutter?' Eddie asked, gambling that the small world of the mercenary might provide common ground – and a way to keep Maximov distracted.

'Strutter, yeah! A *zhópa*, but I meet Stikes through him, so not all bad.' They passed the kitchen, the Russian going to another door. 'Okay, here.'

Eddie decided not to feel too annoyed that he would have found the stairs to the cellar immediately if he had turned right instead of left to begin with, instead following Maximov down into the mansion's bowels. His new companion could have his uses, even if only as a human shield. He turned the knife in his hand.

Maximov led the way along a white-painted passage, his elbows brushing both walls, and stopped at a door. 'When did you meet Suarez?' he asked as he opened it.

'Year or so back, at some United Nations thing,' Eddie said, taking in the room. Three small cells had been installed, metal bars reaching from floor to ceiling – and each was occupied. Suarez in the middle, Kit to one side . . . and Nina lying on the floor at the other.

There was also a guard, who stood and gave the two men a suspicious look. 'Why are you here?' he asked.

'To talk to him,' said Maximov, pointing at Suarez. Then he saw Nina and reacted in surprise. 'Hey! It's you!' She in turn jumped up in astonishment.

The soldier saw her unexpected reaction. 'What are—'

Eddie stepped behind him and with a quick, deadly motion drove the knife deep into the base of his skull.

The Venezuelan collapsed instantly, the hilt buried in his neck. Eddie grabbed the soldier's AK-103 off his shoulder as he fell and pointed it at Maximov. 'Okay, drop your gun. And the grenade.'

'Little man!' said Maximov, sounding shocked and even hurt by the sudden betrayal. 'What are you doing?'

'Rescuing my wife.' He nodded towards Nina, then Kit. 'And my friend.'

Suarez pushed his face against the bars. '*Y a mi?*' he asked hopefully.

'Nope, sorry, mate,' said Eddie as Maximov reluctantly dropped his weapons to the floor.

'Oh.' Now it was the President's turn to look offended.

'Eddie, we have to rescue him,' Nina insisted. 'And by the way: *Eddie!* Oh my God!' She broke into a huge smile. 'I – I thought you were dead! How did you find us?'

'Long story, and it'll have to wait.' He nudged the soldier's twitching body, jingling his keys. 'Okay, Max – let them out.'

Scowling, Maximov took the keys and unlocked Nina's cell. She rushed out to embrace her husband, but he waved her back. 'Get the gun,' he told her. 'Can't have post-rescue sex until we're actually post-rescue.'

'I wasn't planning on dropping my pants right here in the cells,' she said as she picked up the pistol. Maximov opened the other cells, eyeing a fire alarm on one wall, but a wave of Eddie's gun discouraged him from activating it. 'What about the others? Is Macy okay?'

'Macy's fine – she's waiting for us with Mac.'

'What? Mac's here too?'

'Yeah. I called for some help. Left Osterhagen and Becker at a hospital down south – hopefully Callas's lot didn't find them. Oscar's dead, though. So's Loretta.'

The news muted Nina's joy at being released. Kit collected the stun grenade. 'Eddie, what's happening outside? If they've kidnapped the President, I assume things are not good.'

'We've got a full-blown military coup under way,' Eddie told him, gesturing with the AK for Maximov to enter a cell. He slammed the door behind the furious Russian and locked it, then turned to Suarez. 'Okay, Mr *Presidente* – looks like you're coming with us, so where's the best place for us to head for?'

Suarez stared at him in incomprehension. '*Qué?*'

Eddie looked to the ceiling in dismay. 'Oh, fucking great. He's from Barcelona!'

'It's your accent,' Nina said testily. 'I don't think he's spoken to many Yorkshiremen.' She faced the Venezuelan, talking slowly and clearly. 'Mr President, do you speak English?'

'I speak, ah, ah . . .' He held his thumb and forefinger a short distance apart. 'A little, *sí?*'

'Okay, we're going to get you out of here – where should we go?'

He nodded at the door. 'We go, yes, go!'

'No, go *where?*'

'*Qué dijiste?*'

'I said – ugh! Dammit, we need Macy.'

'Let's go and meet her, then,' said Eddie. 'Nina, give Kit the gun – you take that stun grenade, we might need it on the way out. Once we reach the car, Macy can ask el Prez here where to go. If we can meet the militia, he might be able to drum up some support against Callas.' He started for the door.

Nina tugged his sleeve. 'Eddie, wait – we need to get something first.'

He halted and pursed his lips. 'You're going to say we need to pick up those fucking statues, aren't you?'

'Well, ah, yeah . . . but they're not the main thing!' she hastily clarified. 'Callas and Stikes met with a guy called de Quesada—'

'De Quesada?' echoed Suarez with distaste, clearly familiar with the name.

'Yeah, he's a drug lord, and he's helping fund Callas's coup. But de Quesada is blackmailing Callas too. He's got a video recording of something – I don't know what, I didn't see, but it made Callas mad as hell. And the disc is still here!'

'If it was broadcast, if the people of Venezuela had proof that Callas was working with drug lords,' Kit immediately realised, 'it would cripple his support.'

'And Callas was worried that it would force the US to intervene,' Nina added. 'We have to get it.'

Eddie frowned, but Kit was right. It could destroy Callas – if they lived to show it to anyone. 'Where's the disc?'

'A room upstairs, overlooking the golf course.'

The small staircase he had seen was at the rear of the house – and would also hopefully see less foot traffic than the main stairs. 'Okay, I know a way up there. Kit, watch our backs.'

Maximov banged a fist angrily against his cell door, rattling the bars. 'I kill you for this, little man! I thought you were good guy!'

'I am,' Eddie told the giant. 'Nothing personal, Max, but you're on the wrong side. You should find someone better than

Stikes to work for.' The glowering Russian wasn't impressed by his career advice. 'Okay, come on.'

They left the makeshift prison, closing the thick wooden door behind them, and moved quickly to the stairs. Eddie paused at the top. The hall was empty. He went through, the others following.

Clung.

A deep metallic thump from the cellars. And another. 'Shit!' said Eddie, realising what it was. Maximov was trying to use his enormous strength to rip the bars out of the floor.

'Should I go back and stop him?' Kit asked, raising the gun.

Eddie closed the door. The sound dropped, becoming barely audible. 'No time. Let's just get that disc – and hope those bars were cemented in properly!' They hurried to the staircase and went up it.

Nina recognised her surroundings from earlier in the day. 'Through there.'

AK-103 at the ready, Eddie went to the door Nina had pointed out. He shoved it open and darted through. Nobody there.

Nina and the others entered, Eddie remaining on guard at the entrance. 'Callas threw it over here somewhere,' she said, starting to search. Suarez, meanwhile, hurried to the windows and looked out in dismay across the city. The lights of Caracas glistened before him . . . as did the ominous red glows of fires, speckling the vista like sores.

'Nina,' said Kit, from the other side of the room. 'I've found the statues.' He picked up the case.

'Great,' Eddie said impatiently, 'but what about that disc?'

Nina dragged a potted plant away from the wall to find the DVD behind it. 'Here!' she cried, snatching it up. There was a scuff mark and several greasy fingerprints, but it hadn't been chipped or cracked by its flight.

Kit opened the case. 'Put it in here,' he said. Nina found a place where it would be cushioned by the foam without being scratched by the statues, then closed the lid.

'We ready?' Eddie demanded. Nina nodded. 'Good, let's go. Oi, Manuel!' he called to Suarez. '*Vamanos!*'

They hurried out, Suarez complaining in Spanish – though whether about the state of the city or the Englishman's less than respectful attitude the others weren't sure. Eddie led the way back to the stairs. 'Okay,' he said as they made a quick descent, 'we'll go out past the pool and climb over the wall to the next house.' Suarez spoke again; Eddie glanced back at him as he reached the bottom of the stairs – and ran into someone.

'Hey, watch—' said Baine – only to freeze in shock. '*Chase?*'

The collision had knocked Eddie's gun down across his stomach at an awkward angle; not enough space between the two men for him to bring it round and shoot. Instead he whipped it upwards against Baine's chin with a crack of teeth. Before Baine could recover, Eddie swung the AK and hit him in the temple with its stock. He fell against the wall. A boot to his stomach knocked him to the floor.

Eddie was about to finish him off, but Nina and Suarez were already rushing for the lounge. 'Shit, wait!' he hissed, kicking Baine in the head to make sure he stayed down and starting after them—

A loud bang from deep in the building. Metal falling on concrete. Maximov was free.

A moment later, the strident clamour of a bell filled the hallway. He had reached the alarm.

23

Nina and Suarez stopped at the door to the pool. The TV at the poolside showed a view from a building's upper floor of soldiers warily facing off against a crowd of civilians. 'Which way?' Nina asked.

Eddie took the lead. 'Over that wall,' he said, pointing the way as he ran outside – to find three soldiers pounding towards him, less than fifteen feet away.

The Venezuelans were surprised by his sudden appearance. He swept round the AK to cut them down—

The gun fired only once. A soldier tumbled into the pool, trailing blood, but the other two brought up their own Kalashnikovs when they realised his had jammed. The magazine had been jarred loose when he hit Baine, only the already chambered round firing.

Beside him, Nina saw the gunmen – and kicked the catering trolley. Plates flew as it skittered across the poolside and hit the nearer of the soldiers. The impact knocked him back against his partner. Both men toppled into the pool, arms flailing almost comedically.

Eddie wasn't laughing, though. They still had their guns, and a Kalashnikov could fire even after being submerged. He yanked his own rifle's charging handle. A round was wedged in the receiver, refusing to come loose. 'Kit!' he shouted, but Suarez had frozen in the doorway, blocking the Interpol agent inside.

The men surfaced, spluttering angrily. One shook the water from his AK, swinging it towards the group—

Eddie booted the television into the pool.

There was a bang and a sizzling crackle. The soldiers withed and spasmed as power surged through their bodies with heart-stopping force. After a moment they fell still, bobbing in the electric-blue water.

'Don't say it,' Nina warned Eddie.

'What, shoc—'

'I said *don't*.'

'You're no fun.' He finally managed to eject the stuck round, the next slotting into the chamber with a reassuring clack.

Kit shoved past Suarez. 'Eddie, look out!' More soldiers were running from the helipad, alerted by the gunshot.

There was no way they could reach and climb the wall before being shot. 'Come on, round the front!' Eddie shouted, pushing the President in the right direction. 'Nina, give me that grenade!'

Stikes and Callas rushed into the Clubhouse's entrance hall, finding several soldiers milling in confusion – and Maximov, barging them aside as he ran to his employer. 'Boss, boss!' he called over the noise of the alarm. 'The cells – it was Eddie Chase!'

'*What?*' Stikes couldn't conceal his shock. Chase was a resilient little bastard, but the idea that he could not only have survived a plane crash, but then found his way to Caracas and penetrated Callas's headquarters, was almost too much to accept. 'Are you sure?'

'Yes, yes! I know him – he said he knew you!'

'What about Suarez?' Callas demanded.

'He let him go!' Callas's eyes widened in dismay. 'And the others too. He tricked me!'

'Not exactly the hardest thing he's done recently,' Stikes growled. The big Russian was a recent recruit to 3S – and, it seemed, the company could have found better. 'How long ago?'

'Just a minute or two. And boss, they said they had to find some . . . some disc, I don't know what.'

If Callas's eyes had been wide before, they were now practically bugging from their sockets. 'De Quesada's DVD – it's still upstairs! If they get it to a TV station . . .'

Rojas ran in through the front door, shouting urgently in Spanish. 'Shots from the side of the house,' the general reported to Stikes. He started to issue orders—

A piercing bang came from outside, followed by screams.

'Get in!' Eddie yelled, pointing at the armoured car in front of the house. A soldier had been leaning through its open rear hatch, asking others nearby what was happening – until the stun grenade tossed into the middle of the group blasted their senses into oblivion.

Eddie ran for the V-100, unleashing a burst of fire at the guards near the gate to force them into cover behind the parked Tiunas, then blew away a soldier running through the mansion's front door. He hurdled the man who had fallen from the hatch and took up a defensive position as Nina, Suarez and finally Kit piled into the vehicle.

'There's a guy in here!' Nina shouted. The V-100's driver was still in his seat, hands clamped to his ears in agony.

Kit shoved the case containing the statues and DVD under a narrow metal bench. 'I'll get him.' He and Suarez dragged the driver from his seat, then bundled him past Nina and threw him out of the back.

Eddie shot another soldier lurking in the doorway, then hopped into the V-100 and hauled the heavy hatch shut. 'I'll drive,' he said, making his way to the front. He couldn't help noticing that the armoured car had an extremely vulnerable spot; part of its roof was completely open so that a gunner could stand on a step to operate the machine gun. A grenade tossed into the parapet would kill them all.

He would have to make sure nobody got close enough to throw one. 'Hold tight!' he warned as he dropped into the driver's seat. He had driven similar armoured vehicles in the past; the controls would be heavy, but once it got moving it would be almost impossible for anyone – or anything – to stop it.

The engine was already running. He put it into gear and stepped on the gas.

The Commando's acceleration wouldn't break any records, the vehicle weighing over nine tons. Eddie swung it towards the gate, peering through the narrow slot of toughened glass that acted as a windscreen. The men ahead had regrouped, taking up positions behind the Tiunas.

Rifles ready. Flames blossomed ahead as they opened fire.

Nina shrieked and ducked as bullets clanged off the V-100's sloping front and ricocheted into the night. More impacts struck the APC's rear as soldiers poured out of the mansion and joined the attack. The noise was like being trapped in a steel drum during a hailstorm.

Despite this, Eddie almost laughed. 'Takes more than an AK to get through this much armour.'

Kit looked through one of the small rear windows as the V-100 picked up speed. 'I think they have something more!'

Stikes's mercenaries emerged from the Clubhouse, pushing the soldiers aside. Their M4s were, if anything, less powerful than the Venezuelans' AK-103s – but the M203 grenade launchers beneath their barrels were another matter entirely.

Eddie couldn't see what was happening to the rear, the V-100 lacking mirrors, but from Kit's alarm he could make an educated guess. Foot pressed hard on the accelerator, he spun the wheel back and forth. More shots grazed the APC's flanks as it swung from side to side. The armour might be able to withstand a grenade impact, the hull angled to deflect incoming fire away – but he was more worried about the wheels. They could still run on the reinforced tyres even if they were punctured by bullets, but a grenade explosion would destroy them.

Kit dropped flat. 'Incoming!'

Eddie hunched down, Nina and Suarez shielding their heads as an M203 round hit the back of the armoured car – and spun away to explode on the lawn. The hull had done its job.

But they might not get lucky a second time. Eddie yanked the wheel hard over, the Tiunas looming—

Another grenade hit, this time solidly. The explosion rocked the vehicle, shockwaves through the metal causing scabs of paint to spit across the cabin like razor-sharp splinters. Kit cried out as one sliced the back of his head, another catching Suarez's hand. The V-100 rang like a gong.

But it was now too close to the soldiers ahead for the mercenaries to risk firing any more grenades. Eddie raised his head as more bullets banged off the forward armour – then the firing ceased as the Venezuelans realised he wasn't stopping and bolted. 'Hang on!'

The APC was barely doing thirty miles an hour, but with nine tons of weight behind it even the bulky Tiuna might as well have been a matchbox. The V-100's prow bowled the Jeep on to its roof before the armoured vehicle crushed it beneath its huge wheels. The Commando's occupants were thrown about the cabin, Eddie clinging to the steering wheel.

The gate was right ahead—

If the Tiuna had been a matchbox, the gate was made from

toothpicks, bursting apart as the V-100 ploughed through it. Eddie brought the vehicle into a hard turn.

Lights flashed in a driveway, and Mac's rented Fiat came into view. Eddie braked to meet it. 'Open the side hatch, quick! It's Mac and Macy – let 'em in!' He hopped from the seat as Nina and Kit levered the hatch open. 'Get in here!'

'No, you get in here!' Mac yelled back at him.

Holding his bleeding hand, Suarez looked through the rear window – and saw the second Tiuna peel out of the ruined gate. '*Vienen!*'

'Shit!' Nina yelped, glimpsing the approaching 4×4. 'If that means "they're coming", then yeah, they're coming!'

'Get fucking in here, *now!*' Eddie roared, before jumping back into his seat.

By now, both the Fiat's occupants had seen the Tiuna and hurriedly evacuated their vehicle, racing for the open hatch. 'No need to be rude, Eddie,' Mac chided as he pushed Macy inside, then clambered up behind her.

Eddie set off as Kit shut the hatch. 'Sorry, but we're in kind of a rush! Grab on to something—'

A storm of bullets struck hammer-blows against the armoured car's rear, harder and louder than before. The rear window crazed into a spiderweb with a frightening crack.

Nina risked a look through the damaged glass. Rojas was standing in the Tiuna's top hatch, blasting away with a pintle-mounted machine gun. The spray of gunfire hit the Fiat, blowing out its windows and puckering the bodywork with holes, and then the ruptured fuel tank caught fire and exploded, flipping the flaming car on to its side.

Mac looked in chagrin through a porthole. 'There goes my damage deposit.'

'That Hertz,' said Eddie.

More rounds hit the V-100 – lower down. 'He's shooting at the tyres!' Kit warned.

A machine gun had a much greater chance of chewing up the reinforced rubber. 'Mac!' Eddie called, looking over his shoulder. 'There's a fifty-cal up there – get on it.'

Mac peered up through the hole. The parapet was essentially a box of armour plate eighteen inches high around its top. 'It's a little exposed.'

'We'll be more exposed if he knocks out a wheel and chucks in a grenade!'

Mac grimaced and grabbed a handrail to lift himself on to the step. 'I'll see what— *Eddie, look out!*'

Eddie whipped back round – to see the V-300 that had left the Clubhouse earlier blocking the road ahead. Its turret turned to track the APC with its main gun.

Nowhere to go, high walls hemming them in on both sides . . .

He spun the wheel regardless – and drove the V-100 through a wall.

The impact was far more punishing than the collisions with the Tiuna or the gate. Only Mac's grip on the handrail prevented him from being flung against a bulkhead. Behind him, Macy screamed as she was thrown to the floor, Suarez landing on top of her. Smashed brickwork bounced off the APC's prow, fragments clattering into the cabin through the open roof.

The dust cleared, revealing another well-kept lawn around a mansion rivalling the Clubhouse in extravagance. Beyond it, the hillside dropped away to the golf course. 'Mac, are they still following?'

Mac looked cautiously over the parapet. 'That Jeep's coming through the hole in the wall after us.'

'What about the armoured car?'

A crash from outside gave him the answer. 'It made its own hole,' Mac reported – then, with considerably more urgency: 'Gun tracking!'

Another pull on the wheel, Eddie turning the V-100 to present the smallest possible target—

A loud boom from behind, something searing past just inches from the Commando's side – and an explosion blew a hole in the mansion's front wall as the 90mm shell detonated. Eddie swore. His vehicle could withstand bullets, but a direct hit from a gun that size would blow it to pieces.

Beside the house was a garage, room for at least four cars inside. 'Hang on!' he shouted. '*Ramming speed!*'

Everyone scrambled for handholds as the armoured car thundered at the garage—

The metal door folded like cardboard as the V-100 hit it. Eddie caught the briefest glimpse of a bright yellow Ferrari California before the crumpled door rode up over the windscreen, the jolt of a collision telling him that the sports car had been batted aside like a toy. Another, harder impact – then they burst back out into the open, more pieces of brick and wood raining down through the roof.

Eddie swerved, trying to shake off the metal blocking his view. 'Mac, I can't see! What's in front of us?'

Mac pulled himself up to look over the parapet, then hurriedly dropped down again. 'Wall!'

'*Shiiit!*' They were at the edge of the hill above the golf course. Eddie stamped on the brake—

Too late. Another eruption of shattered bricks as the armoured car ploughed through the obstacle, then tipped sharply downwards. The door blocking his view fell away, bushes and trees rushing at him in the V-100's headlights. He yelled, pumping the brake and swinging the heavy vehicle between the trunks.

The Commando crashed back on to level ground in a shower of torn turf. They were on a long fairway, city lights visible in the distance beyond the green. 'Macy!' Eddie shouted. 'Ask el Prez where to go! We've got a DVD that can fuck Callas up – where's the best place to take it?'

Macy shook brick dust from her hair, then pulled herself out from under the Venezuelan president and spoke to him in Spanish. 'He says we should take it to the state TV building,' she told Eddie. 'It's in the same part of town as our hotel.'

'I remember it,' said Eddie. 'What's the quickest way?'

Another rapid discussion in Spanish. 'He says to go north until we get off the golf course and he'll direct us from there.'

The great dark mass of a mountain north of the city was an unmissable landmark. Eddie accelerated along the fairway, swerving to avoid a bunker.

'Eddie, they're coming down the hill!' Nina shouted.

Mac hopped back up into the parapet. 'Two Jeeps!' The Tiuna that had departed earlier had caught up with Rojas's vehicle, both 4×4s slithering on to the fairway in pursuit.

'What about the armour?' Eddie demanded.

'Still at the top of the hill – *shit!* Incoming!' He dropped back into the cabin, bracing himself as Eddie swerved.

The V-300's 90mm gun roared again.

Even though it only scored a glancing impact, the shell still delivered a punishing blow. The V-100 lurched violently, the force of the explosion almost smashing the suspension – had it been an unyielding road beneath the wheels rather than soft earth, it would have been crippled.

It still took damage, though. The hull buckled, rear windows shattering and the aft hatch bursting open, and shockwaves through the armour causing more than mere paint chips to spall away.

Coin-sized shards of shrapnel clanged through the cabin, one stabbing metal splinters into Nina's shoulder as it shattered against the cabin wall, another punching a hole through the shin of Mac's prosthetic leg.

A third hit Suarez.

The President screamed as the chunk of metal ripped a bloody inch-wide gash from his left forearm. Macy shrieked. 'Keep hold of it!' Nina ordered over her own pain. 'Stop it from bleeding.' With deep reluctance, Macy gripped the wound, blood oozing around her fingers.

Eddie regained control, looking back to check on the condition of his passengers – and his vehicle. A glance told him that everyone was still alive, but of more immediate concern was the rear hatch. It had opened about a foot before the deformation of the hull jammed it; more than enough for their pursuers to spray bullets into the cabin if they found the right firing angle.

Which they were trying to do. Rojas's machine gun chattered again, rounds clonking off the armour.

'Mac!' Eddie yelled. 'Get on that fifty and take out those fucking Jeeps!'

'You know, my retirement's been more dangerous than my career thanks to you!' the Scot snapped as he climbed into the parapet once more. The .50-cal was mounted on a semicircular track running around one side of the opening; he pulled back a spring-loaded pin to free it, then slid it to the rear of the armoured pulpit. A round spanged off the protective plating; Mac ducked, but it was just a stray, Rojas concentrating his fire on the vulnerable hatch.

He looked over the top. The Tiunas were practically side by side, gaining fast. Further back, he saw the V-300's lights as it rolled down the slope.

Rojas released another burst, and Mac saw a man in the top hatch of the second 4×4 about to join in the attack. Both Tiunas were angling across the fairway, trying to shoot through the open door—

Mac swung the machine gun round and opened fire.

The flash and recoil from the thudding .50-cal made it almost impossible for him to aim accurately, but with this amount of firepower even a single hit would be horribly destructive – and he scored several as he hosed the Tiunas with thumb-sized bullets. Rojas had seen him aim the weapon, and yelled for his driver to brake and duck behind the other vehicle, which took the onslaught's full force.

Rounds smashed through the engine block, meaning the Tiuna's pursuit was already over, but another bullet punching through the windscreen, the driver's chest, his seat, the leg of the standing soldier, *his* seat and the fuel tank hammered the fact home in no uncertain manner. The 4×4 slewed off course, then plunged nose first into a bunker and exploded, sending blazing wreckage cartwheeling down to the next tee.

'That'll affect his handicap!' Mac cried, hauling the gun towards his other target.

Rojas fired first. Mac ducked, a bullet singeing his grey hair. More rounds struck the armour, knocking dents into it with piercing clangs. The Scot fired blindly, but this time without success – and if he raised his head to find Rojas, he would get it blown off.

'Slight problem,' he told Eddie as he bent back down into the cabin.

'Only one?' Nina hooted.

'Nope, more than that.' Eddie saw the green coming up fast. Beyond the circle of perfectly manicured turf were trees – then buildings. 'We're out of course!'

The V-100 sliced across the green, bounding over the rougher ground beyond as it ripped up bushes. More shots hammered against the rear hatch. A wooden fence disintegrated into splinters, and the APC was in a garden behind a house. There was a driveway down one side of the building; Eddie swerved for it, barging a Mercedes aside before bringing the APC squealing on to a residential street.

Kit looked back at the sound of another collision. The Tiuna shoved past the crumpled Mercedes and skidded after them.

Quickly gaining. On a paved road, it could reach its top speed, which was considerably higher than that of the vehicle it was chasing. Rojas aimed his gun at the damaged hatch. 'Eddie, he's right on us,' the Indian warned.

No way to outrun or evade. Instead, Eddie braked hard. The V-100 screeched to a standstill. The Tiuna's driver was forced to swerve past it.

Eddie saw the vehicle overtake, Rojas clinging to the machine gun to avoid being thrown off. 'Mac, now! Get him!'

Mac tried to slide the .50-cal back to its original position, and found that the pin locking the gun in place had stuck. He turned the weapon on its mount, but it only had a hundred and eighty degree firing arc. He couldn't bring it to bear.

The Tiuna made a shrieking handbrake turn to point back at the stationary V-100. Rojas righted himself and opened fire once more.

Mac hurriedly retreated into the cabin. 'I can't bring it round, it's jammed!'

'Eddie, that tank's back!' Nina gasped. The V-300 crashed out of a driveway, scattering shrubs and garbage cans.

Eddie made a split-second decision and shoved the V-100 back into gear, putting his foot to the floor. Rojas aimed at the armoured car's slit-like windscreen. More rounds thunked off the forward armour – and the toughened glass began to craze.

The crazing became cracks, cracks spreading and widening—

Eddie ducked as the pane blew apart, glass chunks slashing at his face. Everyone dropped as low as they could as the gunfire continued.

It suddenly wavered, the stream of bullets sweeping across the V-100's front—

The Tiuna's driver had remembered what had happened to its sister vehicle at the Clubhouse when confronted by a charging Commando and set off again, jolting Rojas. Eddie popped his head up. The 4×4 was coming at him, trying to swing past on one side.

He turned hard—

The two vehicles hit head on at a closing speed of over sixty miles an hour. The Tiuna took the brunt of the collision, the vastly heavier V-100 flipping it up over its wedge-shaped prow to smash down, inverted, on the still moving APC's roof. The .50-cal was crushed, its severed ammo belt whipping down into the cabin like a brass snake.

Something else had come through the hole. Rojas. He hung upside down from the wrecked Tiuna's top hatch, by some fluke having landed squarely on top of the open parapet. Dazed, he tried to wriggle free – then his eyes snapped into shocked focus as he realised he was looking directly at Suarez.

The wounded President stared back at him. For a moment everyone in the cabin was frozen . . .

Then Rojas yanked his pistol from its holster and pointed it at Suarez's head.

24

E ddie stomped on the brake.

The V-100 screeched to a stop, tossing its occupants forward – and sending the mangled Tiuna sliding off its roof.

Rojas had just enough time to scream before the 4×4 dragged him away with it, breaking his back against the parapet – and slicing off his outstretched arm. The vehicle crashed down in front of the APC, the severed limb landing with a thump before Suarez. The President hesitated, then plucked the gun from its dead fingers.

'Okay, he's disarmed,' said Eddie, restarting the Commando and flattening what remained of the Tiuna and its passengers. 'Nina, where's that tank?'

She searched for the V-300. 'Behind us!' The six-wheeled armoured car was thundering up the street in pursuit.

Eddie threw the APC into a turn on to another road as the V-300 fired, the shell shrieking past and blasting a crater out of the tarmac. Suarez spoke urgently, Macy translating for Eddie. 'He says to take the next left – we've got to cross a bridge.'

Eddie swung the V-100 left at the next junction, the V-300 briefly coming back into view. 'He's still following,' Nina warned.

'Ask him which way once we're over this bridge,' said Eddie, getting directions in return. 'Okay, we – bollocks!' The bridge ahead was blocked, troops manning barriers across it. A small crowd faced them, but the soldiers' weapons deterred them from advancing.

Mac looked into the parapet. 'We've lost the fifty.'

'Just have to go straight through, then.' He examined the controls. 'Does this thing have a horn?'

'I think they know we're coming,' said Mac. The crowd hurriedly parted as the V-100 charged at them. Bottles and bricks thudded off its armoured hide. 'Hrmm. Seems we're not popular.'

'This ought to change their minds.' Eddie aimed the APC directly at the barricade. The soldiers fled as the hulking machine demolished it and swept across the bridge. Cheers rose in its wake.

Suarez spoke, drawing Macy into a brief argument. 'He wants to put his head out the top so everyone can see him,' she complained.

'Might be useful at the right time,' said Mac. 'Not just yet, though.'

Nina looked back. The crowd was running for the bridge, only to scatter before the oncoming V-300. 'It's still coming!'

Eddie turned again to keep out of the larger armoured vehicle's line of fire. But they were still a couple of miles from the TV station – and would almost certainly encounter better-defended roadblocks along the way.

At the Clubhouse, Callas banged an angry fist on a table at another radio report. 'They have crossed the river! This is insane! Why can't we stop them?'

'How far are they from this TV station?' Stikes demanded.

'Less than three kilometres – and we still do not have control of it. The crowd protecting it keeps growing.'

'Then tell your men to fire into the crowd.'

The general's expression went from rage to hesitancy. 'If I don't have popular support, I will not be able to hold on to power – the army is not strong enough to control the entire country by force.' He pointed at a television showing a live broadcast from the government-controlled station – the stand-off between civilians and military outside it. 'That is going out across the country – across the *world*. If my troops are seen slaughtering unarmed civilians, I will lose.'

'So make sure they're not seen doing it,' said Stikes with growing impatience. 'Destroy the transmitter.'

'It's on the roof,' Callas snapped back. 'And before you suggest using tanks to destroy it from the ground, they can't get line of sight on it! There are too many other buildings nearby.'

'Then destroy it from the air . . .' Stikes began, before tailing off.

Callas saw his calculating look. 'What is it?'

'A way to kill two birds with one stone.' He turned to Baine, who had a savage bruise across his jaw and cheek. 'Tell Gurov and Krikorian to get the Hind ready for takeoff!'

Despite Eddie's best efforts, he couldn't shake off the V-300. The heavily armed vehicle was slowly but relentlessly gaining, its more experienced driver extracting every morsel of speed from his vehicle as he chased the smaller APC through Caracas. And the chaos in the city was not helping; Eddie had several times been forced to slow or swerve to avoid fleeing civilians, while the other vehicle ploughed on without a care for collateral damage.

Suarez's directions, relayed through Macy, brought them on to an overpass bridging a wider avenue below. Traffic on the lower road was at a standstill, open doors where drivers had abandoned their vehicles showing that the situation was far worse than Caracas's usual gridlock.

A roadblock ahead. The soldiers had been warned about the stolen APC and were readying weapons . . .

More vehicles emerged from behind buildings.

Very large vehicles.

'Buggeration and fuckery!' Eddie gasped as a pair of T-72 tanks clattered to a stop at the roadblock, chunks of torn asphalt spitting up from their tracks. The Russian behemoths were dated compared to modern Western armour, but there was a reason they had been in continuous production for four decades: they were still tough and deadly. Their turrets rotated, bringing their 125mm main guns to bear on the approaching V-100.

And there was no way to retreat. The V-300 reached the overpass, its own gun swinging towards its target.

A glimpse of red and white on the road below, a familiar logo on the side of a stationary truck . . .

Eddie swerved the V-100 towards the overpass's low wall. 'You're probably getting sick of me saying this, but really, *really* hang on!'

He aimed for the trailer, bracing himself.

The V-100 smashed through the wall and plunged towards the road below.

Everyone screamed—

There was a colossal *crump* of metal as the APC landed on the trailer, nine tons of steel crushing it and blowing its contents apart in an explosion of brown liquid and froth. The truck was a Coca-Cola transporter, the trailer a forty-foot-long advertise-ment for its cargo, tens of thousands of cans stacked to the ceiling. The cans flattened and burst under the V-100's immense weight – but, with so many pallets on top of each other, each layer cushioned the falling vehicle just a little bit more as it dropped.

Even so, the impact when the armoured car hit the floor was still shattering. The trailer's suspension collapsed, and the trailer itself sheared in half behind the prime mover's rear wheels. The unsupported end slammed down, digging a foot-deep gouge in the road surface. On a foaming carpet of squashed red and white aluminium, the V-100 slithered down the makeshift ramp until its wheels touched the avenue.

Dazed, Eddie lifted his head. 'Wow. That actually worked.' He put the APC back into gear. 'Mac, what're those tanks doing?'

Mac peered through the parapet as the V-100 ground out of the wreckage. One of the T-72s appeared on the bridge, its turret tracking them, but its gun couldn't angle down far enough to lock on. 'We're too low for them to shoot.'

'What about the other APC?'

Nina shouted in alarm. 'You're not gonna like this!'

The V-300 burst through the wall after them, intending to use the same trick to soften its landing—

It landed on the back of the crushed trailer with a colossal bang, flipping the front end up like a see-saw. Thousands of Coke cans flew into the air, metal confetti raining down on the tanks above. The first APC's landing had mashed the trailer flat, leaving nothing to absorb the impact of its larger and heavier cousin. All six of the V-300's wheels were ripped from their axles, the turret jolting out of its mount to clang down like an enormous hammer amidst a snowfall of cans.

Eddie looked back at his shaken passengers. 'Well, that's them sorted, so cheer up! Have a Coke and a smile.'

Macy regarded him woozily. 'Only if they have Diet.'

'Eddie, over there,' said Mac, pointing at an exit.

The Englishman made the turn, barging cars out of his path.

The T-72's gun followed it, but still couldn't angle low enough to take a shot. 'Macy, I need directions.'

Suarez gave Macy instructions. She relayed them, then added, 'He says it's less than two kilometres to the TV station.'

Just over a mile. Eddie recognised some of the taller buildings ahead. People were still running through the streets, but there was no immediate sign of the military. They would have to break through the troops attempting to take the television station *and* the civilians and militia defending it, but with Suarez's presence the latter would be easy. They might actually make it!

A basso rumble of thudding blades from above—

The road ahead exploded, sending a car barrelling through a store's windows. Rubble showered the V-100.

Eddie knew the cause. Stikes's Hind.

Stikes squinted into the wind as he looked down from the gunship's open hatch. The stolen APC had just made a desperate turn to avoid the craters torn from the asphalt by the Hind's rockets. Krikorian fired again, another two S-8 missiles streaking from their pod on the stub wing, but these missed by a wider margin, a van blowing apart in a sheet of flame. Panicked people scattered.

'Did you get them?' demanded Callas, strapped firmly into the seat beside him. Baine, Maximov and the other mercenaries craned their necks to watch events below.

Stikes shook his head, shouting 'You're too high!' into his headset. The rockets weren't guided, relying on the gunner's skill to fire them when the pod was pointing directly at the target. 'Go lower and line up properly.'

'We're already too low!' protested Gurov from the cockpit. 'We could hit a power line or a building.'

'I hired you because you claimed to be good enough to avoid that,' Stikes said scathingly. Nevertheless, he saw the Russian's point; they weren't far above the rooftops, and Caracas had enough high-rises to turn the sky into an aerial maze. 'Krikorian, use the cannon,' he ordered instead.

In the forward cockpit, Krikorian grinned and switched weapons, the targeting cursor flashing up in his helmet sights.

He brought it over the fleeing vehicle, then pulled the trigger.

Eddie swerved the V-100 to evade further rocket fire. But none came – maybe the Hind couldn't get a lock amongst all the buildings—

That hope was shattered a moment later, along with a chunk of the Commando's armour, as a stream of 12.7mm cannon fire hammered the vehicle's rear. Nina screamed and dived away from the damaged hatch as metal fragments spat into the cabin. More scabs of steel peppered the APC's occupants, dents appearing in the roof as round after round slammed down.

If any came through the open parapet . . .

Eddie turned sharply at a corner, not going round the building on it, but through it. The V-100 demolished the shop's frontage, scattering shelves and shoes before bursting out of the other side.

Above, Stikes saw the armoured car's destructive shortcut. 'Must be Chase driving,' he said. 'Gurov, follow them.'

Despite the danger, Mac looked up through the parapet to find the new threat. The Hind roared into sight. 'He's coming!'

Eddie sent the V-100 lurching across the street as the gunship opened fire again. Everyone had retreated from the rear hatch, and with good reason: the buckled door juddered violently as

317

more bullets struck it – then with a piercing screech and a spray of sparks it ripped loose and clanged along the road behind them.

The onslaught continued, weaving along the hull towards the open parapet—

A wall dead ahead. Eddie didn't brake – instead he drove the APC straight into it.

Mac ducked as more debris and clouds of plaster dust showered through the open roof. Outside, the orange glow of sodium streetlights was replaced by the off-white of fluorescent tubes as the V-100 ploughed through an office. Desks were crushed under the APC's wheels, a couple of late workers who had stayed inside when the violence started running for cover.

He saw an exterior door in the far wall and aimed for it. Another huge crash, and they were back in the night air, the wind quickly sweeping the whirling dust out through the gaping rear hatch.

Mac irritably tried to brush himself down. 'Another suit ruined. I should start charging you for my expenses.'

'We'll pay for the dry-cleaning,' said Eddie. He recognised a skyscraper ahead as being close to their hotel – and the television station. 'We're not far off. Get ready to run when we get there.'

'*If* we get there,' Nina said. The Hind came back into view, descending towards them. 'The chopper's coming!'

Eddie turned into the first street he came to, the V-100 demolishing a payphone as it rode over the corner of the sidewalk. They were out of the Hind's sight, but that wouldn't last long. Ahead was a wider, tree-lined boulevard – with people running in both directions, some trying to escape whatever was happening further along the avenue, others angrily racing towards it. Some jeered at the armoured car as it rumbled towards them.

More quickly joined in. 'Shit, they're not moving!' Eddie gasped. The crowd was forming a human blockade, trying to stop the military vehicle from reaching the main road. He braked, knowing he could hardly mow them down – but also that the gunship was closing with every second.

He looked at Suarez. 'Macy, tell *el Presidente* to get his arse up in the turret!'

'What?' said Macy, confused.

'If he wants to make a speech to his people, now's the time – they're blocking the way!' Stones clattered off the APC's prow.

'Let's just hope they're all on his side,' said Kit as Macy hurriedly passed on Eddie's instructions.

Still clutching his bloodied arm, Suarez stood. 'I talk to them,' he said.

Over the crowd's shouts and the clonks of thrown stones, Nina heard the Hind's rotor thrum. 'He'd better make it a really short speech!'

A couple more rocks clanged from the parapet as Suarez emerged – then the barrage abruptly stopped. Even dishevelled and covered in dust, he was still one of the most recognisable people in the country. His name quickly spread through the crowd, first in shock and disbelief, then excitement.

Macy translating for the benefit of the armoured car's occupants, Suarez's well-practised orator's voice boomed over the V-100's idling rumble. 'People of Venezuela, my friends! Yes, it is I, your president!' He paused to take in the cheers – and a couple of boos, which were quickly silenced by kicks and punches. 'Earlier tonight, I was kidnapped by traitors and murderers, who want to take power for themselves. But I

319

escaped! I am free, I am here, and I need your help to fight back!'

The rotor noise grew louder. Nina made a frantic 'wind it up' gesture at Macy, who tugged the President's sleeve and hissed at him to talk faster.

Suarez took the hint. 'I need to get to the television station,' he said, pointing down the boulevard, 'to expose these traitors and tell the country that I am safe, and I am! Still! *President!*' Another, louder cheer rose from the crowd. 'First we retake the TV station, then we retake our country!'

A great roar told those in the APC that he had convinced the throng to help. 'He's bloody done it,' said Eddie, almost surprised, as people cleared a path.

'Yeah, but he's left it too late!' Nina cried. The gunship's roar rose as it closed in – and shot overhead, disappearing again behind another building. The pilot had been aiming to intercept the APC further ahead, expecting them still to be moving, and had been caught out by its non-appearance.

'They've lost us!' cried Kit.

'Not for long,' Eddie said grimly as he turned on to the boulevard. Ahead, he saw the television station's jumbotron screen. It showed a view of the street from one of the building's upper windows, which ironically gave him a better idea of what was going on than he could get through the V-100's narrow windows. The TV station was protected by a human ring of protesters and militia, facing off against soldiers backed by numerous Jeeps and Tiunas. The arrival of more people coming to join the studio's defence meant that the soldiers were caught between two hostile groups: an almost certain flashpoint for violence.

And the spark had just arrived. 'Get him back inside before some sniper blows his fucking head off,' he told Macy. Now that Suarez was here, a confrontation was practically inevitable.

Macy pulled the President into the cabin. Mac took his place, searching for the Hind. The helicopter had turned above the boulevard, the image on the big screen changing as the cameraman tracked it. He jumped back down. 'Chopper's coming straight at us!'

The crowd reacted in confusion, not sure what to make of the aircraft. Clarification rapidly came as it fired two rockets, which exploded short of the APC and sent bodies and pieces of bodies spinning into the air. Eddie flinched. 'Jesus!'

The survivors broke away in panic, people trampling each other as they tried to escape the battle. Taking it as a signal, the soldiers opened fire into the crowd. The television camera zoomed in to record the carnage.

The Hind fired again, this time with its gun. Tracer lines seared down at the V-100, blasting off more chunks of armour. Eddie swerved as he accelerated towards the line of troops, the bullet hits stitching a new line down the APC's left flank—

Blam!

A deeper detonation shook the vehicle, the steering wheel jerking in his hands. The armoured car veered to one side. One of the huge tyres had finally succumbed to the assault and blown out. Its reinforced structure was just about holding it together – but every revolution was shredding it, and total failure was inevitable.

'We're gonna crash!' he yelled—

The tyre disintegrated, pitching the wheel down on its steel run-flat insert – which had also been damaged by the gunfire. The hub sheared away from the axle.

Unbalanced, the V-100 toppled heavily on its side. It ground along the road in a huge shower of sparks, narrowly missing a fleeing group of civilians, then continued towards the soldiers.

The troops also ran from the sliding slab of steel – and the fusillade of fire spraying down from the Hind. Then the blaze stopped as the gunship passed overhead. The APC crashed into one of the Tiunas, bowling the military 4×4 over before finally coming to a stop.

For a moment, everything was unnaturally still, people on both sides paralysed by shock. Even the gunfire had ceased. The only thing moving was the Hind, which increased power and gained height to turn for another pass.

Then a figure crawled from the overturned APC. Suarez.

The civilians and militia saw him first, immediately surrounding the armoured car to protect him. The soldiers held their fire, unsure what was going on and waiting for orders.

More people emerged from the wrecked V-100. Kit flopped out of the rear hatch, Macy following Suarez from the parapet. Hands lifted them up; anyone who had helped rescue the President would get the same protection as their leader. Next out of the top hatch was Mac, crawling, one trouser leg dragging limply behind him – the straps securing his artificial leg had broken in the crash, the prosthesis still in the cabin.

He was followed by Eddie. 'Evening,' he said blearily to the two men who picked him up, wincing as he realised his forehead was bleeding from a deep cut. He looked for his friends. All were in similarly beaten states.

Where was Nina?

He shook off the supporting hands and staggered to the APC's mangled rear to find Kit, a palm pressed against his bloodied head. 'Where's Nina?' he asked the Interpol officer.

'I – I thought she was behind me.'

Eddie pushed past him. 'Nina!' he shouted as he looked through the hatch, fearing what he might see . . .

A hand held up the case containing the statues. 'Hold this, will you?'

'Oh, for Christ's sake,' Eddie grumbled as he took it. Nina clambered out, her clothes ripped and smeared with blood from several cuts. 'We're in the middle of a fucking warzone, and you *still* make me carry stuff for you!'

She gave him a pained but genuine smile. 'Love you too, honey.'

'Yeah, I know.' He gave her back the case and pulled her to the throng surrounding Suarez. The Hind was coming back. 'Macy, we've got to get into that TV station *now*.'

Macy passed on the message. Suarez nodded, then exhorted the crowd to come with him, rousing cheers and yells of '*Viva Tito! Viva el Presidente!*' Their leader at their centre, his followers moved en masse towards the building, Nina, Macy and Kit going with him.

'I think I'll stay here,' said Mac, sitting back against the wrecked V-100. He looked morosely at his left leg. 'A hopping man's not much use in a situation like this.'

'You still kicked arse even with only one leg,' Eddie assured him. 'See you soon.'

'Fight to the end, Eddie.'

'Fight to the end.' He shared a look of brotherhood with the older man, then pushed through the mass to join Nina.

'They're out of the car,' Stikes told Callas. 'Krikorian, use the rockets, take out everybody within fifty metres—'

'No!' the general cut in. 'If we do that, it will turn the people against me – even some of my soldiers.'

'In that case,' said the mercenary commander through his teeth, 'we should destroy the TV station, and *then* take out the crowd.'

Callas shook his head. 'No. Land this thing. I will take command of my forces from the ground. We can still capture Suarez – then I can make him turn power over to me legally. On television, in front of the whole world. No one will be able to challenge me.'

With barely contained contempt, Stikes said, 'As you wish. We'll circle to give you fire support if you need it.' Callas nodded impatiently. 'Okay, Gurov, find us a place to touch down.'

Nina looked back in dreadful anticipation, expecting the Hind to attack, and was startled to see it instead moving in for a landing. 'What's he doing?'

'Callas must want to finish us off personally,' Eddie replied. 'Macy!' he shouted. 'Tell him to move faster!'

She did so. Suarez boomed out more orders, and the multitude ahead parted to clear a path to the studio entrance. The big screen above showed the scene from an elevated angle, the movement looking almost like a zip being teasingly unfastened.

The soldiers could see what was happening too. 'Stay close,' Eddie warned Nina as he pushed up behind Suarez.

The Hind landed, rotors still whirling ready for a quick takeoff as Callas jumped out. Soldiers ran to meet him. He jabbed a hand towards the studios, ordering them to move in and take the building – and Suarez.

Alive if possible . . . dead if necessary.

Stikes watched Callas head away with his troops, then turned to Maximov. 'You get out too.'

The giant Russian stared back, bewildered. 'Boss? What do you mean?'

'I mean I don't employ idiots. This is all your fault – if you hadn't let Chase trick you, Suarez wouldn't have escaped. You're fired. Get out.'

'But—'

Baine pointed his M4 at Maximov and flicked off the safety. 'You heard him. On yer bike.'

Maximov's scarred face tightened angrily, but he unfastened his seatbelt and squeezed out of the cabin. '*Zhópa*,' he growled. 'What am I supposed to do now?'

'I think we can rule out a career in rocket science,' said Stikes with a mocking smile. 'Gurov, take us up.'

The Hind left the ground, blasting Maximov with dust. He shook an angry fist at the departing chopper, then looked round. The soldiers nearby regarded him with suspicion. The Russian hesitated, then turned the other way and hurried along the boulevard, disappearing into the approaching crowd.

The group was almost at the entrance. Nina saw the big screen tracking their approach. The shouts of Suarez's name had become almost a ritual chant. The last clump of people in front of the building pushed back to make way for them—

Someone stumbled, almost knocking her over. The case was wrenched from her grip as the man fell. She tried to go back for it, but the crowd swept her along like driftwood. 'Eddie! The case!' she cried, but she had lost sight of it . . .

Kit held it up. He shoved past the fallen man to her. 'I think you dropped this,' he said. 'We don't want to lose the statues after everything we've been through.'

'Or the disc,' she added as he handed the case back to her.

He seemed almost to have forgotten about it. 'Or the disc, yes!'

They reached the doors. They opened, station employees

hurriedly pulling away their makeshift barricades of desks and vending machines. Eddie looked back as they entered. The soldiers were advancing. No shots had been fired . . . yet. But the two opposing forces would meet in seconds.

Clutching the case, Nina pushed through the doors behind Suarez. There were about twenty people in the lobby. 'Can anyone speak English?' she called.

'I can,' said a middle-aged man in a yellow tie. He did a double-take. 'Are you Nina Wilde?'

'Yeah, I am – but never mind that!' She held up the case. 'I've got a DVD in here – there's a recording on it that'll destroy General Callas. You've got to get it on the air as soon as you can!'

Shots cracked outside, people screaming. 'Shut the doors!' Eddie yelled.

Suarez joined Nina, adding his own instructions as she took out the DVD. 'How long will it take you to start broadcasting?' she asked.

'Two minutes, less,' said the man. 'What is on it?'

Nina shrugged helplessly. 'I dunno – just something really bad for Callas.'

He looked uncertain, then took the disc and ran for a set of double doors. Suarez followed as the staff restored the blockade.

There were several large plasma screens in the lobby, all showing the station's current output: a view of the street outside. Eddie joined Nina and watched, seeing a phalanx of soldiers driving through the crowd, clubbing them with their rifle butts. The protesters pushed back, throwing stones and garbage.

More shots. Muzzle flashes flickered across the screens, people falling dead to the ground. Nina gasped and clutched

Eddie's hand. Macy put a hand to her mouth in horror, look-ing away. Some of those nearest the soldiers tried to retreat, but the weight of people behind them left them with nowhere to go. Others, trapped, threw themselves at the troops, armed with nothing more than their fists and feet. They were brutally battered to the ground as other soldiers fired into the mob.

One screen briefly showed a test pattern before switching to a studio. The image jerked about before the camera operator finally fixed on a chair. Someone ran up to it, waving – then Suarez appeared. He took the seat, holding his wounded arm with the blood clearly visible. The camera tipped up as if to frame it out, but Suarez shook his head. The picture tilted back, making sure the injury the President had sustained – and seemingly shaken off – was in plain view. Even in a crisis, Suarez still knew the value of creating an iconic image.

Nina looked at another screen showing the fighting outside. The soldiers were much closer. 'This barricade won't keep them out, will it?'

Eddie shook his head. 'Just hope whatever's on that DVD does the trick.'

Suarez started to speak. All but one of the screens changed to show him, the broadcast going out live to the country. His voice echoed from the loudspeakers outside. Macy gave a running translation, despite her nervous glances at the doors. 'People of Venezuela, today has been a dark day for our country. Traitors have attacked Miraflores, and tried to kill me.' He held up his injured arm. 'A man I thought was a friend, Salbatore Callas, led this revolt . . . funded by criminals and drug lords. I have the proof – and now I will show it to you.'

Suarez then spoke in English. 'Dr Nina Wilde . . . I hope you are right.'

'Oh, great,' said Nina. 'Now if it turns out to be Callas's boudoir tapes, *I* get the blame!'

The president gestured to someone off-camera. The image changed.

Nina recognised the Clubhouse balcony where she had met de Quesada. The drug lord was seated at the very edge of the picture, almost out of shot and distorted by the fisheye effect of a wide-angle lens; the video had been shot on a concealed camera amongst his belongings. Callas, however, was almost dead centre, instantly recognisable in his uniform.

De Quesada had apparently edited the raw footage down to the most incriminating highlights. Again, Macy translated. 'So, just to be perfectly clear about our deal,' she said as de Quesada spoke, 'in return for twenty per cent of the value of my drugs that cross Venezuela, you will give them completely unrestricted passage from the Colombian border to the ports where they are shipping to America and Europe. Yes?'

'Yes, agreed,' said Callas.

'And what about the DEA? If you take power from Suarez—'

'*When* I take power.'

'When you take power,' de Quesada corrected himself, 'you will not let them back into your country?'

Callas smiled. 'I only want the Americans' money, not their policemen.'

A cut, the Colombian leaning forward in his seat. 'And what about Venezuelan drug policy under your rule?' he asked. 'It's not a big market, but it's still worth millions of dollars a year. Since I'm helping you, I don't want to have my . . . subcontractors being arrested.'

'Your dealers will have immunity,' said Callas, though with evident distaste. 'Providing they keep a low profile.'

'They will be very discreet, I assure you.' De Quesada smiled again, then stood. 'So,' he said, extending his right hand, 'we have a deal?'

Callas shook it. 'We have a deal.'

'Thank you.'

The screens went black, then Suarez returned, looking off to one side at a monitor and seeming as astounded by what he had just seen as those in the lobby. But Nina was more interested in the one TV still showing what was happening outside. 'Eddie, look!'

The soldiers were staring up at the big screen beneath the cameraman's vantage point. The protesters were doing the same, everyone's attention captured by the broadcast. The camera zoomed in on the troops. Confusion was clear on their upturned faces . . . quickly turning to shock and outrage.

Eddie watched as the new emotions rippled through Callas's forces. 'This should be interesting . . .'

Callas, standing with a group of his commanders amongst the military vehicles, struggled to conceal his dismay as Suarez returned to the giant screen. Part of him knew that the game was over; the incriminating recording had just been broadcast to the entire country, and more worryingly to his forces outside the television station. While he was using carefully chosen corrupt men to ensure that narcotics traffic across the Orinoco followed his rules, he knew that the vast majority of Venezuela's soldiers despised the drug lords.

But another part refused to give up. He had come so close! And Suarez was inside the building. He could still be captured, some fairy tale about the recording being faked with computer graphics and a vocal impersonator concocted. 'Well?' he snapped. 'What are you waiting for? We'll take the building – I want Suarez to pay for these lies!'

A young captain faced him. 'General, was that – real?'

'Of course it wasn't real!' But Callas could see that doubt had taken root. He decided that sheer volume was the best way to overcome it. 'You idiots! This is exactly what Suarez wants, for you to think I'm in league with drug lords.'

'But that was the Clubhouse, I recognised it.' Other men nearby voiced agreement.

'Never mind that.' He jabbed an angry finger at the studios. 'I want Suarez captured, now!' Nobody moved. *Do what I tell you!*

Other soldiers closed in, faces dark, betrayed. Another officer spoke. 'We want an explanation, general. Did you really make a deal with some Colombian so he could sell drugs to our children?'

'Get back,' Callas warned. The advance continued, more troops surrounding him. 'I'm warning you, do as I say!'

'Get him,' growled the captain.

Several men lunged at Callas. He grabbed for his sidearm, but they pinned his arms behind his back. 'You bastards!' he snarled. 'Suarez will wreck the entire country – I'm its only hope! Everything I do is for the good of Venezuela!'

The captain stood before him, lips tight. 'Let's find out who is telling the truth.' He nodded to the men holding the general. 'Bring him.'

Stikes observed the scene below through binoculars as the Hind continued its orbit. 'Looks as though we're out of pocket on this job, boys,' he said coldly as he watched Callas being frogmarched through the crowd. 'Gurov, get us out of here.'

The gunship changed course, sweeping away into the darkness over the city.

★

'It's Callas!' Nina said as the cameraman zoomed in on the man being forced towards the building. 'They've arrested him!'

'We'll see,' said Eddie, more wary. 'It might be a trap.' But the gunfire had stopped, and the soldiers were retreating to leave a space outside the entrance. The two sides genuinely seemed in a state of uneasy truce.

Suarez hurried into the lobby, followed by the man in the yellow tie, now powering up a professional video camera. The President ordered that the barricades be moved from the doors.

'You sure that's a good idea?' Macy asked him.

'I want to see him face to face,' came the reply. 'And the people have to see that I am still in charge.' Then he addressed the little group of foreign visitors in English. 'I have not said thank you – you saved my life. You saved my country. Thank you.' He added something in Spanish, then strode to the doors as the blockade was cleared.

'What did he say?' asked Kit.

'That we're heroes of the socialist revolution, and we'll all get medals,' Macy told him. She grimaced. 'That's not something I'm gonna be wearing around Miami.'

'I can see it wouldn't be too popular,' said Nina, amused.

Eddie huffed. 'Can't we just get money?'

The station personnel opened the doors. There was a moment of tension as Suarez was revealed to the world outside, standing in plain view of any potential assassin, but it passed. People began to cheer. Suarez waved his hands for silence as he stepped into the open. The cameraman bustled after him to record the scene.

The soldiers brought the struggling Callas to a stop in front of the President. Nina and Eddie watched as the two men faced each other. Suarez spoke first. 'Salbatore. I never thought it would be you who turned against me.'

'That's because you're blind, Tito,' Callas spat. 'You're living in a fantasy world.' Sarcasm twisted his lips. 'All your glorious revolution will do is make *everyone* poor. Our country needs strength, not dreams!'

'The strength of the dictator?'

'Isn't that what we have now?' the general countered.

Suarez drew in a long breath, his expression cold. 'Salbatore Delgado Callas,' he said. 'You are under arrest. Your crime is treason.' He nodded to the soldiers. 'Take him away.'

They turned, pulling Callas with them. He resisted – causing one of the soldiers to stumble.

It was enough for Callas to break one arm free.

He snatched the pistol from the captain's holster and whipped it round at Suarez—

A single gunshot cracked across the plaza. In Suarez's hand was the pistol he had taken from Rojas. The soldiers holding the general jumped back in shock. Callas stared at the bullet wound in his chest, mouth wide in silent pain.

He looked back at Suarez, trying with his last breath to bring up his own gun and pull the trigger . . .

Then he collapsed at his enemy's feet, blood pooling around him.

The coup was over.

25

'So, Mac,' said Eddie, with a twinge of stiff and bruised muscles as he raised a glass of beer, 'how does it feel to be back in action?'

The Scot regarded him through narrowed eyes. 'What, you mean apart from the injuries, the fear, the gunshots and car crashes and explosions, and losing my leg – again?' He thumped the heel of his reattached prosthetic limb on the floor.

'Yeah, apart from all that.'

Mac smiled and raised his own drink. 'Rather good, actually. Cheers!'

'Cheers.' The two men clinked glasses.

Over twenty-four hours had passed since the end of Callas's attempted revolution, and the pair were sitting in the hotel bar. It had been a busy day for all of the group. In addition to receiving medical treatment for their numerous battle scars, the various members had then had to deal with officialdom, both Venezuelan and from their own countries. Eddie and Mac had been summoned to the British embassy, Kit went to make his report at the local Interpol headquarters, and Nina and Macy were whisked away by a cavalcade of black SUVs to deal with the US ambassador. The meeting for the two Brits had been relatively short; as Mac had told Eddie, the United Kingdom's interest in Venezuela was minor, and beyond expressing a regret that Suarez hadn't suffered an injury that would force him to leave office, the MI6 officer debriefing them stuck to obtaining a purely factual account of events.

The debriefing for the two Americans would, Eddie suspected, be more politically charged. 'How long do you reckon they'll keep Nina and Macy, then? Or will they just ship 'em straight off to Guantanamo? They could put them in Sophia's old cell.'

Mac smiled. 'Maybe they'll become the next communist icons. You might see Nina's face on a T-shirt, like Guevara.'

'Oh, she'd love that,' said Eddie with a laugh. 'Now Macy, she'd probably go for it.'

'She might at that.' Mac sat back, his expression turning wistful.

'What is it?'

'At the risk of sounding like a broken record, I wanted to say that, once again, you've done damn good work, Eddie. Whatever we may think of Suarez politically, he's not a murderer like Callas. Stopping Callas from taking power will have saved God knows how many lives. Well done.'

'I learned from the best,' said Eddie. 'And you helped.'

'Well, just a tad.' Mac waved a hand in false modesty. 'But yes, it was reassuring to know that I've still got it. Getting old doesn't mean we become useless.'

'We? You saying *I'm* getting old?' Eddie asked, grinning.

'It happens to us all, in the end. If we're lucky.'

'Speak for yourself. Soon as Nina finds the Fountain of Youth, I'm going to drink out of it from a bucket!'

Kit entered the bar, accompanied, to Eddie's surprise, by Osterhagen. 'Kit, mate! How did it go with Interpol?'

'As well as could be expected,' the Indian replied. 'I had a teleconference with my superiors – they were confused about how an investigation into artefact smuggling turned into the prevention of a coup d'état, but I think I explained everything. As far as I can comprehend how I ended up in this situation myself.'

'You'll get used to it. You've known Nina for eight months and had this kind of mad shit happen to you twice. I've known her for five *years*, so think how much I've been through.' He turned his attention to Osterhagen. 'Doc! How are you?'

'Good, thank you,' said the German.

'What about Ralf? Is he okay?'

'Yes. He is being flown back to Germany and his family.' He sat down beside Eddie. 'I heard you had an eventful night.'

Eddie chuckled. 'You could say that.'

'But you rescued Nina and Mr Jindal safely.' He looked round. 'Where is Nina? I heard she recovered the statues and the khipu. I have a theory about the khipu, and want to discuss it with her.'

'We recovered the statues . . .' Eddie admitted.

'And the khipu?'

He grimaced. 'Er . . . no.'

'What? Then where is it?'

'Probably best to ask Nina that yourself,' Eddie told him, seeing his wife and Macy enter. 'Bloody hell, about time! What kept you?'

Nina shook her head in exasperation. 'From the way the people from the State Department were carrying on, you'd think we personally expropriated the plantations of United Fruit or something. They were one step away from accusing us of being communists because we didn't throw Suarez under a bus when we had the chance.' She squeezed between Osterhagen and Eddie. 'I've had it with debriefings.'

'No you haven't. You've got one more debriefing to come tonight.'

'Huh?' He waggled his eyebrows lasciviously, and after a moment she picked up on his double entendre. 'Oh. Oh!' She blushed a little. 'Well, ah, it's been kind of a long day, and I need to get some sleep, and ah . . .' Macy mouthed *Go on!* at her. 'But we have been through an incredibly intense experience, I suppose, a lot of pent-up tension to get rid of, and, ah, somebody please stop me babbling before I make a total ass of myself?'

Everyone laughed, and Eddie put his arm round Nina and kissed her. Osterhagen gave the couple more room. 'I suppose we can discuss the khipu tomorrow,' he said.

'What about the khipu?' Nina asked.

The German saw Eddie's glare. 'It . . . can wait.'

'Are you sure? I realised something about it at the Clubhouse, how it relates to the map. I think the knots are—'

The glare took on a death-ray intensity. 'No, really, it can wait!' said Osterhagen, throwing up his hands. 'You know, I would like a drink.'

'Me too,' said Macy. 'In fact, I'd like several drinks.'

Eddie gestured towards the bar, catching the attention of a waiter. 'Suarez is paying for everything, so have whatever you want.'

'Seriously?' He nodded; she beamed. 'Awesome! Champagne, then!'

'You want anything?' Eddie asked Nina.

Now it was her turn to look libidinous. 'Yes, but I think we should put it on room service.'

He cackled, standing and pulling her up with him. 'Well,' he said, clapping his hands, 'we'll see you all in the morning!' With that, he scooped the surprised – but excited – Nina up in his arms and carried her from the room.

Mac, amused, held up his glass to the pair as the door swung shut behind them. 'Here's to young love.'

★

Eddie tossed Nina on to their suite's big bed, making her whoop and giggle. 'All right, love,' he said, a grin splitting his face. 'Get your kit off.'

Nina started to pull off her clothes as Eddie jumped on to the bed beside her, unfastening his belt . . . until he saw her bare arm. The red lump of the scorpion's sting was still clearly visible. From its size, he immediately knew it was more than a mere insect bite. He frowned. 'What the hell's that?'

'It's, uh . . . nothing. Don't worry about it,' she replied – partly because she didn't want events redirected from where they had been heading, but mostly because she knew how Eddie would respond.

He wasn't having it, however. 'My arse, nothing.' He examined it more closely. 'That looks like a scorpion sting! Where the fuck did you get that?'

Nina sat up, half clothed. 'The Clubhouse,' she admitted.

'How did you get a scorpion sting at the Clubhouse?'

'They . . .' She still didn't want to reveal the truth, now because of her unwillingness to replay what had happened in her mind. But Eddie's increasingly outraged expression made it clear that he would guess for himself soon enough. 'They used one to torture me, to find out about the statues and El Dorado.'

'They *tortured* you?' Eddie rolled from the bed and paced across the room, furious, before whirling to face her. '*Who* fucking tortured you?'

Her answer, when it came, was in a very small voice. 'Stikes.'

'*Stikes?* Fucking—' He was so apoplectic that for a moment he couldn't speak. Then his voice went unsettlingly cold. 'Wherever he is, whatever he's doing, I'm going to find him.

And I'm going to kill him. I'm going to hunt that bastard down and put a bullet in his face.'

She knew that he meant it. 'Eddie, Eddie, it's okay.' She got off the bed and went to him. 'I'm all right.'

'It's *not* okay. That *fucker*.' He almost spat the word. 'He's going to get what he deserves.'

'Aren't you the one who once said that revenge isn't professional?'

'Depends what it's for. And he's done plenty. Time it stopped.'

'That'd just make you a vigilante. No better than Jerry Rosenthal back in New York.'

He shrugged. 'Nothing wrong with that. He's a sound bloke.'

'Who's going to be found guilty of murder.'

'What, for doing the right thing? Dealing with some rapist scumbag who got off on a technicality?'

'I don't—' Nina forced herself to calm down, lowering her voice and putting her arms round her husband. 'Eddie, I don't want to argue. Not now, not after everything that's happened. I've had enough fighting. I want . . .' She looked into his eyes. 'I want you.' She kissed him. 'Please.'

His face softened, a bit. 'Are you sure you're okay?'

'Yeah. I'm fine, and I just . . . I just want to think about something else tonight.' A twitch at the corner of her mouth quickly broadened into a sly grin. 'I want you to take my mind off everything except one thing.'

Eddie's anger faded, replaced by a lecherous smirk. 'I think I can manage that.' He turned Nina round and gave her backside a gentle slap to direct her back to the bed. 'You were taking your top off, I think.'

'Yeah?' She peered back at him coquettishly over her

shoulder as she undressed. 'And so were you.'

'So I was.' He removed his T-shirt, revealing the bandages and bruises on his body. 'Ow! Bloody hell,' he muttered at a twinge of pain.

'You okay?'

'Yeah, it only hurts when I breathe. Although . . .' He regarded the bed. 'I think I might want to stay on the bottom.'

'Lie down, then,' said Nina. She grinned again. 'I'll do all the work this time. You deserve to relax.'

Eddie laughed as he took off the rest of his clothes, then climbed on to the mattress beside her and shuffled round to lie on his back. He stretched, nestling his head into the plump pillows. 'Oh, God. This is a really bloody comfy bed.'

'Hey!' Nina protested. 'Don't you *dare* fall asleep.'

'Don't worry,' said Eddie with a huge smile. 'That won't happen until after we're done.'

Despite everything she had been through in the previous few days, Nina felt extremely relaxed the following morning.

That said, it proved impossible for her not to feel a resurgence of nerves at a meeting in Interpol's Caracas offices. The events at the Clubhouse were discussed, inevitably bringing back memories of her incarceration and torture by Stikes. Eddie noticed her tensing up and put a reassuring arm round her. But the mercenary was not the primary topic, nor even his late employer.

As well as Kit, several other Interpol officers were attending the meeting, along with a number of Venezuelan officials and a diplomat from the Colombian embassy, who had flown in with a representative of the US Drug Enforcement Administration: a craggy-faced man called Joe Baker. On a wall-mounted screen was a still frame from de Quesada's incriminating DVD, the drug lord frozen as he shook hands with Callas.

'This man is called Francisco de Quesada,' explained Baker, pointing at the screen. 'Colombian drug lord, with an estimated personal fortune of over half a billion dollars. Most of the world's cocaine is made from coca plants grown in Peru; after the Colombian government, with the DEA's help as part of Plan Colombia, cracked down on production in Colombia itself, the drug lords switched to Peru as a manufacturing base. De Quesada controls most of the supply routes from Peru through the Colombian jungle into Venezuela, from where the cocaine is shipped to other countries.'

Eddie had a question. 'If the Colombians cracked down, why don't they just arrest this guy?'

The Colombian official answered, his air of annoyance suggesting this was a political sore point. 'He has the best lawyers money can buy. American lawyers. Every time we have tried to bring de Quesada to trial, they got him off.'

'Ah,' said Nina scathingly. 'An export Uncle Sam can be really proud of.'

Baker jerked a thumb at the screen. 'We got him now, though. That DVD you recovered puts de Quesada square in the frame. He's confessing on camera to high-end involvement in the international narcotics trade. Right now, the Colombians are putting a case together, and this time it doesn't matter how many lawyers he hires or who he tries to pay off or threaten. With evidence like that, he's going down.'

'Won't he just flee the country?'

'He can try, Dr Wilde, he can try. But he'll have one hell of a job even fleeing his *house*. He's got a place on Colombia's Caribbean coast, and we're watching the only road, we got ships offshore, we got satellite surveillance . . . he ain't going anywhere. And as soon as our Colombian friends get all the right names on the dotted lines, we're gonna go in and get him.' He nodded towards one of the Interpol agents, a man Nina and Eddie had met before; Walther Probst, a tactical liaison officer. 'We'll have a SWAT team made up of DEA, Interpol and Colombian forces. We'll bag him.'

'But,' said Kit, standing to address the room, 'he also has the treasures that were stolen from Paititi – the sun disc and the khipu. Considering their enormous value, the Venezuelan government understandably wants them back.'

'I'm sure the Peruvian government'll have its own opinions on who owns them,' said Nina, raising some muted laughter.

'That's for the international courts to decide,' said Kit with a smile, before becoming serious once more. 'But for now, they're worried the treasures could be damaged or destroyed during the raid.'

'We'll aim to minimise that possibility,' said Baker, folding his arms.

'Even so, there's still a risk.' He turned to Nina. 'Which is why President Suarez has personally requested that Dr Wilde, as director of the IHA, oversees their safe recovery.'

Nina, who had been taking a sip of water, coughed it out. 'Wait, what?'

'Nice of him to tell us!' Eddie hooted.

'You won't be going in with the SWAT team,' Probst assured them. 'Once we have secured de Quesada and the house, you will come in to locate and identify the artefacts.'

'You don't need us there for that. Big sun made of solid gold, thing like a hippie belt with loads of strings hanging off it. They should be a piece of piss to spot.'

'All the same, it would be good to have your help,' said Kit.

'Interpol and the IHA started this operation together, so it makes sense for us to see it through to its conclusion.'

Eddie looked dubiously at the image of de Quesada. 'What kind of fight is he likely to put up?'

'His house usually has seven or eight bodyguards,' said Baker, going to a laptop and tapping its keyboard. The freeze-frame was replaced by an aerial photograph of a small island. Shaped somewhat like a kidney bean, it was cut off from the high cliffs of the mainland by a narrow, curving channel. The island was a sea-worn stack, sides almost vertical; its flat top was slightly lower than the nearby land, a bridge sloping down to it across the channel's narrowest point. The island itself, however, was completely dominated by a palatial Spanish-style white house. 'But the bridge is the only way on or off the island, apart from a jetty on the seaward side. So he either stands and fights, which means he'll die, or he runs. And these drug lords ain't big on self-sacrifice. So we think he'll get his men to try to hold us back while he runs for a boat.'

'What if he gets away?' Nina asked.

Baker snorted faintly. 'Doesn't matter if he's got the fastest boat in the world, Dr Wilde – it won't get far with a fifty-calibre hole through its engine block. We'll have snipers on the cliffs. Like I said, he ain't going anywhere.'

Eddie had another question. 'What about his bodyguards? What's their armament?'

'Based on the information we have,' said Probst, 'most likely assault rifles and shotguns, handguns, maybe grenades. But we will have superior numbers, snipers, tear gas – and the advantage of surprise.'

'And when were you planning on doing all this?' Nina demanded.

The Colombian official answered. 'We are getting the warrants signed by judges now. The operation will take place tomorrow.'

'Great,' said Eddie. 'You know, I was hoping for a bit of recovery time. Like a month. In Antigua.'

'You'll still be going to the Caribbean,' Kit pointed out. 'So will you come? Having the IHA there to verify the identity of the stolen artefacts will be very helpful.'

Nina looked at Eddie, who gave her an 'I guess' shrug. 'All right,' she said. 'But we're not going to be involved in the actual SWAT raid, okay? I've had enough of that kind of thing lately to last me a lifetime.'

'We'll take care of all that, Dr Wilde,' said Baker confidently. 'Don't you worry.'

'Famous last words,' Eddie muttered.

After the Interpol meeting Nina and Eddie returned to the hotel, where Osterhagen was waiting.

'I am glad you are back,' he said excitedly, following them to their suite with a wad of papers clutched in his hand. Macy, who had been helping the German with his work, tagged along. 'The khipu – you said you thought the knots are connected to the map at Paititi. I believe you are right. Loretta's camera was recovered from Callas's headquarters, and I have been examining the pictures of the map. I think the khipu is the key to deciphering the markings on it. With the map and the khipu, we can find the lost city!'

'Well, that's a bit of a problem,' said Nina as she entered the suite. 'A Colombian drug lord called de Quesada bought the khipu off Callas. Paid two million dollars for it.'

Osterhagen was horrified. 'What? But – surely he couldn't know its importance?'

'He doesn't,' said Eddie. 'The only reason he bought it was to piss off one of his rivals.'

'Pachac,' Nina added. 'The guy who brought the helicopter to the military base.' The German's grim look told her that he remembered the murderous Peruvian all too well. 'Seems that there's bad blood between them. De Quesada bought the sun disc because he knew it would drive Pachac mad to know that he owned a symbol of the Inca empire. Same with the khipu.'

Osterhagen flopped down glumly on a sofa. 'Then we cannot decipher the map.'

'Not so fast, Doc,' said Eddie. 'That's why we were just at Interpol. They're going to raid his home – partly because he admitted to being a drug smuggler on national TV, but also because Suarez wants those Inca treasures back. I think he's a lot more bothered about getting his hands on two tons of solid gold than the khipu, but they'll be a package deal. We'll get them both.'

' "We"?' said Macy, surprised. 'You're going too?'

'So it seems,' Nina replied with a faint sigh. 'They want someone from the IHA to take charge of the artefacts once they've been secured. Specifically, me.'

'Huh. You're not going to have to get all dressed up in body armour, are you?'

Eddie smirked, giving his wife's body an exaggerated once-over. 'I dunno, some women look really hot in combat gear . . .'

Nina huffed. 'Oh, God. Just when I think I know everything about you, you always come up with some new fetish! But,' she went on, turning back to Osterhagen, 'if everything goes to plan, we'll have the khipu back in our possession soon.'

'Excellent,' he said, relieved. He held up his notes, which included colour printouts of the painted wall. 'I think I have worked out how the knots on the khipu relate to the markings on the map. Once we have the khipu, it should, I hope, be quite straightforward to calculate the location.'

'Can't we just use the statues?' Eddie asked. 'I mean, the other half of the last one should be in El Dorado. You can just use your magic mojo to point to it.'

'Not without knowing where to find another earth energy source,' Nina reminded him. 'We only know about Glastonbury, and we can't triangulate a position without one. Unless you want me to wander around South America holding the statues out in front of me until they start glowing.'

'I suppose. It'd be pretty funny to watch, though. So, we get the khipu back, work out the map, and then . . .'

'And then,' said Nina, 'we find El Dorado.'

26

Colombia

Francisco de Quesada leaned against the door frame, hoping the view would calm his frustration and anger. It wasn't so much the scenery he was admiring – though the impossibly blue sweep of the Caribbean beyond the clifftop edge of his *palacio*'s infinity pool was certainly something to behold – as the occupants of the pool itself, a pair of stunningly beautiful women who had responded to his click of the fingers by entering a passionate, lip-locking embrace, making a show of unfastening each other's bikini tops. There was normally nothing like a pair of twenty-year-old bisexual models to take his mind off life's burdens.

Not today, though. The weight hanging over him was too heavy to ignore. Annoyed, he turned back to his guests, who were studiously attempting to ignore the display in the pool. 'I don't see why you can't make this go away,' he snapped. 'You have done before – why not now?'

His visitors shifted uncomfortably, and not solely because they were wearing formal suits in the humid heat. 'The thing is,' said Corwin Bloom, the bald and doleful chief representative of the American law firm de Quesada had on permanent standby, 'with all the previous charges against you, the evidence could be made out to be tainted and therefore inadmissible, or witnesses, ah . . . dealt with. But on this occasion you were seen by millions of people on national television making a deal with General Callas.'

'That was in Venezuela, not Colombia. Surely that doesn't count as admissible evidence?'

'The DEA submitted it,' said Bloom's assistant, Alison Goldberg, a starchy young woman in black-rimmed glasses and stiletto heels. 'Under the rules of Plan Colombia, evidence obtained by the DEA, no matter from where in the world, is admissible in Colombian narcotics-related cases.'

Bloom put down his briefcase on a table and opened it, handing a document to the drug lord. 'This is a memo we, ah, obtained from within the Ministry of Justice, from the minister himself.' De Quesada began to read it, his expression rapidly darkening as he flicked through the pages. 'To summarise, they think they have you.'

The Colombian hurled the papers to the floor. 'No one has me!' he snarled, snapping his fingers angrily at a broad-shouldered bodyguard standing near a drinks cabinet. By the time de Quesada reached him, the man had poured a large glass of Scotch and soda filled with clinking ice cubes. He downed half the amber liquid in a single gulp, and crunched a cube between his teeth.

'We also learned there is a plan in motion to take you into custody,' said Goldberg.

De Quesada whirled on her. 'And you didn't tell me this the moment you came through my door?' He looked in alarm at the bodyguard, who hurried away to alert his comrades.

'They're waiting for the final warrants to be signed,' said

Bloom. 'We have a source inside the Ministry who will alert us as soon as this happens. You'll have ample warning.'

'Not if they're already here.' He crossed to a window and looked suspiciously out at the cliffs across the channel.

'We didn't see anyone when we arrived,' said Goldberg.

'No. You wouldn't.' De Quesada finished his drink, chewed another ice cube, then waved for the Americans to follow him. 'Tell me what my options are.'

They entered a broad hall, the walls decorated with artworks old and new – and the khipu, pinned to a board like a giant bedraggled moth. 'There is the usual ploy of dragging the matter out in court, of course,' said Bloom. 'Challenging of evidence and witnesses and so forth—'

'I don't want this to even *get* to court,' de Quesada growled. 'I meant, what are my options for leaving the country?'

'Limited,' Goldberg told him. 'It would give the American government the excuse it needed to freeze your assets world-wide. And then there's the issue of extradition . . .' She tailed off as the Colombian went into a white-tiled room – and unzipped his fly.

'What? Haven't you ever seen a man take a piss before? Keep talking,' he demanded. But both lawyers had been left speechless by the bizarre nature of his bathroom. Rather than a lavatory, the room housed a sunken square four feet to a side. Incredibly, set into its floor was the stolen sun disc. An unimaginable fortune in gold, a priceless cultural treasure . . . now acting as a urinal.

Hearing no further legal advice forthcoming, de Quesada looked over his shoulder. 'Oh, this?' he said, anger briefly diminishing as he took the opportunity to boast. 'A little trinket I bought in Venezuela. I thought it would take weeks to arrive, but my new shipping company was very efficient.

Now every time I take a piss, I'm pissing on the culture of my old friend Arcani Pachac! I may even send him a picture – although I doubt he has good cell reception in the mountains of Peru.'

'Ah . . . quite,' said Bloom, as de Quesada shook himself off and zipped up. 'But on the subject of extradition—' His phone trilled. 'Excuse me.'

Now de Quesada was all business, watching intently as the lawyer listened. 'Was that your man?' he said as Bloom terminated the call.

'I'm afraid so. The warrant has been signed.'

'This way,' the drug lord ordered, pushing past them and continuing down the hall.

Two of his men met the trio. '*Jefe!*' said one. 'I just talked to someone in the village. He said some trucks went down your road and haven't come back.'

'When?'

'About two hours ago.'

De Quesada glared accusingly at the two lawyers. 'I told you, we didn't see anyone,' Goldberg said, trying to conceal her sudden nervousness.

De Quesada whispered to the bodyguards, who nodded and jogged back to the room overlooking the infinity pool. 'In here,' the Colombian said, leading the Americans to a set of arched double doors. He opened them to reveal a large room that was a combination of luxurious lounge and office, leather armchairs and couches laid out before a black chrome desk with a top of polished granite. Along one wall was a bar with hundreds of different bottles arranged behind it – and above them a large, yet seemingly empty, aquarium.

Goldberg regarded the glass tank curiously, but de Quesada passed a second archway to the hall and went behind the bar to the shelves at its end. He pulled out one particular bottle – which only slid so far before stopping with a click. 'My vault,' he told the intrigued pair. 'There are some documents I don't want them to find, you understand?'

'Perfectly,' said Bloom.

'Good.' He swung the shelves away to reveal a small room hidden behind them. Goldberg tried to peer inside, but at his stare switched her attention back to the aquarium. 'You like my pets?' he asked. Both lawyers were puzzled, seeing nothing. 'There, in the middle.'

Goldberg stepped behind the bar, finally spotting one of the tank's occupants: a little yellow octopus, two of its suckered tentacles holding it to the transparent wall. She leaned closer, hesitantly tapping the glass. The octopus leapt away, turning a far brighter yellow with rings of black and vivid blue appearing all over its body. Eight limbs pulsing in unison, it shot towards the surface.

'Don't stand too close,' said de Quesada. 'It's a blue-ringed octopus – one of the world's deadliest creatures. If it bites you . . . you'll die.'

'The glass looks quite thick,' she said, covering her brief shock with haughty indifference.

'Maybe, but the tank has no top – and they can climb.'

She hurriedly retreated. De Quesada laughed harshly. 'Now, here is what I want you to do,' he said. 'Wait on the bridge for them to arrive, and do not let them pass. Say you need to check the warrant, any legal shit you can think of, just hold them up for as long as you can.'

'This . . . isn't really what you hired us for,' said Goldberg.

'I hired you to keep me out of prison, and I pay you a lot of money to do it. So do it. Consider it part of your client service.' The bodyguard entered, carrying Bloom's briefcase. 'Take your case and go. Keep them busy.' When they didn't move immediately, he barked: '*Now!*'

Affronted, Bloom collected his case and the lawyers departed. The bodyguard waited until they were gone, then went to the bar. 'Did you do it?' de Quesada asked.

'Yes, *jefe.*' He handed the drug lord a small remote control unit. 'Everything is set.'

'Good. Tell the others to arm up. And bring Alicia and Sylvie here – I want them as my last line of defence.' A cruel smirk. 'No man would dare shoot them.' He returned to the hidden vault. 'I have to destroy the hard drives. Get ready – they will be coming!'

'The guy may be a criminal,' admitted Nina, 'but he's got a gorgeous house.'

The combined force from Interpol, the Drug Enforcement Administration and the Colombian police – and the two representatives of the International Heritage Agency – was concealed amongst the trees along the clifftop, looking at the little island below. De Quesada's villa had been impressive enough in photos, but in reality it was magnificent; white walls gleaming in the sunlight.

'Nice taste in bodyguards, too,' said Eddie, taking a closer look through binoculars.

Nina could guess at what – or whom – he was looking. 'Give me those,' she snapped, wresting the binoculars from his grip as the two young women emerged from the infinity pool and padded, still topless, into the building. 'And I'm pretty sure they're *way* below your "half the man's age plus seven years" rule.'

Eddie grinned. 'No harm in looking.'

'There will be if I catch you doing it again.' She panned

along the house to the crossing. While it seemed solidly built, it was still merely a footbridge, too narrow to accommodate vehicles. The drug lord's cars were kept in a garage on the mainland, outside which an SUV had stopped and disgorged a suited man and woman about twenty minutes earlier.

She moved her view back to the island. At each end of the bridge were tall and stout wooden poles, a cable that she guessed was a power line hanging between them. Near the far pole was the house's main entrance – the doors of which suddenly opened. 'Someone's coming out.'

It was the suited couple. 'De Quesada's lawyers,' said Baker.

'They don't look happy.' The pair were in the midst of an agitated discussion.

'I think I know why.' Nina looked round to see Kit, holding several sheets of paper, and Probst slipping through the bushes. 'This just came through over the mobile fax.'

Baker took the pages. 'Outstanding.'

'The warrant?' Eddie asked.

'Signed, sealed and delivered. We now have full authority to go in and get that son of a bitch. Okay, Mr Jindal, Dr Wilde, Mr Chase, wait here until we're done. Walther, are the snipers covering the jetty?'

Probst nodded. 'We can take out the boats any time.'

'Great. Okay, time to kick ass . . .' He stopped, seeing that the lawyers had come to a standstill three-quarters of the way across the bridge. 'Now what the hell are those two doing?'

The answer came as the man called out in American-accented Spanish. 'Well, shit!' exclaimed Baker.

'What's he saying?' Eddie asked.

The DEA agent shook his head in disgust. 'They want to talk to us. Guess they heard about the warrant.'

'So much for the element of surprise,' Nina said gloomily. 'Now what do we do?'

Probst surveyed the house. 'I don't like it. It could be a trap.'

'We outnumber them three to one,' Baker said dismissively, 'we've got an elevated position and superior firepower, and all their escape routes are cut off. That son of a bitch is just trying to buy time so he can destroy anything incriminating. Mr Cruz!' he called. The head of the Colombian SWAT team, who had been standing beside a six-wheeled truck giving last-minute instructions to his men, hurried over. 'You and four of your guys, come with me. We'll see what these clowns have to say. Get the rest ready to move in. Walther, keep your guys on lookout.'

Cruz signalled to his unit, and four black-clad cops joined him. Baker summoned four more DEA agents, and the ten men, weapons at the ready, headed for the bridge. Probst and Kit moved away to organise the Interpol team.

'Not keen on this,' Eddie muttered.

'You think it's a trap too?' asked Nina. The two lawyers were still waiting on the bridge.

'Yeah, but . . . I don't know what this arsehole's got planned. And that worries me.' He took the binoculars back from Nina and checked the villa once more.

Inside the house, de Quesada looked back at him through his own binoculars from behind a Venetian blind on the upper floor. One of his bodyguards had spotted movement in the trees. With their cover blown, the intruders were less concerned about secrecy.

Which could be their fatal mistake. 'How many?' he asked.

'At least fifteen people,' his bodyguard replied, hefting his M16 assault rifle. 'Probably more.'

The drug lord clicked his tongue, not liking the odds even with his contingency plan ready to go. 'They'll be watching the boats . . .' He stopped when he picked out a dash of contrasting colour amongst the greenery. A woman, her fiery red hair standing out clearly.

A familiar woman. 'What's *she* doing here?' he asked himself, recognising Nina Wilde from their meeting at the Clubhouse. Why would an archaeologist be accompanying a police raid?

The answer was obvious. 'Wait here and get ready to shoot,' he ordered as he headed downstairs to the hall. Two more armed bodyguards lurked near the front door; he ignored them, instead going to one of the artworks.

The khipu. He plucked it from the board, then hurried back to his office, glancing into the bathroom as he passed. The sun disc was obviously far more valuable, almost certainly the main reason for Wilde's presence, but unlike the khipu it could hardly be slipped into a pocket. Wilde had told him that the lengths of string were potentially worth millions to the right buyer; he might soon need the cash.

But first, he had to make sure he remained free. He entered his office, where he found the dark-haired Alicia and the blonde Sylvie waiting for him. He gave their naked breasts an appreciative look. 'You know what to do?'

'Yeah, babe,' said Alicia, raising her imposing weapon: an AA-12 automatic shotgun, its twenty-round drum magazine making it look like a futuristic gangster's Tommy gun. Sylvie was similarly armed, and both women's wide-eyed, hyper expressions told him they had just snorted considerable amounts of confidence-boosting cocaine off the marble table. 'We won't let anyone in until you're done.'

'Good.' He kissed her, then did the same to Sylvie before going through the hidden door.

It was a shame to lose such hot companions, he thought as he placed a small thermite block on top of the computer containing his financial records. But then, he could always find more.

A CCTV monitor showed him the bridge, Bloom and Goldberg still standing partway across it. As he watched, the cops finally revealed themselves, ten armed men trooping to the crossing.

He tugged out a tab to light the thermite's fuse and retreated to the bar, shielding his eyes. The block ignited, sparks spitting as the matchbox-sized incendiary device almost instantly melted through the plastic case, the hard drive inside it and the shelf on which the computer was sitting, and finally made a sterling effort to burrow into the concrete floor.

The girls gave him worried looks, but he smiled reassuringly and, wafting away the smoke, returned to the vault. In an ideal world he would have closed the door to ensure total security, but the stench of vaporised plastic and metal was choking in the confined space.

Another look at the screen. The SWAT team was now on the bridge, marching to meet the lawyers.

He gathered up the items he needed – a clutch of passports, a flash drive containing Swiss bank account details, an encrypted cell phone, a wad of high-denomination banknotes of assorted currencies, and the khipu – and sealed them in a watertight Ziploc bag, then held the remote. Any second now . . .

'Are you with the DEA?' asked Bloom, blocking the SWAT team's path.

Baker tapped the huge DEA logo emblazoned across his body armour. 'What gave it away?' he asked sarcastically. 'Let us through.'

'You're not taking another step across this bridge until we see a warrant,' Goldberg said firmly. 'We have reason to believe that our client's rights are being violated by the issuing of an illegal search order, and we demand to inspect said order before we allow you on his property.'

'In accordance with the Colombian legal code,' added Bloom.

Baker looked irritably to Cruz. 'Is that right?' The Colombian nodded. 'Well, good thing I brought these.' He thrust the faxed documents at the lawyer. 'Read fast, 'cause one way or another, we're crossing this bridge.'

Bloom handed the papers to his partner. 'I need my reading glasses,' he said, opening his briefcase.

It contained a laptop, several folders of documents, assorted pens and a spectacle case, for which Bloom reached . . . before he registered something extra amongst his belongings. A book-sized block of a dull yellow putty-like substance, to which was taped a small electronic device, a red light glowing on it.

He stared at it in bewilderment. 'What—'

The brick of C-4 plastic explosive detonated.

27

In the vault, de Quesada pushed a button on the remote, and watched the image of the bridge – and the twelve people on it – vanish in a flash of light. An explosion rattled the building. He smiled. 'Now that's what I call client service.'

He pulled a cord on the back wall. Another concealed doorway opened, revealing a rocky passage descending steeply into the island's heart. He started down it. Below, the sound of waves echoed through a large enclosed space.

Eddie and Nina raised their heads. The bridge had been obliterated, only truncated stumps left at each end. The two power poles rocked, the cable flapping between them like a skipping rope.

Of the people on the bridge, nothing remained but a red tint to the drifting smoke.

'Jesus Christ!' Eddie gasped. Half the assault force had been wiped out in a single blow.

And the other half was under attack. Crackles of automatic gunfire came from the island. Nina shrieked and ducked again as bullets thwacked the vegetation around them.

'It's suppressing fire,' Eddie realised. The drug lord's men were trying to force the surviving SWAT members to stay down while they escaped.

Probst, with three members of his team by the trucks, had

reached the same conclusion. 'Sniper unit!' he shouted into his radio. 'Take out the boats!'

Further along the cliff, beyond the broken bridge, two more men lay in the concealment of a bush, their monstrous Barrett M82 rifles on bipods before them. While the huge weapons were generally used in a sniper role, they were also often applied to anti-materiel tasks; a single .50-calibre round could destroy the engine of any unarmoured vehicle, and quite a few armoured ones.

The snipers already had targets. A jetty, reached by a zigzag path down the island's less steep seaward side, had three speedboats moored along it. The first man targeted the outboard motor of the boat closest to shore. Even with the waves causing the vessel to bob in the water, at a range of less than three hundred metres it was a simple shot. 'Firing,' he said, warning his companion to brace himself as he pulled the trigger.

A burst of flame eight feet long exploded from the Barrett's muzzle. Looking back through his scope, the sniper saw a hole through the engine wide enough to see blue water. The speedboat wasn't going anywhere.

His companion lined up the next shot . . .

A new sound over the bursts of fire from the house – a low, flat *whoosh*—

They looked round – and an RPG-7 round struck the cliff between them, tearing both men apart.

Eddie grimly watched the RPG's smoke trail drift away. The snipers' first shot had revealed their position, and de Quesada's men had responded with immediate overkill.

'Keep down,' he told Nina, crawling through the bushes to

Kit and Probst. 'They got your snipers,' he told the Interpol officers, who reacted with shock. 'They'll be going for the boats.'

'I'll tell the Coast Guard to intercept,' said Kit, going to one of the group's Ford Expedition SUVs.

'How far away are they?' Eddie asked.

'There's a cutter three kilometres off the coast.' The Indian began speaking into the radio.

'Why the fuck are they so far out?'

'We didn't want to alert de Quesada,' said Probst in disgust. 'For all the good that did.' He turned to the other men. 'We have to make sure nobody gets away. Get the rest and go along the cliffs. But keep spread out – they might have another rocket.'

'Anything I can do?' Eddie asked as the team moved off.

'I'm not sure there is even anything *we* can do,' the German replied, following his men.

'Great,' Eddie muttered. He checked the trucks in the hope of finding a spare weapon, but found only the now worthless tear-gas launchers.

Kit finished his radio call. 'The Coast Guard are on their way.'

'How long?'

'Six or seven minutes before they're close enough to take any kind of action.' He drew a pistol. 'Stay here with Nina. I'll be with Walther.'

'Be careful, okay?' said Eddie.

A humourless smile. 'I'm not wearing body armour. I will be *very* careful!' He hurried after Probst.

Eddie watched them go, frustrated. There had to be *something* he could do. But with the bridge destroyed, there was no way on or off the island except by boat . . .

Something about that troubled him, but he wasn't entirely sure why. He returned to Nina. 'Have you seen anything?'

She shook her head. 'After that rocket fired, all the guys at this end took off.'

'Going for the boats.' He considered that. 'Which . . . doesn't make any fucking sense.'

'What do you mean?'

'This de Quesada blew up the bridge deliberately, so the only way to escape is by boat – but the path down to them's way too exposed. He must have known we'd try to cover 'em.' As if to illustrate his point, more gunfire started, this time from the shore. The remaining members of the SWAT team had reached positions from where they could see the path down to the jetty, and opened fire. A scream echoed off the cliffs: one of de Quesada's bodyguards had been hit. The drug lord's men shot back, dust and chipped stones spitting from the clifftops.

'So, what, you think he's using his own men as a decoy?' Nina said dubiously.

'The guy's a drug lord – he'd probably use his own grandma as a human shield. He wants us looking at *that* end of the island, so he can do something at *this* end.'

'Like what?'

'I dunno. Maybe he's not really leaving – he's just going to hide in a panic room until everyone's gone.' He regarded the house – then stood.

'Get down!' Nina yelped, yanking at the sleeve of his battered jacket. 'They'll see you.'

'There's nobody there. They're all by the boats to give de Quesada time to do whatever he's doing. I need to get over there before he does it.'

'And how are you going to do that?' Even at its narrowest point, the channel was still over fifty feet across. 'The bridge has gone, and I don't think high-diving into the sea to swim across would be a good idea!'

He pointed. 'That cable. I can slide down it.'

'Are you *kidding*? It's probably got ten thousand volts running through it!'

'Then I won't touch it.'

'If you don't touch it, how are you going to slide down it?'

Rather than answer, he hurried back to the parked vehicles and climbed into the truck's bed. As well as carrying the Colombian SWAT team, it had also transported the weapons, including the Barretts. But it wasn't their now empty cases Eddie was interested in; rather, the ratchet straps used to secure them. 'Here we go,' he said as Nina arrived, detaching one. It was six feet long, made from a heavy-duty polyester. 'It's insulated, so I can chuck it over the wire and use it as a zipline.'

Nina wasn't impressed. 'And if the line doesn't hold?'

'Let's not worry about that, eh?' He headed for the stub of the bridge.

She followed. 'Oh, you know me, I worry about everything. Especially you!'

Eddie reached the pole supporting the power line, looped the strap round the pole and held the ends tightly together. 'Okay, stay low, just in case I'm wrong and there's still someone over there. Once I'm across, use the radio in the truck to tell Kit what I'm doing. Back soon.'

'How?' she demanded. 'You're going to slide *up* the line?'

'I'll think of something.' He kissed her, then, using the strap for support, climbed until he reached the metal pegs that acted as a ladder. Warily eyeing the power line on its ceramic insulators, he scooted round to the pole's seaward side.

It was his first clear view of the channel far below. Waves

churned and frothed, and the rocks poking from the water suggested it was not especially deep. High-diving definitely wasn't a good idea. The open sea was visible at the far end to his left; to the right, it curved out of sight towards the jetty. Gunfire was still being exchanged, but less frequently than before – the two sides seemed caught in a stand-off.

Which wouldn't last long. Beyond the island, Eddie saw an approaching ship: the Colombian Coast Guard. The drug lord's bodyguards would soon be forced to make a break for the boats, or be trapped.

Which suited Eddie. Their attention would be focused well away from him. He hooked the strap over the power line, applying experimental pressure. It seemed secure. Nina watched anxiously from the trees; he gave her a thumbs-up.

A deep breath, and he shifted his weight to the strap. The line pulled tight, but still held. He fixed his eyes on the house, not looking at the dizzying drop. '*High* voltage,' he muttered. 'Okay, let's slide . . .'

He threw himself off the pole.

The cable twanged and juddered with the extra load as he slid down it. The cliff-edge rolled past beneath his feet, nothing below for over a hundred feet. The island loomed ahead . . .

The strap rasped against the cable. He slowed . . . and stopped.

Ten feet short of the far side.

'Shit!' He tried to jolt free, but the line wasn't steep enough for him to overcome the strap's friction. Another futile jerk, then he changed tactics. Legs together, he brought them gently back, then kicked sharply. He jerked forward by about a foot. Another kick, and another—

The insulator on the pole ahead sheared apart.

He dropped.

*

Nina barely contained a scream as the line gave way, Eddie plunging towards the water – then the sagging line snapped taut again. His fall gave him a boost of speed.

Too much speed.

All thoughts of concealment gone, she ran to the edge as he hurtled helplessly at the cliff.

Eddie whipped up his feet just before he hit the rock wall. The collision was a hammer-blow against his soles, crashing up through his knees and hips. The cable shook, the strap squirming in his grip.

Another jolt – and he fell again, dropping by a foot before the line jerked tight once more. The power cable ran from the pole to a transformer on the villa – and one of the brackets securing it had just broken. His weight was now being taken by the insulator on the mainland side and the transformer's connector, neither of which were designed to support the extra load.

Even through the strap, he felt the cable straining—

He swung sideways and lunged to grab an outcropping with one hand – just as the connector gave way. The strap flapped free, spiralling towards the churning waters. The drooping power line hung so close that he could hear the faint hum of current flowing through the cable.

If it sparked, the shock would kill him.

Very carefully, he scraped his boots against the rock until he found a toehold. He edged sideways, free hand clawing blindly for purchase. A crack in the cliff; he squeezed his fingertips inside, pulling away from the deadly line.

Another stretch, and another, and he struggled upwards to the stub of the bridge. Once he had a secure hold, he paused to catch his breath, then climbed to level ground.

★

Nina watched, relieved beyond measure, as Eddie waved to her before jogging to the villa's front door. She sagged against the pole, looking at the waters below as she gathered herself—

Something moved.

It took her a moment to realise what; at first, it seemed as though the rock face just above the waterline was morphing like plastic. A blink, and the bizarre sight made sense. It wasn't rock, but something made to look like rock, slowly being pulled away to reveal darkness behind it. Metal tracks led from the shadows into the sea.

What the hell was going on?

De Quesada shut off an electric winch, allowing himself a moment of pride as he admired his emergency escape route. Nobody else knew of it, except the men who had built it – and they were no longer able to tell others, or indeed do anything other than decompose.

The cave below was naturally hard enough to spot, in perpetual shadow amongst the cliff's folds, and his camouflage had made it almost invisible. The entrance was concealed by a heavy tarpaulin hanging down like a stage curtain, painted in browns and greys to match the surrounding rock.

Hidden inside was the vehicle that would take him to safety; not a boat, but a Cessna Skyhawk floatplane, the little white-and-yellow aircraft perched on a set of rails down which it would slide into the channel. From there, he would turn west while his attackers were distracted by the boats at the island's northeastern end, taking off as soon as he reached open ocean. He would leave Colombian airspace within fifteen minutes. By the time the authorities in Panama had been alerted, he would have already reached a safe house, where he would change identities before sneaking out of the country.

He descended a ladder to the cave floor and put the bag containing his belongings in the cockpit before starting the pre-flight checks for the plane's short voyage.

Eddie found himself in a broad hall, paintings on the walls. No sign of anybody, but he was still cautious, moving quietly.

Shimmering reflected ripples through one door told him that the room beyond opened out on to the infinity pool; an open arch to his right led into what was apparently a lounge, a bar visible through the doorway. He edged towards it. As he approached, he picked up a smell, faint but distinctive: chlorinated water. The girls from the pool?

Back against the wall, he moved closer, listening for movement inside the room . . .

Something crunched under his foot.

Rock salt, almost invisible where it had been scattered over the pale marble. A simple but effective warning system.

He backed up—

Boom!

A hole almost a foot across was blown through the wall just in front of him, spraying him with fragmented plaster and wood. He stumbled in shock, slipping on the hard floor and landing on his backside – as a second hole exploded right above his head. '*Shit!*' he yelled, scrambling backwards.

The shooter had anticipated his retreat, another two holes bursting open behind him.

He slithered round, rock salt digging into his palms, and launched himself like a sprinter past the archway.

His brief glance into the room told him plenty. He had expected to see a gunman, but it was actually two gunwomen, the topless water babes from the pool, blasting away at him –

Jesus, with AA-12s – as he hurtled past the entrance. One woman was behind the bar, the other beside a couch. Shotgun fire ripped more holes out of the wall in his wake. There was a mahogany door at the end of the hall – wherever it led, it had to be safer than this—

He passed a second open archway and reached the door.

Locked!

Both AA-12s swung to track him—

He dived into the lounge, slamming against the back of a leather armchair. Shots shredded the expensive piece of furniture as the women kept firing. Eddie had instinctively been counting shots – each AA-12's drum magazine held twenty rounds, and they were rapidly chewing through them, but they would reduce his cover to matchwood long before they ran dry. He needed something more solid.

A granite desk, between him and the killer bimbos. Not ideal, but all he had—

The armchair thumped against him under the force of another shot. Eddie pushed hard at the disintegrating seat, sliding it across the room. Another round blew off an entire corner of the backrest. He kept pushing – then grabbed the chair's base and bowled it at the dark-haired woman as he rolled under the table and strained to tip it on its side. It crashed down with a bang.

The brunette shrieked and leapt away as the tumbling chair bounced past her. The blonde behind the bar kept firing. The granite slab took the impact – but Eddie, pressed against it, still felt as though he was being kicked in the back with each shot.

'Go round it and shoot him!' the blonde yelled. Another shot – and the granite cracked, a plate-sized chunk barely missing Eddie as he jerked sideways.

A slap of feet as the brunette moved. He was running out of time—

The quickest of glances through the broken section of desk revealed a fishtank set into the wall behind the blonde. He grabbed the hunk of granite and hurled it with all his strength.

The blonde ducked as the stone flew over her and hit the glass – which shattered, bursting outwards. She was knocked down by the deluge, shards and marine life hitting her near-naked body.

Eddie was already running. If he could disarm her before she recovered . . .

A horrific scream filled the room. He dived as the blonde's AA-12 barked again and again, her finger clenched on the trigger and firing off its remaining rounds on full auto. Shredded debris spat across the room. The screaming continued, Eddie wondering what the hell was happening. Maybe she was *really* fish-phobic . . .

He got his answer as he scrambled behind the bar. Clamped to the woman's right breast was a small octopus, patterns on its body pulsing furiously as it bit her again and again.

The shotgun clicked, the drum empty. The blonde's movements were already weakening as the deadly paralytic flowed through her system, her screams fading to choked gurgles.

'*Sylvie!*' shrieked the dark-haired woman in genuine anguish. She swung her AA-12 at the bar and fired. 'You bastard, you killed her!'

Bottles and glasses exploded above Eddie. 'Jesus!' Ricocheting pellets rained down on him like embers.

The firing stopped. Twenty rounds gone. Eddie vaulted the bar. The woman was still uselessly pulling the trigger, in her anger only belatedly realising she was out of ammo. She tried to club Eddie with the shotgun, but he easily dodged the blow. There was a time and place for chivalry, but this wasn't it: he punched her in the face, knocking her down on the couch.

He grabbed her by the throat. 'Where's de Quesada?'

'Fuck you!' she spat.

He squeezed harder. 'Where is he?'

'Go fuck yourself!' Eddie pulled back his fist, then thought better of it and released her, hurrying back to the bar. With a brief chill of revulsion, he took hold of the octopus by its body and plucked it off Sylvie's breast. It squirmed, suckers clinging to his skin. The little monster writhing angrily, he went back to the couch. The other woman struggled upright; he pushed her down again and held the octopus just above her face.

Tentacles lashed out and stuck to her, the creature's venom-filled beak snapping less than an inch from her cheek. She shrieked. 'Tell me where he is, or I'll let it bite you!' Eddie shouted.

'In there!' she wailed, pointing at some shelves behind the bar. 'He's in there!'

She was too terrified to lie, Eddie decided. He pulled the octopus away and tossed it across the room into the tank's remaining water – then punched the woman again, knocking her out. 'Sucker,' he said as he went to the shelves.

Close up, they were revealed as a disguised door, the sharp stench of melted plastic coming from inside. No way to know if de Quesada was armed and waiting within. He yanked it open, ready to dive—

The room was empty. Smoke belched from the smouldering remains of a computer, a hole burned right through it. Thermite; de Quesada had been in here to destroy anything compromising on his hard drive.

He wasn't here now, though. But he was sure the woman hadn't lied – and why would she and her friend have been defending an empty room?

A panel not quite flush with the wall, a cord attached . . .

He pulled it. The panel swung outwards, revealing a rocky passage leading downwards.

The coughing grind of an engine came from somewhere far below.

'Oh, you are *not* doing a fucking runner after all this,' Eddie growled, ducking through the opening.

Nina also heard the noise. Eddie had been right – the drug lord was using his own men as a decoy while he escaped in a hidden boat.

Only it wasn't a boat that slid down the rails, but a light aircraft, riding on elongated pontoons. It reached the water's edge, a brief snarl of power to the propeller pulling it into the channel. A door opened and the pilot clambered along a pontoon to detach the runner that had guided it down the tracks.

Even from high above, Nina recognised him. De Quesada.

Descending through the narrow tunnel, Eddie dropped on to a ledge. He was high up in a large cave, its mouth opening into the channel. A glance through a wide crack in the rock revealed the source of the noise: a floatplane bobbing on the water outside. De Quesada ducked beneath the rear fuselage and hopped from one float to the other, crouching to unfasten something from it. As soon as the drug lord finished whatever he was doing, he would be able to escape.

He had to be stopped.

A piece of equipment was bolted to the rock wall – an electric winch, hooked to a painted tarpaulin that had been pulled away from the cave mouth. Eddie checked the rope. Brightly coloured marine line, strong and hard-wearing.

He looked back outside. De Quesada was returning to the cockpit.

Eddie unhooked the rope from the tarp, then switched on the winch, reversing it to unspool the line. He looked back through the opening. Below, the Colombian climbed into the plane. 'Come on, come on!' he snarled, tugging at the rope. He needed more slack—

The engine revved. Out of time.

Pulling the line after him, Eddie leapt from the crevice, aiming to land on the fuselage—

The rope pulled tight, stopping him short. He hit the wing's trailing edge and fell backwards, landing hard on the tail of the port pontoon.

De Quesada, startled by the unexpected impact, turned and saw the stowaway. He jammed the throttle forward, the propeller screaming to full power as he steered the plane down the channel.

Eddie flailed, about to slip off the float . . .

His foot caught the rearmost strut connecting the pontoon to the bottom of the fuselage. He used the tenuous hold as leverage to sit up. The winch was still unspooling the rope – there was just enough slack for him to reach the support.

He lunged, clanking the hook on to the strut—

The line went taut again with a whipcrack. The plane jolted, but didn't slow – it was now unwinding the rope from the winch reel. Eddie dropped to keep his head clear of it. If his plan worked, when the line ran out it would either bring the plane to a stop, or rip out the strut, making it too dangerous for de Quesada to risk taking off.

The Skyhawk headed for the open ocean beyond the cliffs on each side. It picked up speed—

The reel reached its end.

For an instant it held . . . then the entire winch was torn from the wall, flying out of the crack and splashing down in the water.

The plane lurched, pitching Eddie into the sea.

Churning wake filled his nostrils, choking him. The Cessna surged away. He kicked, trying to get his head above the surface.

Something brushed his legs.

The rope—

A loop closed round his ankle, the weight of the winch pulling it tight – and he was dragged along by the plane, bouncing helplessly through the waves.

28

Nina watched in horror as her husband was hauled along behind the floatplane. The Seahawk accelerated, but was still a long way short of its sixty-four knot takeoff speed in the confined channel.

It had to be stopped. But how?

The waterway narrowed just before its end . . .

She ran back to the trucks and scrambled into the lead SUV. The key was in the ignition; she turned it, the big V8 roaring in response. Into drive, apply the gas—

The Expedition surged forward, flattening bushes and saplings as Nina turned to follow the plane. A small tree tumbled with a crack of shattering wood – and she was at the cliff, the drop looming. She swerved to drive along it, the right front wheel thumping over the ragged edge before finding solid ground. Craning her neck, she saw the floatplane was ahead of her – with Eddie skittering in its wake.

She accelerated. Past thirty – and gaining. The Expedition crashed over rocks and roots, slamming her against the door. Ignoring the pain, Nina stayed focused on the cliff ahead – and the plane below. She was almost level with the aircraft. Forty, and the 4×4 was airborne for a moment as it hit a bump, smashing down more shrubs as it landed.

Past the plane, but the end of the channel was just ahead—

Nina opened the door and jammed the steering wheel hard to the right as she threw herself out.

The Expedition shot over the edge and plunged towards the water.

De Quesada adjusted the rudder to keep the Cessna in the centre of the channel. The cliffs were far enough apart to accommodate the Skyhawk's ten metre wingspan, but after having someone jump on his plane, he didn't need any more close calls—

An SUV fell from the sky directly ahead and hit the water with a colossal eruption of spray.

'*Mierda!*' he shrieked, yanking back the throttle and applying full rudder to swing round it. But the vehicle was buried nose-down in the mud beneath the shallow water, blocking his escape route.

The only way out was back the way he had come. Keeping the rudder hard over, he reapplied power in pulses, swinging the plane around to reverse course.

A man was in the water, directly in his path.

Eddie gasped for breath, shaking water from his eyes. The rope was still looped round his leg, coils bobbing on the surface around him. He reached down to untangle it, looking for the plane.

It was powering towards him.

Nina had crashed through a stand of bushes to a soft, if messy, splashdown in a glutinous pool of mud. Bruised, face cut, she dragged herself from the mire and staggered to the cliff edge.

Her plan had worked. She had blocked the exit from the narrow canyon, forcing the plane to stop . . . but it had turned round and was now heading straight for Eddie.

It accelerated, about to mow him down—

★

Eddie abandoned his attempt to untangle himself and dropped underwater, kicking downwards. The float's keel bashed against his foot as it passed just inches above him in the shallow channel.

He surfaced, heart pounding – then realised the danger was far from over as the colourful line skimmed sinuously past him, still hooked to the strut. He grabbed the rope as it jerked into motion, friction burning his palms.

But at least now he wasn't a helpless dead weight. He pulled himself along the rope towards the float.

Something yanked hard on his entangled leg – the winch. It had sunk when the plane stopped, and was now being towed along behind again. Eddie grimaced, but kept reeling himself in. He was almost level with the Cessna's tail, the float just feet away.

The cave passed by to his left, the channel ahead curving round the island. Over the engine's roar he heard gunshots echoing from the cliffs.

Despite the best efforts of Probst and his team, two of the bodyguards had reached a speedboat and started it. The cops concentrated their fire on the vessel as it moved from the jetty – but this allowed another two thugs to reach the bottom of the path and find cover, shooting back.

Kit ducked as bullets smacked into the cliff in front of him. He wiped away grit and opened his eyes – to see the floatplane approaching.

Probst spotted it too. 'De Quesada, it must be!' He swung round his rifle and opened fire.

'No!' said Kit, batting the weapon upwards. 'You'll hit Eddie!' He pointed at the man who had just pulled himself on to one of the floats.

Probst swore in German, then shouted to the others: 'Don't shoot the plane! Chase is aboard!'

'He'll get away!' Cruz protested.

Kit looked out to sea. The Coast Guard vessel was coming in at speed. 'Forget the speedboats – tell them to block him before he can take off!'

Clinging to the float, Eddie winced as bullets struck the plane – then the barrage stopped. Hoping that meant he had been seen, he hooked an elbow round the diagonal brace connecting the float to the wing and freed his leg from the rope. It whipped away as he released it, the heavy winch still acting like an anchor.

He saw the jetty ahead, one of the speedboats moving away.

Into the plane's path.

De Quesada had seen it too. The engine note rose, the wing flaps clunking to their full extent as he tried to give the plane as much lift as possible.

Eddie moved forward and briefly raised his head to glance into the cabin. He was surprised to see the khipu in a plastic bag on the passenger seat, but was more interested in the drug lord. The Colombian was concentrating on getting the plane into the air.

He advanced again, reaching for the door handle . . .

Wind whistled through a bullet hole in the cabin roof. Ten centimetres over, and the round would have struck de Quesada himself. Blessing his good fortune, he looked round to see where else the plane had been hit . . .

The top of a head, short dark hair fluttering in the wind, was visible through a window. Edging towards the passenger-side door.

Jaw set, de Quesada gripped the control yoke tightly with one hand, his other clenching into a fist . . .

Eddie pulled the door open, thrusting himself into the cramped cabin – and was punched hard in the face.

Caught completely by surprise, he toppled backwards, clawing for a handhold but only managing to snatch up the bag on the passenger seat. With nothing to support himself, he fell . . .

His empty hand caught the rope just as the drag of the waves snatched him from the float. He slid back down the line. Even wet, it burned his skin again before he managed to get a grip with his other hand, using a corner of the large bag as a makeshift glove to protect his palm. He hung on tightly, gasping in the spray.

The spray suddenly stopped as the Cessna took off.

'Oh, *shiiiiit!*' Eddie yelled as he was pulled from the water. He was heading into the sky – but if he let go of the rope, he would slam into the speedboat directly ahead like a torpedo.

The men in the boat were forced to duck as the Skyhawk roared barely a foot above. One realised it was trailing something and raised his head to see what—

Eddie pulled up both feet and kicked the bodyguard in the face, backflipping him out of the boat in a spray of blood and teeth.

Behind him, the rope rasped over the speedboat's side—

The winch smashed through the hull – and snagged. The boat flipped over, flinging the other man screaming into the sea, and landed upside down, carving a great swathe out of the ocean as it was dragged behind the floatplane.

The extra weight threw the Cessna out of control. It yawed sideways as the boat pulled it back down.

Eddie hit the waves again, this time managing to stay upright and holding his legs out straight in front of him to use his feet as impromptu waterskis. Each crest pummelled him as he was pulled along.

He saw the Coast Guard cutter looming ahead. The Cessna levelled, then regained height. The rope tightened. In another second, he too would be airborne—

He let go.

Arms windmilling, Eddie skied along the water for over a hundred feet, finally losing his balance and falling over. He skipped like a stone, bouncing once, twice, before hitting the cutter's side with a *thunk*.

Above, de Quesada had been forced to roll the Cessna almost on its side to avoid a crash, shooting between the cutter's elevated bridge and radar mast with less than a foot of clearance. He straightened with an exultant whoop, turning the plane towards Panamanian airspace—

The speedboat, still bounding along at the end of the rope, collided with the cutter.

The Coast Guard boat rolled with the impact – but the plane fared worse. The float was ripped away – along with a chunk of the wing at the top of the support brace and a large section of the fuselage floor.

De Quesada screamed as he suddenly found himself with nothing but open air beneath his feet. The yoke went slack, control cables severed. The ailerons drooped, sending the crippled aircraft inexorably towards the glittering water—

It smashed into the sea at over eighty knots. The impact crushed the damaged fuselage like a beer can, impaling de Quesada on the control yoke. Fuel lines ruptured, avgas gushing over hot metal. What was left of the Skyhawk exploded in a flash of orange fire and oily black smoke.

Eddie surfaced beside the cutter, broken bits of boat raining around him. He spotted the plastic bag containing the late drug lord's belongings floating nearby and swam to collect it before shouting up to the deck. 'Oi! Man overboard!'

One of the boat's stunned crew peered down at him, then tossed a knotted line over the side. Eddie clambered up. The Cessna's burning remains were strewn along the water in the distance. 'Bloody hell,' he said to the crewman. 'That's the last time I fly on a no-frills airline.'

The villa's interior was every bit as expensive as its exterior suggested, but one room stood out above all others. Nina gazed down at the golden sun disc set into the bathroom floor. 'Unbelievable,' she said, half in amazement, half in disgust. 'Spending fifty million dollars on one of the most incredible Inca relics ever discovered . . . and then doing *this* with it?'

'If you've got more money than you can ever spend, I suppose you get daft with it eventually,' said Eddie, drying his hair with one of de Quesada's towels. After his rescue, the Coast Guard ship had landed at the island, and the surviving members of the drug lord's gang had surrendered. The remaining speedboat had been used to ferry Nina and the SWAT team from the mainland. 'So, we found the sun disc, and I got the khipu off el druggio. Plus we saved the world the cost of the bastard's trial. Job done, I think.'

'Is the khipu okay?'

'Far as I know. It was sealed in a bag with a bunch of other stuff – passports, cash, stuff like that. Kit's checking through it all.'

'And are you okay?'

He patted his jeans. 'Bit damp, still. Banged-up, shot at, the usual. Nothing too serious.' In truth, one knee had a searing ache from his impact with the cliff and the friction burns on his palms still stung, but he covered the discomfort. 'What about you?'

Nina's hand went to the Band-Aid one of Probst's men had applied to a cut on her face. 'I'm okay. Just had a scratchy landing when I bailed out of that truck. But it was pretty muddy, which broke the fall.'

'You're lucky you didn't break the rest of you,' Eddie said. 'It was a bloody stupid risk.'

'Oh, kettle, pot!' she snapped. 'And if I hadn't done it, de Quesada would have gotten away – and you would have been dragged along behind his plane like a banner advertising balding Englishmen.'

'The difference is, this kind of stuff is what I do.'

'No, it isn't! Not any more. You work for the United Nations now, not a stunt troupe. Every time I watch you doing something like this, I almost have a heart attack because . . .' Her voice fell. 'Because I'm scared that I'm about to watch you die.'

'I'm not gonna die, okay?' he said firmly. 'Just 'cause I don't bounce as much as I used to doesn't mean I'll smash like Humpty bastard Dumpty if I take a bit of a fall.'

'There's a difference between a bit of a fall and a hundred-foot drop off a cliff,' Nina pointed out. 'And when people are actively trying to kill you . . .'

'You'd think they'd learn,' Eddie snorted. 'Anyone who tries to kill me gets fucked up.'

'Who's trying to kill you?' Kit asked, appearing in the doorway.

'Nobody at the moment, thank God,' said Nina. She gave Eddie a look that promised the discussion was not over, then turned to the Interpol officer. 'Have you searched the rest of the house?'

'Yes. Some of his other artworks are on the CPCU's list of stolen items, although nothing on the scale of that.' He indicated the sun disc. 'And the bag Eddie recovered contained a phone with a list of de Quesada's contacts around the world – that should be very useful.' His optimistic look clouded. 'I just wish it hadn't cost twelve of the good guys' lives to get it.'

'Almost thirteen,' Nina said quietly. Eddie decided to ignore her.

'There's another thing,' Kit said. 'Eddie, can you take a look at something?'

'What is it?' asked Nina.

'Just . . . something Eddie might be able to identify with his military experience. Nina, can you photograph the sun disc so we can send pictures to Interpol and the UN, please?' He handed her a digital camera.

She realised Kit was being evasive, but nevertheless took the camera. 'What about the khipu?'

'It's with de Quesada's other items. You can examine it as soon as we've finished checking them.'

'Okay . . .' She exchanged curious looks with her husband as Kit led him from the room.

'So what've you found?' Eddie asked as they walked down the hall.

'It was in de Quesada's office, among his papers.' Kit stopped outside the arched doorway, glancing almost furtively into the room to make sure the other agents were occupied before taking something from a pocket. 'Here.'

Eddie took it: a plastic evidence bag, containing a business card. 'What's so special . . .' he began – then he read it. He said nothing for several moments.

'It's . . . it *is* your father's, isn't it?' Kit asked, breaking the silence.

'Yeah,' said Eddie, voice flat. 'Yeah, it is.' The card was identical to the one his father had given Nina, which had been taken from her by Stikes. It definitely wasn't the same card, though, this one pristine and uncreased. 'Think I'll have to have words . . .'

29

Bogotá

Larry Chase poured himself a whisky from the minibar, then sat back in an armchair and took a drink, the warm glow as the spirit went down his throat adding to his sense of satisfaction. Not a bad few days' work, considering the ridiculously tight schedule. But for the amount of money on offer – which was now in the company's bank account, as promised – he would have been an idiot to turn it down.

So the clients had hardly been savoury. So what? In his line of work, that was often a given. He was simply providing a service. The seller had an item at point A; the buyer wanted it at point B as quickly – and quietly – as possible. That was all it was, just business.

He had to admit that he was quite proud of himself. Getting something that weighed two tons out of Venezuela, just before the country exploded, and into Colombia had called upon all his years of moving through the more slippery lanes of international shipping, and even necessitated calling in several favours. But he had done it. Which would be good for future business, now that he had proved himself the equal of that fat bastard Stamford West in Singapore. Granted, he wouldn't be getting any future custom from General Callas, but Francisco de Quesada had certainly seemed impressed . . .

Someone knocked on the door. Larry was surprised; he hadn't ordered room service, and as far as he was aware nobody at the hotel knew him. 'Hello?'

No answer, just another knock. Irked, he put down his drink and answered it.

'Evening, Dad,' said Eddie in a scathing voice, pushing past him. 'How's things?'

'Uh . . . fine,' said Larry, shocked. 'What are you doing here?'

'Here on business. You?' Eddie dropped into a chair, gesturing for him to retake his place.

'Same here. How did you know I was here?'

'Found something you left behind.' Eddie held up the business card, still in the evidence bag. His father froze for the briefest moment before lowering himself into the armchair and picking up his drink. 'So I called your home number to see where you were. Spoke to Julie, said hi.' He returned the card to a pocket of his battered and seawater-stained leather jacket.

Larry downed another slug of whisky. 'How's Nina?'

'She's fine, doing her thing – working out how to find lost cities in Peru, recovering stolen treasures. Stolen *Inca* treasures.'

His father was composed enough by this time not to react. 'Inca treasures, eh? Sounds interesting. Like that cartoon you watched when you were a kid.'

'Wow, you remembered something about my childhood? Must have been one of the three days you were actually there for it.'

Larry gave him a cold look. 'Despite what you think, I wasn't a bad father. At least Elizabeth—'

'Turned out okay?'

'I was going to say had no complaints, actually.' Another swig. 'But I get the feeling you've got some, and they're nothing to do with your opinion of my parenting skills.'

'You could say that.' Eddie produced an envelope and took out two photographs, which he tossed on to the table beside Larry. 'Recognise those?'

Larry didn't look at them. 'There's not much point me answering, is there? Since I'm sure you think you already know the answer.'

Eddie laughed sarcastically. 'Don't worry, I'm not fucking taping you. You don't need to get all evasive.'

Larry sat forward. 'What's this all about, Edward?'

Eddie did the same, fixing him with a stony stare. 'It's about whether you're going to do the right thing. For once in your life.'

'Don't you talk to me like—'

'Shut up!' Eddie barked.

Larry flinched, then stood, bristling. 'I don't take that kind of attitude from anybody. Least of all you.'

Eddie didn't move, eyes locked on his father's. 'Sit down. Or I'll *make* you sit down. And you know I'll do it.'

His jaw tight with anger, the elder Chase returned to his seat. 'Get to it, then,' he growled. 'What do you want?'

'First off, I want you to look at those photos.' His father picked them up. 'The big gold face is an Inca sun disc – religious thing, their version of a cross. The other thing's called a khipu. Not as impressive, since it's basically a load of strings, but this one's important 'cause Nina thinks it's the key to finding El Dorado.'

Larry raised an eyebrow. 'What, *the* El Dorado?'

'No, Elvis's Cadillac.'

'You can be sarcastic or make your point, Edward. I'm not going to listen to you do both.'

'All right. My point is that they were stolen from an archaeological site in Venezuela, and that you shipped them out of the country. And when I say shipped, I mean smuggled. 'Cause let's not beat around the bush – that's what you do, isn't it?'

'You don't have a clue what you're talking about,' said Larry. 'I don't handle anything illegal.'

'What about those?' Eddie demanded, indicating the photos. 'They're stolen goods – I'd call that illegal right off the bat.'

'Stolen? From who? I've got access to international watch lists from customs, police, insurers – neither of these things were on any of them. Due diligence; I carry it out before taking on any job.'

'That's a technicality and you bloody know it. It'd never stand up in court.'

'As a matter of fact, it has, on more than one occasion. I know what I'm doing. I'm very good at it.'

'So good that you don't care who you work for as long as they pay well?' Eddie said. 'That guy you gave your business card to was a fucking drug lord!'

'How he makes his money isn't any of my concern. All I was doing was delivering a cargo to him – a cargo that as far as I knew was totally legitimate. If it had been drugs I wouldn't have touched it. Do you think I'm a fucking idiot or something?'

'You're something, all right. Didn't it even cross your mind that the job was a bit dodgy when Diego del Cocainio rings up out of the blue from South America and asks you to shift some merchandise for him, no questions asked?'

Larry almost laughed. 'As a matter of fact, the whole thing was arranged by a friend of yours.'

That caught Eddie totally off guard. 'What're you talking about?'

'Your old SAS mate.' Eddie was left even more bewildered. *Mac?* Relishing the fact that the balance of power had shifted somewhat back in his direction, Larry continued, 'Alexander Stikes.'

'*Stikes?*' Eddie exploded. 'Stikes is no fucking friend of mine! The bastard tried to kill me!'

'Really? Well, obviously I'm glad he didn't succeed, but I didn't know anything about that. He actually said you'd recommended me to him.'

'Oh, and didn't *that* give away that something was wrong?'

Larry gave him an icy look. 'I thought maybe you were attempting to apologise by putting some business my way. But I checked out his company, and everything seemed legit, so I had no reason to doubt him. He put me in touch with Callas and de Quesada, so all I did was act as middleman and ship some goods between them.'

'Without them being checked by customs.'

A contemptuous snort. 'You seem to be under the impression that if something crosses a border without a seventeen-point customs check, that means there's been some great conspiracy. Do you have any idea how many items actually *are* checked by customs? Maybe one in twenty – and that's in the West, where they have the technology and manpower to do even that many. Really, all they're looking for are drugs. Down here, it's more like one in a hundred. I just make sure that my clients' cargoes are in the other ninety-nine per cent. A word in the ear of the right person is usually all it takes.'

'And a bribe?'

'I prefer to think of them as favours. You know, customs men are almost universally underpaid and under-appreciated. I just show a little gratitude for the job they're doing.'

'And what about you, then?' Eddie demanded. 'You don't have any problems with taking money from a drug lord?'

'As I said, his business isn't my business. He was just another client. The only questions I ask are where, when, and how much?'

Eddie stood, voice low and harsh. 'I've got a new question you should ask yourself: am I going to give every penny I got from this job to the British Legion or Help For Heroes, or am I going to jail?'

A startled pause. 'You – you're *threatening* me?'

'That's right.'

Anger flared in the older man's eyes – and defiance. 'You've got no proof.'

Eddie took out the business card. 'You dealt with de Quesada.'

'Anyone could have given him that card. Besides, he's an *alleged* drug lord, not a convicted one.'

'Well, he's a *dead* drug lord now.'

Larry's expression hovered between surprise and relief. 'So you've got even less proof that I had anything to do with him.'

'Interpol's got his records. And why do you think I kept your card in a plastic bag? So they can get fingerprints off it. Yours and de Quesada's.'

'So . . . they haven't actually fingerprinted it yet?'

'Not yet. But I'll give it back to them if you don't make a very large donation to charity in the next few days.' He returned the card to his pocket. 'I'm giving you a chance here, Dad. You do the right thing. Or I will.'

Larry gulped down the last of his drink, fingers clenched tightly round the glass. 'I'll . . . think about it.'

'Don't think for too long.' Eddie went to the door, looking

back at his father with disdain. 'Have a nice trip.' With that, he left.

Larry banged the empty glass down on the table and jumped up. He paced back and forth across the room, shaking with barely contained fury, before taking a long breath, and picking up his phone. He thumbed through the contact list and dialled a number.

'This is Larry Chase,' he said when he got a reply. 'I need . . . I need to speak to Mr Stikes.'

Nina had already returned to Caracas; Eddie flew back to meet her. She was understandably curious about his side trip to the Colombian capital, but he refused to tell her anything beyond its being connected to Stikes. However, they were both too tired to argue about it, flopping into the luxurious bed in their hotel suite and almost instantly falling asleep.

As soon as Eddie was woken by voices from the next room the following morning, he realised that Nina had something more important occupying her mind than his excursion to Bogotá. Her excitement was clear even through the door. He got dressed and went through to the lounge, finding Nina sitting at a table with Macy, Osterhagen, Kit and even Mac. 'What's this, a remake of *The Breakfast Club*?'

Nina hurriedly gulped a mouthful of toast, washing it down with a swig of coffee. 'Mm, morning! Guess you slept well – you don't normally get up this late.'

'Well, yesterday was kind of knackering. Mornin', all.' He waved to the others, getting greetings in response. 'Why didn't you wake me?'

'I thought you needed a lie-in. And you looked so sweet while you were asleep.'

'Funny, I've seen Eddie when he's asleep,' said Mac, 'and

that's not a word I would ever have used to describe him.'

'Yeah, well, kipping with a bunch of sweaty, farting SAS blokes tends to make you scrunch your face up,' Eddie retorted. He looked at the table, seeing the recovered khipu laid out on a long white board, and a jumble of notes in front of the three archaeologists. 'So, have we got this thing figured out? Hope you're going to wash your hands before you pick it up,' he added to Nina, who was wolfing down another slice of buttered toast.

She waved to Macy for a napkin. 'Yeah, Leonard thinks he's got something.'

Eddie pulled up a chair and sat as Osterhagen, with deep bags under his eyes that suggested he had been working all night, held up a large photo of the map in Paititi. 'We know the start point of the journey,' the German explained. 'Cuzco, of course, the centre of the Inca empire. And we know the end point – Paititi. What we needed were reference points along the way. If we could identify other known locations, it would allow us to work out the code shared between the map and the khipu – directions and distances.'

Eddie nodded. 'So what's you found?'

Osterhagen was about to speak when Macy enthusiastically cut in. 'Only the biggest Inca landmark in the world,' she said, waving at a blow-up of part of the painted wall. 'Machu Picchu!' She pointed out a small illustration amongst the markings, little more than a sketch: two rounded-off conical peaks, one large, one small, with lines presumably representing buildings at their bases. 'It's about seventy miles northwest of Cuzco, along a thing called the Inca Trail.'

'I've travelled along it many times,' said Osterhagen, trying to wrest back the discussion from the perky student. 'I know the landmarks well. Now, the number of these markings here,' he indicated part of the map, 'correspond to the *huacas* along the Inca Trail between Cuzco and Machu Picchu.'

'*Huacas*?' said Eddie. 'Sounds like an Inca puking.'

Those who knew him well either smiled or let his attempt at a joke pass without comment; Osterhagen, however, seemed mildly affronted. 'No, they are sacred sites,' he said. 'The Incas believed that certain places were of spiritual importance. Some were natural features like springs or mountain peaks, some were places of historical importance, and others were burial sites for mummies. Not all of them survived the Spanish conquest, because the Conquistadors tried to eradicate everything associated with the existing religions.'

'But it's kinda hard to destroy an entire mountain,' Macy added. 'A lot of them survived.'

'Got you,' Eddie said, examining the photographs. 'You know where these things are today, so we can work backwards and say this marking means a burial site, or whatever.'

'And the other part,' said Nina, having wiped her fingers, 'is the khipu.' She indicated the leftmost section of the collection of knotted strings. 'This part is a record of the first stage of their journey, as far as Machu Picchu. The number of strings matches the number of *huacas* on the map.'

'A lot of landmarks,' noted Eddie.

'It was a long journey. It's over a thousand miles from Cuzco to Paititi, and that's as the crow flies – the Incas took an even longer route. You see this?'

She pointed further along the Inca artefact's woven spine. Although the strings were dirty and darkened by time, Eddie saw that the various strands were discernibly different. Those up to roughly two-thirds of the way along the khipu's length were a variety of shades, mostly greys and browns and reds with greens and blues interspersed; beyond that point, they were almost entirely of the last two. 'The colours change,' he said. 'What does that mean?'

'We think,' said Osterhagen, 'the colours represent different types of terrain. This section here,' he gestured at a cluster of grey strings in the first section of the khipu, 'corresponds to the highlands along the Inca Trail leading to Machu Picchu. By going back towards Cuzco, we found that other colours match particular features of the landscape.' He gently nudged one of the strands with a toothpick. 'This shade of turquoise seems to represent river valleys, for example.'

Eddie took a closer look. The string had multiple knots of different types along its length. 'So the map tells you what landmarks to look for, the colours of the strings show you the terrain . . . so the knots are, what? Directions? Distances?'

'Both, in a way,' said Nina.

'The Incas had a system of sacred routes radiating outwards from Cuzco,' Osterhagen explained. 'They were called *ceque* pathways, and they connected all corners of the empire. Some were actual roads or paths, but most were just straight lines from one *huaca* to another. We knew that the pathways had ritual significance – the most important ones, the forty-one *ceques* around Cuzco, can be linked to the lunar calendar. But nobody has ever worked out how to connect all the others around the empire.'

'Until now, at a guess,' Eddie said, seeing that Nina was practically bouncing in her seat with excitement.

'You got that right,' she told him with a broad grin. 'Leonard used the data he got by backtracking from Machu Picchu to Cuzco to figure out that the knots closest to the main cord give you directions, based on star charts – the Incas had a very advanced astronomical system.'

'Not as good as the Egyptian one, though,' Macy chipped in,

defending the non-Cuban half of her heritage.

'Maybe not, but still accurate enough to be usable for navigation. So that's part of the key. And the other part is also on the khipu – the rest of the knots. The Inca numerical system was decimal, like ours, and on a khipu it worked like an abacus. The knots represent units, tens, hundreds and so on, depending on their position. If you know the system, you can tell what number's recorded on a piece of string at a glance, or even by touch.'

'Again, because I had reference points,' said Osterhagen, 'we were able to work out what the numbers meant. They are indeed distances. Nina calculated how they relate to *huacas* in the real world. In her head,' he added, impressed.

'So you know the total distance they travelled?' asked Kit.

'Something like seventeen hundred miles,' Nina replied.

'Jesus,' said Eddie. 'And you said it was a thousand miles in a straight line? Seven hundred miles is a hell of a detour.'

'It's because they were sticking to what they knew for most of it,' Macy said. She opened up a large map of South America. 'From Cuzco, they were pretty much heading northwest along the east side of the Andes. I guess they didn't want to go into the jungle.'

'But they had to eventually,' added Nina. She pointed back at the section of the khipu where the coloured threads became predominantly green and blue. 'We think the green ones represent jungle terrain. And the directions at the top of each string almost all indicate northeast. The blue ones, it seems likely that they mean to follow rivers.'

'Makes sense,' said Eddie. 'Not a lot of other landmarks in the jungle.'

'Especially if you're used to living amongst mountains.' She moved her finger back along the khipu. 'So if we backtrack from Paititi, they covered long distances with comparatively few changes of direction . . . and then here' – she indicated the point where the colour scheme reverted to the redder end of the spectrum – 'is where they crossed from the Andes into the Amazon basin. But even up in the highlands, they were still heading mainly northeast . . . until *here*.'

Eddie examined the strings she was pointing out. The exact meaning of the knots at their tops were a mystery to him, but he immediately saw what she meant: those to the right of her finger were tied right over left, while on the other side they were fastened left over right. 'So that's where they changed direction,' he deduced. 'They stopped following the Andes and went out into the jungle.'

Nina nodded. 'That's the dogleg, where the extra seven hundred miles came from. And it's something else too.'

He could tell from her struggle to contain another smile that it was something big. Which, considering what they were looking for, could only be one thing. 'El Dorado?'

'El Doraaaa-do!' she sang, showing him a blow-up of the painted city, the Punchaco – and the final piece of statue – at its heart. Mac chuckled at her unrestrained enthusiasm. 'The number of *huaca* markings on the map before you get there is exactly the same as the number of strings on the khipu up to the point where they turn northeast. They left Cuzco, headed along the Andes, thought they'd found a safe place to hide the empire's greatest treasures . . . then had to move again to avoid the Spanish. But they left some of the treasure behind. And now . . . we can find it.'

Eddie gave her a genially mocking look. 'What, you mean you haven't already? I thought you were supposed to be good at this archaeology lark!'

She pouted. 'Well, we *have* only just had breakfast. At least give us until lunchtime!'

It took rather longer than that, the process of calculating all the directions and distances represented by each thread of the khipu and then relating those to known *huacas* throughout Peru dragging on through the day. But Osterhagen's knowledge of the country and its culture proved an enormous asset, even though he was at times on the verge of falling asleep at the table and had to be prodded awake by the two women. The Incas had illustrated on their map what were now known archaeological sites, and the German's wealth of experience allowed the group to skip long sections of the trek, narrowing the possible location of the lost city each time.

While Nina, Osterhagen and Macy worked in the lounge, Eddie made a phone call from the bedroom. 'Hi, Nan.'

'Edward!' came the delighted voice from across the Atlantic. 'It's so wonderful to hear from you. How are you, my little lambchop?' His grandmother sounded somewhat stronger than the last time they had spoken, if still a little breathless.

'I'm fine, Nan. I was going to ask you the same thing.'

'Oh, I feel a lot better, thank you. I still have to wear this silly mask, but hopefully not for much longer – oh, excuse me.' She stifled a yawn. 'I'm a bit tired.'

'Sorry, I forgot about the time difference!' England was five and a half hours ahead of Venezuela, making it past ten o'clock in Bournemouth. 'I'll call back another time.'

'No, don't be silly, Edward. It's never a problem staying up to talk to you. Where are you ringing from?'

'We're in Venezuela, but probably won't be for long. Nina's on the trail of something.'

'Venezuela!' Nan said, alarmed. 'Is it safe there? I saw all that trouble on the news.'

'Yeah, we saw some of it too,' said Eddie, smiling to himself. 'But everything's okay now.'

'Oh, I'm glad. You do lead an exciting life. But when are you going to be in the newspapers, or on television? Everyone saw Nina in the Sphinx last year, but you were only in the background. Why didn't you say something?'

'I'm not much of one for publicity. Nina isn't either,' he added, 'but she sort of gets stuck with it. Besides, who wants to be famous? I'd rather be rich.'

'Well, you'd better get to work on that. And while you're at it, some great-grandchildren for your old nan would be nice. Before I pop my clogs.'

'Plenty of time for that, Nan,' Eddie insisted. 'But I'll see what Nina thinks once we find what she's after.'

At that moment, Nina burst into the room. 'Eddie, Eddie!' she said in excitement. 'We've found it! Come and see!' She rushed back out.

'She doesn't waste time, does she?' said Nan, amused. 'So, about those great-grandchildren . . .'

'*Eddie!*'

He sighed. 'I'd better go, before she drags me out. But I'll call you again when I get the chance.'

'That'll be lovely. Will you be coming back to England? I'd love to see you again.'

'Yeah, soon as I can. I'll take you for another walk down to the sea.'

'I can't wait. Talk to you again soon, Edward. Love you.'

'Love you too,' he replied. 'Bye.'

'Goodbye, love.'

He hung up, then went into the lounge just as Mac and Kit

entered. 'We were summoned,' Mac told him wryly.

The three men joined the archaeologists at the table. 'So, what've we got?' Eddie asked.

'This is where we're looking,' said Nina, tapping a map of Peru. The area beneath her fingernail was in the Amazonas region, south of the border with Ecuador, on the eastern flank of the Andes. 'Leonard worked out that one of the last places the Incas visited en route was Kuélap, which is a pretty amazing fortress near Chachapoyas.' She flipped open a reference book to show her audience a picture of its imposing outer wall.

'Impressive,' said Mac. 'And it looks in good shape, too. Did the Spanish discover it?'

'Actually, no,' Osterhagen told him. 'Even though they reached that region, they never found it – which is why it has survived so well.'

'Which makes it more likely that they never found El Dorado either,' said Nina. 'The whole region is cloud forest; high-altitude jungle. Very few inhabitants, now or then – and lots of places to hide.'

'So how close have you got to finding it?' Eddie asked.

'We think within a couple of miles. The directions from Kuélap take you more or less due north for about forty miles, until you reach the point where the Incas headed northeast towards Paititi.'

Kit peered at the map's contour lines. 'It looks rather hard to get to.'

Osterhagen shook his head. 'Not as hard as you think. There is a road that runs through the mountains. Well, I say a road, but it will not exactly be an autobahn. It will be narrow, it will be steep . . . and it will be dangerous. Very dangerous.'

'Oh, great,' said Eddie. 'A death road.'

'A what?' Macy asked, alarmed.

'Well, you know how in the States dangerous roads have barriers and warning signs and kerbs to keep you away from massive cliffs?'

'Yeah?'

'This won't.' She appeared unhappy at the prospect.

'Any road is better than no road,' Mac assured her. 'But presumably it can't be too close to the road, or somebody would have discovered it by now.'

'We've got some more clues,' Nina replied. 'The map in Paititi showed that El Dorado was very close to a waterfall.' She nodded towards a laptop. 'We've checked the IHA's satellite imagery, and think we've pinpointed it.'

'And we should be able to drive most of the way,' said Osterhagen. 'There will be a trek through the jungle, but nothing worse than at Paititi. The area around the waterfall is reasonably flat.'

Mac nodded. 'That sounds good.'

'For what?' Eddie asked.

'For me.'

'What?'

'I rather fancied coming along with you this time,' said the Scot amiably.

'Are you kidding?'

'Not at all. I'd quite like to see one of these incredible discoveries first-hand. And to be perfectly honest, that little jaunt around Caracas the other night . . . well, it made me realise that in some ways I rather miss the action.'

'But you really want to come on an expedition?' Nina asked.

'Why not? Dr Osterhagen said the place you'll be exploring is fairly accessible. And just because I've got a tin leg doesn't make me helpless. I've run a couple of half-marathons on it.'

'Well, if you think you're up to it, I'd be happy for you to come with us,' said Nina. She saw from her husband's face that he had a different opinion, but he said nothing. 'So,' she went on, addressing the whole group, 'this could be it. We might actually have found El Dorado.'

'What's the next move?' asked Kit.

'The first thing is to contact the Peruvian government via the UN and ask permission to mount an expedition. Considering what we're looking for, I think we'll get an answer fairly quickly. Once we have that, organising everything shouldn't take too long. As Leonard said, we can drive there.'

'And if we actually find El Dorado?' asked Mac.

'Then we'll probably be sticking around for a while! But you won't have to stay if you don't want to. As much as I love getting down to the real nitty-gritty of archaeological work, I know it's not for everybody.'

'Does that mean I can leave too?' Eddie asked, raising a few laughs.

Kit had more to add. 'When you talk to the Peruvian govern-ment, Nina, make sure you emphasise the need for security. If word gets out about what we're searching for, the entire region will fill with treasure hunters – or worse.'

'Wait, "we"?' said Eddie. 'You want to come an' all? Thought the case was closed now that we've got back the stuff Da— de Quesada nicked.' Only Kit noticed his near-slip, but the Interpol agent's knowing look assured him that their mutual secret would remain that way for now.

'Technically, it is,' said Kit. 'But . . . well, I agree with Mac. I want to see the lost city of gold! And I also want to see what happens when Nina puts all the statues together.'

'Okay,' said Nina. 'I'll talk to the UN tomorrow. Until then, we're still honoured guests of the Venezuelan president, so we might as well make the most of it. Dinner, I think?'

There was a chorus of agreement from round the table. The group broke up, heading back to their rooms to freshen up and change. Eddie followed Mac out, catching up with the Scot in the corridor. 'Mac. A word?'

'Something the matter, Eddie?' Mac asked innocently.

'You know bloody well there is. Why do you want to come with us?'

'For exactly the reasons I told Nina. I'm honestly keen to see what she's going to find. And since I flew halfway round the world, I think it would be a shame to go home right before the interesting part.'

'You didn't think being shot at by a Hind was interesting?'

'There's interesting, and there's *interesting*.' Mac smiled; then his expression became more serious. 'I may be getting on, Eddie, but I'm not some invalid. And I want to make the most of life before I become one. As I told Nina, I ran some half-marathons after I recovered from losing my leg, but I doubt I could manage another one.'

'Good job you don't need to. You've got a free bus pass now.'

'Very amusing. Although I do like being able to get home without having to pay. Once I'm there, though . . .' A regretful tone came into his voice. 'It's rather an empty place, truth be told. Especially in the evenings. I want something to do, and people to do it with.'

Eddie was taken aback by his friend's confession. 'Why didn't you say something before? I could have come over to England more often.'

'I don't want sympathy, Eddie,' Mac snapped. 'I want to play my part!'

'But you do, though. You do that consulting work for MI6,

you've helped me and Nina out of trouble – Christ, you even saved a roomful of world leaders from getting blown up last year.'

'We mostly have Kit to thank for that,' said Mac. 'But the point is, I don't want to suffer a gradual slide into senescence—'

'Into what?'

'Crumbling decrepitude. I'd rather keel over dead on the spot from a heart attack before I reach seventy than shrivel away in a hospital ward stuck full of tubes.'

His words summoned up an image in Eddie's mind: his grandmother, small and helpless in the hospital bed, face covered by an oxygen mask. 'Yeah,' he said quietly. 'That's no way to end up.'

Mac recognised his change of mood, and understood its meaning. 'Sorry. I didn't mean to be quite so . . . blunt.'

'That's okay.' He forced away the depressing mental picture. 'So what you're saying is, you want to fight to the end.'

'To coin a phrase, yes.' A wry smile crinkled Mac's features. 'Although I could do without literally fighting. I've had more than enough of that!'

'But you really think you're up for it? Jungles, mountains, death roads?'

'If I didn't, I wouldn't have asked to go in the first place, would I?' He clapped the younger man on the shoulder. 'I already had you carry me to safety once in my life. Twice would be embarrassing. I still have my pride!'

'Well . . . all right,' said Eddie, feigning grudging acceptance. 'So long as I don't have to share a tent with you.'

'If that were going to happen, I'd back out right now!' They both laughed. 'Better get ready for dinner. See you soon.' He headed down the hallway.

Eddie watched him go, then returned to his own suite.

★

In his room, Kit changed his shirt and put on a jacket, and was about to leave when he paused, thinking, then took out his phone. Listening at the door to make sure nobody was about to knock, he made a call. 'This is Jindal.'

'What is it?' came the terse reply.

'Dr Wilde thinks she has found the location of the last statue segment, in northern Peru. I'll be accompanying her on the expedition.'

'Good. Do whatever is necessary to ensure she recovers it. The future of the world depends on our obtaining all three statues. And, having spoken to her, I think she may be sympatahetic to the Group's goals.'

'I'll see to it,' said Kit, but the call had already ended.

He was taking a huge risk by not telling his paymasters what had happened at the Clubhouse: that Stikes had tortured information about his true mission out of him, despite his best efforts to resist. The mercenary leader now knew of the Group's existence, even if he had no specific details of its plans, for the simple reason that his interrogation subject didn't know them himself. But that alone would be reason enough for the Group to terminate his employment . . . or more. In return for the considerable rewards they promised, they expected – demanded – success.

Which, if Nina's deductions were correct, would soon be forthcoming. Reassured, he left the room.

30

Peru

'So these are cloud forests, huh?' said Macy, surveying the scenery. 'I can see the forest part – but where are the clouds?'

'Don't worry,' said Eddie, driving. 'Once they come down, you won't see anything *but* bloody clouds!'

The seven-seater Nissan Patrol was in the middle of a small convoy, heading north along a dirt road that had split off from a paved highway some thirty miles north of the provincial capital, Chachapoyas. In another off-roader behind them were two Peruvian archaeologists; the tall, thin-faced Professor Miguel Olmedo from the University of Lima, and his shorter, fatter associate Dr Julian Cruzado. A local archaeological presence was both expected and welcome, but Nina was less enthused about their also being accompanied by a senior official from the Peruvian Ministry of Culture, a rather full-of-himself man named Diego Zender who had attached himself lamprey-like to the expedition to claim a stake in the glory if the mythical El Dorado turned out actually to exist. Zender had an assistant, a young, long-haired woman called Juanita Alvarez whose function when not acting as a chauffeuse, as far as Nina could tell, was mostly to stand beside her boss looking pretty.

But freeloaders weren't the issue. More worrying was the profession of the four men in the leading Jeep. Soldiers. Her request for security had been taken seriously, but she couldn't help feeling that the armed group in their military vehicle might draw exactly the kind of curiosity she hoped to avoid. Zender's claim that the troops were necessary to protect them from the terrorists known to operate in the province had not exactly been reassuring.

But for now, Nina was able to forget such concerns and simply enjoy the landscape. The three 4×4s were heading up a long, lush valley, vegetation clinging to practically every non-sheer surface. Unlike the trees in the rainforest around Paititi, those here were rather squat, clawing moisture out of the air when the clouds descended rather than waiting for rainfall, but they were every bit as dazzlingly green in the stark high-altitude sunlight. The river that had carved the passage out of the Andes was over fifty feet below at the bottom of a ravine, but the slope they were ascending was broad enough for them to stay well clear of the drop.

That wouldn't be the case for long, however. In the distance, she picked out the road's brown thread clinging precariously to the flanks of the mountains. Swathes of grey running down the hillside, as if someone had randomly scraped away a top layer of green paint, provided evidence of recent landslides. 'So,' she asked Eddie, 'when you mentioned death roads the other day . . . is that actually what they're called?'

''Fraid so,' he replied. 'Went along one in the Philippines once. Fucking terrifying! Combat's bad, but idiot drivers are worse. The best bits of it, there was just enough room for two cars to get past each other.'

'And the worst bits?' Kit asked from the second row of seats, where he was sitting with Macy.

'Just enough room for *one* car. Only problem is, people still try to pass, 'cause nobody wants to reverse for half a mile. And God help you if a bus or a truck comes the other way – they just go "We're bigger than you, so we've got right of way" and come right at you without stopping.'

'You know,' said Mac from beside Osterhagen on the rear seats, 'I think I'll just sleep until we get there. If we go over the edge, try not to wake me with your screams, hmm?'

'At least there is not much traffic,' Osterhagen said. 'We should not have any prob—'

At that exact moment, the convoy rounded a bend – and the Jeep skidded to an emergency stop. Eddie had prudently kept a safe distance behind it, and was able to bring the Nissan to a halt with ten feet to spare. Unfortunately, Juanita had not been so careful, and the Patrol's occupants took a jolt as her off-roader nudged their bumper.

The driver of the bus lumbering the other way gave the stalled vehicles a baleful glare. 'Everyone all right?' Eddie asked, getting positive responses. He looked back at Osterhagen. 'You were saying, Doc?'

Osterhagen recovered his composure. 'I was about to say that once we get *past* the next village, which is the last settlement for over forty kilometres, we should not have any problems.'

'Of course, Leonard,' said Nina teasingly.

There was a walkie-talkie on the dashboard shelf, letting the three vehicles communicate; it squawked. 'Hey, careful how you drive!' Zender demanded. 'That could have damaged my car.'

'Damage his *face*,' Eddie muttered, picking up the radio. 'Here's a tip – you might want to stay further back and not drive so fast.'

'Juanita knows how to drive,' came the peevish reply. 'Now come on, get going!'

'Think anyone'd mind if *he* went over the edge?' Eddie asked as the bus finally squeezed past. Nobody raised any objections. The Jeep set off, the Englishman pulling out after it. With a lurch, Zender's vehicle followed.

About five minutes later a village came into view, ramshackle buildings clumped haphazardly on each side of the road. The Jeep's driver sounded his horn to encourage a skinny goat to clear out of their path, the blare attracting curious looks from the locals. Once the animal had ambled aside the Jeep moved off again, and Eddie had started to follow when Osterhagen suddenly jumped in his seat. 'Eddie, stop the car!' he cried, pointing. 'Over there, look!'

An elongated, moss-covered rock poked out of the ground like a giant raised finger. 'What is it?' Nina asked.

The German was out of the Nissan before Eddie had brought it to a complete stop. 'It's a *huaca*! On the map, one of the last markings before the Incas reached El Dorado was of a particular type of *huaca*. And this,' he pointed excitedly at the stone, 'is almost identical to one on the Inca Trail – and the marking is the same!'

Nina joined him as the third 4×4 pulled up. 'So you think we're nearly there?'

'Yes, absolutely!' He gazed at the valley ahead. 'Only a matter of kilometres. I am certain!'

Zender's window whirred down. 'Why have we stopped?'

'Navigation check,' said Nina. 'Dr Osterhagen thinks we're getting close.'

The official's impatient expression was replaced by approval. 'Ah! Good, good. Well, lead us there, doctor!'

It was now Eddie's turn to show impatience. 'Are we done?'

'Yeah, we're done,' Nina said. She and Osterhagen re-entered the Patrol, and it continued on its way, Zender's 4×4 behind it.

A scruffy man, the smouldering stub of a cigarette between his lips, emerged from a house to watch the convoy pass. He paid special attention to the Nissan – and the red-haired woman in the passenger seat. Once the convoy had left the little settlement, he stubbed out the cigarette, then took out a cellphone.

Beyond the village, the road steepened – and the ground it traversed narrowed enormously. The ravine carved by the river was now over a hundred feet deep, the drop growing steadily higher as they drove along. The route ahead was not so much running through the mountains as clinging to them by its fingernails.

The convoy slowed as it approached a bend. Poking up from the cliff's edge were several crude wooden crosses. 'Ah . . . what are those?' Macy asked nervously.

'Where people have gone over the edge,' Eddie said, navigating the turn. 'Narrow roads, bad drivers and old cars with knackered brakes aren't a good mix.'

'Yeah, I wish I hadn't asked,' she said, shuffling across the seat away from the edge. 'Couldn't we have gone by helicopter?'

'I don't think the Peruvians' budget would have stretched to that,' said Nina.

'*I* would have paid! I've got money!'

The Patrol's other occupants laughed as it rounded the bend, revealing more of the twisting route. As Eddie had promised, clouds were starting to obscure the valley below, in places the ever-deepening ravine vanishing into a blank grey haze.

Somehow, that made the prospect of going over the edge even more frightening: no way of knowing how long it would take to reach the fall's inevitable conclusion.

Other features were still clearly visible, though. 'Is that the waterfall?' Kit asked, pointing.

Ahead, a great scar ran down the hillside, vegetation and even soil scoured away to reveal the bare rock beneath. It started at the top of a rise a few hundred feet above the road, and descended into the clouds below. A thin waterfall flowed down the centre of the exposed swathe, splashing on to the road. Nina checked her map and satellite photos, puzzled. 'No, this isn't marked.'

Eddie reduced speed. 'Must've been a landslide. Probably a river up there somewhere that overflowed.' The road itself was covered in debris, rocks and thick reddish-brown soil dumped on the already rough surface. Even though the locals had made the obstruction passable by simply shovelling much of the stuff over the cliff, the way forward was still worryingly narrow.

The soldiers in the Jeep also had misgivings, three of them hopping out and leaving the driver to traverse it alone. Nina drew in a sharp breath when the Jeep reached the waterfall and slipped sideways – the constant flow from above had turned the soil to a soft, muddy slush – but a quick burst of power pulled it free, muck spraying from its wheels. Once it cleared the landslip, the soldiers hurried after it.

'Well, us next,' said Eddie cheerily. 'Everyone out. Except you, Nina.'

'What?' she protested as the others exited. 'Why do I have to stay in the car of terror?'

''Cause of that whole "till death us do part" business – it might not be too far off. Nah, I'm just kidding,' he added, at her unamused expression. 'I need you to look out of your side and tell me how close we are to the edge.'

'Too close,' she said, even before he started moving. 'Way too close!'

'Ha fuckin' ha. Okay, here we go . . .'

The Patrol was considerably wider than the Jeep, the wheels on Nina's side coming within inches of the edge – which sagged alarmingly as the truck's weight was put on it, clods of earth falling down the steep slope. Somehow, a stunted tree had managed to cling to a rock outcrop below while everything around it had been washed away, the lone sign of life a silhouette against the clouded abyss. She looked away from the vertiginous view to the sliver of road between the tyres and the long drop. 'About six inches, six inches, three inches – whoa! Minus an inch.'

Eddie turned the 4×4 in as far as he could, trying to keep it in the ruts made by previous traffic. 'That better?'

'Yeah. Relatively speaking.'

They reached the waterfall, the stream drumming off the roof. Nina, still leaning out of the window, gasped as spray washed over her. But the Nissan rolled on, soon clearing the landslip.

'Piece of piss,' Eddie said, cracking his knuckles. 'And we even stayed dry! Well, I did.' Nina glared at him from under damp strands of hair.

The Nissan's passengers caught up, then the last off-roader made the crossing, Zender chivalrously abandoning the passenger seat and allowing Cruzado to act as Juanita's navigator. But she too cleared the landslide safely, and the convoy continued. There was an awkward moment when a pickup truck coming the other way took a 'first come, first served' attitude by swerving to the inside of another tight, unprotected bend marked by more crosses, forcing the three vehicles to creep around it on the outside, but they soon reached the first piece of actual infrastructure along the road: a short wooden bridge across a narrow gap.

'We're getting close,' Nina said into the radio as she found the landmark on the map. 'About another mile.'

The news produced a renewed sense of anticipation, even as the clouds closed in. The road narrowed again, the hillside so steep that a short section had actually been carved out of the rock itself to allow it to continue, thousands of tons of stone hanging above the vehicles. Beyond that, though, the way ahead began to widen out. Another couple of turns . . . and their destination came into view.

'Now that's more like it,' said Mac admiringly. The broad waterfall ahead was much more impressive than the one they had passed on the road, plunging down a vertical cliff for over two hundred feet. Its base was hidden by jungle; the falling water had cut a deep bowl out of the hillside, every square inch packed with plant life. Above the cliff, tall peaks loomed through the clouds, the river feeding the falls flowing through a narrow valley between them.

'This is the place,' said Nina. She passed word via radio to the other vehicles. The soldiers turned off the road and led the way into the little forest, crunching the Jeep up a slope for a few hundred yards, winding between the trees, before the sheer density of vegetation blocked their path. The other 4×4s stopped behind them.

Everyone climbed out, glad the bumpy ride was over. Nina stretched and looked round. The waterfall was now obscured by foliage overhead, but the echoing rumble from up the hill meant it would not be hard to find.

She noticed that Mac appeared a little hesitant on the uneven ground. 'You okay?'

'I just need a bit of extra support,' he said, smiling. 'And there it is.' He picked up a fallen branch and knocked it against a nearby trunk to shake off loose dirt before leaning on it. 'There. A perfectly good walking stick.'

'Tie another couple together and you'll be able to make a Zimmer frame,' Eddie joked.

Mac waved the stick at him. 'Do you want me to kick your arse, Eddie, or beat it?'

'Now, now, boys,' said Nina, amused. She turned to Osterhagen. 'Okay, Leonard. What are we looking for?'

Osterhagen had photo blow-ups of the Paititi map laminated in a folder. 'First, we find the waterfall, I suppose. Then, if the painting was accurate, the ruins should be to one side of it.'

Zender bustled over, Juanita a step behind. 'Is this the place? Have we found it?'

'We haven't even started looking,' Nina chided. 'Okay, to find the waterfall we just need to follow our ears. Then we'll see what else is there.'

The soldiers stayed with their Jeep as the rest of the expedition moved uphill into the jungle. The rumble of falling water soon became a roar, and they emerged from the trees to face its source.

'Now that's pretty . . . wow,' said Macy.

'No kidding,' Nina agreed.

Close up, the falls were even more spectacular than they had appeared from the road. The flow, some ninety feet across, plunged down the wide, almost sheer cliff to crash thunderously over the broken boulders at its base. Spray swirled across the pool carved from the rocky ground, sparkling rainbows shimmering in the sunlight breaking through the clouds. A broad, fast-flowing stream acted as a run-off, water rushing away into the forest.

Osterhagen compared one of his pictures to the view before him. 'It looks a lot like the painting. Don't you think?'

'It's pretty close,' Nina agreed. While the mural was stylised, there were undeniable similarities between it and the real-life features of the landscape.

'So in that case,' said Eddie, 'where's this lost city?'

'Let's take a closer look, shall we?' Nina led the way to the water's edge. 'According to the map from Paititi, it should be off to that side of the waterfall.' She pointed. 'We'll split up and check the cliffs.'

Eddie looked up at the falls. 'Think this really is the place?'

'It could be. I'm getting a vibe.'

'I thought you left your vibe at home?' he said with a dirty smile. Nina shook her head, then directed the others to begin the search.

Despite her gut feeling, however, nothing turned up. The cliffs were conspicuously lacking in golden cities, or nooks and caves that might provide entrance to one. Empty-handed, the expedition members regrouped by the pool. 'I don't understand,' said Osterhagen disconsolately. 'It matches the picture from Paititi. What are we missing?'

'There is nothing here,' said Zender. 'We have wasted our time.'

Nina was losing her own patience with the Peruvian official. 'We haven't finished searching yet. There's the other side of the waterfall to search, for a start. And then there's the waterfall itself. There might be an opening behind it.'

'Easy way to check,' said Eddie. He picked up a stone and flung it into the plunging waters. A faint *clack* of rock hitting rock was audible even over the rumble of the falls. 'Well, that's solid,' he said, picking up a second stone and hurling it at a higher spot. 'And that's . . .'

The second missile was swallowed up without a sound.

'. . . not,' Eddie concluded, surprised. 'Huh. I was only doing that to take the piss!'

'There's a cave behind the waterfall?' Mac asked.

'Maybe . . .' Nina regarded the falls thoughtfully.

Eddie threw another stone, aiming at the same height as before, about sixty feet above the pool, but some way off to one side. Again, the missile disappeared noiselessly. 'It's at least forty feet wide,' he said, bending to pick up a new projectile.

Nina put a hand on his shoulder. 'Save your pitching arm, hon. We've got an easier way to check.'

Amongst the team's equipment was a laser rangefinder, which Nina had requisitioned from the IHA to take measurements of whatever they found. The results took some time to collect; while the device could work through rain, it hadn't been designed to send its beam through a torrent of water. The reading constantly fluctuated as the laser light was refracted by the falls. But she didn't need millimetric precision, only for enough of the beam to reflect off the cliff for her to get a reading . . . or not.

Osterhagen stood beside her as she scanned the waterfall, sketching the results. It became clear that there was indeed an opening hidden behind the deluge – a large one, at that. The cave mouth was some seventy feet wide and at least forty high, its lowest point fifty feet above the pool.

Always fifty feet above the pool. While the outline of the opening was irregular in shape, its base was completely level. 'That's got to be man-made,' Nina said.

'It could have formed along a rock stratum,' said the German. But it was clear he didn't believe it.

Eddie looked at the drawing. 'Be a bugger to get to it. Even if you climb up that high away from the waterfall, you've still got to get across – and that much water coming down'll knock you right off unless you're seriously well attached. That's a job for a pro climber.'

'I used to climb,' offered Cruzado. Everyone looked at the portly, middle-aged Peruvian. 'A long time ago,' he admitted.

Nina continued surveying the cliffs. 'We might not need to go all the way up,' she said, pointing at a spot almost dead centre of the waterfall, and considerably lower. 'There's another opening.'

'It is not very big,' said Osterhagen as she took more readings. He marked it on his sketch. It was roughly twenty feet above the base of the falls.

Nina swept the rangefinder back and forth. 'I think that ledge leads to it. Someone might be able to climb up to it and then go along behind the waterfall.'

'Someone,' said Eddie, with a faint but distinct sigh. 'You mean me.'

'I'd volunteer,' said Mac, 'but, well . . .' He banged his stick against his prosthetic leg, plastic and metal rattling.

'Can you do it, Eddie?' Nina asked. 'With the climbing gear that we've brought, I mean. Or will we need to go back to town for more equipment?'

'No, I can probably do it with what we've got,' he said. 'I'd rather take the chance than drive along that bloody road again!' He looked between the waterfall and Osterhagen's drawing, judging distances. 'We've got enough rope, so . . . yeah, I think I can do it. I'll put in some spikes so I can hook up the line.'

'So that we can get across?'

'I was thinking more so I can get back. It's only twenty feet up, but I don't really want to end up in that pool. There're a lot of pointy rocks.' He gave the cliff one last look, then nodded. 'I can do it. Let's get the gear.'

Eddie, Nina and Macy trekked back to the Jeeps, finding the four soldiers sitting around smoking and looking bored. Their interest perked up when Macy filled them in on developments. The highest-ranking of them, a young lieutenant called Echazu, decided to accompany the group back to the waterfall – purely in the interests of gathering information for his superiors, of course, rather than the hope of being involved in something mediaworthy. Another soldier, a corporal, persuaded him of the benefits of having a second pair of eyes to help with his report, but the two remaining privates were left disappointed as they were told to stay and watch the vehicles.

The soldiers in tow, they returned to the waterfall. Mac and Osterhagen had been to the base of the falls in the hope of glimpsing what lay behind it, but nothing was visible through the water and spray. 'That looks like the easiest way up,' Mac told Eddie, indicating a particular section of rock face.

'Yeah, shouldn't be too hard,' Eddie agreed, before giving the older man a look. 'Been trying to find a nice simple route for yourself, have you?'

'Well, of course! If El Dorado really is hidden behind there, I'm not going to stand outside like a lemon while you and Nina explore it. I want to see the place for myself.'

'That's if there *is* anything back there.'

'There must be,' said Osterhagen earnestly. 'Everything fits – the map at Paititi, the khipu, the trail of *huacas*. This is the place.'

'Then let's find out,' said Nina. She regarded Eddie expectantly.

'Muggins leads the way, as usual,' he said. 'All right, I'll go and find you another archaeological wonder. If I must.' He grinned, then gathered his equipment and went to the foot of the cliff.

The edge of the waterfall was only ten feet from where he began to climb, and spray quickly soaked him. As Mac had thought, the ascent was straightforward; it took barely a minute before he was level with the ledge. It was only a matter of inches wide. Eddie hammered a spike into the rock and attached a carabiner, then threaded the rope through it and dropped one end down so the others could follow him up, tying a knot to secure it. Then, the line coiled over one shoulder, he faced the wall and edged sidelong along the ledge.

Even though the route was set slightly back beneath an overhang, the falling water still pounded at his back. He dug his fingers into cracks in the rock, clinging tightly and advancing step by cautious step.

After about forty feet, the cliff bulged slightly outwards. It would force him directly into the deluge. He tried to look past it to see if the ledge continued on the far side, but his view was blocked by water and spray. Keeping hold with one hand, he took out a second spike and gingerly supported it in the crook of his thumb before tapping it into place with his hammer. Another carabiner was hooked on, and the rope clipped through it. Satisfied it was secure, Eddie took several deep breaths – then found a firm handhold and pulled himself into the deluge.

He almost lost his grip as the full force of the water hit, threatening to hurl him down on to the jagged rocks below. Blinded, unable to breathe, he pressed his chest against the rock and groped ahead. The protruding section of cliff was only short – his hand found clear air again on the other side. He hugged the wall and slid round it, emerging back beneath the overhang.

Utterly drenched, Eddie shook water from his face and

regained his breath before attaching another spike. Holding the rope, he twisted to look at what lay behind the waterfall.

His eyes widened at the sight. 'Well, bloody hell . . .'

Nina's radio crackled, Eddie's voice almost drowned by the noise of the waterfall. 'Nina, you there?'

'Eddie! Are you okay?'

'Yeah, I'm fine. Fucking soaked, though.'

'What can you see?' she asked. 'Is there an opening in the cliff?'

'Nope.'

A shock of disappointment ran through her. 'What? There *isn't* an opening?'

'Oh, there's an opening. There isn't a cliff.'

The group exchanged confused glances. 'What do you mean?'

'I mean, it's not a cliff. It's a *wall*.'

31

Eddie gazed up at his discovery. Behind the waterfall, everything was shrouded in shadow, but there was still more than enough light to see the scale of the wall. Like the ceremonial buildings at the heart of Paititi, it was built from exactingly carved blocks, fitted together with incredible precision. Thirty feet above him was its top, a horizontal line bisecting what had once been an irregularly shaped cave mouth. He couldn't help thinking it looked like a battlement, the almost sheer, incredibly smooth surface making it impossible for anyone to get inside.

Except by the entrance further along the ledge.

The laser rangefinder had been correct; there was a second, much smaller hole. He regarded it with deep suspicion. It was about five feet high by four wide, and as far as he could tell wasn't barricaded. A simple, inviting way in.

Too simple. Too inviting. The Incas wouldn't have built a massive defensive wall, then left a hole through which any gold-hunter could wander. There had to be a catch.

'What do you mean, a wall?' said Nina over the radio.

He described it, then continued along the ledge. 'I'm going to look through the doorway,' he reported as he advanced. A gentle trickle of liquid splashed over his hand as he balanced it against the wall – not from the waterfall, but from a small slot-like opening above. There were similar gaps nearby. 'I think there's water behind the wall as well. I just went under a drainage hole. Hope nobody's still living here – I'll be pissed off if I've been pissed on.'

'At least you'll be able to wash yourself straight away,' said Nina. 'How far to the doorway?'

'Almost there.' He sidestepped along the last few feet, then cautiously peered into the opening.

Nothing leapt out at him, no traps were sprung. The confined stone passage looked empty, extending about twelve feet before stopping at a wall. Taking out a Maglite, he crouched and shone the torch inside. There appeared to be a vertical shaft rising up on the other side of the wall. But to where?

'Okay,' he said, after telling Nina and the others what he had found, 'it looks clear, but I don't really trust it. Were the Incas big on booby-traps?'

Osterhagen took the radio. 'The Incas never developed the wheel, so they weren't able to build complex mechanisms. But there have been simple traps found at some sites – tripwires, balanced stones.'

'Great. Just what I needed to hear.'

Nina's voice came back through the speaker. 'Eddie, wait where you are. I'm coming up.'

'Don't suppose I could persuade you not to? Yeah, thought not,' he added before she could even reply. 'You'll want to put on a rain hat, though.'

It took her ten minutes to get there, holding the rope tightly as she shuffled along the ledge. Even though she had donned a hooded nylon poncho over her clothes, she was still soaked to the skin. 'God damn it!' she said as she reached him. 'This thing was supposed to be waterproof.'

'Even if you wore a full gimp suit, water'd still get in somewhere,' Eddie told her. 'Anyway, this is what we've got.'

He shone his light into the tunnel. 'I risked a look inside while I was waiting. There's a ledge about seven or eight feet up the back wall, some more above that. And there's something else. Have a gander.' He ducked, and moved carefully into the passage, at its end turning sideways so Nina could squeeze past him to see for herself. 'What do you think?'

'I think . . . that looks kinda damn worrying,' she said as she looked up the shaft.

The way up appeared to be stepped; she couldn't see all the way to the top, but at least three ledges were visible above. Anyone trying to ascend would have to jump to grab the lip of the next step, then pull up and repeat the process. It would be a strain for someone of her modest height, but far from impossible.

That wasn't what concerned her, however. The reason for her worry was what faced the ledges, set into the back of the great wall behind her.

Spikes.

The first row was only a foot above her head. She gingerly touched one. The dirt that had built up over the centuries came away at her touch, revealing the metal beneath. 'Oh, my God,' she said. 'It's silver. Solid silver. They all are.'

'Silver?' echoed Eddie. 'But there's dozens of the bloody things – hundreds. They must be worth a fortune!'

'And these are just the defences. Imagine what the treasures they're actually protecting must be.' She tapped the spike's tip. 'Ow! Okay, that's still sharp.'

'Not much of a defence, though.' Eddie leaned across the vertical passage, stretching out one arm to the back wall. 'There's plenty of space. You'd have to be really clumsy or a total fat bastard to hit them while you were climbing up. Maybe the spikes move.' He tested how securely the silver prong Nina had touched was attached to the wall. It was firmly fixed. 'There's got to be something. Otherwise why put 'em here?'

'I suppose you'd hit them if you fell back down the shaft.' The ranks of spikes were angled upwards, as if to catch anything that dropped on to them. 'Or were pushed.'

'Something pops out of the wall?'

'Maybe. I don't know. But it's the only way up.'

Eddie directed his torch back up the shaft. 'I'll have a look at the next level,' he said, stepping out of the low tunnel and standing upright. 'Move back. Just in case anything happens.'

Somewhat unwillingly, Nina retreated. Eddie aimed his torch beam along the lip of the ledge above. No sign of loosely fitted stones that might be triggers. Something as simple as small spikes just behind the edge would prove nasty, so he jumped up as high as he could, looking for telltale flashes of silver. Nothing.

He steeled himself, then leapt again, this time grabbing the edge with both hands. He hung for a moment, listening for any unexpected noises. But there was nothing except the waterfall's constant rumble.

'Do you see anything?' Nina called.

'Just looking now . . .' He pulled himself up. The ledge, a rectangular stone slab four feet wide and three deep, was empty of anything except dirt. 'It's clear.' He climbed the rest of the way.

Nina watched as he used the Maglite to check the walls – and the spikes. 'Is there anything there?'

'Nope.' He examined the ledge above. 'Oh, 'ello! There's something on the next level.'

'What?'

'Statue heads on the back wall.' Still cautious, he climbed up for a closer look. Three stone faces stared coldly at him: sleek, aggressive and feline. 'Big cats – like panthers or something.' He reached for one—

'Eddie, don't touch them!' Nina cried.

His hand froze an inch short. 'What is it?'

'The map, in Paititi – it had jaguars on it. Three of them, at the entrance to the lost city. And something bad was happening. Give me the radio, I need to check with Leonard.'

He tossed it down to her. 'Leonard,' she said, 'do you have the close-up photo of El Dorado from the map?'

'Just a moment,' came the crackling reply. A short while later, the German's voice returned. 'I have it.'

'Good. Look at the section with the three jaguars – tell me exactly what you see.'

'Why? What have you found?'

'Eddie's found the jaguars, but I think we might find something else if we're not careful. What's on the picture?'

'Okay, there are . . . three jaguars sitting in a line. To the left is what appears to be a waterfall, with two men being swept away by it.'

'Eddie, did you hear that?' she asked, looking up. Eddie nodded. 'Is there anything unusual about the waterfall? Any objects or symbols by it?'

'There are . . . small lines beside it,' the older archaeologist said. 'Many of them – twenty or more.'

'Diagonal, pointing up, yes?'

'Yes, that is right. You have a good memory for pictures.'

'No, I'm staring right at them.' She gave the silver skewers a leery look. 'We're in a vertical shaft, and one wall is covered with metal spikes.'

'Wait,' said Eddie, 'so the waterfall comes down here?'

'And washes you into the spikes, yeah.'

'Oh, that's fucking magic! I'm coming back down.'

'No, stay up there,' Nina said quickly. 'Leonard, I'm going to get Eddie to describe what he's seeing, okay?' She held the radio high so it could pick up his voice.

Unnerved, Eddie shouted a description of the three stone heads. 'They're about a foot apart, and . . .' He looked more closely, shining his torch beneath them. 'And it looks like they move. There's a vertical slot underneath each of 'em, like they're on the ends of levers.'

'How far can they move?' Nina asked.

'Not far. Six inches, maybe.'

She thought for a moment, trying to compare what Eddie was seeing with her memory of the picture. 'Leonard, what was on the other side of the three jaguars?'

'A man climbing some very steep steps.'

'And are the spikes on that part of the picture too?'

'Yes.'

'Two sets of stairs?' Eddie wondered.

Nina shook her head. 'There's only one entrance. No, it's something to do with the cats.' She asked Osterhagen to describe the three animals.

'The two on the left are sitting upright,' he told her. 'The one on the right is crouching down.'

'Two up, one down,' she said. 'It's part of the Incas' journey, a clue. But it's like the *huaca* markings and the khipu – they thought it was one only they would understand.'

'Well, if you understand it, I wish you'd tell me,' Eddie said.

'I think it's a key – the way to get into El Dorado safely. The two cats on the left are sitting up, so their heads are held high – at the top of the slots. But the one on the right is looking down at the man climbing up the steps—'

'At the bottom of the slot,' he concluded. 'Like a combination lock. Two up, one down, and that stops you having terminal acupuncture.'

'Exactly. Well, er, I think. I hope.'

'Yeah, I hope too, seeing as I'm the one who's going to have to bloody test it!'

'Are you sure?' she asked. 'We can always go back and try to figure out some other way to get up there.'

'No, I think you're right,' he said. 'They wouldn't have put it on the map if it didn't mean something. All the other stuff on it's worked out so far, so . . .' He straightened. 'Let's give it a shot, then. Here, kitty, kitty . . .'

He put his hand on the rightmost of the three carved heads, hesitated – then firmly pushed it down.

There was a muffled grinding sound from behind the slot, then silence. He looked up. No water erupted into the shaft. 'Is it all the way down?' Nina asked.

'Far as it'll go.'

'So now what?'

'See if it worked, I guess. Okay, let's see . . .' He swept his light along the edge of the third step above him. Nothing out of the ordinary presented itself. He climbed up, finding that this ledge was devoid of any features, only plain walls of intricately arranged blocks.

The top of the shaft was now visible above, the ceiling of a high cave picked out in the half-light coming through the waterfall. Whatever secrets the Incas had left behind were only a matter of feet above.

The thought made him more wary than ever.

He performed another round of checks for potential traps on the fourth ledge. This time, he noticed something different, and unsettling: a gap beneath the slab forming the step. It was only a matter of millimetres high, but compared to the precision of everything else it stood out like a gaping chasm. He took out his knife and probed the narrow opening. It was deeper than his blade could reach. 'Nina?'

'Yes?'

'Go back outside. I think I've found the trigger.'

'No, I'll stay with you.'

'No you won't, 'cause if we've cocked this up, I'll end up stuck on some spikes and you'll get chucked on to those rocks outside! Go back on to the ledge – stand a few feet from the doorway be safe. Go on!'

Nina reluctantly headed down the tunnel. Eddie waited until he was sure she was clear, then turned his attention back to the next step. Could he wedge something into the gap? Maybe, but that seemed a little too obvious.

Besides, he had confidence in his wife. All the puzzle pieces fitted together – it was time to see the full picture.

He jumped up and grabbed the edge of the slab.

A faint creak, just the tiniest hint of give as his full weight hung from the stone . . .

And nothing.

He climbed up to stand on the ledge and a jolt of fear surged through him as the stone tipped very slightly beneath his feet. But again, nothing happened. Either the trap had broken down over time, or the jaguar heads really were in the correct position to stop it from going off. There definitely *was* a trap, though; beneath the slab was a fulcrum, the stone tilting on it like a seesaw. But it wasn't the weight of someone climbing up that would set it off, rather when they stood on the ledge itself, thinking they were safe . . . only for water to explode down the shaft and slam them into the spikes.

'Clever little buggers,' Eddie muttered, turning his

attention to the top of the shaft. As far as he could tell there were no more hidden threats.

He climbed up into the cave itself.

Nina had guessed from the absence of water surging down the tunnel that Eddie had successfully avoided the flood trap. But as minutes passed with no sign of him, she became increasingly worried. Unable to endure the uncertainty any more, she went back through the opening. 'Eddie!' she called. 'Eddie, can you hear me?'

No reply. Concern rising with each step, she peered up the vertical shaft – and Eddie dropped down in front of her, making her shriek in surprise. 'Ay up, love.'

'Jesus, Eddie!' She recovered her composure. 'Are you okay? What took you so long?'

'I'm fine – I was just having a look round.'

'What's up there?'

He shrugged. 'Bits and bobs.'

'What?' Disappointment washed over her, as cold as the waterfall outside. Had the site already been looted – or worse, was it nothing but a decoy, an Inca trick? 'There's no city? Nothing valuable?'

'I dunno, I'm not the archaeologist, am I? Come on, I'll help you up so you can see for yourself. Watch out for the spikes.'

He hoisted her up so she could climb on to the first ledge, then followed. Before long they were at the top of the shaft. 'I'll go first and pull you up,' said Eddie. He climbed into the cave, then reached down for her. 'Ready?'

She nodded and took hold of his arms, then he hoisted her up the final section of wall. Nina stood, eyes adjusting to the grey light as she looked into the cave.

For a moment, she was dumbstruck. Then she finally managed to speak. 'Oh, you son of a bitch.'

Eddie shrugged again, this time with a grin. 'Yeah, I was lying. Just wanted to see your face.'

Filling the great cave was a lost Inca city. El Dorado. The legend was real.

32

An hour later, the other members of the expedition had made their way into the cave.

'Watch out for that,' said Eddie, pointing, as Olmedo climbed up the rope he had secured round a boulder at the top of the shaft. Set into a nearby wall was a large square panel of silver that looked for all the world like an oversized cat flap. 'That's the trap. There's a reservoir behind it – if you trip it, the flap opens and the water shoots down the hole and knocks you into the spikes.'

The trap was not foremost on the minds of the others, though. Instead, they stared, almost mesmerised, at the city before them. The cave floor sloped quite steeply, the Inca settlement constructed in tiers rising back into the shadows. The structures nearest the cavern's entrance were small, like those in Paititi, but they became larger and more grand higher up the hill. Visible near the top was what appeared to be another Temple of the Sun, curved walls standing out amongst the rectilinear buildings around it. Behind it, rising above all else, loomed a palace.

'I have to admit, Nina,' said Mac, taking off his rain poncho, 'this is far beyond anything I expected to see. Anything I imagined seeing, even. Pictures of the places you've discovered are one thing, but actually being here in the flesh . . .'

'It's incredible, isn't it?' she replied, still awed by the sheer scale of the find. 'But it wasn't only me who discovered it, though. If it wasn't for Leonard's knowledge of Inca history and culture, it would have taken years to put together all the clues – if we ever managed to at all.'

Osterhagen was equally effusive. 'No, Nina, you did far more than I. You realised the importance of the khipu – and if not for the IHA, I would not even be here at all. And to think I was angry to be asked to meet you!'

'We both owe a lot to Kit and Interpol as well,' said Nina, turning to the Indian. 'He came up with the connection between the artefacts on the black market and the statues.' The case containing the two – and a half – stone figures was amongst the gear the team had ferried up through the waterfall.

Kit adopted a humble look. 'I only made a suggestion. I had no idea whether or not it would be true.'

'All right, can the mutual admiration society hold its annual meeting somewhere else?' said Eddie as he helped the second of the two soldiers out of the shaft. 'We've still got to explore this place yet.' He noticed Macy's somewhat pensive expression. 'What's up with you?'

'I just thought of something,' she replied, taking out the folder containing the photographs from Paititi. 'On the map, this place is coloured in gold, yeah? Just like the sun disc we found.'

'Yes?' said Nina, wondering where she was leading.

Macy waved a hand towards the waiting buildings. 'So . . . where's all the gold?'

'Maybe it was only symbolic.'

Osterhagen shook his head. 'No, she has a point. The Incas really did put gold on their buildings – the most important ones, at least. The Temple of the Sun in Cuzco was covered in sheets of gold. They were among the first things the Spanish stole and melted down.'

All eyes turned to the silent settlement. Even in the low light, it was plain that the only building material was stone, not precious metal, without so much as a golden glint even from the temple or the palace.

'Perhaps we are not the first to find this place,' said Cruzado.

'No,' said Nina firmly. 'Something this big, there's no way it could have been kept quiet. The Conquistadors would have bragged about finding it to rub in their victory over the Incas, and there isn't a treasure hunter in history who could have resisted the fame of revealing a find like this. Besides, look at it. The whole place is almost intact. If it's been looted, they were very orderly about it.'

It was true. Unlike the ruins of Paititi, where the ceaseless growth of the jungle and the rot of climate and insects had left only broken shells, here the majority of the buildings still had roofs. The coverings of woven leaves had long since gone, but the skeletal wooden beams that had supported them remained in place. 'Then,' said Zender imperiously, 'we must explore the city and find the treasures the Incas left behind.' He paused, then continued more hesitantly: 'What are we looking for?'

'Riches beyond imagination,' said Osterhagen in a portentous voice, sharing a smile with Nina. He pointed up the slope. 'The map from Paititi showed the Punchaco in the Temple of the Sun – and the last piece of Dr Wilde's statues in the royal palace. We start at the top.'

'Ready when you are,' said Nina.

The group set out up the hill. The limited space available to the city's builders meant that the steep streets were even more narrow and twisting than those in Paititi. 'I wish I'd brought my stick,' Mac complained.

'It'd probably be quicker to hop over the roofs,' said Eddie, looking up at the buildings on each side. They splashed through a stream that ran across their path. 'Keep our feet dry, too.'

'I don't think my feet could get any wetter,' Nina complained. She looked back to see where the stream led, finding that it drained into the reservoir. The trap was self-sustaining.

Osterhagen halted beside a small, low structure. 'What is it?' Nina asked.

He shone a flashlight inside. 'A tomb. Look.' She peered through the entrance, seeing huddled shapes within. 'Mummies.'

The sight gave Nina a small chill. Unlike the traditional image of an Egyptian mummy, lying flat and completely swathed in cloth, the bodies of Inca mummies were curled up tightly in their shrouds as if straitjacketed – but with their heads left exposed. The sunken eye sockets of a dead, parchment-yellow face stared back at her, shrivelled lips pulled away to expose its teeth almost with a sneer. Behind it, stacked like sacks of flour, were other bodies.

Macy looked over Nina's shoulder, and wished she hadn't. 'Gross. That's gonna be in my nightmares. How many of them are there?'

Nina looked up the hill, seeing that a whole section of the lost city seemed dedicated to the little mausoleums. 'Dozens – hundreds, even.'

'Is there treasure?' called Zender. 'Have you found any treasure?'

'Depends how you define it,' said Nina, using her own torch to pick out grubby metal inside the chamber. The object seemed like a cross between a knife and a small trowel, a fat blade with a decidedly unergonomic handle in the shape of a heavily stylised human figure.

'It is a *tumi*,' said Osterhagen. 'A ceremonial knife – they have been found with many mummies. Some were made from gold, but this looks more like bronze.'

'Only bronze?' Zender tutted. 'Then it can wait. But we can't. Move along, move along!'

Even Juanita seemed exasperated by his impatience, but none of the Peruvian contingent raised a voice to object; he was, after all, technically their boss. Nina had no such concerns. 'Archaeology isn't like the Olympics,' she chided. 'Bronze isn't the loser's consolation prize.'

Mac chuckled. 'I don't think that's *quite* what the symbolism of the medal ceremony means.'

They continued up the slope. Before long, the pathway became noticeably wider, the surrounding buildings larger. 'Leonard, go right,' said Nina when they reached a junction with a tower-like structure to their left. The route ahead continued uphill, but the alternative seemed to lead to a more open area. 'If it's like Paititi . . .'

It was. They soon emerged on a plaza, built up at the eastern end, dug out of the sloping rock floor at the west to keep the whole expanse flat. A broad stone stairway led to the higher levels. She looked towards the cave mouth, seeing the lower levels of the city spread out below. 'God, they were on the run, and they still put in the effort to build all this. It's incredible.'

'And we haven't even found the really awesome stuff yet,' Macy reminded her, starting for the stairway.

'*All* of this is awesome!' Nina protested with pricked professional pride, looking to the other archaeologists for support. But even Osterhagen was moving with the rest of the group towards the steps, as if magnetically drawn. With a huff, she gave in and followed them.

'This is how I feel when I'm trying to talk to you about footie,' Eddie teased her.

They ascended through several steeply ranked tiers of buildings to the Temple of the Sun. As Osterhagen reached the top, Nina paused. 'Hold on,' she called. 'I can hear water.' Eddie jerked a thumb at the falls. 'Ha ha,' she said, with a very fake smile. 'No, I mean ahead of us. And it's bigger than that little stream we crossed.'

Osterhagen strode along the side of the temple. 'I hear it too. I think . . . ah, of course!' he said as the source came into view. 'Ritual fountains. They have been found at several other Inca sites.'

Beyond the temple was a small square, overlooked by the shadowed palace on the tier above. Several jets of water gushed out of the paving slabs, falling back into rectangular pools to run off into drainage holes. 'This must be what makes the stream,' suggested Kit.

'Yeah, but what's making them?' said Nina. As well as the tinkle and splash of the fountains, there was still the other noise she had heard, considerably deeper. Beyond the palace, at the very rear of the cavern. 'Back there.' She started for the next flight of steps.

'Where are you going?' asked Osterhagen, surprised. 'This is the Temple of the Sun! The Punchaco could be inside.'

'There's something I want to check,' she said. 'This cave was originally carved out by water. I want to find out why there isn't still a river running through it.'

'And I thought you married an archaeologist, not a hydrologist,' Mac said to Eddie with a wry smile.

Zender edged nearer to the temple's entrance. 'We don't

need to wait for her, do we?' Eddie shot him a cold look. 'Ah, okay, okay. We can wait. Just for a minute.'

Nina scurried up the steps and forced herself to bypass the waiting temple and whatever riches it might contain to see what lay behind it. Her ears had not deceived her. A jet of white water, so much pressure behind it that it appeared almost solid, blasted out of a six-inch hole in the cave's back wall into a deep pond, from where channels carved in the rock floor sent it downhill to different parts of the city. It was a primitive water main, a simple but effective piece of Inca engineering.

What was considerably less simple was the way the jet had been created. Surrounding the torrent was not natural rock but a wall, as precisely and solidly built as the towering defence at the cave mouth. It was almost like a plug set into the stone, roughly twelve feet across.

She hurried back to the square. The other team members had put down their gear and were waiting for her impatiently. 'So, find anything interesting?' asked Eddie.

'Yes – I worked out how the Incas built this place,' she said excitedly. 'They must have dammed up the river before it went underground. Then they plugged up all but a little hole at the back of the cave so they'd have a water supply, and after that they built all of this, then demolished the dam. But since the river couldn't flow freely down into the cave any more, it went over the top of it . . . and formed the waterfall. A whole city to hide their treasure, and it's completely invisible from outside.'

Osterhagen was suitably impressed, taking in the ancient buildings surrounding them. 'The Spanish never gave them enough credit for their engineering skills. That they could build a place like this is amazing.'

'Their treasures were amazing too,' said Zender impatiently, once again edging towards the temple's entrance. 'Dr Wilde, are you ready see what is inside? Or is their plumbing more interesting to you?'

Nina was tempted to make everyone wait by exploring the smaller buildings around the square, but decided that since Zender was only here for the glory of finding a big prize, the sooner he saw one the sooner he might leave. 'All right,' she faux-grumbled. 'Let's give baby his bottle.' The group laughed, to Zender's annoyance.

She and Osterhagen led the way to the darkened opening. While the limited space in the cave had forced the Incas to compress most of their architecture, the Temple of the Sun was, if anything, larger than its counterpart at Paititi. A short passage followed the curve of the outer wall before opening into a chamber.

Even before she reached it, Nina saw there was something unusual about the interior. Through the roof's skeletal remains, the light in the passage had the same diffuse twilight cast as the rest of the cave. But the room ahead was different. Not brighter, but somehow *warmer*, almost like a dawn.

Osterhagen had seen it too. He quickened his pace. They entered the chamber . . .

And were bathed in golden light reflected off the object on its western wall.

'*Mein Gott!*' gasped Osterhagen, gasping. Nina was equally staggered.

They had found the Punchaco.

It dwarfed its copy from Paititi. That had been four feet in diameter; the golden disc before them now was nearer nine, and at least twice as thick as its counterpart. It stood almost floor to ceiling, mounted on the wall to face the trapezoidal eastern window. Unlike the smaller sun disc, which while ornate had been fashioned only from gold, this was decorated with hundreds of precious stones around its rim and outlining the great face of Inti, the sun god, that stared from its centre. The greatest treasure of the Incas, weighing tons, had been transported across hundreds of miles to protect it from the Spaniards' gold-lust; a monumental, almost unbelievable journey.

But here it was. And an entire city had been built to house it.

The others filed into the room. 'Jesus!' said Eddie. 'De Quesada would have had a job fitting *that* into his loo.'

Zender's mouth dropped open at the sight. He gabbled in Spanish to Juanita. 'What's he saying?' Mac whispered to Macy.

'He's telling her to start arranging a press conference,' she replied. The Scot made a sound of quiet amusement.

Nina regarded the relief of Inti, then turned to see where the Inca god was gazing. Through the window, she could see the waterfall – and, she remembered, there was a gap between two peaks on the opposite side of the valley. Even though the view would be obscured by the falls, the Incas had still made sure the temple faced the rising sun. 'So what do you think, Mr Zender?' she asked. The Peruvian official had a hand raised to the Punchaco's rim, fingertips hovering just above its surface as if afraid to touch it. 'Worth the trip?'

'Oh, yes, yes,' he said, so transfixed that he didn't even turn his head to address her. He finally summoned the willpower to put his hand against the sun disc. Satisfied that it was indeed real, he looked round. 'Dr Wilde, Dr Osterhagen, this is . . .' He struggled for the right words. 'Amazing!' was all he could manage. 'You have found the greatest treasure in Peru's history. You are both national heroes!'

'Thank you,' said Osterhagen, 'but we are not heroes –

simply scholars. The real heroes were here over four hundred years ago, preserving this place for the ages. They made an incredible journey and took great risks to protect their culture and its heritage.'

Zender nodded, rather calculatingly. 'Yes, yes. If you say that at the press conference, that would be very good!'

'Let's save the media planning until we've found everything, shall we?' Nina suggested. 'There's still a whole city to explore. And there was something else on the Paititi map.' She put down her pack and took out the case containing the statuettes. 'We've got two and a half out of three; let's see if we can complete the set.'

She opened the case, revealing the figurines. The Peruvian contingent looked on in bemusement; Nina had only told a few senior politicians about the IHA's other ongoing mission when requesting permission to mount the expedition. 'What are these?' asked Olmedo.

'Pointers, I think,' Nina said. She picked up the first statue; as she had hoped, it glowed with an earth energy reaction, though not an especially strong one. Even so, in the low light it was perfectly clear, the Peruvians reacting with surprise. 'If I put them all together, I'm hoping they'll show me the missing piece.'

She carefully brought the three carved purple stones together, cradling them in her hands. The glow changed, a brighter band shimmering – pointing at the sun disc.

'It's behind that?' Kit asked.

Nina grimaced. 'I hope not – I wouldn't want to have to damage the Punchaco to get it out!' She stepped across to the side wall. The line of light moved, the parallax shift indicating that the final piece was close by – but it no longer pointed at the representation of the sun god. 'No, I think it's in the palace. Just as the map said.'

'It shouldn't take long to find,' said Macy. 'Not when you've got your own personal weird statue detector.'

Nina addressed the Peruvians. 'This is the main reason the IHA became involved. There's no need for you to come with me to find the last statue piece if you don't want to.'

She had hoped they would take the hint and let her search in peace, but from their expressions – even the two soldiers were intrigued – it was clear they all wanted to satisfy their curiosity. 'Probably shouldn't have shown 'em the glowing statues, love,' said Eddie.

Still carefully holding the circle of figurines, she moved back towards the passage. 'Well, let's see where they lead us, then.'

The others following, she left the temple, heading for the palace at the summit of the hidden city.

In the jungle outside the cave, one of the two soldiers left to watch the team's vehicles looked down the hill. Several minutes earlier, he had thought he heard distant engines, but the waterfall's never-ending rumble made it difficult to be sure. He had dismissed the sound as nothing more than local traffic picking its way along the winding road – but now he was certain he had heard it again, and closer. He stared down the weaving trail of flattened vegetation made by the off-roaders, but saw nothing except greenery.

His companion, leaning against the Jeep, stubbed out his cigarette. 'Why would anyone come up here? Nobody's even supposed to know about this place except those archaeologists.'

'Someone might have seen our tracks going off the road.' The reassuring weight of his Kalashnikov AKM rifle hung from one shoulder; he considered unslinging it and heading downhill to investigate. But there was nothing moving amongst the trees except birds, and the noise had stopped. 'I don't know. But I'm sure I heard a truck.'

He expected a sarcastic retort, but no answer came. Assuming the other soldier was busy lighting yet another cigarette, he continued, 'And I know you're going to say that we almost ran into plenty of trucks on the way here, but I meant it was nearer than the road.' He turned to await a response—

A man in dirty, ragged jungle camouflage was behind his comrade, one hand clamped over his mouth – and the other driving a knife deep into his throat, spraying blood over the Jeep's windscreen.

The soldier grabbed his AKM—

A loud, flat thump came from the undergrowth, and he fell, hit in the back by a bullet. He writhed in pain, trying to scream, but only managed a choked gurgle, blood from a shredded lung frothing in his throat and mouth.

The shooter stepped from the bushes. He was short, barrel-chested . . . and wearing a blood-red beret.

Arcani Pachac.

'Any sign of the rest?' the Maoist leader asked as his scout pulled the knife from the second soldier's neck and let the twitching corpse drop to the ground.

'No, Inkarrí,' the camouflaged man replied. 'Their tracks go to the waterfall, but there's nobody there. They must be behind it.'

Pachac nodded, then almost as an afterthought raised his weapon again. The automatic had been modified with a makeshift silencer, a two-litre plastic soda bottle stuffed with shredded newspaper and polythene bags taped to his pistol's barrel. Smoke coiled from the hole in the end of the bottle where the bullet had seared through; the torn-up scraps inside had caught fire. He pulled the trigger, a second round smashing into the back of the wounded soldier's skull. The shot was still loud, the improvised suppressor too crude to do more than muffle it – but, crucially, it didn't sound like the sharp crack of gunfire. To anyone outside the immediate vicinity, it could be mistaken for a falling branch or other similar natural event. And the waterfall's thunder masked it still further.

He pulled the smouldering bottle from the gun, then unclipped a walkie-talkie from his belt. 'The way is clear. Move up.'

The luckless soldier *had* heard engines. Before long, three off-road vehicles came into sight, following the archaeological team's path. Two were old, battered and unassuming 4×4s – a rusting Ford F-150 pickup with a cargo bed full of rebels, and a long-past-its-prime Toyota Land Cruiser with sagging suspension. Leading the parade, however, was something much newer and more expensive: a bright yellow Hummer H3. Pachac was perversely proud of the vehicle, which his group had obtained by the simple expedient of murdering its owner; the oversized, cartoonish 4×4 was a perfect symbol of the kind of capitalist excess he was aiming to destroy, and it gave him a certain satisfaction to use it against them.

He also got a kick out of driving the huge, opulent vehicle, but kept that to himself.

The crowded trucks stopped behind the expedition's vehicles, and Pachac's men emerged. Like him, all were dirty, their clothes grubby and crumpled from a life spent in the rough and on the run. And like him, all were killers. Though they called themselves revolutionaries, to the Peruvian government the True Red Way were terrorists, and hunted as such.

But this time they were not working alone. Pachac ordered his men to head for the falls, then went to the Hummer. Inside was a high-tech field radio. He took the handset and spoke into it. 'This is Pachac. We're at the waterfall.' He wasn't concerned about the Peruvian authorities overhearing; the radio's messages were encrypted.

'Have you seen Wilde and the others?' the reply came. The voice was clipped. British.

'No, but they are definitely here. My contact in the village described the woman he saw. Red hair, in a ponytail – it must be her. We think they have found a way behind the waterfall.' Pachac looked up at the thrum of an approaching helicopter. 'Is that you I can hear?'

'Of course it is. How many of them are there?'

'My contact counted fourteen people. Four of them were soldiers. We have executed two of them already.'

'We'll take care of the waterfall – then you take care of the rest of them. But I need Dr Wilde and the Interpol agent, Jindal, alive. You understand?'

'I have told my men,' said Pachac impatiently.

'Good.' A bleep told the Peruvian that the call was terminated. He followed his men through the trees as the helicopter moved away.

None of Nina's prior knowledge of Inca civilisation had prepared her for – she realised with amusement that she had started using the name without irony – El Dorado. The other known sites were long-looted and derelict; here, relics of the city's inhabitants still remained. The palace's rooms contained belongings left by its occupants, and she had to force herself to walk on by as she followed the statues' glowing light deeper into the building.

But she knew she could explore the rest of the palace later. For now, finding the final piece was her top priority.

'It can't be much further,' said Kit as the group entered a large room. 'We're almost at the back of the palace.' The hiss of the water jet echoed off the walls.

This deep in the cave, there was much less light than in the Temple of the Sun. Eddie switched on his Maglite. 'Is that something there?'

The beam found an alcove set into the rear wall – familiar markings within. 'I think it is,' said Nina, her pace and heartbeat getting faster.

Osterhagen was right with her. 'Just like the map from Paititi!'

'Only part of it,' said Macy as the others crowded round to look. More flashlights illuminated the painted walls.

Nina knelt to enter the alcove. 'Yeah. The people who made this map, this is where their journey ended. They didn't go on into the jungle.' The golden city marked the end of the trek from Cuzco.

But she was more interested in the nook set into the wall. In it stood a small figure, carved from an unusual purple stone.

Half a figure. The other piece of the last statuette. It had patiently stood here for centuries, waiting to be reunited with its mirror image – and its near-twins. The set was about to be completed.

She put down the other figures, their light vanishing, and cautiously touched the statuette in the niche. It lit up with a rippling glow – strongest in one direction. Towards the sculptures at her feet. 'This is it!' Nina said. 'The last piece.'

'Maybe now we'll find out what all the bloody fuss is about,' said Eddie.

'Let's hope.' She reached for it—

A distant boom, a drawn-out rumble of something enormous tearing apart . . .

The floor shook, little cascades of dust and grit dropping from the walls. The statuettes on the floor clinked against each other. *'Terremoto!'* cried Zender, frantically looking round for shelter.

'It's not an earthquake,' said Eddie, straining to listen over the sound of water. 'More like . . .'

'Artillery,' Mac finished for him.

Another tremor rolled through the ground. A new sound, closer, more frightening. Overhead. Rock straining against rock. 'Shit!' said Eddie. 'The whole fucking place is going to come down! We've got to get out of here.'

'The statues!' Kit almost shouted.

'I've got them,' said Nina. No time to see what happened when they were brought together; she jammed them all into the foam-lined case and closed it. 'Okay, let's go!'

Everyone ran for the exit, Mac and Eddie side by side at the rear. Over the thumps and rumbles of rock, Nina realised that another sound was changing. 'The waterfall – listen!' The thunder of the falls was dying down. 'Come on, we've got to get outside!'

They rushed on to the terrace overlooking the square behind the Temple of the Sun. The fountains were still gushing, fed by the subterranean reserve backed up behind the dam at the cave's rear.

But ahead, the flow concealing the cavern's mouth was weakening, glimpses of the valley's far side visible through the thinning curtain.

The river had been blocked.

Alexander Stikes looked out of the hovering Hind's cabin with a smile. Krikorian had just unleashed a barrage of S-8 rockets into the steep cliffs channelling the river – which had collapsed in a most satisfying manner, thousands of tons of rubble dropping into the narrow waterway. The waters behind the makeshift dam were already rising even as those ahead of it drained away, but the flood would find an alternative route down into the valley long before it could overflow the new obstacle. 'Nicely done, Krikorian,' he said into his headset. 'Gurov, take us back to the falls. Let's see what's behind them.'

The Russian pilot complied, the Hind swinging about and flying along the dwindling river before crossing the falls and hovering over the pocket jungle. Stikes's smile widened as he saw the result of his attack. The strength of the cataract had already diminished enormously, exposing a broad cave mouth behind it – was that a *wall* blocking the lower half? If so, it was an impressive piece of ancient construction work – and the pool at its base was rapidly draining. It would soon be possible to reach the cave without even getting one's feet wet.

Pachac, he saw, wasn't going to wait that long. The terrorist leader, easy to spot in his red beret, was pointing at the wall, directing men bearing assault rifles and rocket launchers across the pool.

Ready to take the cavern and its contents by force.

33

Eddie saw the Hind through the cave mouth. Even with the water still partially obscuring it, he picked out the colours of the Venezuelan flag. 'It's Stikes!'

'What?' said Nina in utter disbelief. 'How the hell could he know we're here?'

The aircraft moved out of sight. 'What is going on?' Zender demanded, caught between confusion and fear. 'That helicopter – it was Venezuelan!'

'It used to be one of yours, but it's gone into the private sector,' Eddie said grimly. He turned to the two soldiers. 'You and you – with me, quick!' The three men hurried away down the steps.

Zender still wanted answers. 'Tell me what is happening!'

'Stikes used the helicopter's weapons to block the river and cut off the waterfall,' Mac told him. 'It'll make it easier for his people to get into the cave.'

'Who is Stikes?'

'A mercenary,' said Nina. 'He was part of the attempted coup in Venezuela – and it looks like he's trying to make up for not getting paid by raiding this place.'

Juanita was scared. 'What – what about the soldiers we left outside?'

'They're dead,' Mac replied bluntly. 'And we will be too unless Eddie and your other men can hold them off.'

'You don't sound confident,' said Kit.

The Hind came back into view outside. 'We *are* slightly outgunned,' said Mac. He looked towards the plaza. 'We need to see what's going on.' He started down the steps, the others going with him. Nina left the case amongst the team's gear before following.

Eddie and the two soldiers raced downhill through the narrow streets. They passed the tombs, seeing the reservoir ahead. 'Where are we going?' asked Lieutenant Echazu.

'There's only one way into this cave,' Eddie answered. 'We need to make sure nobody comes up that tunnel.'

'We? But you do not have a gun!'

'I've got a water pistol, sort of.' They reached the edge of the hidden city, the ground sloping more steeply down to the shaft. 'Okay, cover that hole.'

The soldiers split up to take positions overlooking the entrance. 'What are you doing?' shouted the corporal, Chambi, seeing Eddie running to the shaft itself.

'Making sure they get the point!' he said as he jumped down to the booby trap's trigger slab. There was a rasp of stone, but it stayed in place.

More sounds echoed up the passage. He looked down, seeing torchlight glinting off the silver spikes. The intruders were already at the bottom of the shaft – and he had left them an easy way up. The hanging rope suddenly pulled tight as someone started to climb it.

He jumped down to the next step. Below was the ledge with the three jaguar heads. Another look over the edge – and he saw a man on the first ledge.

Eddie dropped flat on the cramped step, reaching down with one hand. The two jaguar heads that he had left untouched were just within his grasp, but the third, lowered to deactivate the trap, was a couple of inches beyond his fingertips. Swearing under his breath, he leaned further out. The man on the rope was already climbing to the second step—

A torch beam flashed across his face. Someone shouted in Spanish. The climber looked up, saw him – and dropped back down to the first step, reaching for the AK-47 across his back.

Eddie lunged, grabbing the stone jaguar and yanking it upwards – then rolled back as the Kalashnikov roared. Bullets smacked against the wall, sending ricochets screaming up the shaft. The noise was horrific in the confined space.

The thunder faded to echoes, then to nothing. The AK's magazine was empty. He heard metallic clicks from below as the gunman kept pulling the trigger.

Not one of Stikes's men, then – a professional would already be changing the mag. No time to wonder who he might be, though. Instead Eddie leapt and grabbed the rope, swinging round to plant his soles against the shaft's side as he scrambled up. He couldn't touch the trigger slab on the step above.

Kla-chack! The gunman had finally reloaded and pulled the AK's charging handle, chambering the first round—

Eddie heaved himself over the ledge and swung sideways on the rope, thumping against the back wall as another burst of gunfire hammered up the shaft. He was barely an inch above the slab, his leather jacket brushing the stone. A sharp chunk of metal hit his cheek – a bullet had blown the tip off a spike. He flinched, almost falling, straining to hold on . . .

The firing stopped. The rope juddered in his hands as the man below grabbed it and started to climb after him.

Eddie jerked back into motion, pulling himself rapidly up the shaft. He clambered out and drew his knife. The rope was still bar-taut with the gunman's weight; he sawed at it, threads fraying—

It snapped. A yell of fright came from below as the climber fell – followed by a terrible scream as he hit the spikes. The agonised shrieks continued as the man flailed, trying to drag himself off the spears tearing into his flesh. He succeeded – only to plummet down the shaft. The crack of shattering bone as his jaw caught the edge of a step was almost as sharp as the Kalashnikov's shots.

The sound was followed by the real thing as the dead man's companions fired up the shaft. Eddie ran – not because he feared being hit, but because he was only feet from the silver door at the bottom of the reservoir.

If the trap still worked, it would soon open.

The gunshots stopped, replaced by grunts of exertion. Another man was ascending, pulling himself up each step in turn. Shouts followed him as other men crowded into the tunnel to join the pursuit.

He reached the fourth ledge–

The slab tilted under his weight. Only by an inch . . .

But that was all that was needed to release the flap.

The heavy metal door, hinged at its top, flew open under the pressure of thousands of gallons of water. The escaping flood smashed against the great wall before finding an escape route – straight down the shaft.

The deluge swept away the men climbing the steps, dashing them against the spikes and driving the silver points through skulls and torsos. Those at the bottom fared no better, the surge of water pounding along the passage like a piston and flinging them to their deaths on the jagged rocks below.

Outside, Pachac stared at the plume of water gushing from the tunnel in horrified disbelief. He had been about to enter the passage himself – and now all the men who had gone before him were dead! Bodies surfaced and bobbed in the frothing pool, limbs snapped like broken dolls. The rest of his men were equally shocked. 'Inkarrí!' shouted one. 'What – what do we do now?'

The force of the water was already falling. Pachac's face set into an angry snarl. 'As soon as the tunnel is clear, we go in – and make the bastards who killed our brothers pay!'

Eddie reached Echazu, the young officer having found a position in a small house overlooking the shaft. Chambi was not far away, crouched behind the wall of a terrace near their route into the city. 'You got them!' said the Peruvian.

'Dunno if I got all of 'em, though,' Eddie replied. The reservoir was now empty, the silver flap's weight swinging it shut to reset the trap – but it would take hours, even days, for the streams running through the cavern to refill it. 'If I didn't, it won't take long before they come through that hole. If you see anyone, shoot 'em!' He ran along the terrace to give the corporal the same instructions.

From the circling Hind, Stikes watched Pachac and his remaining men climb to the entrance set into the towering wall. The gush of water from it had reduced to a modest stream. 'The Incas didn't leave their city totally undefended, I see.'

Baine, sitting beside him, looked down at the corpses in the pool without sympathy. 'Stupid bastards. Must have run right in without checking.'

'And Pachac's probably about to do the same thing. He said they killed two soldiers, but that leaves another two – and I suspect the other end of that tunnel is easily defensible.' His gaze rose from the wall to the cave mouth above it. With the waterfall all but stopped, the faint shapes of buildings were visible in the darkness. Elevated positions, with plenty of cover . . . 'We might have to give him some help.' He spoke into his headset. 'Gurov, get a good firing angle into that cave.'

Nina looked down from the plaza at the great wall. She had seen Eddie running from the top of the shaft as a massive wave crashed into it, but then he disappeared behind the city's lower buildings. 'Oh God, where is he?'

'He got clear,' Mac assured her. 'He'll be okay.'

The other expedition members joined them at the stone balustrade. 'Look, there!' said Kit, pointing. A man peered cautiously from the top of the shaft before climbing out—

Gunfire crackled from below. Dust and stones kicked up around the intruder – then he slumped to the rocky ground, dead. Another man behind him hurriedly dropped out of sight.

Zender clenched a fist in triumph. 'They got him!'

Nina didn't feel reassured. Even if they could hold off their attackers, they were still trapped inside the city.

And there was another threat. The chop of the Hind's rotors rose as the gunship descended, slowly pivoting to face the cave entrance.

Eddie reached over to Chambi's AKM and turned its firing mode selector from automatic to single-shot. 'You need to save ammo,' he told the surprised soldier, having noticed that both Peruvians were only carrying one extra magazine. 'It'll be more accurate an' all.'

Chambi's grasp of English was apparently not great, but he got the gist. 'You have been in fights before?' he asked.

Eddie grinned crookedly. 'You could say that. Whoa, look out – there's another one.' The barrel of an AK-47 popped up from the shaft, followed by its owner's head, his companions lifting him so he could aim his weapon with both hands.

Chambi fired, the shot accompanied by a crack from Echazu's gun. Eddie wasn't sure whose bullet hit its target, but was happy with the result either way; the man's head snapped back with a burst of blood from his forehead, and he disappeared again, this time permanently.

'Good shot,' he told the corporal, who seemed pleased by the praise. He saw that the first man to emerge had dropped his Kalashnikov when he was shot. An extra weapon would be a huge help – if he could reach it. 'Keep the hole covered – I'm going to get that gun.' He started back along the terrace to tell Echazu his plan.

A change in the Hind's engine noise caught his attention. He had tuned out the gunship while concentrating on the shaft, but it was now hovering, engines straining at full power to support its armoured bulk.

Its cannon turned—

'*Down!*' Eddie shouted, diving flat behind the wall—

The Hind opened fire, the four barrels of its Gatling gun spitting out a stream of death. Echazu, fixated on the shaft, didn't realise the danger until it was too late. The bullets ripped through the little building's doorway, ricocheting shrapnel tearing him apart.

A momentary pause as Krikorian switched targets, then the onslaught began again, this time aimed at the terrace. The wall behind which Eddie and Chambi were sheltering was over a foot thick, but even its blocks splintered and cracked under the pounding storm.

'Jesus Christ!' Eddie yelled, shielding his face from stone fragments. He crawled rapidly towards the steep pathway. The soldier had flattened himself against the wall, too terrified to move – and blocking Eddie's path. 'Stay with me!' the

Englishman yelled, batting at Chambi's legs with a fist. 'If we can get round the corner, we'll be safe – soon as he stops firing, run up the hill!'

The gunfire stopped. '*Go!*' Eddie shouted, springing up like a sprinter off the blocks. He heard Chambi set off, a couple of paces behind.

Three yards, two—

The harsh rasp of the Gatling gun and the explosive crack of bullet impacts returned as Eddie reached the corner, rounds chewing into the wall behind him . . .

And into Chambi.

The young corporal was only one step away from safety when the stream of lead caught up with him. Half of his upper body literally exploded, showering the wall with blood and flesh. What was left of him tumbled on to the path behind Eddie. Horrifyingly, he was still alive.

Briefly.

The firing stopped again, the gunner trying to regain sight of his escaped prey.

Eddie shook off his shock. Chambi's blood-splattered AKM was beside his corpse; he grabbed it and ran up the hill.

In the gunner's cockpit, Krikorian kept the infrared sights fixed on the corner. A glowing splash of hot blood told him that he had hit one of the two running men . . . but the other had gone. He tipped his head to move the cross-hairs up the slope. A brief flash of body heat between two buildings, but it disappeared before he could lock on to it.

'Lost him!' Annoyed, he searched for other targets inside the cave.

A cluster of bright human shapes stood out.

★

Fear for her husband's life had paralysed Nina as she and the others watched the Hind open fire – but the sight of the gunship's cannon turning towards them snapped her back into motion with a surge of adrenalin. '*Run!*'

She and Mac went one way, the rest of the group the other – except Juanita, who started to follow the American and the Scot before Zender's panicked shout of her name made her double back.

The hesitation cost the young woman her life. Tracer rounds seared over the city, catching Juanita as she tried to run. Her body was thrown back along the plaza, a bloodied rag doll.

The line of death pursued Nina and Mac—

'Cease fire, *cease fire!*' Stikes snarled into his headset. 'I need Wilde and Jindal *alive!*' The cannon's roar stopped.

All of Pachac's men had now gone into the tunnel. With the defenders dead they would be able to enter the cave with minimal resistance, but the bloodlust roused by the death of their comrades would almost certainly lead to their killing anyone they found. He had to take control of matters on the ground to prevent that from happening, but it would take him crucial minutes to rope down and catch up . . .

His gaze shifted back to the cave mouth. A moment's thought, then: 'Gurov! What's this thing's rotor diameter?'

Nina pressed against a building, out of the helicopter's sights. Mac joined her a moment later. 'Are you okay?' he asked.

'Yeah, but – oh God, Juanita . . .' The Peruvian woman lay motionless.

'At least it would have been quick,' Mac said grimly. He saw the other expedition members reach cover on the other side of the plaza. 'Everyone else is okay – but why did they stop firing?'

That was not a question high on Nina's mind. 'What about Eddie? Did he get away?' She leaned round the corner – and saw men emerging from the shaft. 'Shit! More of them!'

Eddie crouched behind one of the tombs, looking back. The Hind had stopped shooting and was now hanging almost hesitantly above the trees. There was nowhere to land – was Stikes about to rope down?

Shouts brought his attention to a more immediate threat. More attackers had entered the cavern, and this time there was nobody to stop them. He pulled himself on to the little tomb's roof. From here, he could see the shaft. A man scrambled out of it, then another.

Activity, much closer. Two men were heading up into the ruins. One was armed with an AK-47 – the other a rocket launcher. The first man pointed at the plaza.

Eddie aimed his AKM, but before he could shoot the pair moved out of sight.

He knew what they were doing: finding a good firing position.

Keeping low, Kit returned to the plaza's eastern end. The helicopter was still hovering outside, but its cannon was no longer pointed at him. He raised his head to look down at the city. The shaft was disgorging armed men like an anthill; two, three, four, and no way to know how many were already inside the cave.

'Kit, get back here!' Macy cried. He looked round. She was with Osterhagen and Zender behind a squat building, Olmedo and Cruzado peering from inside its doorway.

'I need to see how many there are,' he replied. A man in a red beret pulled himself out of the shaft. Nobody followed him. But however many intruders had come through the tunnel, it was enough for the explorers to be outnumbered – and very definitely outgunned.

He was about to return to the others when he caught movement in his peripheral vision—

An RPG-7 warhead streaked towards him.

Kit dived as the rocket shot over the balustrade and hit the building sheltering the two Peruvian archaeologists. The explosion blew in one wall, stone blocks and the remains of the roof crashing down on top of them.

The rebel with the rocket launcher looked in satisfaction at the swelling cloud of dust from the partially collapsed building. The job wasn't over, though. 'I think there's still someone up there. Help me reload,' he said, kneeling so his comrade could reach into his backpack.

It contained another two RPG-7 rounds. One was taken out, its fuse protector being removed before the missile was loaded into the launch tube. The rebel looked through its sights. The cloud was clearing – he glimpsed someone behind the ruin and took aim—

Bullets tore into his body as Eddie opened fire from a rooftop several tiers above. The rebel fell, toppling over a wall to end up sprawled on a steep pathway, the launcher still clutched in his dead hands. The other man whirled, raising his AK – only to take a lethal round to the forehead.

Eddie hopped from one roof to another, then dropped down to the ground and ran uphill towards the plaza.

'Macy! Leonard!' Nina yelled across the plaza. She couldn't see anything through the drifting smoke.

She heard coughing: Kit. The dust cleared enough for her to

see him lying by the balustrade, a hand to his head. Chunks of broken stone were scattered around him. He was alive, but clearly hurt, hit by debris.

She was about to run to help him when Mac pulled her back. 'Stay in cover!' he warned. 'The chopper's coming in!'

A shocked glance at the cave mouth revealed that he meant it literally. The gunship was slowly advancing through the opening into the cavern itself.

It took all Stikes's willpower not to show any outward signs of tension to his men as the chopper entered the cavern. The opening was easily large enough to accommodate the Hind – but helicopters were not designed to fly inside enclosed spaces. The enormous force of the rotor downwash could be deflected back at the aircraft in unexpected ways, throwing it into the ancient buildings – or even against the ceiling. He just had to hope Gurov was as good a pilot as he claimed . . .

Wind buffeted the gunship. Shielding his eyes, he leaned out of the hatch for a better view. They were now clear of the wall, and he saw Pachac's men scurrying up through the city. But his attention went to the plaza, the only place the Hind could land – and to his anger he saw that the revolutionaries had already attacked it, the ghostly trail of a rocket-propelled grenade ending at a newly demolished building. If these communist cretins had killed the people he was after—

Bullets clanked off the helicopter's flank. Stikes jerked back. Who was firing?

Somehow, he knew the answer: *Chase!*

Eddie reached the plaza, opening up with his AKM at the approaching Hind. He saw Stikes, his blond hair and tan beret instantly recognisable, duck into the cabin. 'Everyone get out of here!' he shouted. 'Find somewhere to hide!' Nina and Mac were behind a nearby building; across the paved area he spotted Macy, Osterhagen and Zender struggling upright. 'Go on, *run*!'

He was about to follow his own advice when the helicopter swung in his direction—

'Hold fire!' Stikes shouted into the headset – but his voice was drowned out by a hissing roar as Krikorian unleashed an S-8 rocket.

In the time it took to blink, it shot down from the Hind's wing pod and smashed into the plaza.

The explosion flung Eddie off his feet as broken stones were blasted into the air, thrown high and far enough even to hit the Hind. Part of a wall near him collapsed with a ground-shaking crash.

But the destruction didn't end there. The plaza itself trembled, the foundations of its raised eastern end shifting. A great crack lanced across the slabs – towards Nina and Mac.

The cracks of falling debris were overpowered by louder, deeper crunches. Nina jumped back from the building as its blocks rasped and groaned against each other. 'I don't think we're in a safe place . . .'

Mac grimaced. 'Nor do I!'

They leapt over the plaza's edge – as the wall slammed down where they had been standing with an enormous crunch of masonry.

Flying rubble cascaded after them. A piece hit Nina's shoulder like a blow from a baseball bat. Mac fared no better, taking a hit to the stomach that left him winded. A billowing grey cloud swirled over them.

The first of Pachac's men reached the building in which they had landed . . .

And ran past, skirting as far as he could round the rolling miasma. The others behind him did the same, not wanting to risk getting close to a potentially unstable ruin. No one saw the two dust-covered figures inside.

Stifling a groan, Nina listened to the running footsteps move away, then painfully sat up. 'Mac,' she whispered. 'Mac! Are you hurt?'

'Nothing a spot of death won't cure,' the Scot wheezed, wiping his eyes. Nina helped him upright – then they both looked up at a rush of hot, fuel-stinking wind.

The Hind was moving in to land.

Eddie dizzily tried to move, and rapidly regretted it. His entire body felt like one huge bruise. What had happened? He'd shot at the helicopter . . .

The Hind!

It was hovering just feet above the plaza, pointing its Gatling gun at the explorers. Faced with certain and immediate death if they tried to escape, Macy, Osterhagen and Zender had surrendered. Men in black combat gear jumped from the cabin, some aiming at Kit, who raised his hands.

The others came for Eddie.

The AKM was only a few feet away. Ignoring the pain, he crawled towards it—

A booted foot stamped down on the weapon. Eddie twisted to see a gleaming handgun aimed at his head. A Jericho. Behind it was a sneering, aristocratic face.

'Hello, Chase,' said Stikes. 'Fancy meeting you here.'

34

The Hind had landed, Pachac and his men had reached the plaza – and the prisoners were being held at gunpoint.

'Some familiar faces, I see,' said Stikes, giving Macy and Osterhagen dismissive looks before turning rather more attention to Kit. 'There's one that's conspicuously absent, though. Where's your wife, Chase?'

Eddie said nothing, fixing the other Englishman with a defiant stare – which earned him a fierce blow from a rifle butt, knocking him to his knees. 'He asked you a question, Chase!' shouted Baine, following the strike up with a boot to the side. He was about to deliver another kick when a gesture from his commander stopped him short.

'Well?' said Stikes. 'Where is she?'

'Buggered if I know,' Eddie groaned, standing back up. Nina's location had been preying on his mind as well. She and Mac had been beside a building on the plaza's southern side – which had now collapsed.

'You may well be. I doubt Pachac's men have a lot of female company hiding out in the mountains – they're probably desperate enough to find even your hairy Yorkshire arse appealing.' He turned back to Macy. 'But I think it's fairly clear who'd be at the top of their list. Should I give her to them, Chase?' He raised the Jericho to her head. Macy's lips tightened, trembling. 'Or should I just shoot her now? So. Where's your wife?'

'She was behind that building,' Eddie growled in defeat, knowing the former SAS officer would pull the trigger without hesitation. He gestured towards the rubble.

Stikes's eyes flicked towards the wrecked structure. 'Cagg, Voeker, check that. See if she's buried in it.' His two men moved off to search the ruin. Stikes lowered the gun. Macy let out a whimper of relief.

'So you brought this arsehole with you,' said Eddie of Baine, enduring another kick in an attempt to direct Stikes's thoughts away from his hostages. He didn't recognise any of the other mercenaries. 'What about Maximov?'

Stikes scowled. 'I fired him. Anyone stupid enough to be outwitted by you isn't somebody I want on the payroll. And speaking of stupidity . . .' He faced the helicopter. Both cockpits were open, Krikorian examining the nose cannon while Gurov climbed on to the fuselage to inspect a large dent where a flying rock had hit one of the engine intakes. 'Gurov! Is there any damage?'

'I don't know,' the Russian replied. 'I need to check the turbine blades.'

'How long will that take?'

'Twenty minutes.'

'Do it.' Stikes glared at Krikorian, who noticed his employer's ire and shamefacedly moved behind the gunship. Stikes returned his gaze to Eddie. 'Idiot. Firing a missile in a confined space – when I'd already given specific orders that I wanted you taken alive.'

'Nice to know you care,' said Eddie sarcastically.

'Oh, I don't. Not about you, at least.' He looked across at Kit. 'But Jindal and your wife are going to do something for me.'

'What thing?'

Eddie hadn't expected an answer, but his chances of getting even a hint fell to zero as Pachac and a couple of his men hurried down the stairway. 'Stikes!' shouted the terrorist leader excitedly. 'It is here, it is here! The Punchaco!'

'You found it?' said Stikes.

Pachac ran to him. 'Yes, yes! In the temple. It is – it is magnificent! And huge! Three metres high, at least.'

'Over twice the size of the sun disc from Paititi, then,' said Stikes thoughtfully. 'At least four times the volume of gold.'

'At least. And it is covered with gems, diamonds and emeralds and more!'

'That should fund a revolution or two.'

Pachac's enthusiasm dampened. 'The Punchaco is the greatest symbol of my people. I cannot sell it – it would be a betrayal.'

'What about the rest of the gold?'

'There is no other gold,' said the Peruvian. 'Not that we have found.'

Stikes frowned. 'That doesn't seem likely. Since we're standing in the heart of the legendary *city* of gold.' He stood before Osterhagen. 'You're the expert, Dr Osterhagen – where's the gold?'

The Punchaco is the only gold we have seen,' said the German.

'I find that difficult to believe.'

'We haven't had time to explore,' Macy protested. 'You got here right after we did.'

'How *did* you get here so quick?' Eddie demanded. 'Only a few people knew exactly where we were going.'

A smug smile slithered on to Stikes's face. 'I have your father to thank for that.'

'What?'

'He called me after you threatened him in Bogotá. He was rather worried, but I assured him there wouldn't be any problems.' The smirk broadened. 'He also told me that your wife was searching for El Dorado in Peru. And I knew someone with a lot of contacts here.' He nodded at Pachac. 'So I made a deal with Arcani, and he put the word out to his informants, his sympathisers, and most importantly his network of drug dealers to watch for a certain red-haired woman in charge of a team of foreigners. We knew that you'd arrived in Lima, we knew you spent last night in Chachapoyas, and we knew when you passed through the village down the road. But you didn't reach the next village to the north, and there are only a handful of places you could possibly have turned off the road . . . so all Arcani's people had to do was look for your tyre tracks. Simple.'

Eddie held in the surge of rage he felt towards his father, focusing it on more immediate targets. 'So you're in this for the gold? You might have a problem getting your cut if your new mate here doesn't want to sell it.'

Stikes laughed. 'I don't want gold, Chase! Who am I, Mr T? No, the deal was that apart from enough to pay my men all they're owed, plus a bonus, Pachac can keep everything that he finds here . . . except for the three statues your wife is so interested in.'

Eddie reacted with surprise – but noticed that, if anything, Kit seemed even more shocked. 'What the hell do you want those for? They're just bits of stone.'

'We both know that's not true.' Stikes turned as Voeker and Cagg returned. 'Well?'

'She's not there,' said Cagg. 'But there were some tracks in the dust. Looks like she went down the hill.'

Stikes whirled, staring towards the shaft. 'Damn it! We can't let her get away – Baine, make sure she doesn't get out of the cave. Do *not* kill her; I need her alive.' Baine raised his M4, which was fitted with a telescopic sight, and ran to the end of the plaza. The mercenary leader addressed his other men. 'The rest of you, spread out and find her. We need to find the statues too. Where are they, Chase?'

'How the fuck would I know?' Eddie replied as the black-clad men dispersed. 'I was down at the bottom trying to stop you arseholes from getting in.'

Stikes sighed and drew his gun again, pressing it against Macy's head. 'We're not going to have to go through this rigmarole again, are we?'

Osterhagen spoke up. 'Leave her alone. The statues are with our equipment, outside the temple.'

'Show me,' said Stikes. 'Arcani, tell your men to guard the others . . . no, wait. I want to keep Chase in my sight. Bring them with us.' Pachac issued orders, and the rebels pushed their prisoners forward at gunpoint.

'We can't let him take the statues,' Kit protested.

'Don't worry about being separated from them, Jindal,' said Stikes. 'You'll be coming with them.'

'Why do you want him?' asked Pachac.

'I'm a wanted man after the fiasco in Venezuela,' replied Stikes. 'An Interpol officer will be a useful hostage if the police get too close.'

Eddie narrowed his eyes, puzzled. Stikes's answer was a little too glib, too rehearsed. And it didn't even hold water; taking a cop as a hostage was a bad idea, because it ensured that the other cops trying to rescue him would be particularly determined and ruthless. The mercenary had some other purpose in mind for Kit.

Pachac seemed equally doubtful, but was apparently willing to accept the explanation. 'Then what about the gold?' He waved a hand at the silent ruins as they climbed through the tiers towards the temple. 'We are the first people to find this place since the Incas left. There must be more gold than just the Punchaco. I must have it. I need it for the revolution.'

'Revolution?' muttered Zender with contempt. 'You are a drug dealer, nothing more. A common criminal.'

Pachac rounded on him, face twisted with anger. 'I am the Inkarrí!' he snarled. Zender flinched, but stood his ground, almost nose to nose with the terrorist leader. 'I will give back my people the land and power that were stolen from them by the Spanish. By people like you! Bourgeois puppets of the ruling class! The revolution will sweep you away like garbage.'

'There will not be a revolution,' Zender countered. 'This is the twenty-first century! Communism is dead – even the Chinese have rejected Maoism. People want jobs, and money, and homes where they can raise their children. They do not want drug-dealing psychopaths like you!'

Pachac was silent, the veins in his thick neck standing out as his fury rose . . . then with a roar he snatched something from his belt. A metallic *snick* – and he drove his knife into the official's stomach. Zender screamed as the blade slashed deeper into his abdomen.

Eddie lunged at the Peruvian, but was seized by other rebels and dragged back. Macy turned away in horror as Pachac pulled out the knife, then clamped both hands around Zender's throat, spittle flying from his lips as he hissed abuse in Quechua, the Indian language. He squeezed harder and harder, forcing Zender to his knees.

Zender convulsed, trying to force Pachac's hands away, but the muscular revolutionary's grip was too strong. The official's mouth opened wide in a futile attempt to draw air through his crushed windpipe, tongue writhing like a panicked snake. A choked gurgle escaped his throat . . . then his eyes rolled grotesquely up into his head and his entire body sagged into the limpness of death.

Pachac let go. The corpse slumped to the ground. He wiped off his knife, then folded it shut. 'So that was your speciality?' said Stikes. 'Callas told me about it. *Capa* . . .'

'*Capacocha*,' Pachac told him, returning the knife to his belt. 'An ancient Inca ritual. One I will be proud to bring back.'

'Couldn't you have just stuck to playing pan pipes?' Eddie asked, disgusted. The Peruvian's expression made him think that he might also receive a demonstration, but then Pachac turned away and continued towards the temple entrance. His followers shoved the prisoners after him, leaving Zender's body behind.

'Where are the statues?' Stikes demanded as they entered the little square with the fountains.

'Over here,' said Osterhagen, leading him to where the team had left their equipment.

Stikes opened the case to find the statues inside, the set now complete. 'Excellent,' he said, snapping the lid shut and picking up the box. He looked at Eddie. 'So I've got the statues, I've got Jindal – that only leaves your wife.'

'And the gold,' said Pachac impatiently.

'And the gold, yes. But—' He broke off as his walkie-talkie bleeped. 'Yes? Have you found her?'

'Sir!' said one of his men urgently. 'We haven't – but we found two of Pachac's men dead. Their weapons are missing.'

Stikes immediately understood the implications. 'She's not trying to escape – she's going to try to rescue her friends! Everyone get back up here – we're on the level above the plaza.' The case under one arm, he strode back to Eddie. 'Been giving her survival lessons, have you?'

'A few,' said Eddie, wondering what the hell Nina was doing – and Mac, for that matter. 'She knows how to take care of herself.'

'But does she know how to take care of you?' The Jericho was drawn again – but this time it was Eddie, not Macy, who was its target. 'Dr Wilde!' Stikes's voice rose to a shout, echoing through the cavern. 'Dr Wilde, I have your husband at gunpoint. You have ten seconds to make your position known and surrender, or I'll kill him, then move on to the rest of your friends!'

Macy clutched Osterhagen's arm in fear as Stikes stepped closer to Eddie, the gun inches from his face. The first of the mercenaries ran into the square, covering the other entrances and surrounding buildings with their M4s. 'Ten!' said Stikes. 'Nine! Eight—'

'Really, Alexander!' boomed a Scottish voice. 'You always were such a drama queen.'

Everyone whirled to see Mac on the terrace above, an AK taken from one of the rebels Eddie had shot ready in his hands. The weapons of mercenaries and terrorists alike snapped up to lock on to him. Stikes was genuinely thrown by his unexpected appearance, but quickly masked his surprise. 'Well, well. McCrimmon. What in the name of God are you doing here?'

'I'm on holiday,' Mac replied. 'Let them go.'

Stikes laughed sarcastically. 'I don't think so.' The Jericho was still aimed unwaveringly at Eddie's head. 'Now, where was I? Oh yes. Seven! Six! Five!'

'I'm warning you, Alexander!' Mac shouted, lining up his gun's sights on the mercenary leader.

'And I'm warning you. Three! Two! One—'

'Arse!' Mac growled. With a noise of angry frustration, he tossed the Kalashnikov down to the square and raised his hands.

'Hold your fire,' Strikes snapped, the command aimed more at Pachac's men than his own. 'Come down here, McCrimmon.'

Mac started towards the nearest flight of steps. 'So, this is what you've come down to, Alexander?' he said. 'Teaming up with Maoist killers? Robbing and plundering? It took eleven years, but your true colours are finally out in the open.'

'Don't be so bloody sanctimonious,' Stikes sneered. 'You've hardly kept your hands clean, doing all those little jobs for MI6. How many people did you set up to be killed? And as for your favourite poodle here,' he waved his gun at Eddie, 'it's a wonder he hasn't ended up in jail, with all the chaos he's caused around the world.'

Mac managed a sardonic half-smile as he descended the steps. 'I'd hoped that after the official investigation, the difference between legitimate and illegitimate targets might finally have penetrated your skull.'

Stikes narrowed his eyes in anger. 'The only thing penetrating *your* skull will be a bullet if you don't—' He caught himself. 'Oh, very good, Mac,' he continued, voice becoming mocking. 'You almost got me.'

'Got you with what?' Mac asked innocently as he reached the square. Pachac's men surrounded him.

'Got me into an argument about your attempt to destroy my reputation back in the Regiment. That would have kept me occupied for a few minutes, wouldn't it?' He regarded the surrounding buildings suspiciously. 'Enough time for Dr Wilde to do whatever you're both planning.'

'Actually,' called Nina, 'I've already done it.'

Her voice came from above. The people in the square all looked up at the terrace, but saw nothing – until they raised their eyes higher to see Nina on the roof of the palace itself, watching them from the highest point in the city.

And aiming a rocket launcher at them.

'Okay,' she continued, having got their full attention, 'here's the deal. Either you let everyone go, or . . . boom.'

'Er, love,' said Eddie in alarm, 'that didn't work for Indiana Jones, and it won't work for us either!' The kill radius of an RPG-7 warhead was relatively small . . . but still more than large enough to shred the closely packed group in the square, good guys and bad alike.

But then he caught Mac's eye. The older man gave him a knowing look – one that while not exactly reassuring, still suggested Nina had something in mind other than a no-win scenario.

Stikes was unimpressed by her threat. 'You really expect me to believe that you'd kill your husband? And your friends?' He briefly looked round as the rest of his men arrived. They immediately aimed their rifles at her.

'Well, of course not,' Nina replied. 'I just wanted to let them know what I climbed all the way up here to do.'

'Which is what?'

She cocked her head to one side – and smiled. 'Pull the plug.'

And with that she ducked out of his sight, making a half-turn and dropping to one knee to brace herself as she took aim.

Eddie realised what she meant at the same moment as Macy, Kit and Osterhagen. 'We're gonna get wet again—'

Nina pulled the trigger.

The grenade's small expeller charge blasted it out of the launch tube, flying clear of Nina before the main rocket booster ignited and sent the warhead streaking towards the rear of the cave at over six hundred miles an hour. It hit the wall the Incas had built to constrain their water supply – and exploded.

The echoes of the detonation faded . . . to be replaced by another sound. A low, crackling rumble.

Pent up behind the ancient dam were hundreds of thousands of gallons of water. Even with the river blocked, the level had hardly fallen, only having a tiny hole through which to escape.

That hole was now widening.

The cracking of stone blocks grew louder – then with a splintering boom, the wall gave way.

And a tidal wave burst into the cavern.

35

The fountains erupted into geysers as the pressure behind them increased a hundredfold. Water exploded around the palace, sweeping over the terrace and down the broad stairways towards the shocked people below.

Mac grabbed Macy, yelling '*Run!*' She broke into a sprint, the Scot behind her.

Simultaneously, Eddie ran for the closest shelter – the Temple of the Sun. He swatted Osterhagen's shoulder as he passed him, hoping the German would get the message and follow. Kit, further away, also made a break for the entrance.

'Evacuate!' Stikes bellowed, rushing for the steps leading down the temple's side. His men raced after him.

Pachac and his followers were the least prepared, lacking the understanding of Nina's plan or the mercenaries' training. The great wave was almost on them before they broke through their dumbfoundedness and started to move.

Macy leapt on to a wall just as the water thundered past her. Mac, two paces behind and slowed by his artificial leg, was not so lucky. The frothing surge swept him away, also snatching up Pachac and his men, and Kit, bowling them all down the stairway towards the city's lower levels.

Eddie ran into the temple just as the wave caught him and Osterhagen, throwing them against the inner wall. The two men were tossed like driftwood into the Punchaco's chamber.

Outside, Stikes and his men changed direction just before the flood consumed them, running on to a narrow ledge along the temple's flank rather than down the steps. Most of the flow took the steeper, wider route, human flotsam tumbling help-lessly within it – but the rearmost mercenary slipped as a pursuing bore of water washed beneath his feet and fell with a scream into the maelstrom.

Choking, Mac managed to bring his head above the water – and saw danger dead ahead. The path down into the city made almost a ninety-degree turn at the bottom of the stairway. He was about to be flung against a wall.

Two buildings abutted each other to one side, a narrow gap between them—

He lashed out with his left leg. His foot wedged into the crack – and his ankle bent at an unnatural angle as he jerked to a stop.

His prosthetic ankle. The joint creaked and strained, the force of the water threatening to rip the straps securing the artificial limb to his knee. Water pummelling his face, he bent at the waist to grab the prosthesis itself with both hands, taking the weight off the bindings.

A hand clamped around his arm. Pachac, his extra weight about to snap the metal bone – then the Peruvian lost his grip and was gone.

Kit also glimpsed the approaching wall. He held his breath, powerless to prevent the collision—

The current swept the fallen mercenary in front of him, the other man taking the full force of their impact with a crack of ribs. Winded and spinning, Kit saw pillars along the front of a building. He grabbed at them, the water's relentless push forcing his fingers from the first before he managed to get a grip on a second. He hung on as the flood surged past him, carrying the other men away downhill.

Stikes and his remaining men jumped from the ledge as the bore rushed around their feet, landing on the walls of the roofless buildings on the tier below the temple. A waterfall gushed down behind them. 'Fuckin' 'ell!' gasped Baine. 'That ginger bitch is a fuckin' psycho!'

'Keep moving,' Stikes ordered, surveying the way ahead. By moving along the rooftops, they would be able to stay above the water and make their way down to the helicopter. He still had the case containing the statues; he checked that it was securely closed, then took the lead across the ruins.

On the plaza, Gurov and Krikorian had broken off from their checks at the sound of the explosion and rumble of water, but neither had been able to figure out what was happening – until the wave burst over the buildings above. Gurov gaped at the oncoming deluge, then scrambled down to the open rear cockpit. 'I'll start it up!' he yelled at Krikorian. 'You shut the hatch!' The Russian had opened an inspection panel to access the gunship's engines. Krikorian climbed up, slamming it closed and fumbling with the locking bolts as the wavefront swept across the plaza, churning against the Hind's landing gear.

The tsunami swept Eddie and Osterhagen all the way round the chamber's curved inner wall, slamming them against the Punchaco. Eddie gripped the enormous gold disc's thick edge with one hand, the other clawing for a hold before finding purchase on the sun god's open mouth. 'Hang on to me!' he yelled. Osterhagen clung to his waist. The water level was rising rapidly in the confined space, more surging in every second—

The wall beneath the window cracked – and broke apart.

Eddie almost lost his grip under the powerful suction of water rushing out through the new hole. It cascaded on to the buildings below, sweeping the broken stones with it – and exposing something beneath them.

From the palace roof, Nina watched the spreading waters, conflicted. The rocket launcher, now slung over her shoulder, had given Eddie and the others a chance of escape – but they were still in danger. She could see Macy fearfully climbing a building, cut off by the torrent, but the rest of the explorers were out of sight. And the ruins themselves were under threat; as she watched, a wall crumbled behind Macy like a sandcastle in a rising tide.

The palace itself trembled under her feet. She spun in alarm. The building was taking the full force of the escaping water – and a chunk of its rear wall collapsed in a waterlogged implosion. Pillars toppled like dominoes, a chain reaction of disintegrating masonry advancing on her—

She screamed and made a running jump off the roof just as it broke apart, landing painfully on a lower wall. Spray and froth crashed over her. She gasped for breath, then looked back at the fallen section . . .

Her pain and fear disappeared, replaced by utter amazement.

Pachac had been right. There *was* more gold hidden in the ancient city. Quite literally – behind the carefully interlocked stones from which the palace was built, she saw the unmistakable sheen of precious metal, cast into rectangular slabs. The Incas had kept more than the Punchaco hidden from the Spanish, an unimaginable fortune concealed inside the walls. Despite her precarious situation, she actually laughed in genuine delight.

★

In the temple, Eddie had made a similar discovery. 'Doc!' he shouted. 'Look at the wall!'

Osterhagen found secure footing. He turned – and gasped. Jutting from the edges of the jagged hole were large golden bricks, gleaming in the daylight coming through the cave mouth. 'The city of gold!' he cried. 'It's true, the legend is true!'

Suddenly, the light became brighter.

The advancing wave hit the great defensive wall. The reservoir was filled in a moment, a huge backwash exploding into the air as the drainage holes were overwhelmed by the sheer volume of water. More plunged down the shaft, sweeping away the bodies of Pachac's men, but even this was not enough to relieve the pressure.

A huge section of the wall bulged outwards – and toppled with a cacophonous boom. The water rushed down its new escape route, sweeping over the rubble into the drained pool outside. The river channel that had carried away the overflow filled again, a tidal surge charging through the jungle towards the valley.

Almost as if satisfied with its destructive efforts, the flow of water began to ease. Most of the underground reserve had now drained away. The roar fell to a rumbling growl.

Stikes, climbing down to another rooftop, heard the change and looked up the slope. The torrent's fury was dying. There was still a lot of water gushing through the streets, but no longer with deadly force.

That didn't alter his objective. Plenty of damage had already been inflicted on the Inca settlement, the thumps of falling stonework echoing all around him. The sooner he got to the helicopter with his prize, the better.

Prizes, plural. Another sound caught his attention: a coughing groan. Not far away, Kit clung to a pillar as the flood washed around him. Stikes drew his gun and pointed it at the Indian. 'Jindal!' Kit looked up at him through half-closed eyes, confused – then shocked. 'Don't move. We've still got some business together.'

The raging water trying to tear Mac loose subsided. He shifted position, keeping hold of his prosthetic leg with one hand as he used the other to grip a jutting block and pull himself higher. Taking his weight on his right leg, he freed his trapped foot, then splashed down to solid ground. The water reached his shins, but was quickly falling.

He sloshed back up towards the square to search for his friends, discovering to his annoyance that he was limping: the strain had bent his artificial foot out of alignment. 'I'll have a job kicking anyone's arse with that,' he muttered.

Gurov completed his hurried pre-flight checks and twisted in his cockpit seat to look back at Krikorian. 'Come on, close the fucking hatch!'

The Armenian was struggling with a catch. 'It's stuck, I can't lock it!' He bashed at the panel with a fist, trying to force it shut.

Even though the flood seemed to be slowing, Gurov still wanted to get the hell out of the cave. 'I'm starting her. Just get it closed before we take off!'

He flicked switches. With a whine of turbines, the engines came to life, the heavy rotor blades slowly beginning to turn.

Further down the hill, the bedraggled Pachac pulled himself out of the water up a short flight of steps. Another of his men was already there, panting and clutching his bleeding arm, and nearby he heard moans and calls for help. 'Comrades! Can you hear me?' he shouted. 'Who's still with me?'

One by one, his remaining followers responded. Eight men altogether – all that was left of his original force of over twenty. 'What do we do, Inkarrí?' one asked.

Pachac looked towards the cave mouth. Now that part of the wall had collapsed, it would be easy for them to reach the jungle outside. 'We need to get out of here and contact the rest of the True Red Way,' he decided. 'The Punchaco is here – we can't let the government get it. We need more men so we can take it ourselves.'

'But it's huge, it weighs tons!' protested another rebel. 'How are we going to get it down the road?'

'We'll steal a truck!' He pointed at two men. 'Mauro, Juan, when we get outside you guard the cave. If any of the archaeologists survived and try to escape, kill them.'

Heads turned towards the rising sound of the Hind. 'What about the mercenaries?' said the first man.

'Stikes got what he came for, those statues,' replied Pachac. 'If he tries to get anything else . . . we kill him too!' He regarded the broken wall. 'The water's falling; we'll be able to get out now. Come on.'

Eddie waded to the now open end of the temple. Osterhagen followed. 'This is incredible,' said the German. 'If there is gold behind the whole wall, it would be worth hundreds of millions of dollars!'

'If I were you, I'd start negotiating for a finder's fee . . .' Eddie tailed off, the gold forgotten as he took in the view beyond the opening. On the plaza, the Hind's rotors were building up to takeoff speed – and closer, on the maze of rooftops between the temple and the helicopter, he saw Stikes and four of his men carefully navigating the walls to reach the aircraft.

With a prisoner. Kit. Baine held him at rifle point.

'Doc, wait here,' Eddie ordered. Before Osterhagen could reply, the Englishman had climbed through the hole and jumped down on to the skeletal buildings below. He ran along the thick walls after the mercenaries.

The water flowing beneath Nina's position finally looked safe enough to traverse. She dropped down into it and made her way to the terrace overlooking the square.

To her relief, she saw a welcome face below. 'Mac!' she cried, carefully negotiating the waterfall running down the steps and hurrying to him. 'You're okay!'

'My specialist will probably have some harsh words,' Mac replied, raising his buckled prosthetic leg out of the water, 'but apart from that, yes, I'm all right. What about the others? Have you seen them?'

Nina looked to one side. 'I saw Macy over there somewhere – she'd climbed up on to a building, she looked okay. I haven't seen anyone else, though. Do you know where Eddie went?'

'In the temple, I think.' Mac's gaze returned to the rocket launcher. 'Let me have that.'

Nina handed it to him. 'What are you gonna do with it?'

'Stikes's helicopter is getting ready to take off,' he said. 'Hopefully, that spare warhead is still where we left it; if it is, I'll see that he encounters a little turbulence.'

'I'll tell Eddie to find you,' said Nina as she headed for the temple. Mac smiled, then limped as quickly as he could down the hill.

★

A narrow, flooded alley separated two tiers of buildings. Eddie vaulted it, wobbling as he regained his balance on the lower wall, then hurried after the mercenaries.

All five were still armed, and if any looked back he would be in trouble, but their attention seemed fixed on three things: the waiting helicopter, their prisoner, and navigating the walls without slipping. The only thing on Eddie's mind, however, was violence. He rapidly gained on them, cutting corners in pursuit.

Stikes, leading, dropped out of sight on to a lower tier, followed by Voeker. Kit, next in line, hesitated at the jump. 'Get fuckin' down there,' Baine snarled, jabbing his M4 at him. The other two men stopped behind him in a line, unable to get past. Kit glared back at Baine – then his expression changed to one of surprise. Baine turned—

The last man in the line was carrying his rifle over his shoulder. Eddie grabbed it, swung it round, and fired a burst at point-blank range into his back.

The bullets tore through the man's body, exploding messily out of his chest – and hitting Cagg. Even mangled by their passage, the rounds still had enough force behind them to rip into his torso. The mercenary staggered, eyes wide in shock, then keeled over and fell into the waterlogged room below.

Eddie struggled to pull the rifle free of the dead man as he collapsed. Baine brought up his own gun—

Kit body-slammed him, knocking the rifle from his hands. It clattered off the wall and landed near Cagg's body. Baine reeled. Kit grappled with him – and threw him off the wall to the next tier down.

Eddie finally wrestled the M4 free, the mercenary's corpse toppling on to a wooden beam and hanging spread-eagled over it. 'Kit! You okay?'

'Yes. Thank you!' The Interpol officer smiled in relief.

Eddie hurried up to him. Stikes and Voeker came into view below. The ex-officer was still carrying the case. Eddie raised the M4, but before he could fire, Stikes and his companion leapt down to the plaza, shielded by thick stone walls.

Eddie had found a new target, though. The Hind was not yet at takeoff revolutions, needing to be at maximum power to haul itself airborne – and he saw a man in a jumpsuit slam closed a panel on the engine cowling. The forward cockpit's canopy was open: the gunner.

The man who had brought carnage to Caracas. Without hesitation, Eddie aimed and fired. The jumpsuit's jungle camouflage blossomed with dark red. Krikorian crumpled, thumping off the Hind's stub wing and dropping to the ground.

No way to do the same to the pilot; the rear cockpit was shut, impervious to the M4's bullets. But he could still deal with the pilot's boss. 'Get back up to the temple,' he told Kit. 'Osterhagen's in there – see if you can find Nina or anyone else.'

'Where are you going?' Kit asked.

'After Stikes.'

'Are you going to get the statues back?'

'No, I'm just gonna kill him!'

As Kit retreated, Eddie moved to the edge of the wall and pointed his gun at the tier below. No sign of Baine. There was a steep alley between the lower buildings, water still draining downhill with some force. He jumped on to a wall and advanced along it, still searching for the ex-SAS trooper – but then any thoughts of Baine vanished as he spotted Stikes running for the helicopter. He raised the rifle, pinning the mercenary's back in his sights—

Hands clamped around his ankles.

Baine had been hiding, now leaping up to grab him and pulling with all his strength. Arms flailing, Eddie fell.

He landed on top of the mercenary, knocking him backwards. Both men landed in the alley – and were swept away downhill by the rushing water.

Kit made his way back along the rooftops, then realised he had missed the opportunity to arm himself in case Pachac and his men were still around. He was about to turn back to retrieve one of the fallen rifles when a holster on the dead mercenary slumped over the roof beam caught his eye. He pulled out the pistol, a Steyr M9-A1 automatic, and quickly checked that it was loaded with its full fifteen rounds before continuing.

Nina entered the temple to find Osterhagen looking out through the broken wall. 'Leonard! Are you okay?'

The German nodded. 'What about you?'

'I'm fine. Where's Eddie?'

'He shot some of the mercenaries – but he just fell off a wall!'

Nina ran to the opening, ignoring the gold as she searched for her husband. 'Where?' Osterhagen pointed at a lower row of buildings. She saw Kit picking his way along a wall, arms held out for balance like a tightrope walker, but there was no sign of Eddie. 'Dammit!' She ran from the temple, hurrying down the steps.

Macy gingerly lowered herself from her perch. 'Oh, gross . . .' she whispered as cold, muddy water sluiced into her boots. It was now only about ankle deep, the flow like that of a brisk stream, but she was still worried about keeping her footing.

One hand on a wall for support, she started to make her way downhill.

'Kit! Over here!'

The Indian looked round to see Mac emerging from a building. The Scot was carrying the RPG-7 – which was now loaded with the last of the olive-green warheads. 'Mac! I'm glad to see you,' Kit said, relieved.

'You too.' Mac noticed the gun. 'You're armed, good. Come on, get down here. Nina and Macy are okay – have you seen any of the others?'

Kit jumped from the wall and splashed to him. 'Eddie rescued me from Stikes and his men.'

An approving nod. 'Good lad. Where is he now?'

'He went after Stikes.'

Approval turned to a frown. 'Sod it! If he's too close . . .'

'Too close for what?'

Mac held up the rocket launcher. 'I won't be able to use this.'

'You're going to blow up the helicopter? But Stikes has the statues.'

'That's the least of my worries.' He indicated the tower the expedition had passed on their way to the plaza. 'I should be able to get a good shot from there before he takes off. Come on!' He started a limping jog towards it.

Kit followed, his face betraying his secret concern.

Stikes and Voeker reached the Hind and jumped through the open rear hatch. The mercenary leader grabbed a headset. 'Gurov! Take off, now!'

'I can't!' came the reply. 'There's a problem with the port engine, oil pressure. I need to bring it up to speed slowly.'

'How long?'

'A minute. What about the others?'

'There's no one left to wait for,' said Stikes coldly. He put the case down in the empty seat beside him and secured it with the harness straps. 'Besides, I've got what I came for.'

The steep alley ended where it met a wider, shallower pathway, the rush of water bowling Eddie into one of the small tombs. Tightly wrapped mummies, now sodden and waterlogged, crunched underneath him. Bruised and winded by his uncontrollable trip down the hard-sided waterslide, he stood—

Baine slithered into the tomb in a burst of spray and slammed a boot into Eddie's stomach. 'All right, Yorkie?' he cried as Eddie doubled over. He jumped to his feet, delivering another kick to his former comrade's midsection. 'Yeah, 'ave some of that! You broke one of my fucking teeth in Caracas – you know how shit the dentists are down here?' More kicks. Eddie collapsed in a corner, scattering bones and ritual items. Baine moved closer. 'Gonna break your fucking neck—'

Eddie whipped up a length of cloth like a slingshot – with a skeletal arm folded inside it. It smashed against the side of Baine's head. Eddie followed up with a punch. From his awkward position it didn't have much power behind it, but was hard enough to make the bigger man retreat. Eddie held in a groan as he pushed himself upright. 'You couldn't break a fucking *pencil*, you southern ponce.'

Baine balled his fists. 'Always 'ad some fucking smart-arse comment, didn't you? Now me, I stick to—'

He broke off abruptly, driving a fearsome punch at Eddie's head. The Yorkshireman barely managed to dodge, Baine's knuckles clipping his ear. His military training had taught him that the mere act of speaking demanded a surprisingly large part of the brain's processing power, detracting from its ability to react to sudden events – but Baine had the same training and had played on Eddie's expectations to launch a surprise attack.

Another blow, forcing Eddie back a step to avoid it. Baine advanced, fists raised like a boxer. Eddie, realising he was being cornered, brought up his own hands to defend – and took a brutal blow just inches from his groin from the other man's foot. Not just a boxer – a kickboxer. Baine had expanded his skill set over the past decade.

The mercenary grinned malevolently. 'Yeah, weren't expecting that, were you? Feet an' fists – I can take you down with either.' A few feints from both pairs of extremities. Eddie countered, but knew that in the confined space, when the real attack came he wouldn't be able to avoid it. 'You're getting slow, Yorkie! Married life'll do that, turn you into a useless fat fucker.' A glance at Eddie's hairline. 'Makes you go bald too!' He laughed—

Eddie struck, this time landing a solid blow to Baine's upper jaw. The punch split the skin on his knuckles, but the Essex man came off worse, the inside of his lip tearing against his front teeth and the cartilage of his septum snapping. He staggered back, spitting blood.

This time, it was Eddie's turn to deliver a kick – but even through his pain Baine still had the reflexes to twist away from a ball-crunching impact. Snarling, he dived at the Yorkshireman. Eddie punched him again, but couldn't avoid the collision – or stop himself from being driven against the wall.

'Fucker!' yelled Baine as they grappled. His greater size and weight gave him the advantage, pushing his opponent further down into the tomb's corner. He jerked up a knee and hit Eddie squarely in the stomach.

Gasping, Eddie struggled to recover, but Baine shoved his

head back against the stone wall with a crack. Dizzied, he tried to rise—

Baine's forearm pressed across his throat like a steel beam, choking him.

Mac ran up the steps into the tower, Kit behind him. As he had hoped, it gave him an excellent view over the plaza.

The Hind was still on the ground, but the amount of spray being kicked up by its downwash told him that it was almost at takeoff power. He brought up the RPG-7 and looked down the sights. The Russian weapon's aiming system was crude, but at a fairly short distance against a large stationary target he didn't need to do anything beyond point it in the right direction and fire.

'Mac, what if Eddie's down there?' Kit protested. 'You might kill him.'

'He's not on the plaza, so he's safe,' Mac replied. The Hind was fixed in the sights. 'Clear behind!'

'No, Mac – if they know you've got a rocket, we can force them to surrender!'

'Kit, the backblast on this thing will kill you,' Mac snapped impatiently. The helicopter shifted on its landing gear as the rotors reached full speed. It would lift off in a matter of seconds. 'This is our only chance – move!'

He saw in the corner of his eye that Kit had moved out of the rocket's deadly exhaust cone, then turned his attention back to the sights. He flicked off the safety, steeling himself for the jolt of firing as he tightened his finger on the trigger—

Two bullets hit him in the back.

Mac collapsed, searing pain swallowing his senses. Blood gushed from the wounds. The unfired RPG-7 clunked down beside him.

Kit stood frozen, the smoking Steyr clutched in his hand. His eyes were wide in shock at what he had just done. His mouth opened, an apology, a confession, on his lips . . . then it snapped shut. Dismay disappeared, replaced by determination. He ran down the stairs, leaving the dying man behind.

36

Eddie kicked and thrashed at Baine, but couldn't shift the thick arm crushing his throat. Darkness pulsed in from the edges of his vision with each beat of his heart. His hands scrabbled over the detritus of the tomb for anything he could use as a weapon, but found nothing except cloth and desiccated flesh.

The darkness swelled again, narrowing his view to a tunnel: Baine leering down at him, the entrance behind.

Another pulse – and something changed—

He tried to speak, only a raw croak escaping his mouth. Baine leaned closer, cruel smile widening. 'Wassat, Yorkie?'

'Marriage . . .' Eddie managed to rasp.

Puzzled, Baine eased the pressure on Eddie's neck very slightly. 'Marriage? What about it? Makes you fat an' bald – what else?'

Eddie choked out more words. 'Someone – always – got your back.' To Baine's surprise, his grimace turned into a crooked smile. 'Like – *now!*'

A mummified skull smashed down on the mercenary's head.

Nina stood behind him, wincing at the pain in her hand. 'Dammit, that really hurt! Oh, crap,' she added as Baine recovered from the shock and glared over his shoulder at her.

'Yeah, that *did* fucking hurt, you bitch!' he snarled, spitting out more blood. He turned to face Nina. Behind him, Eddie slumped to the water-covered floor, more burial artefacts clattering around him.

Nina brandished the skull, before realising that without the element of surprise it was all but useless as a weapon. She backed towards the exit. 'Great, I had to pick frickin' Yorick and not a gun ...'

Baine advanced, face full of fury—

'Oi!' said a gravelly voice from behind him. '*Twat!*'

Baine spun – and Eddie plunged an ornate golden dagger into his stomach. The mercenary roared as the Yorkshireman twisted the *tumi*, forcing the blade deeper into his body.

But despite the agony, Baine wasn't incapacitated. He caught the still winded Eddie with a savage punch, knocking him down. Another kick hammered into Eddie's stomach, then Baine pivoted to smash his steel-capped combat boot into his face—

The skull cracked down on his head again, shattering into fragments. Baine slumped to his knees, falling forward. Eddie rolled out of the way – and the mercenary splashed down face first, driving the knife all the way into his abdomen. He let out a long, bubbling moan, then was silent. A red circle swelled in the water around him.

Eddie sat up. 'He's got a *tumi* in his tummy,' he groaned.

Nina was too worried to complain about the terrible joke. 'Oh my God, Eddie? Are you all right?'

'Help me up, and we'll see if any bits fall off.'

Nina stepped over Baine's body. 'Sorry about your friend,' she said to the remaining mummies as she pulled Eddie to his feet.

★

With the water level dropping all the time, Macy had been able to increase her pace through the city. She had spotted first Mac, then Nina, hurrying down the hill and decided to follow them, but so far hadn't seen any further sign of anyone. And the two gunshots she had just heard prompted her to duck into hiding. Were Pachac and his people still around?

It was obvious that Stikes and his men were leaving, though. The helicopter rose above the plaza, making a careful half-turn before heading for the cave mouth. One less set of assholes to worry about, then, but she still felt far from safe.

Macy looked cautiously around, seeing nobody, then moved out and continued down the slope. The Hind was approaching the cavern's entrance. Once it left, she might actually be able to hear if there was anyone nearby—

She rounded a corner – and found a gun pointing at her.

Shock and fear quickly turned to relief as she realised it was Kit, who seemed equally startled. 'Jeez!' she gasped, unable to hold back a nervous giggle. 'You scared me!'

For a moment, the gun remained still . . . then Kit relaxed and lowered it, 'Sorry. Are you okay?'

'Yeah, I'm fine. Have you seen Nina or Eddie? Or Mr McCrimmon?'

'No . . . no,' he said, the repetition more firm. 'Eddie went after Stikes – I'm looking for Mac.'

A flight of steps nearby led up to the tower. 'I saw him not long ago – I think he was heading that way.' She started towards them.

Kit shook his head firmly, moving to block her. 'No, I saw some of Pachac's men go up there.' He pointed to a nearby building. 'Wait in there and keep out of sight until it's safe. I'll . . . look for Mac.'

Macy reluctantly did as she was told as Kit ascended the steps. 'Take care,' she called to him.

He didn't reply, or even look back.

'How are you feeling?' Nina asked Eddie as they left the tomb.

'Lighter.'

'Huh?'

''Cause I just had the shit kicked out of me.'

'Very funny.'

They looked up to see the Hind clearing the cave mouth. 'Buggeration and fuckery!' Eddie growled. 'Stikes got away.'

'Well, good!' said Nina. 'If he's gone, we don't have to worry about him any more.'

'He's got your statues.'

'What? Oh. *Oh!* God damn it!' She scowled after the departing aircraft as it powered away. 'Son of a bitch!'

'Does it matter?' Eddie asked as he started to limp back up the slope. 'He can't do anything with 'em, and they helped us find El Dorado – what else can they do?'

'That was kinda what I wanted to find out!'

'Well, you can worry about it when we get back to New York. For now, we still need to get out of here. Let's find the others.'

'Mac had the rocket launcher – he said he was going to try to shoot down the helicopter.' Eddie stopped. 'What?' Nina asked, reading concern on his face.

'He didn't even try – we would have heard it.' He looked around for the most likely spot from which to launch an attack. 'Up there,' he said, indicating the tower. He set off again. 'Mac! Mac, can you hear me?'

★

Kit had halted once he was out of Macy's sight, mind a whirlwind of confusion and guilt – until Eddie's shout snapped him back to full awareness. It wouldn't be long before the Scot was found—

An idea, the Interpol officer acting upon it the instant it formed. He hurried back into the tower. Mac lay unmoving on the floor, blood pooling around him. Kit sat against the wall behind him, fired two shots into the air – then moved the gun to point at his upper arm.

He braced himself – and pulled the trigger.

Eddie broke into a run at the sound of gunfire. He reached the steps, seeing Macy peering fearfully from a nearby building. 'Stay out of sight!' he warned her.

'Eddie, wait!' Nina cried behind him, but he pounded up the steps and raced for the tower, the pain of his beating forgotten. Past a junction, up another flight of steps—

He stopped at the top as if he had slammed into an invisible wall. Kit was slumped on the floor, clutching a bloody wound to his left arm – but all Eddie could think about was Mac. His friend lay face down by the wall overlooking the city, the RPG-7 beside him. There were two bullet wounds in his back, lines of blood oozing from them.

'Mac?' He took a clumsy step closer, feet as heavy as lead. The figure didn't stir. Another step. 'Mac!'

Nina ran up behind him. 'Eddie – oh, God.'

Kit moaned. 'Pachac,' he said weakly. 'It was Pachac . . . caught us by surprise, then ran . . .'

Eddie reached Mac and stood over him, statue-like. Even through his horror, part of his mind was still functioning with trained, robotic clarity, assessing the injuries. The wounds were close together on the left side of his back. They would have hit the lung, probably also the heart. From the amount of pooled blood, there would also be a much larger exit wound in his chest. Even with immediate surgical intervention the chances of survival were extremely low.

But there would be no surgery. They were miles from any help.

He knelt, the blood soaking into the material of his jeans. Movement – slight, but definite. Mac was still breathing. He reached down, finding that his fingers were shaking. A hesitant touch on the older man's shoulder. 'Mac? Can you hear me?'

Silence for several seconds . . . then a faint sigh of drawing breath. Little bubbles formed in one of the bullet wounds. Mac slowly, painfully, turned his head, one half-closed eye blearily focusing on the man beside him. 'Eddie?' His voice was barely a whisper.

'Yeah. Yeah, it's me. It's me.'

The Scot moved his hand, trying to reach up but lacking the strength. Eddie gripped it. The skin already felt cold. 'I'm sorry . . .'

'For what?'

'Stikes . . . Had him right in my sights before he took off, but . . . not fast enough. I let him get away . . .'

'No, you didn't, it wasn't your fault,' said Eddie, shaking his head. 'Look, I'm – I'm gonna try to stop the bleeding.' He knew it was futile, but he had to do *something*. 'Hold still, and I'll—'

'No, Eddie.' Mac groaned, more bubbles rising from the blood-filled holes. 'Not . . . worth it.'

'It *is* worth it!' His voice cracked as he spoke.

'No, not going to . . .' Mac's whole body trembled. His hand now felt like stone. He whispered something.

Eddie leaned closer, desperate. 'Mac, I can't hear you. Stay with me, stay with me!'

With a last agonising effort, Mac turned his head further so he could look up at his friend with both eyes. He spoke again, forcing out the words. 'Fight to the end . . . Eddie.'

Then nothing. The sagging of his body was so slight that it was barely noticeable, but it was all Eddie needed to know without a doubt that he was dead.

'Mac,' he said anyway, pleading for him to return. 'Mac, come on. Mac!'

Tears beading in her eyes, Nina crossed to him. 'Eddie, I . . .' she began, before stopping, unsure what to say. 'I'm sorry,' she eventually whispered, touching his shoulder.

He didn't look up at her, instead staring silently at the man who had shaped so much of his life, the man he had respected and admired above all others. He reluctantly let go of Mac's hand, then reached over and gently closed his eyes. 'Fight to the end,' he echoed, voice hoarse.

Running footsteps. Nina looked back in alarm, but it was only Macy and Osterhagen hurrying up the steps. 'I heard shots . . .' said Osterhagen, before tailing off at the sight of the tableau.

Macy raised her hands to her mouth, horrified. 'Oh no. Oh, God. Is – is he okay? Is he . . .'

Eddie abruptly stood and turned. Nina almost flinched at a frighteningly unrecognisable new aspect to his familiar features. His eyes were wide, clear, intensely focused – but his face was utterly, chillingly blank, devoid of expression. Stone cold. 'He's dead,' he said flatly, pushing past Nina to go to Kit. He picked up the gun from the floor beside him and ejected the magazine. Nine rounds left, plus one in the chamber. He snapped the mag back into place and headed for the stairs, almost barging Macy and Osterhagen aside.

'Eddie, wait!' Nina shouted. 'There are too many of them, they'll kill you!'

But he was gone. 'Shit!' she cried, rushing down the steps after him. 'Leonard, Macy, stay with Kit!'

'I'm coming with you,' Macy insisted, following. Osterhagen went to the wounded Indian to examine his injury.

Eddie ran through the abandoned city, eyes sweeping like radars, hunting for threats. For targets. Nobody there; they had all evacuated the cavern. He reached the reservoir, skirting the top of the entrance shaft to the great gap where the defences had collapsed. He pressed himself against the edge and checked outside.

The jungle's colours were muted, clouds having descended. A great pile of broken rubble was strewn across the pool. On the far bank, about fifty yards away, were two of Pachac's men. Both held AK-47s.

The knowledge that he was outgunned didn't cause even a fraction of a second's hesitation. Eddie whipped round the wall, locking the Steyr on to the centre of mass of the man on the left with mechanical precision. He squeezed the trigger three times. The first shot narrowly missed, kicking up a clod of earth from the ground, but he had already compensated. The second and third bullets hit the rebel in the arm and stomach. He dropped.

The other man raised his AK. Too late. This time, all three rounds hit their target. The revolutionary fell, blood spurting from his chest.

Eddie ran down the pile of stones and splashed through the pool to the bank. The first man was still alive, writhing in agony. Without the slightest emotion, Eddie shot him in the head, then shoved the Steyr into his jacket and scooped up an

AK-47 before continuing into the jungle.

Nina reached the ruined wall just in time to see him disappear into the trees. She called his name, but knew she wouldn't get a response. 'What's he doing?' Macy asked as she caught up.

'He's going to kill Pachac,' Nina answered grimly as she began to pick her way down the unstable slope. 'And everyone with him.'

Pachac, in the Hummer's passenger seat, looked back sharply at the distant echo of gunfire. The shots weren't the distinctive thump of an AK-47 – and the lack of returning Kalashnikov fire suggested that the two men he had left to guard the cave were dead.

He tried his phone. No signal. Even though they had reached the road, there was still no reception; the nearest cell mast was several kilometres away in the village down the winding mountain valley. That meant the survivors of the archaeological team couldn't call for help, but he couldn't summon support for his much-diminished force either.

'Stop the car!' he ordered the driver. The H3 came to a halt. Pachac got out as the other two 4×4s pulled up behind him. 'Somebody's coming after us,' he shouted to his men. 'Make sure they don't catch up.'

They got the message, readying their guns. Pachac climbed back into the Hummer and the convoy set off again.

Eddie reached the spot where the expedition had parked. Their three off-roaders were still there – as were the corpses of the two soldiers who had been left to guard them. A rumble of engines from the direction of the road told him that the revolutionaries had left – probably going to get backup to raid the incredible wealth of El Dorado before the Peruvian authorities could secure it.

But their purpose didn't interest him. All he cared about was catching them.

He ran to the military Jeep, the lightest and fastest of the 4×4s. No key. Who had been driving? One of the privates, he remembered; he quickly searched their bodies and found it. He jumped in and started the engine, reversing into a slithering half-turn on the muddy ground. Flattened bushes to one side marked where Pachac's men had left their own vehicles. Three of them, the tyre tracks told him.

Eddie powered down the slope. The Jeep bounced over rocks and roots, the suspension crashing to its limits. He ignored the rough ride – and the jolts of pain it sent through his body. All that mattered was his new mission: catch the rebel convoy.

Pachac would almost certainly be in the lead vehicle. Eddie would have to fight past the other two to get to him.

No problem. He had enough bullets for everyone.

37

Nina and Macy reached the vehicles. 'Oh, Jesus,' said Macy at the sight of the dead men. 'Why are we going after these guys? We should be trying to get a long, long way *away* from them!'

Nina ignored her, running to the Nissan Patrol. Eddie had left the key in the ignition. 'If you don't want to come with me, then wait here.'

'No, no, I'm coming,' said Macy, the presence of the corpses making her decision easier. She got in beside Nina. The redhead turned the key, then guided the big off-roader down the hill.

Pachac looked at his phone again. Still no signal. Once he got into range of the cell tower, though, he would be able to call in more men within hours. The True Red Way had an active membership of close to a hundred, and several times as many sympathisers. It would be tough to remove the Punchaco before government forces reacted, but the longer he could prevent word of El Dorado's existence from getting out the better . . .

The road narrowed at a bend beneath an overhang of rock ahead – with a truck coming the other way.

'Mother of God!' the driver blurted as he braked hard. Maoism and religion may not have been complementary, but some things were too deeply ingrained to remove. Both vehicles stopped. He leaned out of the window. 'Hey! Back up!'

The sweating, overweight truck driver scowled at him. Under the unwritten rules of the mountain road, the bigger vehicle always had right of way. 'You back up!'

'We don't have time for this shit,' Pachac growled, drawing a gun and firing it out of his window. The truck's windscreen shattered. 'Get out of my way or I'll kill you!'

The terrified driver decided that unwritten rules were made to be broken and put his truck into reverse, backing up as quickly as he dared. 'Move,' Pachac told his own driver. The H3 set off again, almost nose to nose with the lumbering transport. The road widened round the bend, and the driver moved to let the convoy pass.

Even as far over as the truck could possibly go, the gap was actually a few centimetres narrower than the Hummer, nothing but air beneath the rims of its left-side tyres. Pachac's driver cringed as he edged past the truck, looking down at the near-vertical drop into the clouds below. The H3's chromed wing mirror scraped against the other vehicle's cab, and broke off. The driver gave his leader an apologetic look. 'Maybe we should have stolen something smaller?'

'Just get going,' Pachac snapped once they were clear.

Eddie saw a bright yellow Hummer disappear round the overhang about a quarter of a mile ahead, another two vehicles trundling in a line behind it: an old Land Cruiser and a big American pickup truck. Pachac and his men.

He put his foot down, the Jeep jolting over the rutted road. He would soon catch up.

The Land Cruiser slowly followed the Hummer. Even though it was several inches narrower than the American behemoth, its two occupants still tensed as they crawled along less than a hand's-width from the precipice's ragged edge. Next, the pickup truck squeezed through, the rebel in the cargo bed leaning out and shouting instructions to the two men in the cab.

The F-150 disappeared from Eddie's view behind the over-hanging cliff. The time the larger vehicles had taken to squeeze past the obstruction meant that he was now almost upon them.

He slowed to pass the stationary truck, then readied the Kalashnikov.

'There he is!' Macy cried, pointing ahead.

Nina saw the Jeep go out of sight around a narrow bend. 'I just hope we can reach him before he gets himself killed,' she said, guiding the Patrol in pursuit.

The man in the F-150's pickup bed looked back along the road – and saw a military Jeep coming after them. Fast. He banged on the cab's rear window. 'Hey! He's catching up – tell Inkarrí!'

He drew his gun, an old Colt .38 revolver, as the passenger used a walkie-talkie to relay the message to the Hummer.

Pachac listened to the urgent radio report, twisting in his seat. The Land Cruiser filled most of the view behind, but the road's curves gave him a glimpse of what was happening beyond.

He didn't like what he saw. 'What are you waiting for?' he shouted into his radio. 'Kill him!'

Eddie saw the Ford pickup slowing, its occupants getting ready to attack. One man in the back, holding on to the F-150's rollbar, and from the silhouettes it looked like two in the cab.

No rifles; they must have lost them in the flood. The guy in the rear bed was instead taking aim with a pistol—

The Englishman had something bigger. He fired the AK-47 through the broken windscreen.

The rebel got off three shots, but firing single-handed from a jolting vehicle didn't even hit the speeding Jeep, never mind its driver. Eddie's shooting was just as wild – but with far more bullets. One clanged off the pickup's tailgate, another cracking the rear window – and a third tore into the gunman's chest in a gout of blood. The man fell backwards, his clothing catching on one of the rollbar's lamp brackets to leave him hanging against the cab, the revolver clattering to the metal floor.

But the passenger in the front was bringing up an automatic. Eddie fired again—

Two shots – and the Kalashnikov's bolt stopped with a dry *clack*. Out of ammo.

He dropped the AK and ducked as the rebel fired. More bullets struck the Jeep, shattering a headlight, ripping another hole through the already damaged radiator with a shrill of escaping steam.

And hitting a wheel.

The tyre didn't blow out, the thick, heavily treaded rubber only holed, but the effect on the Jeep was immediate. The steering wheel jerked in Eddie's hands as the vehicle pulled to the left, towards the cliff. He dragged it back into line. But the vibration grew worse as the tyre deflated, the 4×4 harder to control with every second.

The shooting stopped. Eddie raised his head. The gunman was fumbling for a replacement magazine.

The Jeep swerved back towards the precipice. He forced the steering wheel hard over to the right, but the tyre was almost flat, weaving on the wheel rim. A few more seconds and it would collapse . . .

He snatched up the empty AK-47 and jammed its stock down on the accelerator. The Jeep surged forward, engine screaming. He wedged the rifle's barrel against the front seat and jumped up, gripping the steering wheel in one hand as he clambered over the broken windscreen on to the bonnet.

The man in the cab had slapped in a new magazine. He turned to fire—

Eddie lined up the Jeep with the pickup, and let go of the wheel as his vehicle rammed the Ford from behind.

He was flung over the tailgate into the cargo bed – and slammed against the corpse hanging from the rollbar. The breath was knocked from him, but the body cushioned his landing, the damaged rear windscreen behind it shattering and spraying the gunman in the cab with glittering fragments.

Eddie dropped heavily into the pickup bed, the angular body of the Steyr inside his jacket digging painfully into his ribs. The revolutionary shook off broken glass and turned again to find his target—

Eddie grabbed the fallen revolver and fired three shots at the cab's back wall.

Bullets ripped through the rebel's seat into his body. He fell against the passenger-side door, which burst open. He rolled out of the cab with a shriek of terror that was cut short as he was crushed under the wheels of the still speeding Jeep.

The 4×4 swerved sharply as it bounded over the human speed bump, veering at the cliff—

'*No!*' Nina screamed as she watched the Jeep sail off the road and arc down into the valley. 'Eddie, oh my God!'

'He's okay, he's okay!' Macy desperately reassured her. 'He jumped into the truck!'

'He what? Oh, Jesus Christ . . .' Nina gasped for breath, the horror of what she thought she had just witnessed still clutching at her heart.

Eddie pulled himself up and pointed the revolver into the cab. 'Stop the truck!' he yelled at the driver.

The rebel instead clawed inside his wet, grubby jacket. Eddie pulled the trigger—

Click. The hammer fell, but the gun didn't go off. All the bullets in the cylinder had been fired.

The driver drew his own gun, twisted—

Eddie dropped and rolled as the rebel opened fire. Unable to turn any further without risking losing control of the truck, the driver unleashed a couple more shots blindly over his shoulder. One hit the floor as Eddie jerked out of the way, the other blasting messily through the dangling corpse's stomach.

Eddie flipped the useless revolver over in his hand. He scrambled forward and lunged through the broken rear window, brutally cracking the empty gun against the driver's head like a knuckleduster.

The man reeled, the pickup swerving to the right. Before he could recover, Eddie grabbed his gun hand and slammed it against the window frame, rasping his wrist against the broken glass. The driver yelled in pain and fired again, forcing Eddie to duck – but not before he pushed the weapon's magazine release button. The automatic's slide locked back as the mag clattered into the cargo bed.

The driver pulled the trigger twice more, getting nothing but metallic clicks in response. By the time he realised his gun was empty Eddie had shoved the corpse over the truck's side and reached into the cab to hook an arm round his neck. Choking, the driver struggled to break free – then saw that the truck was heading for the side of the little wooden bridge. He yanked at the steering wheel—

The F-150 lurched, tilting on its suspension and throwing Eddie sideways. He lost his hold on the driver and reeled across the cargo bed, almost falling out before grabbing the rollbar.

The passenger door swung open and hit the bridge's fence with a huge bang. It was ripped away, spinning backwards. The mangled metal scythed past Eddie, slashing the back of his jacket.

The driver regained control, straightening out. Eddie was about to attack again when he saw something ahead – something that hadn't been there when the expedition drove up the road. A waterfall spewed down the hillside from high above, pounding the road in a swirling cloud of spray.

He gripped the rollbar tightly as the truck drove through the torrent, crashing across the newly created dip where the muddy track had been washed over the cliff. The driver fought with the wheel as the pickup skidded.

Eddie saw his chance. If he got into the cab through the missing door, he could use the Steyr to kill the driver and immediately take the wheel before the F-150 went out of control.

He drew the gun from his jacket and climbed over the pickup's side.

The Nissan rounded a bend. 'Where the hell did that come from?' Macy gasped, seeing the new waterfall.

Nina looked up for its source. There was only one possible explanation: when the river feeding the falls concealing El Dorado had been blocked, the water rose behind the dam . . .

and was now finding other ways downhill. 'Oh God,' she said in alarm. 'This whole valley might flood!'

Eddie swung into the cab, aiming the Steyr at the driver—

The Peruvian hurled his empty gun.

Eddie jerked his head sideways, but the automatic struck his cheek hard enough to draw blood and knocked him backwards. The Steyr dropped into the footwell as he grabbed at the dashboard, missed, toppled through the gaping doorway . . .

His hand clamped round the seatbelt.

It didn't stop him. The reel unwound, pitching him out of the truck—

Thunk!

The seatbelt's inertial lock mechanism activated, yanking him to a stop. One hand clutching the belt, Eddie dangled out of the open door, his back almost parallel to the ground.

Grinning sadistically, the driver turned the wheel to smear him against the rock wall.

Eddie grabbed with his free hand for the seatbelt, the door frame, anything – but there was nothing within reach. The cliff face rushed past, getting closer . . .

Something sticking out of the ground, right ahead—

He snatched up the wooden cross and hurled it into the cab.

The driver had turned to watch Eddie's head hit the wall – but instead took the pointed stake in his left eye. He screamed, reflexively bringing up both hands to pull out the cross. The F-150 swerved away from the wall – and towards the precipice.

The change of direction swung Eddie into reach of the doorframe. He hauled himself inside. The rebel was still screaming, one hand pressed to his face as blood gushed from his eye socket. The truck jolted over the road's crumbling edge—

Eddie grabbed the wheel. The Ford lurched back across the track, throwing the driver against his door. Flailing for balance, he looked across the cab with his remaining eye – to see Eddie twist in the passenger seat and slam both feet against his chest.

The battered vehicle's door flew open, the rebel shooting out of it like a cannonball. With an echoing wail, he vanished into the abyss.

Eddie pulled himself across and took the controls, rounding the next bend to see the Land Cruiser and the Hummer ahead. He shut the door, groped for the Steyr, then accelerated after them.

A radio crackled on the parcel shelf, a voice speaking in Spanish. Pachac.

Pachac looked back at the F-150. Only one figure was visible inside it. 'Mateo, did you get him? Mateo!'

The reply was in English, almost calm despite the struggle that had just taken place. 'No. He didn't. He's dead. And Pachac?'

The terrorist leader exchanged a worried look with his driver before answering. 'What?'

'You're next.'

Pachac stared at the walkie-talkie, then yelled orders to his men in the Land Cruiser. This time, there was no anger in his voice, only fear. 'Stop him! Kill him! *Kill him!*'

Eddie dropped the radio, eyes fixed on the two 4×4s ahead. The Land Cruiser was falling back from the H3. He could see two men inside it, the passenger climbing over the seats into the cargo space.

He also glimpsed the unmistakable silhouette of an AK-47 in the rebel's hands.

The Steyr was wedged under his thigh. He pulled it out and switched it to his left hand. The Toyota was still slowing. The tailgate hatch swung up, the man inside aiming his AK out of it—

Eddie fired his remaining bullets from the side window as he accelerated. The revolutionary ducked for cover behind the lower half of the tailgate. By the time he realised the shooting had stopped and looked up again, the F-150 had caught up—

The Ford slammed into the back of the Land Cruiser. The driver's head whiplashed backwards as he let go of the controls – and the 4×4 swerved towards the rockface. The man in the back was thrown against the side wall.

Eddie saw an opening and swung to pass the Toyota on the outside. The pickup drew alongside the off-roader. The Ford's left wheels were less than a foot from the cliff-edge.

The Land Cruiser's driver shook off his pain and grabbed the wheel, turning hard to sidewipe the F-150—

Eddie did the same thing, trying to ram the Toyota into the hillside. The vehicles clashed together with a crunch of crumpling metal. Eddie's truck was more powerful, but the Japanese 4×4 was heavier. He turned the wheel harder, but the rebels were bullying him inch by inch towards the precipice.

And the man in the back was raising his rifle again.

Death by fall, or by firepower—

Eddie braked hard – then swerved at full throttle to smash into the Toyota's back quarter as it pulled ahead. The 4×4 slewed around, almost side-on to the pickup's blunt nose, before its right rear corner struck the hillside and it abruptly swung back, hitting the rock wall side-on like a door being slammed. The F-150 shot past, ripping off the Land Cruiser's front bumper.

A glance in the mirror told Eddie that it wasn't out of the hunt, though. It bounced back across the road, right side caved in, then the driver caught the skid and turned back into pursuit.

The Hummer was not far ahead, its driver being cautious on the dangerous road. Eddie switched his attention back and forth between Pachac's vehicle and the one in the mirror. Even though he was gaining on the H3, he wouldn't reach it before the Land Cruiser caught up with him.

An AK poked out of one of the Toyota's left-side windows. Eddie moved as far over to the right as he could to deny the rebel a clear shot. But the road's curves meant it would only be a matter of time before he was exposed.

Still closing on the Hummer. Beyond it, he recognised the scenery: they were coming up to where the landslide had deposited tons of mud and stones on the road, the waterfall gushing on to the rubble. The H3 would have to slow to negotiate it – but so would he.

The waterfall—

It had grown enormously since the morning. The stream was now much wider, more powerful.

Realisation of the new threat struck him like the force of the water itself. The flood, caused by the blocking of the river, was building up above, and could overflow at any moment . . .

The Hummer reached the landslide and lurched over the rubble. Eddie speeded up. The Land Cruiser followed suit, still gaining.

Gunfire—

Eddie ducked as bullets clanged off the bodywork behind him. He was almost at the landslip. More shots. The H3 entered the waterfall, spray kicking up from its flat roof. He lined up the F-150 with the ruts carved by other vehicles and pushed the accelerator to the floor. He needed all the momentum he could get—

All four of the Ford's wheels left the ground as it hit the blockage, then crashed back down with a squeal of poorly maintained suspension. It veered towards the drop, Eddie struggling to bring it back into the ruts. Rocks pounded at the tyres, throwing him about in his seat. Despite his best efforts, he was losing speed. The Land Cruiser grew in the mirror, the gunman firing again.

He had almost reached the waterfall—

No. The waterfall had almost reached him.

It grew wider even as he watched, its edge sweeping along the defoliated swathe of the cliff above. Stones tumbled down the mountainside.

The river was about to burst its banks—

The F-150 plunged into the waterfall. The torrent exploded into the cab through the missing door, the force of the water throwing the truck sideways. Eddie frantically spun the steering wheel, trying to turn back towards the cliff-face. He couldn't see anything, froth obliterating all vision. All he had left was his sense of balance, which told him the truck was tipping over as it slid closer to the edge of the road . . .

The sickening feeling of being about to fall suddenly faded. He had somehow found traction in the mud. He didn't know why, but took advantage of his apparent luck, applying more power. The truck levelled out.

The deluge eased, giving him a rippling, distorted view through the windscreen. The Hummer was a yellow shimmer ahead. He looked back – and saw where the extra grip had come from. The pickup bed was full of water, putting well over a ton of extra road-hugging weight on to the rear wheels.

Water sloshed around his feet. He opened the door to let it gush out. The truck was struggling, but continued its lumbering journey.

He emerged from the falls. The Hummer was still negotiating the remains of the landslide. A loud bang from behind, and the F-150 shook violently – he thought a tyre had exploded, until he saw that the tailgate had burst open, the trapped water sluicing out of the back.

A dark shape emerged from the downpour in the mirror. The Land Cruiser was right behind him. The gunman leaned from the window again, AK raised—

A new noise from above, a colossal ground-shaking boom as the weight of millions of gallons of trapped water finally overwhelmed the earth containing it.

The waterfall Eddie had just passed through was barely a trickle compared to the wave that surged over the hilltop. Thousands of tons of soil and boulders were swept down the cliff into the valley below.

Eddie floored the accelerator, aiming the Ford at the Hummer. Shadows swelled around him as the great mass of muddy water descended like a shroud.

It hit the road, blasting away the debris of the landslide as if jet-washing the mountain. A massive rock flattened the Land Cruiser and the two rebels inside it, what little was left of the vehicle whirling away into the maelstrom. More stones hit the pickup like meteorites. The windscreen shattered as the roof buckled under the impacts.

A swelling, churning wave snatched up the F-150. Fear froze Eddie's heart as he thought he was being flung to his death into the void – then he realised he was being carried *along* the road, not off it, the water finding a ready-made channel down which to run. But he was out of control, the truck tossed like a cork on the wavecrest . . .

A flash of yellow—

The pickup hit the Hummer. Both vehicles slewed round, wheels scraping sidelong over the road as the water swept them along. For an instant, Eddie found himself looking straight at Pachac, the Maoist leader staring back at him wide-eyed through the H3's window.

Then the Hummer slipped away – and went over the edge.

Eddie had no time to rejoice, or think about anything but his own survival. The steering wheel jerked in his hands as the pickup was carried down the track. If the tyres could find enough grip for him to steer, just for a second, he could try to wedge the F-150 against the hillside—

He didn't get the second he needed, or even close. The current whirled the truck round. The front wheels dropped sharply, the pickup hanging briefly on the brink . . . then the sodden soil collapsed beneath it and pitched it over the cliff.

38

Nina skidded the Patrol to a desperate emergency stop as the seething wave crashed down the hillside ahead. 'Holy *shit!*'

'Over there!' said Macy, pointing down the steep slope on the far side of the deluge. Nina saw the yellow Hummer skittering down the hill – and the pickup truck following it over the edge of the road.

The truck Eddie was driving.

She wanted to look away, but couldn't.

Pachac and his driver screamed as the H3 picked up speed down the steepening slope. The only thing between them and the clouds filling the valley below was a rocky outcrop, a gnarled tree jutting sidelong from it—

The Hummer hit the protruding rock nose-first. The airbags fired, but with neither man wearing a seatbelt they were still slammed brutally forward. Another impact followed as the H3 tipped back and hit the cliff, ending up wedged against the rockface.

Even through his pain and disorientation, Pachac knew he had to get clear as quickly as possible. He swatted away the airbag's flaccid remains and opened the door. The thin build-up of dirt in which the tree had taken root was already being washed away by the water flowing down the cliff – and with over two tons of automobile on top of it, the rock would probably soon go the same way.

He dragged himself out. 'Come on,' he rasped. 'We've got—'

Noise above. Not water, not rock. Metal. He looked up.

Something rushed down the hillside towards him—

Even as the F-150 went over the edge, Eddie was turning the wheel, trying to aim the truck at a tree he had glimpsed below. His chances of reaching it were almost zero, but a minuscule hope of survival was better than no hope at all. He leaned out of the open door as the abused vehicle rushed down the slope—

The Hummer was perched on the rock supporting the tree – off to the side.

He wasn't going to make it.

Not in the truck—

Eddie dived out, twisting in freefall to land on his back . . .

He hit the Hummer's roof with such force that all its windows exploded, the expanse of sheet metal crumpling beneath him as the F-150 shot past, missing the rock by inches. The pain was so intense it overwhelmed his senses.

Taste returned first, the metallic sting of blood in his mouth. Other pains reported in throughout his body as he tried to move. His spine was ablaze – broken? No, he realised as his limbs achingly responded, but it could hardly hurt much more.

He forced his eyes open. The tree was a wavering blur, the light from the sky beyond its branches almost painful. All his body wanted to do was lie still and fade away . . .

Pachac.

The thought of the Peruvian pulled him back. Where was

Pachac? He had been in the Hummer, and Eddie was now *on* the Hummer. He had a mission. Make him pay for what he had done to Mac. Catch him. Kill him.

The pain made the cold, ruthless detachment of his pursuit impossible to maintain, animal rage sawing at the clinical parts of his mind. He channelled it, controlled it, used it as fuel as he slowly rolled on his side.

Pachac lay on the rock below.

Their gazes locked on to each other. Disbelief filled the rebel's eyes, fury Eddie's. The pain vanished as the Englishman threw himself at the revolutionary leader—

The mangled Hummer tipped into the abyss behind him with a grind of metal and the driver's petrified scream, but Eddie didn't even notice, fixated on Pachac. The Peruvian managed to scramble aside as he landed, the desperation of self-preservation overcoming his own pain. He jumped up and backed towards the tree, fumbling in his wet clothing as Eddie advanced. 'The rock is going to fall!' Pachac cried as stones clattered down around him, dislodged from their homes by the muddy deluge. The waterfall's full force was already fading, the bulk of the flood released in a single great burst, but it would be some time before all the escaped water found its way down to the bottom of the valley. 'If we fight here, we both die!'

'So long as you go first,' Eddie growled.

Pachac flinched as he backed against the tree. His search became more panicked as Eddie drew closer – then he found what he wanted.

His knife.

The savage blade snapped out. Eddie stopped, eyes fixed on the weapon, waiting for Pachac to make his move.

The Peruvian misinterpreted his hesitation as fear, a sneering smile creeping on to his face. 'Yeah, you should be scared,' he hissed, stepping forward. 'You know how many I have gutted with this knife?' The smile widened into a twisted, demonic grin. 'I don't know myself. I stopped counting at twenty.' Another step, the knife sweeping from side to side like a cobra assessing its prey.

Eddie held his ground, still watching the weapon. The blade kept moving, left, to right, to left . . .

Forward—

The knife jerked at his stomach, but Eddie's hands were already in motion, grabbing Pachac's wrist and deflecting the attack. Even so, the Peruvian's brute strength almost caught him, the blade stabbing through the sodden lining of his jacket.

Still clutching the rebel's arm with his left hand, he lashed out with his right to chop at Pachac's throat. Pachac jerked back, but still took the edge of Eddie's palm to his larynx. He gasped, choking.

Eddie smashed Pachac's knife hand down against his knee, trying to force him to drop the blade. Another hit, but the Peruvian's fingers were still clenched tightly round the hilt. A third blow, and it slipped—

The knife clattered on to the rock just as Pachac recovered his breath and lashed out with his other arm, the muscular limb thudding against the base of Eddie's neck like a club. Eddie struck back, trying to crush Pachac's nose, but only hit his chin. Another blow dropped the Englishman to his knees. Pachac's own knee crashed against his head. Eddie fell on his back, struggling to get up—

Pachac's hands locked around Eddie's throat and squeezed.

The strength of the Peruvian's fingers was incredible. Eddie clawed at them, but they were as unyielding as steel. '*Capacocha*,' the revolutionary leader snarled. 'This is what happens to all enemies of the Inkarrí!'

Eddie tried to bend back and snap one of his little fingers, but even that was too strong for him to move. He shifted his hands to the rock, groping for a weapon – a fallen stone, a piece of wood . . .

But his fingers found nothing. He flailed, writhing along the outcrop in a last desperate attempt to break free. Pachac moved with him, mouth widening into a triumphant grin—

Eddie felt a spike of pain in his hand. Something very sharp.

He grabbed it, striking with the last of his strength—

The knife stabbed into Pachac's arm, tearing between the bones to burst out from the inside of his wrist in a spray of blood. He screamed, releasing his hold and stumbling away.

Still clutching the bloodied knife, Eddie sat up, straining to draw air through his bruised throat—

The rock jolted.

A split opened up where it jutted from the cliff, flowing water eagerly rushing into the new space and washing out the earth acting as natural mortar. The outcrop dropped a couple of inches, halting with a crunch. The rebel fell on his back.

Eddie jumped up and hurdled Pachac, making a flying leap at the tree—

The rock dropped away from under him, ripping out of the cliff like a tooth from a diseased gum. He hit the tree, grabbed it – and slipped.

Falling—

He caught a protruding root with one hand – and slammed the knife into the wood with the other, arresting his fall.

Then was almost torn loose.

Pachac's hand was locked round his ankle.

Some of the roots had wound their way into the cliff's cracks, holding the tree in place, but the men's combined weight was pulling them out. Eddie kicked at the Peruvian's fingers, hearing a cry from below, but before he could strike again Pachac managed to grab his boot with his other hand. Even with an injured wrist, his grip was still fiercely strong.

Another snap of roots. 'Pull us up!' Pachac cried. 'The tree is going to fall – pull us up!'

Eddie looked down at him . . . and the anger returned. Not taking his eyes off the revolutionary, he jerked his hand from side to side, working the knife out of the root.

Pachac saw the movement. 'What – what are you doing? No! You'll kill us both!'

Eddie said nothing, still tugging at the knife. The wood creaked, splintering – then the blade pulled free.

Both men swung away from the cliff, Eddie supporting them with only one hand. The tree swayed sharply. Pachac stifled a shriek, toes scrabbling at the rock. He knew that if he risked finding a handhold, his other hand would be kicked until his fingers broke.

Straining, Eddie reached down as far as he could, and slowly, painfully, pulled up his legs to bring Pachac into range of the knife. The Peruvian realised what he was about to do, and his face filled with helpless horror. 'No! Don't do it! Please!'

Jaw clenched, Eddie held the knife poised above the other man's hand. 'This is for what you did to Mac.'

Pachac tried again to find a foothold, failed. 'Who? Who is Mac?'

'My friend. You killed him.'

'The government man?'

Disgust rose inside Eddie. The bastard didn't even remember! He dug the knife's point into the back of Pachac's hand, making him gasp. 'Grey hair! Beard! Know who I mean now, you fucking piece of shit?'

'The old man?' There was genuine confusion behind the fear. 'But – I never touched him!'

'No. You shot him. In the back.' He slowly turned the knife. Blood ran from the wound, oozing down Pachac's arm. 'But I want to look you in the face . . . when I do *this*.'

He stabbed the knife through the Peruvian's hand and twisted it, hard. There was a sharp crack of bone. Pachac screamed in agony and terror as he lost his grip. He hung for a moment on his injured arm – then Eddie smashed his heel down and snapped two of his fingers. Pachac dropped away, Eddie watching coldly as he vanished into the clouds below. The scream continued after he disappeared, fading to nothing.

The tree shook violently with the release of weight. Eddie stabbed the knife back into the root, pulling himself up. Dirt and grit showered over him. At any moment, it would rip away from the cliff—

He lunged for a solid nub of rock to one side, clawing at the stone as the tree plunged into the valley. Branches slashed at him as the tree fell, trying to drag him down with it. He yelled, battling to keep his grip – then it was gone, tumbling down the cliff to be swallowed by the blankness beneath.

Eddie dangled, recovering his breath. His anger receded as the reality of his situation sank in. The road was sixty or seventy feet above. How the hell was he going to get up there? He scraped his boots against the rock, but only found enough purchase to support the tip of one foot. Bracing himself, he experimentally reached higher for a handhold. All his fingertips found was slick, treacherous wet mud caking every surface. Unclimbable.

'Well,' he muttered, 'buggeration and f—'

Clank!

A noise above. Metal on stone. He looked up – and saw a

hook scraping down the cliff towards him.

Nina! It had to be. He waited until the hook, at the end of a steel winch cable, was within reach, then grabbed it with one hand and tugged repeatedly to signal that he had a firm hold. It stopped. He locked his other hand over the first, then pushed himself out from the rockface with his feet.

The cable retracted. He rose with it, boots rasping over the rock. Before long he saw the expedition's Nissan Patrol at the edge of the road – and a familiar face gazing anxiously down at him.

'Eddie!' Nina shouted. 'Oh, thank God, thank God!'

'Are you okay?' he called.

Macy was at the 4×4's winch, relief plain on her face. 'Are *we* okay?' she said in disbelief. 'You just went over a cliff, and you're worried about us? We didn't even know if you were still down there!'

'Then why'd you throw down the cable?'

'Because I was sure that you were,' said Nina, pulling the line to help him up the last few feet. He scrambled on to the muddy road, looked into her eyes . . . then, wordlessly, they embraced.

Macy eventually broke the silence. 'What happened to Pachac?'

Eddie's voice was flat. 'He's dead.'

Nina eased her hold and leaned back. 'What about you? How . . . how are you feeling?'

It took a few seconds for him to provide an answer. 'I'm okay.' In truth, he didn't know what he was feeling – or even if he felt anything at all. He had expected some sort of catharsis at Pachac's death, a release of anger or satisfaction or a sense that justice had been done . . . but there was nothing, just an empty numbness.

'You sure?' There was concern in her voice.

'Yeah.' He looked away, at the Patrol. 'Get the satphone. We need to call this in.'

The chatter of rotor blades echoed off the cliffs around the entrance to El Dorado. This time, though, the helicopters were not gunships but transport aircraft, both civil and military. Nina's call to the Peruvian government, telling them what had happened – and what she had found – brought a rapid response, the first soldiers arriving to secure the area within an hour.

More troops soon followed, accompanied by civilian officials. Taking charge of the operation was Felipe Alvarado, Zender's superior and head of the Ministry of Culture. In his late fifties, he had a weary, cynical face that suggested he'd seen it all – but his astounded expression when he emerged from the cave proved that that was not the case. 'Dr Wilde!' he cried. 'This is amazing, incredible! El Dorado, real – and in my country!'

Nina was too exhausted to respond with similar enthusiasm. 'Yeah. It's a hell of a thing.'

'The lost city of gold – it is almost too much to believe. I admit, when the IHA first asked permission to search for it, I did *not* believe it.'

'Is that why you sent Zender instead of coming yourself?'

Alvarado's gaze moved to the edge of the drained pool, where several forms lay beneath sheets: some of those killed inside the cave, recovered by the soldiers. 'Oh, Diego,' he said with a tinge of sadness. 'He wanted to be in the news, for everyone to know his name. But not like this.'

'Nobody wants to be remembered like this,' Nina said.

'No.' He gazed at the bodies for a moment, then looked back at the cavern. Several soldiers were making their way down the collapsed wall, bearing more corpses on stretchers. The first was dressed in dirty and mismatched camouflage gear; one of the revolutionaries. 'But something good has come from this,' Alvarado continued. 'Pachac and his butchers are dead. You have done my country a great favour by killing them.'

'I'm sure my husband'll be thrilled to hear that,' said Nina bitterly, eyes fixed on another of the bodies being brought out.

Mac.

'He should be,' said Alvarado. 'But I am sorry for the loss of your friends.'

'Thank you.'

He was about to add something when an official called out to him. 'Excuse me,' he said, moving away to speak to his subordinate. On the way he passed Eddie, returning from having his injuries treated by a Peruvian army medic. The Englishman stopped when he saw Mac, watching as he was placed alongside the other corpses. A soldier prepared to pull a sheet over the unmoving figure.

'No!' Eddie snapped, hurrying over. 'I'll do it.' He crouched and took hold of the sheet . . . but didn't pull it up. Instead, he stared down at his friend's still, pale face.

Nina joined him. Seconds passed, Eddie still holding the sheet in silence. Finally, she spoke. 'Eddie?'

He twitched, as if surprised to hear her voice, then abruptly pulled the sheet over Mac's head and stood. 'What?'

'I'm so sorry. Are . . . are you okay?' She gently touched his arm.

He pulled away – only slightly, but enough to give her a shock of dismay, rejection. 'No. I'm not.'

'What can I do? Do you want anything?'

'I just need to think.' Face set and unreadable, he turned away and limped towards the nearby trees.

'Eddie . . .' Nina said quietly, her voice tailing off with the hopeless feeling that nothing she could say would help.

'Nina?' Macy, approaching with Kit and Osterhagen. 'Is everything okay?'

'Not really,' Nina replied, still watching Eddie's retreat.

Macy's lips quivered as she realised who was under the sheet. 'Oh, that's . . . Mr McCrimmon. Oh . . .' Tears welled in her eyes.

Kit, looking equally stricken, put a hand on her shoulder. His sleeve had been cut away, the bullet wound to his arm bandaged. 'It shouldn't have happened,' he said quietly, as much to himself as to her.

Osterhagen was also solemn as he regarded the bodies. 'None of this should. So many deaths. All because of gold, the greed for gold.'

'Five centuries, and nothing's changed,' Nina said sadly.

'Maybe some day it will,' said Kit.

'I wish it could. But I doubt it. People never change.' She looked back at her husband, seeing him standing at the edge of the clearing, head bowed. 'I need to be with Eddie,' she said, starting after him. But she had no idea what she could possibly say to comfort him.

A Peruvian official bustled past her, holding a satellite phone. 'Mr Jindal! A call for you. From Interpol.'

Kit took the phone. 'Yes, this is Jindal.'

'This is Alexander Stikes,' said the crisp English voice from the other end of the line. Kit froze. 'I'd like to offer you a deal . . .'

39

The panoramic windows of the villa in which the Peruvian government had housed the surviving explorers looked out across Lima from the city's southeastern hills, but even though he was facing the view Eddie's eyes weren't taking in the spectacular burning sky of a Pacific sunset beyond the darkening capital. His focus was directed inwards.

Kit hesitated at the door before steeling himself and entering. He stood beside Eddie's chair, gazing in silence at the vista outside for a long moment, then finally summoned the courage to speak. 'Eddie?'

Eddie didn't seem to have registered his presence, until a fractional tilt of his head brought the Indian into his eyeline. 'Eddie,' Kit repeated, 'I just wanted to say that . . . I'm sorry. I'm sorry about Mac. It shouldn't have happened.'

'No. It shouldn't.' There was an odd, almost mechanical feel to Eddie's eventual response, rusty gears slowly grinding to life.

'If he hadn't decided to destroy the helicopter, if he hadn't been in that place at that time . . . it wouldn't have. He'd still be alive. If he hadn't gone after Stikes . . .'

'Stikes.' The word was a growl. 'You shouldn't talk to me about Stikes.'

A cold fear swept through Kit's body. Eddie couldn't possibly know about the phone call – could he? 'Why not?'

'Because you're a cop. And I'm going to murder that fucker.'

He tried to conceal his relief. 'I think this is one occasion where I would be willing to look the other way.'

Eddie nodded, then sank back into silence. Kit felt compelled to keep speaking. 'He was a good man. Brave and honourable.' He looked down at the floor, shaking his head.

Someone tentatively cleared their throat. Kit turned to see one of the villa's staff, a pretty young maid, standing in the doorway holding a cordless telephone. 'Excuse, please, Mr Jindal?' she said. 'Telephone for you.'

Kit glanced at Eddie, then went to her and took the phone. 'Hello?'

'Jindal.' It was Stikes. 'Have you discussed my proposal with your superiors?'

He took a breath before answering. 'Yes.'

'And?'

Another look at Eddie, this time surreptitious, to make sure he wasn't listening. But he appeared completely detached from the rest of the world. 'Yes, they agree.'

'Good. And did you tell them I want to meet one of their representatives in person? Not an errand boy like you.'

'I did,' Kit said through his teeth. 'Someone is on the way.'

'Excellent. In that case, there's a town called San Bartolo, twenty miles south of Lima on the Panamerica Highway. About two miles past it is a pumping station for the gas pipeline, number fourteen. Meet me there in one hour.'

'San Bartolo, station fourteen,' Kit echoed. 'All right, I'll be there.' He returned the handset to the maid. 'Eddie, I have to meet some people from Interpol. I think we might have a lead on the statues. Will you be all right?'

The Englishman remained still, not even moving his eyes to look at him. 'I'll be fine.'

'Okay. I'll see you later.' He turned to leave, then paused at the doorway. 'Again, I'm so sorry about Mac. I'm sorry.'

Eddie didn't reply.

Freshly showered and in clean clothes, Nina left her room and went downstairs to look for Eddie. Instead, she found Kit in the villa's hall, donning a jacket. 'Are you leaving?' she asked.

'I have to meet someone.'

'Interpol?'

A conflicted look crossed his face. 'Not exactly,' he replied after a moment. 'Look, don't say anything to Eddie, but . . . it's about Stikes. He's offered to hand over the statues.'

'What? You're kidding!'

'No, I think he really means it. He wants to make a deal – in exchange for immunity.'

Nina frowned. 'I don't think the Venezuelans will be thrilled about that.'

'I'm not happy about it either. But nothing has been finalised. I'm on my way to meet . . . his representative, to see what his terms are. If Interpol accepts them, he'll give us the statues.'

Nina was torn by the prospect. 'As much as I want them back, I don't like the idea of that son of a bitch getting an amnesty. But . . .'

'If there is a chance we can recover the statues, I think we should take it. At least that way, the people who died trying to find them won't have given their lives for nothing.'

'People like Mac,' she said unhappily. 'Is that why you don't want to mention this to Eddie?'

'Yes. I was talking to him a few minutes ago, and he got angry just at the mention of Stikes's name. If he found out we were negotiating with him, I think his reaction would be a lot stronger.'

'I don't doubt it.' She looked down the hall. 'Is he in the lounge?' Kit nodded. 'Let me know what happens. And good luck.'

'Thank you.' Kit departed, and Nina headed for the lounge.

She found Eddie still in the same chair where she had left him, contemplating the sunset. 'Hey,' she said, perching on the chair's arm and gently resting her hand on his chest. 'You okay?'

This time, at least he didn't pull away from her touch, but neither did he respond to it. 'I know what you're feeling right now,' she continued. 'I've been there; I've lost people who were close to me. I just want you to know that I'm here for you, and I always will be. Whatever you need, just ask me.'

He stirred, jaw muscles tightening. 'I didn't lose Mac,' he said in a low voice. 'He was taken.'

'I know. And I know what that's like too. It happened to Rowan, remember?'

'It's not the same. It's—' He stumbled, struggling to put his thoughts into words. 'Mac was different. You don't know what it was like, what he meant to me.'

'He was my friend too, Eddie. I'm going to miss him just as much.'

Now there was a distinct edge to his voice. 'No, you won't. Mac wasn't just a friend. I would've—' He choked off, taking a sharp breath. 'I would have died for him. That's what he meant to me. And he would've done the same for me. You wouldn't understand.'

Nina tried to suppress a flare of anger. 'I *do* understand. And I *do* know what it feels like. My parents were murdered, remember?' She experienced a sudden resurgence of loss, rising on the back of her current feelings. 'I *know*. Believe me, I know.'

They both fell silent. For a couple of minutes, the only sound was their breathing. Then: 'Excuse, please?'

Nina looked round to see the maid. 'Yes?'

'Telephone, from IHA.' Nina held out a hand, but the maid shook her head. 'For Mr Chase.'

Slightly surprised, Nina passed the phone to Eddie. 'Hello?' he said. 'Lola, hi. What is it?'

He listened to Lola. 'But it's the middle of the night over there,' he objected. Nina could faintly hear her assistant's voice as she replied; even at this level, she detected a worried urgency. 'Okay, thanks,' Eddie said, disconnecting, and punching in a new number.

'What's wrong?' Nina asked.

'Lizzie's been trying to get hold of me. Lola said it's urgent.'

'Nan?'

Eddie's look said as much as any words. He stood and put the phone to his ear, anxiously awaiting an answer. 'Lizzie, it's me,' he finally said. 'I just got your message. What is it?'

He paced back and forth before the windows as he listened to his sister. Nina watched with growing concern as his expression became increasingly stony, his interjections more terse – a sign that he was putting up his shields as a reaction to bad news. Finally he stopped, and with a simple 'Okay. Right,' ended the call.

Nina almost didn't want to ask the obvious question, because she was sure she already knew the answer. But she had to. 'What did Elizabeth say?'

'She said . . .' Eddie began, before his voice shrank to a dry croak. He swallowed, then spoke again. 'She said that Nan died today.'

Even though it was expected, the news was still a painful shock. 'Oh, God,' said Nina. 'Eddie, I'm sorry.'

'It wasn't her lungs,' he went on quietly. 'They thought she was responding well to the oxygen therapy. But apparently there's some side effect of emphysema, something about blood building up in the liver – I dunno, I didn't really understand it. But that suddenly got worse, so they took her to hospital, and that's . . . that's where . . .'

Abruptly, he hurled the telephone at the wall. It shattered. The maid shrieked in fright, then fled as Eddie grabbed the chair and flung it across the room. It hit a small table, wood flying as both pieces of furniture smashed. *'Fuck!'* he roared, running after the chair and stamping on its remains in a fury.

'Eddie, stop!' Nina cried, hurrying to him. 'Please, stop! Please!'

He dropped to his knees amongst the wreckage. 'Oh, *God!*' he gasped, voice trembling. Tears rolled down his cheeks.

Nina crouched, putting her arms round him. 'I'm here, I'm here. It's okay. Everything's going to be okay . . .'

'No it's not – it's *not* going to be fucking okay!' He pulled away from her and stood, kicking away debris. 'You know what one of the last things Nan said was? Just before she died? She asked where I was. She wanted to know why I wasn't there with the rest of her family. I should have been there – I *could* have been there if it hadn't been for your *fucking statues!*'

Nina recoiled, shocked, as his rage was turned on her – then stiffened as the injustice of the accusation stoked her own suppressed anger. 'That's not fair.'

'Isn't it? If you hadn't been looking for them, Mac wouldn't have come to South America, and I would have been able to stay in England with Nan.'

'We had to find them. That's part of the IHA's job – making

sure things like that don't fall into the wrong hands.'

'And Stikes is the *right* fucking hands?' he yelled. 'If we'd just left everything alone, things would have been fine! We had two of them, Callas didn't give a shit about the first piece, and nobody would ever have found the second one! What's all this got us, except for people killed?'

She struggled to keep her temper under control, knowing that he was under immense emotional pressure. 'We've been here before, Eddie. When Mitzi died, while we were looking for Excalibur. Remember?'

'Course I fucking remember. And you know who got me through it? *Mac!* Who's going to get me through this?'

'I will!'

'But it's your fucking fault!'

Nina felt as though she had been slapped. 'I can't believe you said that.'

It looked for a moment as if even he knew he had gone too far . . . but then his gaze snapped to something behind her. 'What?' he demanded.

Nina turned to see the maid waiting almost fearfully in the doorway, clutching a replacement telephone handset. 'I'm sorry, but . . . another telephone call. For Dr Wilde.'

'Tell 'em to fuck off,' Eddie snarled.

'No, but . . . it is the president of Peru!'

'And? Tell him to fuck off!'

The young woman seemed on the verge of tears. Nina shot Eddie a furious look, then went to her. 'I'll take it,' she said.

'Work always comes first with you, doesn't it?' Eddie said bitterly. Nina held in an angry reply as she took the phone.

The call was short, but straight to the point. 'I have to go,' she told Eddie with reluctance. 'The President wants to see me.'

'Now?'

'Yeah.'

'You should have said no.'

'I can't face having two arguments at once.' She returned the handset to the maid, who made as rapid an exit as etiquette would allow. 'They're sending a car. I'll be back as soon as I can. We can talk then. If you've calmed down.'

'Never been calmer,' rumbled Eddie, tapping a piece of the broken chair with his foot as she left.

The sky over Lima had darkened, the city coming alive with sparkling pinpoints. But Eddie now had his back to the view, sitting on a couch in the fading half-light. The smashed furniture was still strewn across the floor, the maid not having dared return to clean it up.

He heard footsteps and raised his eyes to see Macy at the doorway. 'Eddie? Why are you in the dark – jeez!' She saw the wreckage. 'What happened?'

'I had words with the chair,' Eddie said drily. He had managed to recover his composure since Nina's departure, but was still simmering inside, grief and anger and confusion all swirling in a toxic mix.

'Uh-huh . . .' Macy entered cautiously. 'Where's Nina?'

'Busy.' He said the word with a caustic sourness. 'She went to talk to the President.'

Her eyebrows shot up. 'Of America?'

'Of Peru.'

They fell again, considerably less impressed. 'Oh.' She went to the window, twitching fingers betraying her awkwardness before she finally spoke her mind. 'I, ah . . . heard you two arguing. While I was in the shower, so I guess it must have been a big one.'

'You could say that.'

'What was it about?'

Tact and subtlety had never been Macy's strong points, but Eddie managed to hold back a scathing reply; she was also genuinely concerned. 'Doesn't matter,' he said instead. 'All started because I got some bad news.'

'What?'

He took a deep breath. 'My nan died.'

'Your nan? Oh!' exclaimed Macy, as she realised she had met her. She hurried to the couch and sat beside him. 'Oh no, I'm sorry. That's terrible. She was so sweet!'

'Yeah, she was,' said Eddie.

'God, I'm really sorry. And right after Mac as well—' She clamped her mouth shut, appalled at her own insensitivity. 'Sorry,' she mumbled. 'I didn't mean . . .'

Eddie gave her a small, sad smile. 'Don't worry about it. This really has been a fucking shitty day all round. At least it can't get any worse.'

'I'm still sorry,' she said. 'Can I – is there anything you want?'

'My nan back. And Mac.'

Macy wasn't sure how to react to that, until Eddie eased her mind with another faint smile. 'Mr McCrimmon really meant a lot to you, didn't he?' she said. 'How long have you known him?'

'A long time. It was . . .' He worked it out. 'Christ, over sixteen years, when I first joined the SAS. God knows why, but he took me under his wing.'

'He must have seen something good in you,' Macy suggested.

'Again, God knows why. But yeah, he sorted me out. I was a bit of an arsehole when I was younger. Bad attitude, aggressive . . .'

She glanced at the demolished chair. 'You don't say.'

'Oi! You want me to have words with you too?' But it was said lightly, not with anger. 'He got me through a lot of stuff. I'd be dead ten times over if it hadn't been for him – not just when I was in the Regiment. He taught me pretty much everything I know. And I don't mean about being a soldier, I mean about . . . about being a good person. About doing the right thing.'

'I don't think that's something you can teach,' Macy said quietly. 'It's something that's there already.'

'But he brought it out, taught me to never give up. "Fight to the end", that was his motto. It—' He broke off, voice catching. 'It was the last thing he said before he died.' He lowered his head. 'Christ. I shouldn't have left him. I shouldn't have let him come at all, but . . .' He sat up, misery returning with self-recrimination. 'If I'd gone with Kit to find him instead of going after Stikes, he'd still be alive. I had an AK, I would have been able to take out Pachac, and Mac could have blown up the chopper before it took off. But I didn't, and Pachac shot him and Kit – so Stikes got away. It's all my fault.'

'It wasn't,' Macy insisted. 'You can't blame yourself. And it couldn't have . . .' She paused, frowning.

'What?'

'I'm not sure, but . . .' The frown deepened as she tried to remember the sequence of events in the lost city. 'Pachac couldn't have done what he did until *after* Stikes got away.'

'No, he must have done,' Eddie countered. 'Mac told me he was about to take out Stikes's chopper when he got shot. Kit said so as well – Pachac caught them by surprise.'

Macy shook her head. 'No, that's wrong. I met Kit just as the chopper was going out of the cave, and he hadn't been hurt yet.'

'You sure? Maybe you got things mixed up.'

'A helicopter taking off is kind of memorable,' she said testily. 'It was already in the air when I met Kit. And he definitely hadn't been shot. But he said—' Her confused look returned.

'What?'

'He said that Pachac and his men had just gone past – up to where we found him and Mr McCrimmon.'

'But Mac wasn't with him?'

'No. Actually, he said he hadn't seen him.'

'And this was after the gunship took off?'

'Yes, I'm sure of it.'

He leaned forward, thinking. If there was one person in the world he trusted to give a completely accurate account of events, even on the brink of death, it was his former commanding officer. Mac was right. Therefore Macy had to be wrong.

'That doesn't make any sense,' he said. He hadn't meant to say it angrily, but the image of Mac's bloodied, pain-twisted face as his life ebbed away put a harsh edge to his voice.

Macy pulled away. 'I'm not lying! I know what I saw.'

'Sorry. I didn't mean it to come out like that. I wasn't saying that you were lying . . .' He tailed off.

Mac. Kit. Macy. Three different accounts of the same events. But two of them contradicted each other. He had assumed that Macy's was the odd one out.

What if it wasn't?

To him, Mac's version was the inviolable truth. What about the others?

Macy first. She saw the helicopter take off and leave the cavern, then encountered Kit, who told her he was looking for Mac. The next time she saw him, he had been shot – and so had Mac.

Now Kit. He was with Mac when Pachac and his men

attacked, shooting the Indian in the arm – and the Scot in the back.

But Mac had been shot *before* the gunship took off.

The idea that someone might have lied about events simply hadn't occurred to him until Macy put it into his mind. Why *would* anyone lie? It made no sense.

But nor did the contradiction. And Pachac had denied killing Mac. He'd had every reason to, considering his situation at the time . . . but his confusion at the accusation had been genuine.

And the revolutionary leader and his men had already escaped the cave and reached their vehicles by the time Eddie started in pursuit – but the gap between his hearing the gunshots and finding Mac had been maybe thirty seconds. Even taking into account the time he spent with the Scot as he spoke his last words, Pachac couldn't have got so far ahead so quickly. Which meant he had to have left earlier.

Which meant he couldn't have killed Mac.

Eddie felt a cold tightness close around his chest. If Pachac hadn't killed Mac . . . that left only one other possibility.

Kit.

Mac had been shot in the back. And Kit had been behind him. Shot in the arm . . . the *left* arm. Kit was right-handed. And the injury was only a flesh wound, a single shot. Mac had taken two fatal bullets.

Ten bullets left in the Steyr he had taken from Kit, out of fifteen. Five used; one for the flesh wound, two fired off as decoys . . . and the first two, before Kit encountered Macy, used to kill Mac.

It couldn't be true, though. *Why?* What reason could he have?

His thoughts went wider . . . and came up with more questions. Kit had been pulled out of the group by Stikes, not once, but twice – with a very feeble excuse the second time. And Stikes himself had initially wondered why Kit was on the mission at all.

Why *was* the head of Interpol's Cultural Property Crime Unit personally accompanying an archaeological expedition? His interest had been . . .

The statues.

It was Kit who had suggested – no, *pushed* a link between Nina's discovery at Glastonbury and South America, responding immediately to the IHA's report. Kit who had proposed a joint Interpol/IHA mission. Kit who had been determined to accompany the explorers to El Dorado even though the smuggling case was closed. Kit whose first concern when an apparent earthquake shook the cave was the statues.

And Kit who had gone to follow a lead on the location of those same statues.

Which had been stolen by Alexander Stikes.

'The statues . . .' Eddie jerked upright as realisation struck him. 'The fucking statues!'

'What?' Macy asked, startled. 'What is it?'

He ignored her, the answer burning in his mind. It was the only possible explanation for what had happened at El Dorado.

Kit and Stikes were working together.

Stikes had already announced that he was going to take the Interpol agent with him, giving weak reasons that not even Pachac believed, when Nina flooded the cave. Then, as Stikes tried to escape in the Hind, Mac had been about to destroy the gunship – until Kit shot him in the back. To save Stikes and the statues.

And now . . . they were about to meet again.

Eddie stood and ran from the room, the bewildered Macy

following him. 'Hello?' he called. 'Hey, housekeeping! Miss Maid, are you there?'

The maid nervously emerged from a side room. 'Yes?'

'Look, I'm sorry I shouted at you. And don't worry about the chair, I'll clean it up later. I just need to ask you something. Do you know where . . .' He struggled to recall Kit's half-heard telephone conversation. 'San Barn, Bart . . . San Bartolo. Do you know where San Bartolo is?'

She nodded, still timorous. 'It is a town on the sea. About thirty, thirty-five kilometres south of the city.'

'Does it have a railway station?'

'No.'

'Okay, so do you know what station fourteen is? What kind of station is it?'

'Station? I don't know, it . . .' She thought, then her face lit up. 'No, I know. A gas station.'

'Gas station? What, selling petrol?'

'No, no. The gas, the . . .' She made a hissing sound. 'The gas, in the pipes! To cook with.'

'A gas pipeline?'

'Yes, yes! My brother, he work on the pipeline. It comes all the way from the jungle to Lima. There are stations on it, they pump the gas.'

'Get me a taxi,' he ordered. 'And make sure it's someone who's willing to break the speed limit.' The maid scurried away.

'Eddie, what's going on?' Macy asked.

His expression was now utterly cold, determined – just as it had been when he went after Pachac. 'I'm going to look for Kit. If I find what I think I'm going to . . .' He didn't need to complete the sentence for Macy to be fully aware that it was a threat.

'I'm coming with you.'

He fixed her with a look so chilling that she felt genuine fear. His voice made it clear that he would not accept – or even tolerate – any argument. 'No. You're not. Stay here.'

Eddie turned away, leaving an unnaturally quiet Macy with the frightening feeling that she had just seen the face his enemies saw – before he killed them.

40

Station fourteen of the natural gas pipeline that ran along the Pacific coast towards Lima squatted behind a high chain-link fence, a cluster of dull grey metal tanks and rumbling pumps. It was a lonely outpost, a few kilometres beyond San Bartolo in the crumpled foothills of the Andes, and the sense of isolation was increased by its being completely automated. The status of the pumps was monitored from Lima, only closed-circuit television cameras watching over the remote compound.

The cameras were just one of Kit's concerns as he turned off the Panamerica Highway and drove his car, a loaner provided by Interpol, down the access road. If he were caught on video, it might raise questions he would rather not answer. But then he noticed that the chain securing the gate had been cut – and that the gate was in plain view of a camera. Presumably Stikes had sabotaged or hacked the CCTV in some way.

All the same, he kept his head down to conceal his face as he left the car. This close, he could hear not only the thrum of machinery, but a continual low rushing sound – the noise of hundreds of cubic metres of gas flowing through the great stainless steel pipeline every second. He looked through the chain-link for any sign of Stikes. The tallest tanks were at the northern end, a catwalk running round them above numerous pipes and valves. The walkway continued above the main pipeline to what he guessed was a control station. The whole facility was bordered to its east by a low escarpment, and a flight of metal steps led up it from the controls. He now realised why Stikes had chosen this particular place to meet: the plateau served as a helicopter landing pad.

The empty pad wasn't for the mercenary's Hind, though. It was for the person the Interpol officer would soon be summoning . . . if Stikes lived up to his end of the deal.

Where was he? Kit surveyed the pumping station. Since it was automated, there were only a few lights, and they were more for the benefit of the surveillance cameras than visitors. Reflections glinted off pipes, picking out a steel maze amongst the shadows . . .

Stikes came into view, climbing a ladder up to the central catwalk. He gestured impatiently for Kit to approach. With a wary glance at the nearest camera, Kit opened the gate and crossed the dusty ground to the machinery. He ascended a ladder, feeling the pulse of the pumps through the metal.

Stikes waited for him, dressed in dark military fatigues, beret on his head. The Jericho gleamed in its holster. At his feet was the case he had taken from El Dorado. 'You're late,' he said.

'I had to organise a car,' Kit explained.

Stikes regarded the Indian's vehicle. 'Did you come alone?'

'Yes, of course. Are *you* alone?'

'Of course not.' The Englishman smiled coldly. 'Two of my men are covering you with rifles. See if you can spot them.'

Kit turned nervously, eyes darting across the pipework. So many hiding places . . . but a sniper would need to be in an elevated position to avoid having his aim blocked by the steelwork. He raised his gaze, finally seeing one of the men: a ladder led up one of the smaller gas tanks to a narrow platform on top of it. A dark shape was barely visible against the clear night sky, the station's lights reflecting faintly off a rifle barrel.

'One on the tank,' he said, continuing his search, 'and . . .' He was forced to admit defeat. 'I can't see the other.'

'You wouldn't,' said Stikes. 'Gurov's outside the fence.' His gaze briefly flicked towards the escarpment.

'So are they going to shoot me?'

'Only if you don't give me what I want. So.' Stikes straightened, putting his hands on his hips. 'Am I going to be introduced to the Group?'

'Have you brought the statues?'

Stikes nudged the box forward. Kit crouched and opened it. The three statues were inside; two intact, one split in half, but both the pieces present. He picked one up, feeling the weight of the stone, the texture of the ancient carving. They were genuine.

Finally reunited.

'Well?' Stikes demanded. 'Satisfied?'

'Yes,' said Kit, standing.

'Good.' He produced a satellite phone. 'Make the call. I'm sure you remember the number.'

The meeting with the president of Peru had been relatively brief and, to Nina's mind, entirely unnecessary, accomplishing nothing that couldn't have waited until the following day. Though ostensibly to congratulate her on discovering El Dorado, it was actually a far more political affair, the country's leader firmly planting the flag of Peru on the lost city and the incredible wealth it contained, while simultaneously making it clear that the IHA's role would be downplayed as much as he could get away with. Zender and the Peruvian archaeologists had already been elevated to the status of national heroes, brave explorers who had sacrificed their lives to bring the incredible find to the world.

Nina was too tired to raise more than a token objection, but in truth was neither surprised nor particularly bothered by the land-grab. She had experienced similar attempts by governments to claim credit for her discoveries – the Algerians for the Tomb of Hercules, the Egyptians for the Pyramid of Osiris – but so long as she could put her own account out via the UN, the countries involved could spin events however they liked. Ultimately, what mattered was not who had found a treasure thought lost to time, but that it had been found at all.

A government car brought her back to the villa, where she met Osterhagen as he descended the stairs. The German looked utterly exhausted, apparently having slept from the moment he was shown to his room. He was still in the same crumpled, torn clothes, too weary even to undress before collapsing on the bed. 'Nina,' he yawned. 'Where have you been?'

She gave him a precis of the meeting. 'Ah, yes,' he said with faint amusement, 'I have experienced the same thing. An occupational hazard.'

'Ain't it just.' Macy hurried into the lobby, looking anxious. 'Hey, Macy. What's up?'

'It's about Eddie.' With an apologetic smile to Osterhagen, Macy hastily guided her away from the German archaeologist, who shrugged and went in search of the kitchen. 'I'm worried about him.'

'Me too. I think it'll take a while before he can deal with everything that's happened today.'

'No, no, that's the thing – the day's not over. He's gone!'

'What? Gone where?'

'Some place called San Bartolo. We were talking, and he

suddenly went all weird, and started asking one of the staff how to get there.'

'Weird how?'

'I mean, he was *pissed*. But scary-pissed. Like he was so angry that it wasn't showing on the outside, you know?'

Nina did know; she had seen that kind of cold fury before, not least earlier that day, and it never boded well. 'Why was he angry? What were you talking about?'

'About what happened at El Dorado – something to do with Kit. I told him what I was doing just before Mr McCrimmon got shot, and he got mad and kept saying I was remembering it wrong. Then he went quiet, like he was working something out, and then he found the maid and wanted to know how to get to San Bartolo.' She thought for a moment. 'No, not San Bartolo; somewhere near it, a pumping station on some gas pipeline. Station fourteen.'

'What's it got to do with Kit?'

'I don't know. But it seemed like he was comparing what I told him with what Kit told him, and then he said something about the statues – and that's when he got angry. He took a cab.'

The statues. Nina made the connection. 'Oh God.'

Eddie had somehow realised what Kit had been trying to keep from him: that Interpol was making a deal with Stikes to recover the statues. But Eddie would only be interested in revenge – for her torture, for Mac's death. And he would be going after Stikes.

And if his anger was because he believed Kit had betrayed him by dealing with the mercenary – or worse, that he was somehow in league with him . . .

'When did he leave?' she asked Macy urgently.

'I don't know – a half-hour ago? What is it?'

'I think Eddie's about to do something he'll regret. How do we get to this pumping station?'

'That is it,' said the taxi driver, pointing.

Eddie saw a handful of lights in the darkness off the Pan-america Highway. Gas tanks and pipes behind a fence, a small cliff beyond the facility. A car was parked outside the gate.

Except for the burning coal of his fury, his mind was completely analytical, assessing the scene from a tactical perspective. The car had to be Kit's, and if he was there, Stikes would be too. But it was unlikely he would have come alone. So where would the other mercenaries be?

Elevated positions, where they could both cover their boss and watch the road. On top of the tanks, on the cliff. No way to know how many – but Stikes's forces had been winnowed down at El Dorado, and it was unlikely he would have been able to drum up more at such short notice. He had left the cavern with only the Hind's pilot and one other man . . .

The driver started to slow for the turning on to the dirt road. 'No, keep going,' Eddie told him. He looked down the highway, seeing taillights disappear round a curve in the distance. 'Stop once we get round the next corner.'

He turned his attention to the rugged landscape. Scrubby bushes, small trees. Adequate cover. It would take him ten to fifteen minutes to make a stealthy crossing.

The taxi passed the pumping station. Eddie looked back, seeing movement. Two figures on an elevated walkway. Even at this distance, he recognised them both.

Stikes. And Kit.

His fears had been confirmed. They *were* working together.

The coal inside him burned hotter.

★

Stikes's satellite phone warbled. The mercenary answered it, then gave Kit a crooked smile. 'It's for you.'

Kit took the phone, listened to the brief message, then disconnected. 'The helicopter is on its way,' he reported. 'It should be here in about twenty minutes.'

Stikes checked his watch, then nodded.. He noticed Kit looking towards the gate. 'Something wrong?'

'The security cameras. It could be hard for me to explain to Interpol what was going on if this is recorded – and the Group's representative certainly won't want to be seen.'

Stikes tutted. 'Do you think I'm an amateur? The camera at the gate is sending a looped recording – and as long as we stay away from the pumps,' he gestured at the machinery behind Kit, 'none of the others can see us. I don't particularly want to appear on *Candid Camera* either.'

'I suppose not.' He turned his gaze back to the gate and the road beyond, seeing a lone car pass out of sight round a bend.

'You want me to wait?' asked the taxi driver.

'No, that's fine,' said Eddie, paying him and providing a generous tip before getting out. The driver shrugged, then drove away.

Eddie started uphill through the undergrowth towards the escarpment.

With no time to go through the rigmarole of obtaining a car through government or United Nations channels, Nina and Macy had followed Eddie's example and got the maid to summon a taxi. It was now heading through Lima's southern outskirts for the Panamerica Highway. 'How long before we get to this station?' Nina asked.

Macy put the question to the driver in Spanish. 'About

twenty-five minutes,' she said after getting an answer. 'And yes, I already told him that we're in a rush.'

Nina tapped her foot in impatience – and worry. Would they get there in time to stop Eddie making a mistake?

Kit broke off from pacing the catwalk to check his watch. Over twenty minutes had passed since the phone call, and there was still no sign of a helicopter. The Group's representative might simply be being cautious . . . but might also have decided that the risk was too great and abandoned the meeting.

And their operative. The thought twisted his stomach into a knot. He glanced at the gas tank. Stikes's sniper was still lying on the platform. The Interpol officer had no doubts whatsoever that Stikes would kill him the moment he felt things had gone wrong . . .

A new sound over the unceasing rumble of the gas pumps. Rotor blades. The helicopter.

Unable to conceal a sigh of relief, he looked for the noise's source, seeing strobe lights in the sky to the west.

Eddie also heard the incoming chopper, and froze behind one of the tanks. Stikes and Kit showed no signs of surprise or alarm, so they were expecting it. Who was aboard?

For now, that was irrelevant. What mattered was that it gave him a deadline: it was no more than two minutes away from touching down. He had to be finished before it arrived.

He set off again, moving through the pumping station's shadows until he reached the ladder up one of the tanks. From here, the sound of the pumps was a steady, churning rumble, backed by the low-frequency hiss of gas rushing through the main pipeline. It would mask the sound of his climb – and better yet, he realised as he took hold of the ladder, there was a vibration running through the framework that would camouflage his steps.

He began to climb. The tank was about thirty feet high. As he approached its top he slowed, cautiously peering on to the platform.

A man dressed in black lay upon it, back to him.

One of Stikes's men, armed with a SCAR rifle with a telescopic sight. He wasn't looking through the scope, though; he was watching the approaching helicopter.

Eddie waited, poised at the top of the ladder. If he climbed any higher, the man might catch him in his peripheral vision and raise the alarm. The chopper was now only a minute out. *Look away, dammit!*

After another agonising few seconds, the man finally moved his eye back to the sight. Eddie carefully climbed the last few rungs to crouch on the platform just behind the sniper . . .

Then he lunged, grabbing the mercenary's head and yanking it back as hard as he could, wrapping an arm tightly round his throat.

The sniper made a choked gurgling sound, dropping the SCAR and trying to claw at his attacker's face. Eddie squeezed harder, twisting sharply – and a crunch of crushed cartilage came from the sniper's neck, followed by the muffled snap of bone. The man went limp.

Eddie dropped him and caught the SCAR by its strap just before it tipped over the platform's edge. He lay beside the dead man, recognising him as Voeker, and quickly and expertly checked the gun. A full load of thirty 5.56mm rounds, and the scope was a high-quality night vision unit, a sharp red chevron superimposed over the centre of the shimmering green image.

He lined up the chevron's point on Stikes's head. The mercenary leader was completely unaware of him, a sitting duck. All he had to do was pull the trigger . . .

It wasn't mercy that stopped his finger from tightening – he had already decided that Stikes was going to die. Instead, it was the urge to find out what was going on, to catch everybody involved. The helicopter swung overhead, kicking up dust as it settled on the pad. Stikes picked up the case, and the two men on the catwalk headed for the metal stairs.

Eddie moved the sight to the helicopter. A young, beefy blond man in a dark suit climbed out. Was this the contact? No – he hurried round to the aircraft's far side to open the door for another passenger.

At first, all he could see beneath the fuselage was a pair of black stiletto-heeled boots. Then the new arrival strode into view.

He was so shocked that he almost dropped the rifle.

The person meeting Stikes was someone he knew. Someone he thought was dead.

His ex-wife. Sophia.

41

'I know you,' said Stikes with a suspicious frown as Sophia Blackwood descended the steps, her long black coat billowing in the idling helicopter's rotor wash. 'You were Chase's wife.'

'I know you too,' said Kit, alarmed. 'You tried to set off a nuclear bomb in New York!'

Stikes's frown deepened. 'You're also, if I remember correctly, supposed to be dead.'

Sophia smiled, coming fully into the light at the foot of the stairs – revealing that her beautiful face was marred by a deep, crooked scar that ran from an inch behind her left eye down her cheek and on to her neck, disappearing beneath a black scarf. The rest of her outfit was also black, including a pair of expensive leather gloves. 'Gentlemen, I'm all those things, and more,' she said. 'But right now, I'm the person *you* wanted to meet' – she turned away from Stikes and looked at Kit – 'and, like it or not, *your* superior. So shall we get to business?'

'As you wish, *Lady* Blackwood,' said Stikes. There was a faint tinge of mockery to the word; the British government had stripped Sophia of her title following her failed attack on the United States. She gave him a cold look. 'I assume Jindal told you what I want in exchange for these.' He held up the case.

'I know what you want,' said Sophia. 'However, the people I represent are more curious about *why*.'

'It's simple, really. When I first met Jindal in Venezuela, I knew something wasn't right. Interpol division heads don't go out and do fieldwork – and they certainly don't do fieldwork that's only tangentially related to their job. He gave me some cock-and-bull story about the archaeological expedition being connected to a smuggling investigation, but he obviously had some other motive for being there. So I had a little chat with him, and learned about your organisation. The Group.'

If Sophia's look at Stikes had been cold, the one she directed at Kit was positively icy. 'Funny. He somehow forgot to mention that.'

'I was tortured!' Kit protested. 'If I hadn't said anything, he would have killed me. And I didn't tell him *why* the Group need the statues. How could I? I haven't been told myself.'

'You told him more than enough, apparently.' She turned back to Stikes. 'So, you have some idea of the Group's objectives. What do you want from them? Your wanted status with international law enforcement to disappear, perhaps? Or is it just about money?'

'Only indirectly,' said the Englishman. 'I'm actually offering them my services.'

Sophia arched a perfect eyebrow. 'Are you now?'

'Yes. I have the experience, the connections and, frankly, the ruthlessness to be a great asset. From what Jindal told me, what they're planning will genuinely change the world. I want to make sure I'm on the side that benefits when it happens.'

'Everyone will benefit. Or so they say.' There was a glint in her eye that suggested she had a different opinion.

'They will,' insisted Kit. 'I wouldn't be a part of this if I didn't believe it would help the world.'

Stikes rattled the case. 'But they need these first, don't they?'

Sophia glanced back at the blond man watching from the top of the steps. 'There was a suggestion – not mine, I'll point out – that we should take them from you by force.'

Stikes gave her a lupine smile. 'That would be a bad idea.'

'I know. We used a thermal scanner to see who else was here before landing. Mikkel is very good, but I doubt even he could pick off all three of your men before they killed us.'

'He'd be lucky to draw his—' Stikes broke off abruptly. '*Three* men?'

Sophia responded in kind to his sudden concern. 'What is it?'

'I only have *two* men.'

'Then who's the third?'

'Ay up,' said a Yorkshire voice.

The trio whirled to see Eddie climb on to the catwalk, carrying a SCAR. Mikkel's hand flashed into his jacket to draw a gun – but Eddie had already whipped the rifle up and fired. The blond man collapsed, two bullet wounds in his chest.

The SCAR came back to the three people on the walkway. 'So,' said Eddie, advancing, 'interesting little meeting. My ex-comrade, my ex-wife, and,' a searing glare at Kit, 'my ex-friend.'

'Eddie, this isn't what you think,' said Kit, raising his hands. 'Interpol authorised me to make a deal with Stikes for—'

'*Shut up!*' Eddie roared. Kit flinched. 'Don't give me any more of your fucking lies and bullshit. You've been working with him the whole time to get those fucking statues – and you killed Mac for them!'

Silence, Kit frozen with an expression of shocked guilt. Stikes finally broke it. 'McCrimmon's dead? What a shame.'

Eddie's mouth tightened with anger. He snapped up the rifle and fired. Stikes's beret flew off and disappeared into the darkness. The mercenary staggered, dropping the case and clutching his head as blood ran down his face.

'You missed?' said Sophia, affecting casualness as she recovered from the shock of the gunshot. 'Not like you, Eddie.'

'I don't miss what I'm aiming at from this range,' he growled.

Stikes felt the wound. The bullet had carved a deep gash in his scalp, red spreading through his fair hair like ink on tissue paper. 'That was a mistake, Chase. If you want to kill me, you should have done it then. You'll never get another chance.'

He stared at the other former SAS man, anticipation growing as he waited for the crack of a distant rifle, an explosion of blood and bone . . .

His expectancy faded. Nothing happened.

'Oh, were you waiting for one of your sniper mates to shoot me?' asked Eddie sarcastically. He held up the SCAR. 'Got this off the bloke on top of the tank. And I killed the guy on the cliffs over there before I got here. You're getting sloppy, Stikes, putting your men in the most obvious positions.' A gesture with the rifle. 'Okay. Weapons. Chuck 'em.'

Stikes reluctantly pulled the Jericho from his holster and tossed it past Eddie, where it hit the machinery below the catwalk with a dull clank. Eddie moved the gun on to Kit. 'I'm unarmed,' he said.

Eddie nodded; the Indian wouldn't have had the opportunity to acquire a new weapon. The SCAR lined up on Sophia. 'So am I,' she said.

Her ex-husband gave her an irritated look. Sophia sighed and reached into her coat, drawing out a matt-black Glock 36 compact pistol, which she dropped over the edge of the walkway. There was something odd about her left hand, Eddie noticed; some of her fingers seemed unnaturally stiff inside the leather glove. And looking more closely, besides the scar, there was something different about her face: her cheekbones looked sharper, the line of her nose more curved. Had she had plastic surgery?

'So, what are you going to do now, Eddie?' she asked. 'Are you going to kill us?'

'Him?' said Eddie, nodding towards Stikes. 'Yeah. For what he did to Nina. You, I haven't decided yet. Since I already thought you'd died twice, might have to make it third time lucky – but I wouldn't mind seeing you back in prison either.' He rounded on Kit. 'As for you, though . . . I *should* kill you. But first, I want to know why. Why did you do it – why shoot Mac? Why?'

Despite the cold wind blowing down from the hills, Kit was sweating. 'I didn't want to do it, Eddie, you have to believe me. But he didn't give me any choice. He was going to destroy the helicopter – and the statues.' His eyes flickered towards the fallen case.

'The statues,' Eddie echoed quietly – before suddenly erupting. 'Those fucking statues! Am I the only one who doesn't put all this stupid archaeological shit above people's *lives*? What's so important about the fucking things?' He aimed the rifle at the case. 'Give me one good reason why I shouldn't blow them to fucking pieces right now.'

He noticed Sophia tense – she had a reason, at least. But Kit spoke first, taking a step closer with his hands spread, almost pleading. 'I . . . I can't tell you, Eddie. I wish I could. But it'll change the world. We have to have the statues. For . . . for the sake of all humanity.'

Eddie regarded him for a moment . . . then his eyes narrowed. 'Not good enough.' His finger tensed on the trigger—

Bright lights washed over him.

He looked round. Another car was pulling up beside Kit's—

The instant of distraction gave the Indian an opening. Kit leapt at him, one hand grabbing the SCAR and shoving it away from the case. Eddie fired, a burst of bullets twanging off the pipework below. Stikes jumped away from the line of fire, Sophia hurriedly taking cover behind him.

With both hands on the rifle, Eddie couldn't defend against a punch that jarred his vision. He and Kit grappled for control of the SCAR, lurching back along the catwalk. The gun's ejection port was facing the Interpol officer; Eddie pulled the trigger again, more rounds ripping into the pumping machinery – and showering Kit's face and neck with searing cartridge casings.

Kit shrieked and jerked back, still trying to wrest away the SCAR. Another burst of fire, but this time the spent brass sprayed over his shoulder as he forced the gun upwards. Eddie kicked at his legs, trying to trip him—

A shrill screech came from a pipe below, followed by an earth-shaking thud and a thunderous roar of flame.

The bullets had damaged one of the pumps, gas escaping through a cracked valve . . . and igniting as more red-hot rounds flashed through it.

Nina and Macy exited the taxi – and jumped in shock as an explosion rattled the vehicle, a fireball boiling skywards from the pumping station. Beneath it, a forty-foot-long line of fire blasted out almost horizontally from the machinery, the force of the flame seething against a complex knot of pipes.

Stikes and Sophia recoiled from the heat. The two fighting men were almost directly over the burning gas jet – which was acting like a blowtorch, slicing into the neighbouring pump's pipework.

'Time to leave, I think,' said Sophia. She reached for the case – but Stikes was quicker. The former soldier snatched it up and opened it, moving as if to tip its contents over the guardrail.

'Do we have a deal?' he demanded. 'Because if not, I'm going to throw these things into the fire and get the hell out of here before this whole place goes up!'

Sophia gave him a sour look, then nodded. 'We have a deal.'

'Excellent. Then I'd appreciate a lift!' He looked at the helicopter, which was already rising from an idle to takeoff revolutions as its pilot realised the danger.

'Well, it does seem that I have a spare seat.' She hurried up the steps with Stikes behind her, passing Mikkel's body without a second glance.

Racing through the open gate, Nina saw someone jump into the helicopter. A man, blond hair standing out in the firelight: Stikes? The brief glimpse wasn't enough for her to be sure.

Macy, behind her, looked fearfully around the compound. 'Do you see Eddie or Kit?'

Dismay filled Nina's voice. 'Oh, yeah. I see them.'

'Where?'

She pointed above the flame as she ran faster. 'Take a guess!'

The detonation had knocked both Eddie and Kit down – with the Indian landing on top. He threw another punch at Eddie's face, knocking the Yorkshireman's head back against the walkway's grillework floor. Eddie's grip slackened, and Kit managed to prise one of his hands off the SCAR. He struck at the Englishman's face again, bloodying his mouth, then rolled back on to his haunches, pulling the gun with him.

He turned the bulky weapon round, pointing it at the man who had been his friend—

The conflict in his mind made him hesitate, just for a split second. He didn't want to do this, but he *had* to – Eddie had deduced the truth of what happened to Mac, had seen him with Stikes and Sophia Blackwood. It was the only way to maintain his cover at Interpol and prevent anyone else from learning of his involvement with the Group.

The only way, he told himself. Finger on the trigger—

One of Eddie's legs lashed upwards, striking the rifle just as it fired. Two shots exploded from the barrel, whipping just above his head – then the SCAR clicked impotently, its magazine empty.

Eddie didn't hear it; the gunshots, practically in his face, had left him deafened and half blind from the flash of the muzzle flame. But he could still see well enough to slam his other foot hard against Kit's chest. Kit fell backwards, head smacking against the guardrail.

Spitting out blood, Eddie kicked the other man again before using the railing to pull himself to his feet. The heat from the flame jet was like standing at an open oven.

He looked along the catwalk. Stikes and Sophia were gone – as was the case containing the statues. The chopper was at full power, about to take off. No way he could stop them from escaping.

That left Kit.

Even as part of his mind protested at leaving Mac's killer unpunished, Eddie knew he would have to bring Kit in alive. He was the only link to whatever the hell was going on, the only way to learn the truth behind the Scot's murder. He grabbed Kit by his black hair and slammed his head against the railing again, then hauled him upright—

A sudden noise, loud enough to break through even his addled hearing. Straining metal, something giving way under immense heat and pressure . . .

Nina was almost at a ladder up to the catwalk, Macy a few yards behind, when a very threatening sound made her stop abruptly. 'Get back!' she shouted, turning and diving to the ground—

The damaged pump exploded.

Shattered sections of pipe were thrown hundreds of feet into the air as a pillar of fire blasted skywards like an erupting volcano. The entire facility shook, the noise of burning gas a jet-engine roar as it sucked in air to feed the conflagration. The explosion was powerful enough even to jolt the helicopter as it took to the sky and wheeled away.

Eddie's slowly recovering hearing had been obliterated again – but that was the least of his worries. The new geyser of flame was forty feet away, but he didn't need to touch it to be burned. The combined heat from it and the ruptured pipe below was horrific. He could feel his exposed skin stinging, his hair scorching.

But worse was to come. The walkway juddered, joints snapping—

The world suddenly rolled around him, a whole section of catwalk giving way like a giant hinge. He fell, hitting the guardrail – which broke. Nothing below but the blazing gas—

He jerked to a painful stop as one of the severed rail's stanchions speared through his flapping leather jacket, almost wrenching his shoulder from its socket. Six inches to the side, and it would have gone through his chest. Eddie hung helplessly, dangling only feet above the line of flame . . . then with an agonising effort managed to twist and claw the fingers of his right hand into the grated floor.

The catwalk was tilted at a seventy-degree angle. Eddie pulled himself higher, shrugging his left arm out of his ruined jacket and finding a secure hold with that hand before tugging the other sleeve inside out to free himself. Something dropped from one of the pockets.

His father's business card, still in its evidence bag. It landed in the fire and was instantly incinerated.

He would go the same way if he didn't move fast. The grillwork cutting into his fingers, he hauled himself up until he could stand on the support, and looked round. An intact section of the walkway was six feet away in one direction; in the other . . .

Kit hung from the catwalk's edge, his feet closer to the flame jet than Eddie's had been. He struggled to climb, but couldn't get a firm enough grip.

His panicked eyes met Eddie's.

The Englishman hesitated, looking across to the nearby catwalk, and safety . . . then he stepped across to the next stanchion to reach Kit.

Ears ringing, Nina sat up to see a spear of fire at least a hundred feet high roaring into the dark sky. Smaller blazes were already spreading across the pumping station as debris fell all around like burning hailstones.

She heard a shriek, and whipped round to find Macy clutching her thigh where she had been struck by a piece of smouldering shrapnel. 'Macy, get out of here!' Nina shouted, waving towards the gate – where she saw the taxi rapidly making a skidding turn as the driver fled.

'What about Eddie? And Kit?'

'Just go!' She stood, flinching as another chunk of pipe smacked down nearby, then started back towards the ladder.

To her horror, she saw that a section of catwalk had partially collapsed – and someone was hanging from it over a searing fire. Kit. A moment of sickening fear – where was Eddie? – then she made out her husband through the broken walkway's gridwork floor.

He was moving towards Kit. Was he going to rescue him, or . . .

She scurried up the ladder, recoiling from the heat at the top. A security camera watched her. The pipeline's operators *had* to know by now that something was badly wrong, and be trying to stop the flow of gas.

Unless they couldn't.

The fires were spreading, getting closer to the gas tanks. If one exploded, it would take the others with it, obliterating the entire area.

'Eddie!' she cried. But he didn't hear. '*Eddie!*'

Kit finally got a firm hold on the grating. He dragged himself up, looking for anything that would assist his climb.

A small pipe to one side, connecting two larger conduits running from the pump. He shifted his weight towards it, finding a foothold – and something else.

Stikes's gun was wedged between the two main pipes, just within reach.

Despite the danger, he was thinking one step beyond immediate self-preservation. He still had to protect his cover. Which meant he still had to deal with Eddie—

A foot on the stanchion. Eddie loomed over him.

Kit made his decision – and grabbed the gun.

★

Nina hurried along the catwalk, holding up her arms to shield her face from the almost unbearable heat. Her eyes stung – she rubbed them and blinked, seeing Eddie standing over Kit—

Eddie was about to reach down to Kit when he realised the Indian's hand was already moving. Not towards him, but to something under the catwalk, nickel glinting on the steel pipes . . .

Stikes's Jericho, now in Kit's hand.

The Indian twisted his wrist, aiming the pistol upwards—

Eddie's foot snapped out, catching Kit hard in the face. Blood sprayed from the Indian's nose, shock causing him to lose his grip. He fell.

Into the fire.

For a fraction of a second, Eddie saw his expression in the inferno's light, a mixture of pain and anger and terror – then he was gone, vaporised by the fury of the escaping flame. The Jericho dropped with him, vanishing into the fire.

He turned, starting back towards the intact section of catwalk – and saw Nina standing there, staring at him in utter disbelief.

Even in the searing heat, Nina somehow felt cold, as if her blood had been replaced by icy water. Her mind refused to accept what her eyes had just witnessed. It couldn't have happened. It couldn't!

But it had. Eddie had just climbed over to the helpless, flailing Kit . . . and kicked him to his death.

He came closer, the stanchions shuddering under his weight. 'Give me a hand!' he called as he reached the end of the broken section and tried to clamber up. She didn't move. 'Nina!'

She broke out of her freeze and pulled him up. 'Oh God, what did you do? *What did you do?*'

'We've got to go!' he shouted, looking towards the spreading fires. 'Run!' He pushed her ahead as he raced along the walkway. The security camera looked on with its glazed eye.

Nina reached the ladder and hurried down it, jumping off halfway. Eddie followed. They ran for the gate, the roar of the fires now accompanied by the squeals and groans of warping metal. The gas tanks were giving way . . .

Through the gate. Macy sprinted for the highway ahead of them. The squeals turned to shrieks—

One of the gas tanks blew apart in a seething white ball of fire, the others following it in a chain reaction. A shockwave erupted outwards, whipping up a wall of dust and blowing Nina and Eddie off their feet. A roiling mushroom cloud rose into the night sky, a marker visible for miles around for the crater that had once been station fourteen.

It took minutes before Nina felt composed enough to speak, or even think. She had a vague, confused memory of Eddie carrying her along the dirt road, Macy running back to help them, then sitting beside the highway trying to recover from the shock.

Not merely the shock of the explosion. Her memory of what had happened on the catwalk was crystal clear. It kept replaying, unbidden, in her mind: Kit dangling from the walkway by one hand, struggling to get a grip on a pipe with the other, Eddie's foot lashing out, Kit's face filling with horror as he dropped into the fire . . .

Vigilante justice. Revenge-driven murder. Just like Jerry Rosenthal in New York. Only this time it wasn't a mere moral talking point, a topic of argument. It was something her husband had done right in front of her.

Someone sat beside her. Eddie. The light from the still burning pipeline revealed his scorched clothes and reddened skin. 'Hey,' he said, putting his arm round her shoulders.

She pulled away.

He looked startled, then hurt. 'What's wrong? Are you okay?'

'I'm fine,' Nina said curtly, standing. In the distance, she saw flashing lights – emergency vehicles coming along the highway.

Eddie stood as well. 'Then what's the matter?'

'What's the *matter*?' she cried. 'You murdered Kit, that's what's the matter!'

Macy, sitting nearby, reacted in disbelief. Eddie's response was only slightly less surprised. 'What?'

'Eddie, I was right there! He was hanging off that walk-way, and you – you kicked him into the fire!' Saying the words out loud brought back her shock at what she had seen, full force.

'He was trying to kill me!' Eddie protested. 'He had a fucking gun in his hand!'

Nina shook her head. 'He didn't have a gun.'

'He did – how could you not have seen it? You were right there, you *must* have seen it!'

'He didn't have a gun,' she repeated forcefully. 'And why would he have been trying to kill you?'

''Cause he was working with Stikes,' said Eddie, anger rising. 'He was all along. All they wanted the whole time was those statues. Kit killed Mac to protect them, and tried to kill me because I figured it out.'

It was now Nina's ears, not her eyes, that she doubted. *Kit* had killed Mac? The idea was impossible to believe. More than that, it was . . .

Insane? The word sent another chill through her. Could Mac's murder – compounded by the news of his grandmother's death – have possibly affected Eddie so badly? 'Why?' she asked.

'How the fuck would I know? I wasn't in on whatever they were doing. But I'll tell you who else was,' he added. 'Sophia.'

Nina stared at him. 'Sophia?' she said after a pause. 'Sophia, as in your ex-wife Sophia?'

'Yeah. She was the one who wanted the statues.'

'You mean Sophia Blackwood?' said Macy, bewildered. 'The terrorist? I thought she was dead.'

'She *is* dead,' Nina told her. 'And Eddie should know – he threw her off a cliff!'

Eddie looked in frustration between the two women as the wail of approaching sirens reached them. 'She was here – she took off with Stikes in that chopper. Don't tell me you didn't see her either!'

'I saw Stikes – I think.' Nina glanced at the now empty helipad. 'But the only other people I saw were you . . . and Kit.'

'There! Kit and Stikes were working together, like I told you! That's why he kept the whole meeting a secret!'

'He told *me* about it.' Eddie's face revealed his shock. 'Stikes offered Interpol a deal – immunity in return for the statues. Kit didn't tell you because he knew how upset you were about Mac, and thought you'd react badly if you knew he was talking to Stikes.' Nina let out a short, bitter laugh. 'And he was right!'

'No, that isn't – that's not what happened,' Eddie insisted, desperation entering his voice. 'Kit wasn't negotiating some immunity deal. He was working with Stikes and Sophia!'

'Stikes and Sophia,' Nina echoed. 'Two of the people you hate most in the world – and they're both involved in a conspiracy to cover up Mac's murder? By *Kit*? Eddie, this whole thing, everything you're saying, is just, just . . .' She didn't want to say the word.

He knew exactly what she meant, though. 'I'm not fucking mad, and I didn't fucking hallucinate this.' He grabbed her by her upper arm. 'Kit killed Mac! And he would have killed me too, if I hadn't killed him first!'

Nina recoiled with a gasp of pain as his fingers dug into her. 'Eddie, let go,' she said. It was the first time she could remember that he had ever physically hurt her. 'Let go of me!'

He opened his hand, and she jerked away, almost tripping as she scurried backwards. 'Jesus Christ, Eddie! You killed a policeman – you murdered your friend!'

'That's not what happened!' he shouted, starting to follow her.

'Don't touch me!' Nina brought up her hands, balled almost into fists. Eddie stopped as she continued to retreat. 'Get away from me! I don't – I don't even know you any more! What have you *done*?'

Eddie stayed still, stricken, as the first emergency vehicles reached the dirt road. Leading was a yellow van bearing the gas company's logo, which tore past and headed for what was left of the pumping station. Behind it was a police car, which screeched to a stop at the roadside. Two cops jumped out, running to the group and drawing their guns. They shouted orders in Spanish.

'What the fuck's this?' Eddie demanded, raising his hands as the men fixed their weapons on him.

Macy translated. 'Oh, my God. Eddie, they say they're

arresting you for murder!' She ran to the cops and asked panicked questions in their language, getting brusque responses. 'The gas company saw you and Kit on the security cameras!'

One of the cops approached Eddie. He gestured for the Englishman to hold out his hands, ready to be cuffed. The other hung back suspiciously, unsure what to make of Nina and Macy and splitting his attention between the three.

'I didn't murder him,' Eddie said – to Nina, not the cops. 'He was trying to kill me. You've got to believe me.'

'I . . . I don't know if I can,' she whispered.

The first cop waved his gun impatiently. Eddie gave Nina a long, saddened look, then held out his wrists. The cop fumbled one-handed for his handcuffs, glancing down as they caught on his belt—

And was sent reeling as Eddie's fist crashed against his jaw, his other hand wrenching the pistol from his grip.

The second cop hurriedly brought up his gun – but found his partner between him and their intended prisoner. He hesitated, then clumsily sidestepped to get a clean line of fire—

A single gunshot, and the second cop's weapon spun away with a crack. He screamed and clutched his hand. Eddie's bullet had shattered on impact with the pistol's harder steel, sending shards of metal spearing into his flesh.

'Tell 'em not to move,' Eddie barked to Macy as he rounded the two men, smoking gun covering them, and headed for their car.

'Uh . . . I think they figured that out for themselves,' she said, shocked.

Nina was stunned, struggling to take in the latest turn of events. 'Eddie, what the hell?'

'Kit killed Mac, and he tried to kill me,' said Eddie, reaching the car. Its engine was still running. 'He was working with Stikes, *and* Sophia. And I'm going to prove it. I don't have a fucking clue how, but I'm going to prove it to you.' The gun still raised, he slid into the driver's seat. 'Only I can't do that from inside a Peruvian prison. So . . . I guess this is it.' He put the car into gear and reached to close the door – then spoke again just before it slammed shut. 'I love you.'

And with that the car peeled away, swinging across the central divider and heading at high speed back north, leaving the overwhelmed Nina behind.

Epilogue

England

The last time Eddie saw the English Channel, it had been a brilliant blue beneath a sunny sky. Today, though, the sea beyond the harbour entrance was as grey and leaden as the thick clouds overhead, a stiff breeze stirring up whitecaps.

He watched as a boat slowly approached the quay. The white motor yacht had left Poole Harbour an hour earlier, heading a few miles out to sea on its short, solemn voyage. Its screws reversed, churning up white foam, and it came to a stop at the quayside. A crewman quickly tied it up, then positioned a gangplank so the passengers could disembark.

Eddie counted a dozen, all dressed in mourning black. Most he didn't recognise; elderly people, friends of his grandmother's. But four he knew. His sister, his niece . . . and his father, accompanied by Julie.

He checked that nobody nearby was paying him any undue attention, then left the doorway in which he was waiting and crossed to the quayside to meet the group as they came ashore. Holly was the first to see him, crying out 'Uncle Eddie!' in a mix of surprise and shock. Even after several days, his bruised face still bore witness to the beatings he had suffered in South America.

'Hi, Holly,' he said. 'Lizzie. Julie.' He deliberately didn't acknowledge his father . . . yet.

Elizabeth was just as startled as her daughter, though far less enthused. 'Eddie, what the hell are you doing here? The police came round – they told us to tell them if we heard from you. They said you killed someone!'

'I came to say goodbye to Nan.' Elizabeth was holding an empty cremation urn, the family having carried out Nan's wish to have her ashes scattered at sea. 'Was it a good service?'

'As far as any service can be said to be good, yes,' said Elizabeth tightly.

'I'm sorry,' Eddie told her. 'I wish I could have seen her before . . . before. You know.' Holly, red-eyed, tried to stifle a sniff as new tears welled. 'I should have been there. But . . .'

'But you were busy,' said Larry. 'More important things to do.' Sarcasm entered his voice. 'Saving the world, no doubt.'

Eddie rounded on him, fists clenched. 'No, I was watching a friend die.' He looked at Elizabeth and Holly. 'Mac. Jim McCrimmon, you remember him?' Both women reacted in dismay. 'He was murdered, shot in the back.' He faced Larry again, anger rising. 'Because of you!'

'What?' said Larry. 'What are you talking about?'

'You talked to Stikes after I saw you in Colombia, didn't you?'

'Well . . . yes. But he was a client, so I had every right. I don't see how—'

'You told Stikes that Nina was looking for El Dorado in Peru. And guess what, he turned up at the site with a helicopter full of mercenaries and a truckload of terrorists! A lot of people died – and it was your fault!'

Larry bristled, rising to his full height. 'You told *me* what Nina was doing. I hardly think you can put all the blame on me.' His mouth tightened accusingly. 'I'm sorry about your friend, but it's your fault too.'

Eddie stared at him . . . then a surge of fury overcame him. Before he even knew what he was doing, he swung with his full strength and punched his father in the face. Larry flew backwards and thumped down on the damp dockside. Julie screamed.

Eddie moved as if to kick him into the water – but Holly rushed forward to crouch in front of her grandfather, looking up at her uncle in disbelief. 'No, leave him alone!'

'Edward! Elizabeth shrieked. 'What are you doing?' People on the quay turned to see the cause of the commotion. One of the mourners took out a phone and hurriedly dialled 999.

Larry put a hand to his face, stiffly moving his jaw before wiping blood from his mouth. 'Pretty good punch,' he gasped as Julie knelt to help him.

The burst of rage that had fuelled Eddie faded as he took in Elizabeth's and Holly's appalled expressions. He looked down at Larry. 'I'm . . .' he started to say, but even now he couldn't bring himself to complete the apology.

'I think you should go,' said Elizabeth coldly. She clutched the urn protectively to her chest. 'Before you do anything else that Nan would have been ashamed of.'

Eddie regarded all the faces looking at him with horror, shock, disgust, then walked away, disappearing into the port's narrow streets.

Another day, another funeral.

Eddie lurked in an alley across the street from the small church as Mac's coffin was raised by the pallbearers and placed in the hearse. He knew several of the mourners; Mac's ex-wife Angela was among them, as were a number of his former military colleagues. On the group's fringe was a man with whom Eddie had in the past had decidedly mixed dealings; Peter Alderley. The MI6 officer's drooping moustache made his downcast expression look even more doleful. As Eddie looked on Alderley twitched, then edged away from the others to take a vibrating phone from his jacket. A brief conversation, and he retreated into the church.

Eddie shook his head at the disrespect, then watched as the coffin's loading was completed. Angela spoke with some of the mourners, then she and a couple of others entered a Rolls-Royce, which followed the hearse as it slowly moved into the London traffic. He gazed after the cortège until it was out of sight. 'Fight to the end,' he said quietly.

'Fight to the end,' echoed a voice behind him.

Eddie whirled to find Alderley in the alley, rapid breathing suggesting he had got there in a hurry. 'Well, look who it is,' Eddie said, trying to cover his surprise that the MI6 man had managed to sneak up on him. 'James Bore.'

'I thought you might turn up here, Chase,' said Alderley. 'Once we knew you were back in the country after that contretemps with your dad, it seemed likely. I had a couple of spotters looking out for you.'

'You did? Thought that was MI5's job on home turf.' Eddie glanced into the street, but saw no signs of large men moving purposefully towards him.

'It is, normally. But I've got a personal interest in this one.' He briefly looked in the direction of the departed hearse. 'My men are hanging back – for the moment. I wanted to talk to you first.'

'About what?'

'A few things. First, how you managed to get from Peru back to England when Interpol has a red notice on you for murder.'

Eddie shrugged. 'I know a few people.'

'Like Bluey Jackson?' A half-smile at Eddie's discomfiture; the Yorkshireman had contacted the Australian, not for the first time, to obtain fake identity documents, which had then been couriered to Lima. 'I thought so. One of these days, we really should tell the Aussies about his little false-passport factory. But . . .' Another humourless crease of his lips. 'Not today.'

'So what else is on your mind?' Eddie asked, not sure where the discussion was leading. Alderley could already have had him arrested – and still might – but clearly wanted something first.

'Mac. What happened to him?'

'What did they tell you happened?'

'That he was killed by Peruvian rebels, who also wounded an Interpol officer – the same man you later killed.'

'Yeah, that's what everyone thinks. Even Nina.' He couldn't keep bitterness from his voice.

Alderley noticed, but didn't comment. 'And you know differently?' he asked instead.

'Yeah. It was Kit – Ankit Jindal, the Interpol agent – who killed him. Shot him in the back, and then gave himself a flesh wound to make it look like the rebels did it.'

'Why?'

'You know that Alexander Stikes was involved too?'

Alderley nodded. 'I read the statements Interpol took from everyone. Including Nina. She told them what you told her.'

'Stikes was in a chopper that was about to take off, with these statues that everybody's so bloody keen to get hold of. Mac had an RPG lined up on it – and Kit shot him to save Stikes and the statues. They were working together. I don't know if they were all along, but they definitely were by the time they met up at that gas plant. And there's something else. Sophia's involved too.'

Alderley's eyebrows rose. 'Sophia Blackwood? I thought she was dead.'

'So did I. Apparently not. I don't know what she's up to or why she wants the statues, but she and Stikes went off with them – and Kit tried to kill me to cover his tracks. If I hadn't done what I did, I'd be a charcoal fucking briquette right now.'

Alderley rocked on his heels, thinking. 'So . . . what are you going to do about it?'

'Find Stikes and kill him, mostly. I hadn't thought much past that . . .' He tailed off as he realised the subtext of the MI6 officer's words. 'Wait, what do you mean, me?'

'I can't do anything – officially, at least – until I have some actionable evidence. All I have so far is your word, and you're, well, a wanted fugitive. Your stock isn't at its highest at the moment. But if you get some proof for me . . .'

Eddie made a disbelieving face. 'You're going to let me go? Why? You can't stand me!'

'Just because I don't like you doesn't mean I don't trust you. Mac, God rest his soul, always believed in you, one hundred per cent. And I always believed in Mac.' His expression became more mournful than ever. 'You're not the only person who's lost a friend, Chase. You say Mac was killed as part of some conspiracy? I'm willing to take you at your word. I want answers as much as you do. So go and get them. Find Stikes, and he should lead you to whoever else is involved.'

'Me, working for MI6?' Eddie said dubiously. 'Christ, and I thought I was already badly off!'

'Amusing as ever – i.e., not at all,' said Alderley with a

disparaging sigh. 'But you really should get moving, before my men come looking for me.'

'So are you going to give me anything to help? An Aston Martin that turns into a helicopter?'

'Just a head start, I'm afraid. When you run, go right; my men are in a car down the street to the left.' Alderley took a breath, then braced himself. 'Make it look convincing. But try not to break my nose again. Oh, and . . . don't enjoy it too much, will you?'

Eddie managed a faint grin. 'I'll do my best.'

It was the second time in as many days that he had punched someone he knew. As Alderley hit the ground, he sprinted out of the alley into the world beyond to begin his hunt.